WINTERSET

OTHER BOOKS AND AUDIOBOOKS
BY TIFFANY ODEKIRK

HISTORICAL

Summerhaven

Summerhaven: Collector's Edition

CONTEMPORARY

Love On Pointe

Love Unscripted

Love Sidelined

WINTERSET
TIFFANY ODEKIRK

PROPER ROMANCE

SHADOW
MOUNTAIN
PUBLISHING

For Kevin, who knows all my secrets
and
for Lexi, my talented little artist

© 2025 Tiffany Odekirk

All rights reserved. No part of this book may be reproduced in any form or by any means without permission in writing from the publisher, Shadow Mountain Publishing®, at permissions@shadowmountain.com. The views expressed herein are the responsibility of the author and do not necessarily represent the position of Shadow Mountain Publishing.

This is a work of fiction. Characters and events in this book are products of the author's imagination or are represented fictitiously.

Visit us at shadowmountain.com

PROPER ROMANCE is a registered trademark.

Library of Congress Cataloging-in-Publication Data
Names: Odekirk, Tiffany, 1985– author.
Title: Winterset / Tiffany Odekirk.
Description: Salt Lake City : Shadow Mountain Publishing, 2025. | Series: Proper romance | Summary: "Katherine Lockwood is forced into hiding when Oliver Jennings returns to Winterset. Desperate to protect her secret existence to save her life, she devises a plan to drive him away. But as Oliver uncovers the truth behind his estate's 'haunting,' their lives collide. With danger closing in, they must navigate a perilous game of survival while untangling their growing attraction for each other"—Provided by publisher.
Identifiers: LCCN 2025006661 (print) | LCCN 2025006662 (ebook) | ISBN 9781639933228 (trade paperback) | ISBN 9781649333094 (ebook)
Subjects: BISAC: FICTION / Romance / Historical / Regency | FICTION / Gothic | LCGFT: Romance fiction. | Novels.
Classification: LCC PS3615.D435 W56 2025 (print) | LCC PS3615.D435 (ebook) | DDC 813/.6—dc23/eng/20250325
LC record available at https://lccn.loc.gov/2025006661
LC ebook record available at https://lccn.loc.gov/2025006662

Printed in the United States of America
Publishers Printing

10 9 8 7 6 5 4 3 2 1

CHAPTER ONE

Kate

Northern England, October 1820

THE PROBLEM WITH DRAWING FLOWERS was that they were constantly being blown about by the breeze. I could successfully sketch one petal, but by the time I was ready to draw the next, the flower would be posed in a completely different manner. I loved drawing in the walled garden, but how was I ever supposed to improve my art when all I had to work with were such unruly subjects?

I frowned at my little daisy muse.

Well, not my *muse* so much as my de facto model. I'd never really cared to draw still life. I could not capture the personality of a peony nor convey the emotions of a foxglove's face.

With a sigh, I set aside my sketch and lifted my chin toward the sky, searching for warmth. If only I could be satisfied to admire great works of art instead of attempting to create them, I might find some measure of contentment, if not happiness. But no matter how vexing the effort, I couldn't bring myself to quit; I loathed the act but loved the art. A paradox, to be sure.

Summer was surrendering too soon this year. The once warm breeze had already turned into cool gales, and the sweet scent of flowers had given way to the earthy fragrance of fall foliage. In a few short weeks, my beloved walled garden would lie dormant for a season.

Determined to capture its beauty before it did, I returned to my drawing. I successfully sketched another petal, but halfway through the next, wind swirled through the garden again.

Drat!

What I wouldn't give to have a willing human model to sit for me. It wasn't that Mrs. Owensby was *un*willing, but as Winterset's housekeeper, she was forever at work cooking, cleaning, and tending to everything in her path. And Bexley, Winterset's butler, was constantly occupied with everything else it took to keep the manor from falling into complete ruin. Heaven knew I was grateful for them, but in my most selfish moments, I did wish for more.

But dwelling on what that dark day two years ago had deprived me of would do me no good. Time had taught me that it was better to focus on whatever was before me. At present, a daisy.

Most people would probably view the small, scraggly weed as nothing more than a nuisance. But I admired how it survived against all odds, the way it clung to life between the cobblestones. Its beauty was worthy of being committed to paper, even if all I had were the pages in Papa's old books and a bit of charcoal.

It wasn't ideal to draw in a book. My art obscured the text, and the text interfered with my art. I did feel guilty about it, but I took comfort in knowing I wasn't damaging the books beyond their intended use. If ever someone wanted to study—I peeked at the cover of the book I was using as my sketchbook—*A Compendium of Domestic Accountancy*, they could. Although with such a stuffy title, I doubted anyone ever would. I always replaced the book on the shelf in Papa's study once I'd filled the pages.

Straightening the book in my lap, I lowered the charcoal to the page, but before I could make my mark, a conspiracy of ravens rushed from a nearby tree, and their caws set my heart to racing.

I froze and listened for whatever had frightened them to flight.

At first, I heard nothing. And then, faintly in the distance, the clatter of a horse's hooves coming toward Winterset broke the silence.

I sprang to my feet, abandoning my art, and hid behind the leaning willow tree near the wall. Even though the garden's interior was not visible from the road, panic pulsed like poison in my veins, making me weak and shaky.

We never had visitors. Nor deliveries. Nor anything that would cause anyone to come to Winterset.

But someone was here.

Perhaps it was a person seeking employment. Or a neighbor finally curious enough to come see about the state of the house.

It couldn't be *him*, could it? No, not after all this time.

Taking care not to be seen, I scooted up the tree's tilted trunk and peeked over the garden wall.

It was only a post-boy. He was entering the courtyard through the servant's gate, skipping no less.

My whole being relaxed with relief.

But . . . why was he here? We rarely received mail, and what we did receive was never delivered directly to us but to the postmaster in town. So again, why was he here?

The boy quickly disappeared around the side of the house to make his delivery at the servant's door. A minute later, he reappeared and left the way he'd come, the servants' gate clanging closed behind him.

I waited a few minutes to be sure he would not return, then crept from behind the willow tree and padded down the cobblestone pathway to where my art supplies lay in a heap.

I knelt to assess the damage. Papa's book and my unfinished drawing were unharmed, save a wrinkled page. But my model, my flawless daisy, was crushed. I gently straightened it, but as soon as I withdrew my support, the flower fell.

I plucked it from its stony crevice and tucked it between two pages to press. It would be safe there, damaged but not discarded.

Too curious to be creative, I replaced my slippers and bonnet and made my way to the garden door. I wound my way through the tall hedgerow maze, and at the exit, I glanced around the edge, surveying the courtyard. Ivy covered the front gate like a curtain, which suited my purposes, but it pained me to see the overgrown carriageway, the shuttered windows, and the filthy fountain.

Certain I would not be seen by passersby, I hugged my art supplies to my chest and walked from the hedgerow to the house. Like always, I entered through the servant's door. The familiarity of the kitchen was always a comfort. But rather than the typical warm welcome from Mrs. Owensby, I was instead greeted by a cloud of thick smoke and the scent of burning bread.

"Mrs. Owensby!" I called, rushing into the kitchen. "Bexley, help! Quick!"

In the hearth, a pot bubbled over, steaming and spewing soup onto the hot coals. In the brick oven, bread burned, black smoke curling out of the opening. I hurriedly retrieved the baking peel, snatched the loaf from the oven, and set the blackened lump on the worktable.

With still no sign of Mrs. Owensby or Bexley, I then grabbed the poker from the hook next to the hearth and pushed the cast-iron arm holding the soup pot out of the fire.

Situation in hand, I went in search of the servants.

"Mrs. Owensby?" I called as I climbed the kitchen stairs, my voice carrying up to the vaulted ceiling in the dining hall. "Bexley?"

Though they gave no response, I heard their hushed voices and followed the sound to the entrance hall, where I found them huddled together. "There you two are," I said.

Mrs. Owensby startled and spun to face me. "Kate." She held one hand to her bosom and used the other to tuck something into the back of her apron. "You mustn't sneak up on an old woman."

"You are not old, and I did not sneak. On the contrary, I have been calling out for you both for help. The pot was bubbling over, and the bread is . . . well, coal."

"Dear me," Mrs. Owensby said and moved immediately toward the kitchen.

"I saw to it," I said, stepping in front of her to block her escape. "What were you two up to?"

"*Up to?* What are we always up to, dear? Cooking, cleaning . . ." Her sentence stretched, and she glanced at Bexley for assistance.

Bexley cleared his throat and added, "Polishing."

"Really?" I said, suspicion mounting. Bexley hated polishing the silverware and always left that chore until the end of the week. It was only Tuesday. I glanced over my shoulder into the dining hall and saw that the table was barren. They were definitely up to something nefarious.

"I saw the post-boy," I said. "What did he deliver?"

Bexley's Adam's apple rolled with a swallow, and Mrs. Owensby shifted uncomfortably beside him. "A missive," he said simply.

"I am sure. What did it contain?"

"Nothing you need mind, dear." Mrs. Owensby patted my shoulder like I was a small child, not a grown woman, and her fingers brushed my hair.

I flinched.

She gave me a sympathetic smile. "I would love to style your hair for you."

As kind as her offer was, I could think of nothing worse.

Well, that was not precisely true—I could think of many things much worse—but having my hair touched was not something I would enjoy.

I fingered my hastily woven plait and felt a twinge of sadness. It felt like another lifetime ago that Molly, my former lady's maid, had stood behind me at the vanity and tamed my curls into an intricate coiffure. How I missed her.

I pushed away the memory and met Mrs. Owensby's gaze. "That is kind of you, Mrs. Owensby. Thank you. But taking pains in my appearance when I do not grace anywhere but these halls would be a waste of both our time."

With a knowing nod, she withdrew her hand. "If you will excuse me," she said. "I must see if I can salvage dinner."

As she walked past me, I wickedly plucked the letter from the back of her apron and started up the western side of the double staircase.

"No, Kate," Mrs. Owensby called, her footsteps hurrying after me. "You mustn't! Bexley, stop her!"

Bexley, despite his age, obediently sprang toward the steps to intercept me. But I was faster and well ahead of him.

The missive felt soft and smooth in my hands. It had been an age since I'd had the use of paper so fine. Hopefully, the writer would be brief so I could use the rest of the paper as a canvas.

The seal had already been broken, so I quickly unfolded the letter. Every inch of the page was filled with precise, elegant script, leaving only a small portion of the outside part of the paper without mark. Drat!

Dear Mr. Moore,

I frowned at the salutation. Who was Mr. Moore? Had this letter been delivered to Winterset in error? I glanced at the bottom of the page to see who had sent it. It was signed, x*Mr. Oliver Jennings.*

Winterset's rightful owner.

Absent owner. He'd never bothered to show his face here.

I gritted my teeth. Was Mr. Jennings really so arrogant that he could not learn the correct names of his household servants?

I rolled my eyes and continued reading.

As you requested in your last letter, I am sending you notice that my Grand Tour of the Continent is soon ending. I shall take up residence at Winterset in four weeks' time. Staff should ready the manor for my imminent arrival. I require the following: French-milled lavender soap, Scottish salmon, Portuguese port wine...

The list continued, but I scarcely skimmed a few lines before the letter slipped from my fingers and fluttered to the floor.

Bexley and Mrs. Owensby reached the top of the stairs, where I stood.

"Mr. Jennings is coming," I said, and the reality that my safe situation was coming to an end made me sway. I grabbed the railing to steady myself, but the truth was just too heavy, and I lowered myself to the floor.

Bexley crouched in front of me. "Kate," he said softly, and the concern in his eyes reminded me of the way Papa used to look at me when I was frightened during lightning storms.

Mrs. Owensby sat beside me and wrapped me in her arms. "It will be all right, child."

"Will it?" Winterset was the only home I'd ever known, but it did not legally belong to me. It belonged to Mr. Oliver Jennings, however unworthy I believed him to be. I'd hidden here these past two years because I'd had no other choice, but now that he was taking up residence, what would become of me?

"Of course, it will. He has never shown up when he's promised. He was supposed to come to Winterset after your father"—she paused to clear the emotion from her voice—"after your father's lease ended, but he did not. Last year, we expected him to come, and again, he did not. Perhaps we will yet again be lucky."

"In the past, his *mother*, Lady Winfield, wrote that he would come," I said. "This time, *he* has written. And not only that, but he has also included a detailed list of instructions. How he has the audacity to demand such luxuries when he has not sent a single cent to care for his estate is beyond my comprehension. We barely have any money to buy the essentials."

Mrs. Owensby worried her lower lip.

I shook my head. As upset as I was about Mr. Jennings's failings, his many faults were not my current concern. The only thing that really mattered right now was the fact that he was coming, and I was about to be displaced. "What am I to do?" My voice broke.

"We will find another place for you," Mrs. Owensby said.

"You know as well as I that there is no other place for me," I said. By necessity, everyone who had ever known and loved me believed I was dead. My life, as I had known it, had ended two years ago when I'd caught my intended, Mr. Cavendish, taking the moonlight with a maid in the garden a few days before our wedding at our engagement ball.

He'd insisted I still marry him, that the banns had been read, and he would *not* be made a fool. When I refused and tried to walk away, he retaliated by grabbing a fistful of my hair and yanking me back to him. Then he'd ripped my bodice and kissed me against my will. When Papa and a small group of other attendees found me, Mr. Cavendish made a convincing display of debauchery, ruining my reputation and trying to trap me into marriage. I'd been crushed by his callous cruelty and had thought my life could not get any worse. But my sorrows had been multiplied when Papa had challenged him to a duel to defend my honor and died later that day from his wounds.

The world felt cold and empty without Papa, the weight of my guilt and grief crushing.

On his deathbed, Papa had told me that as long as I stayed within Winterset's walls, I would be safe from Mr. Cavendish. I wasn't sure why he'd believed I would be safe here, perhaps because he knew and believed in Mrs. Owensby's and Bexley's care of me, or it could have been because Winterset had been a safe haven for so many people before me. I didn't know, but miraculously, I had been kept safe in hiding here.

Mr. Cavendish had come to claim me that very day. He'd stood at the door, his sinister face a mixture of anger and triumph. As if in his killing Papa, I'd had no choice but to marry him. I had again refused. He'd told me he would not allow me to tarnish his family's good name and threatened that if I didn't marry him, I would meet the same fate as my father. Terror had gripped me. I had not known what would become of me, but I would not marry that monster.

So, like Joseph's brothers of old, I had faked my death by throwing my pelisse, stained with Papa's blood, over a cliff to the seashore below. When the garment had been found by local townspeople, a brief investigation had been conducted, and I had been presumed dead.

I knew I could not remain at Winterset forever, but neither could I have left. I'd had no money and no one to turn to, so I'd stayed under Mrs. Owensby's and Bexley's care.

For weeks, I worried that Mr. Cavendish would figure out the truth and come for me. I stayed strictly in the attic, watching from a small window. But . . . he never did. And neither did Mr. Jennings.

Weeks passed, then months. Ivy grew over the gate, creating something of a sanctuary, and I began to trust Papa's promise and to feel safe.

Safe, so long as I stayed within Winterset's walls.

For nearly two years, I had lived one day at time, praying Mr. Jennings would stay away and that he would not claim his inheritance, but now that he was indeed returning to Winterset, I did not know what to do. I should not stay, but nor could I go.

"I promised Papa I would stay within these walls," I said, my voice a weak whisper.

Mrs. Owensby's gaze softened. "This is not the life your father wanted for you, Kate. He wished for your safety, yes, but not your seclusion. You cannot become who you are meant to be living in the shadows."

"Papa is dead, Mrs. Owensby, and that is entirely my fault. The least I can do to honor his sacrifice is to remain here alive. It might not be the life he wished for me, but at least I *am* alive."

A sorrowful look passed between my guardians.

I hated to put them in this position. They'd already given up so much these past two years to hide me away and ensure my safety. But what choice did I have?

Bexley cleared his throat. "If Mr. Jennings does indeed take up residence, then you will indubitably be discovered."

"Not necessarily," I said, a plan forming in my mind. "What if we make Mr. Jennings not *want* to stay?"

"What do you mean?" Bexley asked warily.

I needed to tread carefully. What I had in mind was unconventional, at best, and criminal, at worst. "Well, a man like Mr. Jennings, who has made the world his home these past years, could not be content to live so far from London Society and, thanks to his neglect, in an estate in such disrepair."

Mrs. Owensby gave me a disapproving look at my lack of respect for the supposed gentleman.

"It is true, is it not?" I said.

She said nothing in reply. She couldn't because Mr. Jennings *had* let the estate fall into disrepair. When he'd inherited Winterset, he'd not come to care for the estate, nor had he hired a steward to care for it in his absence. He'd not sent one penny to pay for the upkeep of Winterset. All the maids and footmen had long since left, the grounds keeper too. Had it not been for me, even Mrs. Owensby and Bexley would have sought employment elsewhere.

To pay for the necessities of life these past two years, I'd had them quietly sell Mother's jewelry several towns south of Winterset. Bexley had farmed much of our food in the kitchen garden, and Mrs. Owensby had sold the surplus at market. It was not a bounteous life, but we'd managed to survive.

Our funds were growing scarce though. Mother's jewelry was gone, but I still had a few family possessions left to sell that would fetch a price.

I could always sell the *other* items I'd found in the attic. They did not belong to me—they belonged to *him*, even if he did not know of their existence—but they would sell for a significant sum and could sustain us for a very long time. Perhaps the rest of our lives if we were frugal.

I did not like the idea of taking more from Mr. Jennings than was owed to the servants for their work these past two years, but if worse came to worst, I would have no other choice.

What type of man could allow his estate to go to rot and to slight his servants? I didn't know, nor did I wish to. In truth, I'd forgotten Mr. Jennings as readily as he'd forgotten Winterset. And now he wanted his servants to shine his home, order him special soap, and prepare his favorite meals?

Over my missing body.

I would not let the irresponsible Mr. Jennings displace me from my beloved Winterset.

"The estate *is* in disrepair," Bexley hedged. "It is possible, I suppose, that he might take one look at Winterset and decide to leave."

"He might," I agreed, "but we cannot leave it up to chance. We must do all we can to make Winterset inhospitable. We must drive Mr. Jennings away."

Mrs. Owensby sucked in a breath. "Kate, we cannot—"

"We can. We *must*. Did you not read his list of demands: French-milled soap? Portuguese port wine? A man of his breeding could *never* be happy here. We will help him realize it sooner. And until we can drive him away, I will stay out of sight. I will hide."

"What if Mr. Jennings discovers you before we can drive him away?" she asked.

The truth hung above our heads like a noose. "I won't let him find me."

"How could you help it?" Bexley asked. "Mr. Jennings will walk these halls every day."

"*I* have walked them my whole life. I know every secret passageway and priest hide."

"You cannot hide forever," Mrs. Owensby said.

"I don't intend to, just until Mr. Jennings leaves."

"And then what?" Mrs. Owensby asked, her voice gentle. "Even if we are successful in making Mr. Jennings leave, he would likely let the house or try to sell it."

"If that happens, we will scare-off potential renters or buyers just as we did him." It was not a perfect plan, it was not even a good plan, but I was desperate to hold on to my home and safety. To hold on to the promise I'd made Papa. I gathered Mrs. Owensby's work-worn hands into mine. "I know I have asked for so much these past two years, but I cannot stay here at Winterset without your help. I promise I will not let harm come to you or Bexley. I will do everything in my power to protect you."

"It is not *us* I am worried about." She looked down at our clasped hands, and her thumb traced over my charcoal-smudged knuckles. "*I* would protect *you* with my life, Kate."

"As would I," Bexley said, placing his hands around mine and Mrs. Owensby's.

Tears filled my eyes. "It won't come to that," I assured them, blinking away my emotion and standing to pace. "Not if we make his life miserable here."

Mrs. Owensby nodded. "His letter said he would arrive in four weeks. That should be enough time for a sufficient layer of dust and cobwebs to form."

"And I could track mud throughout the manor and ruin the carpets," Bexley suggested.

"No. Don't do anything Mr. Jennings might blame you for." My conscience could not bear it if anything happened to them because of me. "Besides, a dirty house is easily set to right. We must make him feel every discomfort the country has to offer."

"Such as . . . ?" Mrs. Owensby asked.

"Well, for starters, you should not do a thing to ready the house, seeing as neither you nor Bexley received a letter from Mr. Jennings informing you of his arrival, nor any money to pay for such provisions."

Mrs. Owensby's brow furrowed. "But we did receive word. And should he ask, the post-boy could confirm it."

"Actually, the letter was addressed to *Mr. Moore*," I said. "A pity he wasn't here to read it."

"That is true," Mrs. Owensby said. "But we opened the letter to discover the sender's identity, and when we saw Mr. Jennings had sent it, we did read it."

"*I* know that, but Mr. Jennings does not. Therefore, you must do nothing on his ridiculous list to prepare. Don't remove the Holland covers from the furniture or make up his bedchamber. Don't buy his precious soap or his delicious port wine. And once he is here, with all the work you will have to do with his unexpected arrival, Bexley will probably have to take on the duty of preparing Mr. Jennings's meals."

"I don't know how to cook." Bexley frowned.

"That is precisely the point." I smiled.

"But what if his discomfort makes him dissatisfied with us?" Mrs. Owensby said. "He could release us from his service."

"You need not worry about that," I said. "Even if Mr. Jennings wishes to let you go, there is not much skilled help nearby to hire a replacement, *none* who know and care for this manor as you do. And if by chance he did manage to find someone, you need only tell them of his treatment of you these past two years, and they would seek other employment."

She nodded, appearing mildly reassured.

"At every turn," I continued, "we will only help him see *his own* poor decisions and neglect."

"Except for all the dismal meals," Mrs. Owensby said.

"Yes, well, you are his housekeeper, not his cook, so even that will highlight his mismanagement," I said. "If we work together, we will be rid of him quickly, and things can return to normal."

My guardians nodded in understanding and agreement, silently vowing their support to do whatever was necessary to get Mr. Jennings to leave. Together we would make his life miserable, and he would return to his sophisticated life in the city.

And despite everything I had lost these past two years—my dear papa, my future, life as I'd known it—as we made a plan for my protection, I felt gratitude. Gratitude for the servants who had loved me my whole life and were now, in all respects, my family. Gratitude for Winterset. Gratitude that I was alive.

I would not give up these blessings so easily. I would not be turned out without a fight.

CHAPTER TWO

Oliver

Society could forgive a gentleman many faults so long as he possessed a title and a grand estate. Regrettably, I did not have—and never would have—a title, but I did have an estate, though it was not grand.

Winterset Grange.

Although the manor was old and far from London, at least it was mine.

Had Mother possessed brothers or the property an entailment, I would have been forced to earn a living—an unappetizing prospect for any man of gentle breeding, to be sure. Thankfully, there was neither. Which meant The Grange, as Mother lovingly referred to her childhood home, and all its possessions now belonged to me.

If I survived the long trip north, that was.

Several days into this jarring journey and, still, the carriage clattered on. Over stone, under bridge, and through countless villages. It seemed my valet, Charlie, and I would never reach our destination.

It had been over twenty years since I'd last visited my inheritance with Mother for the funeral of my maternal grandmother, and I remembered very little of the estate: the misted moors, the stone eagles that stood sentinel atop the gateposts, and the medieval wood door.

Winterset was beautiful in its way, but it was not Summerhaven, my childhood home, and that would take some—perhaps a lot—of adjusting to. And with a name like The Grange and an address so far from London, how was I ever meant to attract a suitable wife, let alone entice her to live there?

With a sigh, I stretched my legs and bumped Charlie.

"Sir?" He blinked into consciousness.

"My apologies. I did not mean to wake you," I said, but seeing as both of us stood over six feet tall and were folded into a tiny conveyance, it could not have been helped.

"It's no problem." Charlie sat upright, stretching. "I wanted to finish this poem before we arrived anyway." He retrieved his notebook and pencil from the bench beside him and began writing. His poems never made much sense to me, but they were humorous.

Charlie had been my valet for years, since Cambridge. We were near in age, height, and intellect. The only things that differentiated us were our incomes and social standing. He was my friend—perhaps my only friend these days—as much as he was my valet.

After I'd finished my schooling, he'd continued as my valet, accompanying me first to my set of rented rooms at Albany in London, then on my Grand Tour of the Continent. After two years discovering the wonders of Italy and France, settling at Winterset was likely as unappealing to him as it was to me, but Charlie was nothing if not loyal, and I was grateful not to be embarking on this final venture alone.

I had always pictured returning to Winterset with a wife, but Miss Amelia Atherton had declined my suit. The rejection did not fester. I hadn't loved her, and she hadn't loved me; neither of us wished for the difficulties that love brought into a marriage, which was why I had thought we would make a good match. But in the end, she had not wanted to live so far from her family. Although I could not relate to *that* sentiment, I had wished her well, and we'd parted as friends.

It was better this way.

Amelia would have been miserable so far from London. No, that fate was for me alone to endure. A penance for past deeds, probably.

Then, two years ago, I'd had my opportunity at happiness with my closest childhood friend, Hannah, but I'd been blind to her feelings for me. When I'd finally realized them and offered for her hand, it had been too late; she had fallen in love with my elder brother, Damon. It had been an uncomfortable situation, and to be honest, I'd already struggled to feel like I fit within my own family at Summerhaven; I was always out of step and out of place. The spare. They didn't need me, and they never had. So I'd set off on my Grand Tour.

I had not seen Damon and Hannah since the day of their marriage two years ago, but I did not begrudge their happiness; in fact, it was one of the many reasons that I stayed away from Summerhaven. I did not wish to cast a shadow on their contentment. My feelings for Damon were complicated, but even I could see how in love they were.

I'd never felt that kind of love. Not even for Hannah. Flirting was a favorite pastime of mine, and London had offered plenty of opportunity, but I'd never really loved a lady, and a lady had never loved me. But in two years, I had certainly changed, and now I hoped that one day my circumstances with love would change too.

Now, more than anything, I wanted to fall in love and marry. I wanted to find someone who I could settle down with and start a family, to have a place where I belonged. I'd gone about marriage wrong in the past, courting women not because I felt something for them but because of what they could offer me. I had been selfish and shortsighted. While I'd acted as so many of the *ton*'s gentleman did, I had not acted as a gentleman ought, something I deeply regretted. I'd worked hard to cultivate change within myself these past two years, though, and I was determined to court the right woman properly next time.

The carriage clattered on, with long stretches of travel, quick stops to change horses, more monotonous miles, day after torturous day. The farther we ventured north, the rougher the roads became. Mine and Charlie's horses, which were tied behind the carriage, protested the unsteady terrain with snorts of displeasure and frustrated neighs, their impatience mirroring my own.

I stared out the side glass.

As a boy, the untamed land surrounding Winterset had terrified me. The wild way the wind had whipped over the grass and through the gardens, how it had howled through Winterset's halls and hearths. Echo Ridge, where Winterset was built, was as beautiful as it was haunting.

At last, we came to the covered stone bridge that marked the southeast border of my estate. It wouldn't be much longer before Winterset came into view.

I did my best to smooth my cuffs and cravat, limp from hours of confined carriage travel, then donned my silk topper. It was the latest fashion, boasting a tall stove-pipe design and a bell-shaped brim, and had been made for my particular use by the finest hatter in all of London, Mr. James

Lock. It was a bit luxurious for traveling, but I wanted to arrive at Winterset in a manner befitting its master.

I could scarcely wait to enjoy a warm, well-cooked meal and to sleep in a comfortable bed. I'd written to Mr. Moore, the steward I'd hired to care for Winterset in my absence, notifying him of my arrival date, and I was not a day late. He would likely be waiting for me at the manor, eager to show me the many improvements he'd overseen there.

I'd written extensively to Mr. Moore in my last letter to him about my preferences to make the transition easier for the servants. *A gentleman could never be too prepared*, Father had obsessively preached, although only to Damon, not to me. As his second son—his spare—I'd always been beneath Father's notice, but I'd learned what I could from his overheard lectures.

My lack of preparation was one of the reasons I'd stayed away from Winterset so long.

When I'd come into my inheritance, I'd known I wasn't ready to take up my duties. I'd been ill-prepared and prideful and so deep in my cups that my whole world had wavered. The house had been blessedly let at the time, so I'd planned and paid for my Grand Tour of the Continent. But then Winterset had become unexpectedly vacant. I thought I would have to cancel my tour and see to the duties of running the estate.

Thankfully, Mr. Moore—the previous tenant's butler—had appeared like a godsend and offered me the perfect plan: hire him as steward to care for the estate and I could go on my Grand Tour, as planned. Mr. Moore's knowledge of the house had been second only to his love for the property, so I'd hired him.

With him to oversee Winterset's many repairs and refurbishments these past two years, I'd been able to enjoy my tour, confident that all was being taken care of in my absence.

Hiring him had been the best decision I could have made for Winterset, the one thing I was proud of.

After two years abroad, I had gained experience and perspective, and I was finally ready to take the reins, eager even. I wanted to make Winterset the pearl of the north. And perhaps, one day, if I worked hard enough to make something of this house and of myself, Society would overlook my lack of title.

The carriage continued through a small village. There weren't more than a dozen shops, and I did not see a hat shop, only a general haberdasher—a disappointment, to be sure. Next, we passed through woodland, then by several tenant farms. My tenants, I realized with some trepidation. And then, at last, looming in the distance was Winterset.

The sight sent a chill down my spine. The gray stone house stood ominously afar off. Its stacked stone chimneys stained black from more than three centuries of smoke looked like skeletal fingers reaching skyward. An intricate cornice adorned the roof like a rough-cut crown. And below, oriel windows jutted from the facade like the eyes of a haunted soul. The closer the carriage came to the manor, the heavier the air hung. It felt like the house itself was holding its breath.

The carriage swayed around the final bend and then suddenly stopped. The forceful motion all but threw me from the seat, and my hat toppled to the dirty floor.

Charlie looked up from his notebook. "Have we arrived?"

"It would seem so." I retrieved my hat from the ground and brushed off the dust. "Although we have not yet passed through the gateway." I righted myself and opened the door to inquire of the coachman. "Why have we stopped?"

"Gate's closed, sir," the coachman called back in a thick Scottish brogue.

"Can you not open it?" The coachman had not seemed a simpleton when I'd hired him, but one never could tell whether a servant was worth his wages until he'd been proven.

"'Tis grown over with ivy," he said.

Grown over? He must be mistaken. "Certainly a little ivy can't stop us from passing through," I said, but when I leaned out the conveyance to get a better view, I found that he was correct. It was *not* a little ivy. It was a curtain of ivy that covered the entirety of the gate. The scrolling iron, the red brick pylons, even the stone sentinels were completely cloaked.

"What the devil?" I hopped down from the coach, my boots sinking into the rain-softened soil, and strode quickly to the gate to search for the handle. In tearing away the vines that clung to the iron bars, I discovered the gate was chained and locked.

I stepped back and stared at it, utterly perplexed.

"Strange no one's here to greet you," the coachman called down to me.

"Quite." I stared hard at the padlock.

I'd written to Mr. Moore weeks ago, instructing him to have the servants prepare the house for my arrival. I'd not received a response, but I hadn't expected one, as I'd been traveling. Besides that, he was a man of few words, writing only when funds were needed for repairs or improvements. I'd appreciated his brevity while I'd been traveling the Continent, but now it worried me.

An uneasy thought crossed my mind: Perhaps I'd been too hasty in hiring Mr. Moore with only his own reference to recommend him.

Charlie joined me and stared at the gate too. "Perhaps Mr. Moore did not receive your letter?" he said.

"It's possible. But that fact hardly matters. If my steward cannot be trusted to keep my estate in readiness while I am away, he is not worth his wages."

Still, *a gentleman should never be too hasty in his judgment*—another lesson I'd overheard Father teach Damon. I dashed it away, determined not to let Father's voice overrun me now.

It was possible the gate was locked for a reason. What reason, I couldn't imagine, but it *was* possible.

"I need to see the state of the grounds and manor," I said, stepping closer to the gate.

It took considerable effort, but I made a small viewing hole through the intricately woven ivy. Though I could not see much through the defense foliage, I saw enough: an overgrown carriageway, a filthy fountain, which I had paid to have him refurbish last past spring, and boarded windows.

"Devil take it!" It was worse than I could have imagined. It looked as though not a single shilling I'd sent Mr. Moore—if that was even his name—had gone to Winterset's upkeep.

I'd trusted him! And I'd paid him handsomely to serve as my steward and to care for Winterset in my absence.

Evidently, I'd made a grave mistake.

Mr. Moore was not a steward but a thief!

What an imbecile I was! Every person who had passed by this blasted gate these past two years knew it too.

How humiliating!

"Do you want me to search for another entrance?" Charlie asked. "I can see if there are any other servants to help clear away the ivy so the carriage might enter the drive."

What I wanted was to go back in time two years and shake myself out of my liquor-induced stupor so that I could see clearly enough to discern Mr. Moore's true character and not have hired him. But since *that* wasn't possible, Charlie's plan would have to suffice. "Yes, Charlie. Thank you."

With a nod, he followed the fence line in search of the servant's entrance. And when he disappeared around the corner, I turned back to glare at the gate.

Pacing now, I prayed the inside of the manor did not match the exterior. If it did, I did not know what I would do, or rather, what I could afford to do. So much of my savings had been spent.

Several more minutes passed and, with it, the remainder of my patience.

If I could not pass *through* the gate, I would climb *over* it.

CHAPTER THREE

Kate

Rising to my tiptoes, I peered through the dirty diamond-paned window and tried to glimpse Mr. Jennings—a difficult task, considering the overgrowth.

"Careful," Mrs. Owensby said. "You mustn't let Mr. Jennings see you."

"I am well enough concealed." From the attic window where we stood, he could not see me. I could only just make out Mr. Jennings's ridiculously tall top hat moving back and forth as he paced in front of the gate. Truly, the crown of the hat must stand more than eight inches from the base.

How foolish he looked.

I hadn't stepped foot in Society for nearly two years, and even *I* knew his expensive-looking topper was more appropriate for promenading around Hyde Park than for cross-country travel. Was he so arrogant that he must always wear such a pompous hat? Who was he trying to impress out here in the country?

Insufferable man!

The sooner he left, the better.

I returned my gaze to the gate and gasped. "What in heaven's name is he doing?"

The gate pulsed with movement, and a moment later, Mr. Jennings's hat appeared over the ivy. Then two hands grasped the top of the gate. As he hoisted himself up, broad shoulders came into view. One long leg swung over the gate and then the next, and with one swift movement, Mr. Jennings jumped to the ground.

"My, but he is nimble." Mrs. Owensby sounded far too delighted for someone whose home was being invaded by the enemy.

I was *not* amused.

Yet I could not look away. Mr. Jennings stood on the overgrown carriageway, weeds up to his knees. From this distance, I could not make out the features of his face, only his form, which was, in a word, *ideal*.

Objectively, one might find him pleasing to look upon. Not me, of course, but someone. The impressive breadth of his shoulders was balanced by his statuesque height, which could not be less than six feet. And while many men who stood so tall tended to look long and lanky, like the cattails that grew near the pond, Mr. Jennings's limbs appeared perfectly proportioned.

Like Michelangelo's *David* come to life, he was a study of masculine form.

Mr. Jennings was probably missing teeth or hair or both. Perhaps he wore such a silly hat to distract from his less desirable features, details that I could not make out from here.

Hands set on hips, he turned in a slow circle, inspecting the courtyard.

"Oh, Kate," Mrs. Owensby said, pulling me from my thoughts. "He looks displeased, does he not?"

"Indeed, he does. *Quite* displeased. How distressing it must be for him to come face-to-face with the consequences of his own neglect."

"Now, Kate. You must not be unkind."

Mr. Jennings attempted to press through the weeds with little success. He made it only a few paces before abruptly stopping. At this rate, he might concede the fight before he even entered the house. Had his boot gotten stuck in the mud? His body jerked once, twice, and then he stumbled forward.

A smile tugged at my lips.

Perhaps I should have quelled my amusement, a proper young lady would have, but it had been such a long time since I'd had occasion to smile, and it felt so nice.

"I do hope our plan works," Mrs. Owensby said, her tone worried.

"It *will* work." Once Mr. Jennings stepped inside the house and saw that the manor had not been readied to his specifications, he would leave. Perhaps not tonight but by the end of the week, for certain.

We'd planned nothing malicious, only minor annoyances and discomforts. He would not be permanently affected, only permanently removed. Anywhere but Winterset would be quite acceptable to me.

"You've hidden the wax candles?" I asked Mrs. Owensby.

"Aye. Only the tallow candles remain."

"Very good." A well-bred man like Mr. Jennings would hate the stench of the cheaper tallow candles. They might even turn his sensitive stomach. "And his ancestors' portraits?"

"Bexley has removed them from the walls and packed them safely in the attic." She indicated over her shoulder to the far corner of the cramped space, where we now stood. "And every member of the Lockwood family is now proudly displayed in the entrance hall."

I nodded my approval. "An army of my grim-faced Lockwood ancestors will be the perfect welcome party, don't you agree?"

"I most certainly do," she said.

"And tonight's dinner—"

She held up a hand, stopping me. "Bexley has taken care of everything."

"You see? We have nothing to worry about. We will soon be rid of our unwelcome guest," I said, but despite my confident words, I could only hope that proved true.

Now was not the time for fear but faith.

I did not like the idea of creeping through the narrow servants' passages or crouching in cramped priest holes, but I would not have to live like a ghost forever, only until Mr. Jennings retreated back to his fancy London lodgings.

Beside me, Mrs. Owensby wrung her hands. "I must admit, I'm having misgivings. I do not like lying to the master of the house, Kate."

"Nor I," I said. "But it is for our mutual benefit. A gentleman accustomed to the finer things in life, like Mr. Jennings is, could never be happy here. We are only helping him reach that conclusion sooner and saving him a great deal of time and effort."

"I'm sure you are correct, but I do hate the thought of treating the master poorly."

"You need only remember how poorly *he* has treated Winterset." I turned away from the window to face her. "Two years Mr. Jennings has traveled the Continent, and not once did he send funds to care for his estate. His behavior was dishonorable, and he is unworthy of your respect."

"That may be true, but I still don't know if I can do this." She pressed a hand to her stomach, as if to still her nerves.

"Because you, unlike him," I glared out the window at Mr. Jennings, "are a person of the highest integrity."

It was true. Everything Mrs. Owensby did, she did with dedication. Seeing Winterset fall into such a sad state, even if by no fault of her own, had been unbearably hard for her, for all of us. She took pride in her responsibilities, and that included serving the master of the house, even if he did not deserve it.

I inched closer to the window to view Mr. Jennings's progress to the door.

Mrs. Owensby gave me a disapproving look. "You must be careful—"

"I will be careful. I promise."

With a nod, Mrs. Owensby walked to the stairs and took hold of the rope railing to safely descend.

I lingered at the window, wanting one last look at the man who was about to invade my home before I hid.

He was inspecting the fountain now and shaking his head. The pump had broken not long after Papa's death, and without funds to fix it, it was now filled with stinking sludge. I'd considered cleaning it myself but had decided the stench would keep would-be intruders away.

A moment later, Mr. Jennings stepped back, his gaze rising up the house.

I dashed the curtain closed before he could see me and pressed my back to the wall.

The time was nearly upon me, and I needed to hide before he entered the house.

The smart thing for me to do would be to lock myself in the priest hide up here in the attic. It was well hidden, and I doubted he would inspect this part of the house anytime soon. I glanced at the book on my bedside table. *The Mysteries of Udolpho* by Ann Radcliffe. The book had belonged to Mother. I'd planned to reread it for what had to be the fiftieth time in the past two years to pass the time, but if I was going to get Mr. Jennings to leave, didn't I need to know as much about the man as possible? Although I would not be able to see him, as I would be concealed in the priest hide, I'd at least be able to hear him. It did not feel right leaving Bexley and Mrs. Owensby to deal with this on their own. It was, after all, my plan. I wanted to help in some small way, so I decided to hide on the ground floor and gather information to use later.

I descended the attic stairs two at a time, then hurried down the corridor toward the main staircase, which led down to the entrance hall. No sooner had I reached the landing than the knob on the front door rattled, as though Mr. Jennings were attempting to open the door. Luckily, at least for me, it was locked. Then an ardent knock on the door sounded from below. It had been two years since anyone had darkened our doorway, save the post-boy, and my heart felt as if it would beat out of my chest.

Bexley was already halfway to the front door when I started down the stairs. He must have heard my steps because both he and Mrs. Owensby stopped and spun to look at me.

Mrs. Owensby's eyes widened. "Katherine Lockwood!" She gritted the words through her teeth. "You must be jesting." And when I reached the base of the staircase, she gave me such a stern look that I had half a mind to march back up the stairs and hide in the attic.

I might have done so, but then another knock came at the door, sharp and insistent.

"The priest hide," I said. "Behind Papa's portrait. Help me inside."

With a nod, we hastened across the entrance hall. My hiding spot would likely be the first thing Mr. Jennings laid eyes on when he stepped inside the manor, although he would not know it, as the priest hide was concealed by clever paneling and Papa's portrait.

Mrs. Owensby pressed the timber, and it swung out, exposing the small space within the wall.

The dark hide was much smaller than I remembered. Was there even room for me to climb inside?

When I was a young girl, Papa and I played hide-and-seek. Back then, it had been a most diverting game. But now, I dreaded experiencing this hide's true purpose: protection. Like the Catholic priests who'd hidden here three hundred years before, I now hid to protect my life.

"Quickly now," Mrs. Owensby said.

I crept slowly forward.

Bexley cleared his throat as if to hurry me.

Knowing I must obey or be found out, I climbed inside the priest hide and closed my eyes.

CHAPTER FOUR

Oliver

I rapped again on the weather-worn door, not knowing whether anyone was even inside to open it and receive me. Charlie still had not returned, but I hoped he'd found an entrance and, God willing, servants.

I'd provided funds to Mr. Moore to retain a housekeeper, a butler, several servants, *and* a grounds keeper to keep Winterset in good repair in my absence. But if none of the money I'd sent Mr. Moore to pay the servants had even made it to them, why would they have remained?

I raised my hand to knock yet again when the door groaned open on its hinges, revealing a grim-faced man.

"May I help you, sir?" the man said.

"I certainly hope so. I am Mr. Oliver Jennings, Winterset's master."

The man's gaze sharpened as he looked me over, from hat-covered head to mud-encrusted boots.

And when he offered me no welcome, I said, "And who, sir, are you?"

"Bexley, sir. I am the butler."

"A pleasure, Bexley."

He did not return the sentiment, only a stony stare.

"Bexley, do you know what has become of Mr. Moore? The previous tenant's butler."

"*I* was the previous tenant's butler, sir."

"Has a Mr. Moore ever been employed in any capacity at Winterset?" I asked.

"No, sir," he answered, confirming my fears.

I swore beneath my breath. And although Bexley's expression did not change at my directness, I got the distinct impression that he thought me slow of mind.

Perhaps I was.

Had I any sense, I would not have hired a charlatan such as Mr. Moore.

I had not expected a warm welcome, considering the state of things, but as a gentleman, I did deserve respect. It was not polite to leave a man of gentle breeding standing outside on a portico, let alone *his own* portico. "Might you move aside so I may enter my house, please?"

But Bexley did *not* move. In fact, he braced one shoulder against the door, defending against my entering. "Forgive me, sir, but how am I to know you are who you say you are?"

"A wise question,to be sure." One which I wished I had asked Mr. Moore two years ago. It galled my pride to prove to my servant who I was, but since he would not be moved, I produced the necessary paperwork from my breast coat pocket, which I'd kept on my person during the journey so as not to displace it, and handed the document to him.

Bexley looked over Winterset's deed and my inheritance claim, then inspected the seal on the reverse.

I removed my seal from my watch fob ribbon and gave it to him to view so that he might confirm my identity.

Bexley thoroughly inspected that, too, and when he was finally satisfied, he handed back the items and said, "My apologies, Mr. Jennings."

My initial reaction was to express my displeasure with him, but cutting a man down in order to build myself up was something Father would have done. I did not wish for my servants to fear me as Father's had him. I wanted my servants' respect, which meant I needed to emulate Mother's attitudes and actions.

"I appreciate your apology, and I commend you for your judicious protection of Winterset. It speaks well of you."

He blinked. "Thank you, sir. Do come in." He opened the door fully to grant me access.

Behind Bexley stood a woman. The housekeeper, likely. She had a creased, careworn face and a cautious gaze.

Moving toward the threshold, my heart raced with hope that the manor's interior would prove more promising than its exterior. Perhaps it was foolish, given the state of the gate and grounds, but Winterset was the desperate dream of my youth and my only hope for the future.

As I stepped inside, a floorboard groaned beneath my weight, an inauspicious greeting, to be sure. But knowing my servants watched me, I schooled my face into a neutral mask as I took in my surroundings.

The entrance hall boasted two floors. An arched corridor stretched the length of the landing, and a double staircase flowed like waterfalls along the outer walls to the modest entrance hall below. The appointments were adequate, but the space itself was not as large, nor as stately as the manor I'd grown up in.

My boots sounded against the weathered wood floor as I walked to the center of the room.

Directly before me hung not a few gilded-framed portraits. Indeed, there were so many frigid faces staring at me that it felt as though the walls had eyes.

The oak-paneled walls and scarlet-cloaked windows made the space dark and dreary—fitting for my mood, perhaps, but not my vision. I could only hope that when the drapes were properly pulled back, light would flood the room to dispel the dismal darkness.

It was obvious that efforts had been made to maintain the manor. There was not a speck of dust or dirt visible. And the fact that two servants remained at all made me wonder if perhaps Mr. Moore had sent them money. It did not make sense that he would, but why else would they remain here? How could I ask them that, though, without making an even greater fool of myself?

I continued surveying the space. Considerable refurbishments would need to be undertaken to bring this old maid into the nineteenth century. A burdensome task, considering much of my capital now lined Mr. Moore's pockets.

"Might I take your coat and hat, sir?" Bexley asked.

I hesitated, not because I did not want to remove them but because he was not wearing gloves, and I didn't want my new topper ruined.

Living so far from polite society, replacing it would be an impossible task. It was not as if I could step outside my door and walk to No. 6 St. James's Street as I had when I'd resided in my rented rooms at Albany.

Yet I did not wish to offend my servant in our first hour of meeting, so I handed over my belongings, and he moved to put them away.

"Before you go," I said, stopping him. "My valet, Mr. Charles Hanover, went around the house in search of an entrance earlier. Please find him and show him in, and then assist the coachmen in seeing that my belongings are unloaded and brought inside."

"Certainly, sir." Bexley bowed, my coat and hat in hand, and quit the room.

"Might I get you a cup of tea, Mr. Jennings?" the woman asked, not looking at me but at the floor.

Was she afraid of me? I ducked to meet her gaze. "Thank you, Mrs. . . ."

"Owensby. I am the housekeeper. For more than two decades now."

"Very good, Mrs. Owensby. A cup of tea will do nicely. But first, I would like a tour of the house."

Her eyes widened. "The *whole* house, sir?"

"Is that a problem?"

"Only that it is such a large house. And you are, no doubt, famished from your journey."

"That I am. But the cook can see to that."

"*I* am the cook, sir. Also the maid of all work."

Of course my staff would also be victims of that scoundrel, Mr. Moore. I berated myself silently once again. "Good gracious, Mrs. Owensby. That is a great deal of responsibility. I shall hire more staff immediately."

"No, thank you."

"No, thank you?" I blinked at her in surprise.

"Yes, sir. I prefer to work on my own."

"Now that I'm in residence, caring for Winterset will be an impossible task for one person."

"Two, sir. But Bexley also serves as a footman and even helps me in the kitchen on occasion."

I grimaced at the thought. Never in all my life had I heard of a butler serving beneath his station. And Mrs. Owensby certainly needed more help, but to insist on hiring more help when she did not desire it would likely offend her. Heavens. What should I do? This discussion would have to be revisited at a later date. "Only a brief tour," I said. I did wish to eat tonight.

"Very well. We will start right here with the portraits."

In requesting a tour, I had not meant that I wanted to view the manor's details but rather the house in general—the main halls, the private rooms, maybe even the outbuildings, if time remained before nightfall. But if she wished to show me the particulars, I would oblige.

I followed her across the entry hall to view the portraits.

"As you can see," she began, "more than five generations are represented in this room."

"Impressive," I said with more enthusiasm than I felt.

"It is, sir. This wall displays a great many men and women of honor."

"Indeed," I agreed, although I did not know much about my mother's ancestors. When Mrs. Owensby didn't move on, I feigned interest, and with hands clasped behind my back, I bent to inspect the nameplate. *Francis Lockwood, 1589.* Lockwood? I frowned. Though my maternal line was somewhat of a mystery, I was certain there was some mistake. "This man is not my ancestor."

"No, sir. He was your former tenant's ancestor."

"Do all these portraits"—I indicated the other paintings on the wall "—belong to the Lockwood family?"

"Aye." Mrs. Owensby nodded proudly.

"Why do they still hang on my walls?"

"Because the walls in the dining hall and portrait gallery were already covered, sir."

She must've understood my meaning: not why did they hang *here* in the entrance hall, but why did they hang in *my* house at all? "Forgive me, Mrs. Owensby, but where are *my* ancestors' portraits?"

"In the attic," she said as though that should be obvious.

I took a deep breath. "These portraits should have been removed and replaced with my family portraits."

"Had you sent word of your arrival, they would have been, sir."

I had sent word of my arrival, only to Mr. Moore, although I was too taken aback to contradict her. I could only blink. Never in my life had a servant spoken this way to me. Had she meant to be impertinent? It would profit me nothing to reveal my mounting annoyance, so I said calmly, "Well, now that I am here, please have these packed and sent to Mr. Lockwood directly."

"I'm afraid that is impossible," Mrs. Owensby said.

"Why is that?"

"Because Mr. Lockwood now resides in heaven, sir. And no matter how much you might want his ancestors' portraits packed and sent away, I'm not sure how I would do that."

I tried to contain my irritation. "Mrs. Owensby, you must know that I meant for the portraits to be sent, not to the deceased Mr. Lockwood but to his next of kin."

"And surely *you* must know Mr. Lockwood has no next of kin." She spoke slowly, enunciating each word as if *I* were a simpleton.

I did not know how much other masters knew of their tenants, but when I'd come into my inheritance two years previous, I'd been too deep in my cups to learn anything more about Winterset's leaseholder than to ascertain whether or not he was current on his rent.

"Did Mr. Lockwood have any children?" I asked.

Mrs. Owensby hesitated. "None to speak of, sir."

"There must be *someone* who will receive these portraits. A distant relative perhaps? I will have my solicitor search them out. In the meantime, these pictures are to be removed and my family portraits hung in their place."

Mrs. Owensby made a show of wringing her apron.

"What is it, Mrs. Owensby?" I sighed inwardly.

"Removing the portraits of the dead will bring Winterset bad luck."

I sighed inwardly. Was everything I said to be met with this much opposition? "Mr. Lockwood removed *my* ancestors' portraits, did he not?"

"Aye. And that did not end well for him."

I did not know the details of Mr. Lockwood's death, only that he'd died, so I could not argue the point. "Well, we shall just have to hope that when the rightful portraits of *my* family are restored to their proper places, all will be made right."

"I advise against it, sir, but if you insist—"

"I do." I'd never been superstitious, and although I could tolerate those who were, this was *my* home, and I would not have another family's portraits hanging on my walls.

"I will inform Bexley," she said with a submissive bow of her head.

"Very good." I gestured that Mrs. Owensby should continue our tour. She did not put up a fight. A small, if not easily won, victory.

I followed in her wake but made it only a few steps when a young lady's portrait arrested my attention. As I turned to view it, my boot caught a hole in the threadbare carpet, causing my lower half to stop suddenly while the bulk of my body continued forward. Had it not been for my training at Gentleman Jackson's boxing salon, I would not have been quick enough on my feet to catch my fall.

"Are you all right, sir? That was quite a stumble!" Mrs. Owensby exclaimed as I composed myself. "You looked like a caught chicken, the way you flailed about."

A noise that sounded almost like a laugh came from my right.

I glanced around the entrance hall but saw no one. "Is there someone else here?"

"O-only the portraits," she stammered.

"Did you not hear something?"

"Winterset is over three hundred years old, Mr. Jennings. You will hear many sounds: the creaking of the gables. The scurrying of rats."

"This was a voice. A young lady's voice." I was certain of it.

"Perhaps you've seen a ghost," she said, her expression grave.

"*Heard* a ghost," I corrected, and hearing the utter ridiculousness of my words, I shook my head. "I must be more fatigued from my journey than I realized." I rubbed my forehead and returned my gaze to the portrait.

Dark curls, pale skin, and bright eyes.

I leaned forward to inspect the nameplate, but it was missing, the small nail holes where it had been secured now exposed. The only identifying mark on the painting was a date: 1818. The same year I'd left on my Grand Tour.

"Whose portrait is this?" I asked Mrs. Owensby, not taking my eyes off the portrait.

Her eyes flicked to the portrait and then quickly away. "Oh. Well, I suppose it belongs to you now."

Was she being purposefully obtuse? "That is not what I meant."

"Oh. Pardon me. I believe the artist's name is Mr. Colstone."

"Mrs. Owensby, who is the *subject* of this painting?" My question came out more curtly than I intended, but I needed to know the young lady's name.

"Oh. Why did you not ask?"

"I thought I *had*."

Mrs. Owensby smiled as if we'd had a happy misunderstanding, though the mirth in her eyes gave me the distinct impression that she was toying with me. "Why, that is Miss Lockwood."

"Miss Lockwood?" I directed a pointed look at Mrs. Owensby. "Mr. Lockwood's daughter?"

"Aye. She is beautiful, is she not?"

"She is . . . sufficient," I said, but in truth, I was spellbound. Although I'd danced, and even flirted, with many beautiful women both in London and on the Continent, I had *never* seen this young lady's equal. Miss Lockwood was more than beautiful. She was captivating. Something about her big bright-blue-green eyes, her curls cascading down her delicate neck, her heart-shaped mouth—lips that almost smiled but didn't quite—utterly enthralled me. "She laughs at me."

"Aye. That she does, sir." And so did my housekeeper.

"What is Miss Lockwood's Christian name?" I asked.

Mrs. Owensby's brow rose. "My, but you are forward."

I dragged my gaze away from the portrait to look at my housekeeper. "This is a painting, Mrs. Owensby, not a person. I am only inquiring because earlier, you said Mr. Lockwood has no next of kin, yet this portrait proves that he does."

"I did not say he had no children, sir."

"You did," I countered, pointing at her.

"No. I said Mr. Lockwood had no next of kin *to speak of*."

Were we truly arguing over semantics? I heaved a weary sigh and rubbed my temples. If every conversation with Mrs. Owensby was going to be this exhausting, I would need to develop a great deal more patience or, better yet, assign Charlie to the task.

"Mr. Lockwood did have a daughter," Mrs. Owensby continued, "but she is . . ." Her sentence stalled as she bowed her head and circumspectly crossed herself with a whispered prayer.

"Miss Lockwood is deceased?" I could not believe it. Someone so young and lovely as she could not possibly be gone.

But Mrs. Owensby sniffed in acknowledgment.

"Forgive me," I said, feeling badly for making my housekeeper cry, and I quickly handed her my handkerchief. "I did not know."

She took it and blew her nose—several times—then offered it back to me.

"Please. Keep it." I held up my hand, and as she tucked the handkerchief into the front of her apron, I tried not to grimace. "Shall we continue our tour?" I suggested, hoping to extricate myself from this most uncomfortable situation. Then, realizing she was likely to continue in the same detailed way as before, I added, "Though I should only like to view the remainder of the ground floor tonight."

"As you say, sir," Mrs. Owensby said, and as she turned to lead me away, I thought I saw the corner of her mouth twitch.

It was not until later, when I stood in my pitiful excuse for a bedchamber with Charlie, dressing for dinner, that I realized Mrs. Owensby had not told me the young lady's name.

CHAPTER FIVE

Kate

As soon as the entrance hall fell quiet, I shifted in my seated position in the cramped priest hide to relieve some discomfort in my back, but I found no relief.

It felt like an age since I'd climbed inside this cramped hiding spot, and every part of me ached, my lungs most of all. Winterset's walls were so damp and dusty that I was sure I was breathing air that had sat stagnant for more than two centuries.

Best not to think about it.

Instead, I envisioned Mr. Jennings—what was it that Mrs. Owensby had said?—oh yes: *Flailing like a caught chicken.*

My mouth tugged up at the corners, but I denied myself the pleasure of laughing. After my slip earlier, it had been a minor miracle that Mr. Jennings had not discovered me. Mrs. Owensby would surely box both my ears for the mistake.

At least Mrs. Owensby had played her part perfectly. She'd not lied to Mr. Jennings, at least not overtly, and still, she'd made him believe me dead. I did not know how she had managed it, but I was grateful.

At long last, Mrs. Owensby returned to release me. Without a way to keep time in the dark priest hide, I'd estimated that it would be nearing sundown, but when the panel was pressed open, I was surprised to find that it was full dark. The only light in the entrance hall came from the candle in Mrs. Owensby's outstretched hand. I crawled out, my legs weak from being held in one position for so long.

"Are you all right, dear?" Mrs. Owensby whispered, helping me stand.

I started to nod, but even my neck was sore. Drat! I would have to be more selective in where I hid in the future. Winterset had several priest hides—twelve, that I knew of. Some, like the one I'd hidden in today, were tiny and tight, and others, like the one in the attic, were quite large. Well, not *large*, but big enough that Bexley had furnished it with a bed and a bedside table for my few things because that would be my new bedchamber for the time being. It was small, but my mattress was at least comfortable, which was more than I could say for Mr. Jennings's mattress. Still, he was getting the better bargain; he would sleep in a proper bedchamber tonight.

"We must get you a plate of food and sneak you up the servants' stairs before Mr. Jennings or his manservant come down for dinner," Mrs. Owensby said quietly.

Famished, I readily agreed. But before following after her, I removed my portrait from the wall and pushed it inside the priest hide, where it would be safe from Mr. Jennings's critical gaze. *Sufficient*, indeed.

With a sigh, Mrs. Owensby shook her head and turned toward the kitchen.

I followed closely behind, Mrs. Owensby's lone flame our only source of light.

How disconcerting it felt being resigned to the shadows. This morning, I'd walked freely through these rooms. Now I was a visitor. The happy halls I'd known my whole life were suddenly fearsome and foreign.

As we neared the kitchen, a foul scent filled the air, like burned bread and spoiled meat. I lifted a hand to my nose. "What is that horrible smell?"

"*That* is Mr. Jennings's dinner," Mrs. Owensby said. "I think Bexley is almost done. He has been boiling the beef for the better part of two hours."

"Two *hours*?" Mr. Jennings's dinner would closer resemble saddle leather than food.

"Don't worry, dear. I've prepared a tray of finger sandwiches, fruit, and cheese for you to enjoy."

We entered the kitchen to a veritable circus; pots bubbled and boiled over, bread burned in the oven, and a mess of ingredients were strewn across the worktable. And at the center of it all was Bexley, red-faced and frantic.

"I c-cannot be sure," Bexley stuttered, "but I think I may have r-ruined Mr. Jennings's dinner."

"Oh dear." Mrs. Owensby grinned. "I daresay you did."

I pressed my lips together, trying to hide my amusement. I'd not meant for Bexley to cook Mr. Jennings's dinner quite so poorly. I did not wish for Mr. Jennings to stay, but neither did I want for him to starve. There was nothing to be done about it now though. The least I could do was make Bexley feel better. "I can hardly wait to see Mr. Jennings's face when he eats it." Or tried to eat it anyway.

"Certainly not," Mrs. Owensby scolded, tidying the worktable. "You, Katherine Lockwood, will be safely tucked away in the attic long before Mr. Jennings comes down for dinner. Do you understand me?"

"I'd prefer to eat my meal here in the kitchen with you."

"And with Mr. Jennings's manservant?" She huffed a laugh. "I think not."

I'd forgotten about Mr. Jennings's valet.

"Speaking of, you must take your tray and go up the servants' stairs to your new bedchamber before Mr. Hanover comes down to dinner," she said.

Bexley began plating the beef on a serving platter, and a piece fell to the floor. He quickly retrieved it and moved to add the soiled meat to the platter.

"Bexley." I held out my hand, stopping him. My conscience wouldn't allow me to knowingly feed Mr. Jennings soiled food. "You must throw that piece out."

Bexley blinked at the piece of meat, seemingly surprised by what he was about to do, then tossed it aside. He rubbed his brow with the back of his hand. "If I should never cook another meal again, it would be too soon."

"My kitchen agrees with you," Mrs. Owensby said, surveying the chaos.

"But it was a valiant first attempt," I reassured him, and I was about to offer him words of comfort when footsteps sounded on the servants' staircase.

We stilled to listen, and my heart began to gallop.

These stairs connected the house's upper floors to the kitchen and servants' quarters below, which likely meant Mr. Jennings's valet was coming to the kitchen for dinner and that Mr. Jennings himself was finished dressing and would soon be entering the dining hall, which was also connected to the kitchen.

I was trapped.

Mrs. Owensby's panicked gaze shot to mine. "He's much earlier than we expected. Quick, Kate!" She motioned for me to hide behind the worktable even as she stepped in front of it.

"Good evening, Mr. Hanover," Bexley said, attempting a casual tone and subtly positioning himself to block Mr. Hanover's view of me.

"And to you, Mr. Bexley," Mr. Hanover replied, and although I could not see him, his voice painted a portrait of a polite young man, not much older than I.

"This is Mrs. Owensby, the housekeeper," Bexley said.

"Pleased to make your acquaintance, Mrs. Owensby."

"Mr. Hanover," Mrs. Owensby greeted, joining Bexley's side.

"Charlie, if you please."

"Very well, Charlie," she said. "Now tell me, how long have you been employed by Mr. Jennings?"

"Fourteen years," he said, and I detected pride in his voice.

"So long? You can't be but five and twenty years yourself."

"I am eight and twenty, same as Mr. Jennings. My contract with him was rather informal during his time at Eton. I did not come into proper employment until Mr. Jennings's studies at Cambridge."

"My, that is certainly a long time. Mr. Jennings must be a kind and fair master," she said.

"Yes, ma'am. He is not without his faults, but I would not wish to work for anyone else."

What faults did Charlie hint at? Mr. Jennings had already proved himself a neglectful landowner, but did he possess more egregious vices?

"Well, Charlie, we are glad to have you join us. As you can see, we are not large in numbers, but we pitch in wherever needed, and we get by."

"Yes, ma'am. I, too, am happy to help wherever needed."

"With your master's unexpected arrival," Mrs. Owensby said, "we have need to put you to work straightaway."

"Of course, ma'am. But first, I must ask, is that dinner tray intended for me?"

My gaze rose. The corner of *my* dinner tray hung slightly over the edge of the worktable.

"I hate to presume," he said when no one answered, "but after today's travels, I am quite hungry."

"Who else would it be for?" Mrs. Owensby said with false cheer. "Bexley, fetch the tray for Charlie, please."

"No need," Charlie said. "I can get it myse—"

"I insist," she interjected. If he were to come around the worktable, he would see me.

Bexley walked to the worktable, and when he grabbed the tray, I wanted to cry. After a long day of hiding, I was also hungry.

"Charlie," Mrs. Owensby said, commanding his attention away from my direction, "will Mr. Jennings be down to dinner soon?"

"Forgive me for not saying so earlier, but he is already waiting in the drawing room to be shown into the dining hall."

Mr. Jennings wished to be *shown* into the dining hall? Papa and I had always shown ourselves into dinner. Was Mr. Jennings so self-important as to stand on formalities even when dining alone? I looked heavenward and shook my head.

As Charlie sat at the servants' table with *my* tray, Mrs. Owensby came around the worktable, where I crouched. She glanced in Charlie's direction, then tipped her head toward the kitchen door leading to the dining hall.

I hesitated. What if Mr. Jennings had grown tired of waiting and shown himself into the dining hall?

Go, she mouthed.

I peeked around the edge of the worktable. Charlie was seated with his back toward me. Mrs. Owensby moved to block him from seeing me should he turn, and Bexley engaged Charlie in conversation, talking a touch too loudly, no doubt to cover any sound my exit might make.

I quickly but quietly tiptoed across the kitchen toward the servants' entrance into the dining hall. Mrs. Owensby glanced inside the room and, after confirming it was vacant, ushered me inside. "Hide behind the tapestry in the small alcove where the display cabinet used to be," she whispered. "Stay there until Mr. Jennings has retired upstairs for the night. I'll fetch you when it's safe."

I shook my head. "I will go upstairs before you show him in and hide in the attic."

"Don't be foolish. The drawing room where he waits has a clear view of the staircase."

As much as I longed to retire to my bed, she was right. Crossing the entrance hall to the stairs *would* be foolish.

Mrs. Owensby pulled back the tapestry to reveal the small alcove, and I stepped inside.

The alcove was taller than the priest hide in the entrance hall, but it lacked depth, so I would have to stand.

Once the tapestry was back in place and my eyes adjusted to the darkness, I realized the cloth had several small holes that allowed light to shine through. I'd never noticed the imperfections in all the years I'd sat in this hall, but there they were. As I stood staring at the worn tapestry, I felt like I was seeing it for the first time. Were there other things I'd failed to see as they really were?

I leaned forward to peer through one of the holes. I had an unobstructed view of the dining hall, specifically the head of the table where Mr. Jennings would be seated. Indeed, it would be almost as though I were sitting, or rather standing, directly across the table from him, only better because I would be able to see him, but he would not be able to see me.

But what if I sneezed? Or fainted from fatigue? Mr. Jennings would discover me, and then—

I cut off the thought, but my heart continued racing. I closed my eyes, attempting to calm myself, and breathed deeply.

So long as I stayed hidden, I was safe.

Bexley's voice carried from the entrance hall. He was again speaking loudly, no doubt to warn me of their coming. I leaned forward to watch through one of the holes. A few moments later, the door opened, and Bexley led Mr. Jennings into the dining hall.

I sucked in a silent breath at the sight of him.

This man invading my home was *handsome*.

His face was all smooth lines and sharp angles. He had a straight nose and a square jaw. He even had a cleverly clefted chin. Whether he had a complete set of teeth, I wouldn't know until he began his dinner, but he did have hair. And it was lovely hair too: loose, golden curls that were perfectly twisted and neatly styled but not overly so.

His features were so finely formed. He really was as handsome as a man carved of marble.

A pity that sculpture was my least favorite medium of art.

Statues were too perfect to be interesting to me. Stone, like Mr. Jennings's face, lacked a certain humanity. The symmetry was nice to look at, to be sure, but there was nothing uniquely interesting about his features that made me wish to commit his likeness to paper.

His face held no strength, no story that demanded to be told. To me, it was a person's imperfections and the strength they exuded that captured my attention.

Mr. Jennings's gaze—I could not tell what color his eyes were from this distance—swept the dining hall, taking in everything: the molded ceiling, the paneled walls, the gilded chandelier, and finally, the tapestry, behind which I hid.

Did he approve of his new home, or was he disappointed? His face was impassive as he sat at the table.

I wished for him to like Winterset enough to finally take care of her but not so much that he would want to stay in residence.

It was a dichotomous, confusing feeling, to be sure.

Bexley and Mrs. Owensby entered with the food dishes and set them on the table before Mr. Jennings.

Mr. Jennings stared at the food being placed before him, his spine stiff. "Thank you for this . . . meal, Mrs. Owensby," he said, and I noted the absence of praise.

"Actually, sir, Bexley prepared your meal tonight."

Mr. Jennings's gaze shifted to Bexley. "*You* cooked this meal."

"I did, sir."

"While I was giving you the tour of the ground floor," Mrs. Owensby offered as explanation.

"I see," Mr. Jennings said, and he dropped his gaze to his plate and stared forlornly at his dinner.

"Can I offer you some wine, sir?" Bexley said.

"Please," Mr. Jennings replied a bit too readily for a man of gentle breeding, though he would need it to stomach this plateful.

Glass filled to the brim, Mrs. Owensby moved to serve Mr. Jennings's meal. First, a piece of burnt bread, then a chunk of overboiled beef so rubbery that it bounced off his plate onto his lap, then fell unceremoniously to the floor.

"Pardon me," Mrs. Owensby said, sounding more than a little embarrassed as she lowered herself to retrieve the meat. She served him another portion and then stood with Bexley by the wall.

I held a hand to my mouth to keep from laughing—I would not make that mistake again—then watched him eat. It took him considerable time to chew the meat enough to swallow it safely. That he could chew it at all was a testament to the fact that he indeed had a strong set of teeth.

"May I serve you more beef, sir?" Mrs. Owensby asked when he'd finished his food.

"No!" Mr. Jennings said swiftly. "That is, I've had *more* than enough."

I was sure he had. I grinned.

"Would you like dessert?" Mrs. Owensby asked.

"Dessert?" Mr. Jennings said hopefully. "That would be most agreeable. Thank you."

"It is my pleasure, sir. I will fetch it from the kitchen. Bexley, will you assist me?"

"Certainly," he said and followed her out of the dining hall.

As soon as the door closed and Mr. Jennings was alone, or so he thought, he let out a low moan and leaned forward to rest his head in his hands. He sat like that for a long moment, his golden curls poking through his fingers, then heaved a weary sigh and relaxed back into his chair.

He looked exhausted, and his pallor was gray. Clearly, the country did not agree with him. We were doing him a favor in hastening his trip home.

Mrs. Owensby returned only a minute later carrying Mr. Jennings's dessert: headcheese jelly covered in custard and spritzed with lemon. A unique blend of savory, sweet, and sour, which could only loosely be called dessert.

When Mr. Jennings saw the oozing, gelatinous concoction, he held a hand to his mouth as if he might be sick. "Only a small serving, please," he said.

"Nonsense," Mrs. Owensby said. "After the long journey you've had, you deserve a king's portion, you do." She served him a healthy helping, then waited for him to take a bite.

He reluctantly did, appearing to swallow without chewing. He continued in the same way until he'd eaten nearly all the dessert. Then he claimed fatigue and retired to his bedchamber.

I had to give Mr. Jennings credit; despite everything we'd put him through today, he had remained calm and controlled. His cool demeanor would not last long though. I would make sure of it.

CHAPTER SIX

Oliver

Sunlight streamed through the window, and a scratching sound—rats?—roused me from a restless night's sleep.

"Charlie," I groaned, rolling over on my hard-as-rocks mattress. "Close the curtain." But, of course, Charlie could not hear me because his quarters in my new house were below stairs with the other servants.

I wrestled back my covers and stumbled toward the window. After the day I'd had yesterday, I'd wanted to sleep as long as possible. Apparently, Winterset had other plans.

I grabbed the curtain to close it, but when I pulled, the rod broke and the curtains fell to the floor.

Devil take it!

I made several attempts to drape the curtain across the broken rod before giving up the fight and leaning against the window frame, exhausted. Last night, sleep had come in fits and starts, and thanks to Miss Lockwood's portrait and her unsettling smile, it had not been at all restful.

The view from my bedchamber window was nothing special, just the overgrown grounds, but cloaked in morning mist, it appeared *slightly* less unpleasant than yesterday, likely because I could not yet see it clearly. As a boy, I'd risen early every morning to watch the sunrise. It was the most magical, hopeful time of day, but it had been many years since I'd risen early enough to view it.

Before arriving yesterday, I'd been excited to make Winterset the pearl of the north. But now that the estate had proved less a dream and more a nightmare, I wasn't so enthusiastic.

I released a heavy breath, and the warmth fogged the frozen window panes. As I watched the sun rise, some of my agitation settled. Seeing the sun peek over the horizon, the newness of the day, made me feel more serene. Perhaps I'd been too pessimistic yesterday. I had been weary of a week-long journey and tired and hungry. Perhaps the shock of seeing the condition of the courtyard yesterday had clouded my impression of the manor. While I was *still* tired, having seen the sunrise, rude awakening notwithstanding, I felt more optimistic.

I had the sudden urge to see the manor by the light of day and take stock of everything that needed to be repaired.

Not wanting to wake Charlie, I dressed myself, grabbed my notebook and pencil, then crept down the darkened corridor toward the staircase. It was still early, so the candles had not yet been lit, but that was preferable, considering their off-putting odor I'd noticed last night.

I opened my notebook and wrote: *purchase wax candles*, then closed my notebook around my pencil and descended to the darkened entrance hall. When I reached the base, the dining hall door opened, and Mrs. Owensby stepped into the entrance hall.

"Good morning, Mrs. Owensby," I said.

"Mr. Jennings!" She startled, clutching her heart. "You're awake early."

"As are you."

"I've not yet seen your manservant. Shall I fetch him for you?"

"No need. I am well enough dressed for the day, am I not?"

"Indeed," she said even as she eyed my unshaven face with a disapproving look that reminded me pleasantly of Mother. "But a servant should rise before his master. I will wake him and issue a lecture."

"There's no cause for a lecture," I said. "My usual schedule has conditioned him to both rise and retire late. Let Charlie sleep."

Mrs. Owensby's disapproval deepened into a frown, but she said nothing more on the subject.

"Shall we get on with it, then?" I said.

"Get on with *what*, sir?"

"Our tour, of course."

"Surely not before you've eaten breakfast."

I touched my stomach, which was still protesting last night's meal. "After such a *hearty* meal last night, I have no appetite this morning. And

I wish to see every inch of Winterset, so we best begin straightaway. We can start where we left off yesterday, on the ground floor, and work our way up to the attic."

"You don't wish to tour the attic." She shook her head.

"Of course I do." I didn't know why that would surprise her. "I intend to survey every inch of this estate."

"But the attic is . . . well, it is haunted, sir."

I fought a sigh, not wishing to endure another day of my housekeeper's games. Mrs. Owensby was like the matchmaking mamas in London, the way she persisted in toying with me. Perhaps I should play along with her little games as I had with the matchmaking mamas. Then, at least, we'd both have fun. "Tell me more," I said, tucking my notebook under my arm and my pencil into my pocket. "Are you acquainted with this ghost?"

"Indeed, I am, sir. *Well* acquainted."

"Capital." I clapped my hands together, causing her to jump. "In that case, I would like an introduction."

Mrs. Owensby's brow furrowed. "I do not think she would be willing to accept your introduction. Now, if you will—"

"*She?*" I said, my attention piqued. "I have a *female* ghost living in my house?"

Mrs. Owensby blinked, her eyes unnaturally wide.

Oh yes. Teasing Mrs. Owensby was vastly more enjoyable than being teased by her. "You must tell me now whether she is married," I said. "I should hate for her husband to call me out."

Mrs. Owensby looked at the floor, worrying her lower lip.

"That said, if she is unmarried, that, too, would be a problem. Can you imagine the scandal if Society discovered I was residing under the same roof as an unmarried lady? Tell me now, Mrs. Owensby," I said, adopting a serious tone, "is my ghost married?"

"No." She shifted her weight side to side. "Well . . . she was almost married, once."

"How curious," I said, playing along. "My ghost is engaged, then?"

"*Was* engaged."

"More intriguing still. What, pray tell, is my ghost's name?"

She swallowed hard. "I dare not utter it, sir."

"Ah. I see. You are afraid of her," I said. "Never fear. I shall vanquish this ghost from the premises." I opened my notebook, wrote *Vanquish ghost*, and then showed it to Mrs. Owensby for approval.

"Y-you mustn't do that." Her voice trembled.

Gads! I had not mean to frighten the poor woman. Perhaps I'd taken my jesting too far. "My apologies, Mrs. Owensby. I did not mean to make light of something serious to you. However, I do need to survey the attic to ascertain the soundness of the roof. We will do our best not to disturb this ghost."

"That would be in your best interest, sir. Winterset has a tragic enough history already."

"Tragic? How do you mean?"

"You must know this house's history."

"Some of it," I said, but in truth, I knew almost nothing about Winterset.

Mrs. Owensby appraised me, the downturn of her lips suggesting she thought me slow of mind.

Currently, I felt it.

Father never spoke of Winterset, not of its history nor of my maternal ancestors who had lived here. Not ever. Mother spoke of it fondly, though not often. And I hadn't wanted to know; it was Father's surname I carried and Father's family I had so desperately wanted to belong to, not Mother's. Winterset had always been both a blessing and a banishment. Something I had dreamed of but also despised.

I opened my mouth to explain but then closed it, remembering myself. I was master here and did not need to explain myself to my servants. Instead, I made a few more notes about needed repairs in the entrance hall:

Replace carpets
Repair uneven floorboards
Return Lockwood portraits

"Well," Mrs. Owensby said. "I can tell you what I know of Winterset, if you'd like. But I must warn you, it isn't all pleasant."

"Please. Go ahead."

With a nod, she led me across the entrance hall to the study. "Winterset Grange was built in 1485 and originally served as a monastic granary to Blackhurst Abbey up the lane. Sadly, the monastery was dissolved during King Henry VIII's reign, and the crown seized and then sold all buildings."

"Which is when my maternal ancestors came into possession of The Grange," I said.

"No. Both the abbey and The Grange were sold to the Smythes. Two decades later, your ancestors bought Winterset, when Mr. Smythes's financial indiscretions forced the sale. A blow to that family but a blessing to yours."

"Indeed," I said, though it was hard to think of it as such. I knew the pain that a father's financial indiscretions caused; my own family seat, Summerhaven, had been beggared because of Father's debts. The entailment had prevented its sale, and Damon had ultimately found another way to save the estate from complete ruin, but its impoverishment was painful.

"Upon the sale," Mrs. Owensby continued, "The Grange was renovated into a proper manor house, tenant dwellings were erected to provide the new estate needed income, and finally, the grounds were improved."

"An admirable undertaking," I said.

"It was," she agreed.

"Winterset's history is not so horrific; I was prepared to hear a terrific tale."

"Well, I am not finished," Mrs. Owensby said. "During Queen Elizabeth's reign, when religious tensions were high, especially here in the north, Winterset was renovated yet again and served as a safe house for Catholic priests suffering persecution from the newly formed Church of England. Sadly, at least one priest perished while hiding here."

"That is tragic."

"Aye," she said, leading me from the study into the drawing room. "And during the English Civil War, your fourth great-grandmother perished protecting the manor from Roundheads."

"Truly?" I grimaced.

Mrs. Owensby nodded. "She loved and fought for this house until her very last breath."

"How many have died here?" I asked.

"Too many. God rest their souls."

My stomach knotted with guilt. I'd descended from a long line of passionate people. People who had worked to buy and build up Winterset. People who had protected the property and those who had dwelled upon it with their lives. I'd never felt a fraction of the feelings my maternal ancestors had. I'd never loved anything enough to be willing to sacrifice, much less die for it.

Would I ever?

I walked to the window and pulled back the curtain. Outside, it was overcast and dreary, a stark contrast to the inside, where the walls were papered in blue with tiny gold peacock plumes painted in a pattern. Sadly, upon closer inspection, the paper below the window was water-damaged.

Repair water damage, western wall
Remove wall papers in drawing room
Repair window casement

We continued our tour of the ground floor, viewing first the library, then the study, and finally, the dining hall. Every room required repair.

Next, Mrs. Owensby led me through the kitchen and downstairs to the servants' quarters, where she, Bexley, and Charlie slept. The rest of the servants' rooms were vacant and, with all my money now needed for repairs, likely would be for some time.

We climbed the servants' stairs in the kitchen to the first floor.

Winterset boasted four bedchambers, two in the western wing and two in the eastern wing. Mrs. Owensby led me to the eastern wing first. The first bedchamber she showed me was the one I'd occupied last night, thus I didn't spend much time inspecting it. I'd already experienced its dilapidated condition firsthand. I glared at the lumpy mattress and the broken curtain rod, then made a note to replace both.

The second bedchamber was in even worse condition, with peeling wall papers and warped floorboards. I should probably save myself some time and money and declare this side of the house condemned and be done with it.

The wings were connected by a corridor, which also served as a portrait gallery. As we passed through it, I didn't pay much attention to the artwork—more portraits belonging to the Lockwood family—and instead focused on the hall itself. Save a few squeaky floorboards, it appeared in good repair. What a fine billiard hall this space would make. Large enough to host a good-sized party but not so large as to prohibit conversation.

I added *Repurpose the gallery into a billiard hall* to my list, then followed after Mrs. Owensby. But instead of continuing to the western wing, she moved toward the stairs.

"What about the western wing?" I asked.

"That won't be of interest to you. Only two more bedchambers. And besides, it is past time for luncheon." As if the conversation were over, Mrs. Owensby began descending the stairs.

But I did not follow her.

When I was a boy, Father had forbidden me from entering Summerhaven's east wing. For much of my life, I'd felt like a stranger in that house. I would not be made to feel so here in my own home.

I strode toward the west wing.

"Mr. Jennings?" Mrs. Owensby called after me, but I did not stop, determined as I was to discover what she was obviously hiding. "*Mr. Jennings?*" Her footfalls closed in behind me.

Before she could catch up to me, I opened the first bedchamber door and was met with a shock of sunlight. I held up a hand to block the bright light, then blinked, adjusting to it.

My gaze roamed the room, taking everything in.

It was a fine room. Finer than the one I'd slept in last night. *Much* finer. The walls were painted soft white, the ceiling high, the window wide.

Mrs. Owensby caught up to me, slightly out of breath.

"For the record," I said, turning to meet Mrs. Owensby's gaze, "I find this room of *great* interest."

For once, she was silent.

Standing in the center of the room, I surveyed the space. The furniture was draped with Holland covers, which I removed, unveiling a four-post bed in the middle of the room, a vanity and mirror near one corner, and an escritoire under the window. The mistress's room, likely. "This was Mrs. Lockwood's bedchamber, I presume?"

"It was," Mrs. Owensby said. "At least, before she died in childbirth. But most recently, this bedchamber belonged to Miss Lockwood."

At the sound of her name, I glanced around the room like I might find the young lady. But of course, that was impossible.

I turned in a slow circle, taking in the beauty of the space.

It would be a long while before a lady—my wife—would occupy this space. If ever one would.

Such a shame for a space as fine as this to go to waste. Perhaps this room would make a fine room for my hats.

Turn the white room into a hat room

And then, next to the four-post bed, I noticed a second door. "What is through there?" I asked, pointing.

"It's, uh, well . . ." Mrs. Owensby stammered, and as I moved toward the door, she followed on my heels.

I discovered the door led to an intimate sitting room, which contained two overstuffed chairs and a small circular table. There was no direct access to the corridor, only the two bedchambers it discreetly connected.

I continued through the sitting room to another bedchamber. Paneled in English oak and furnished finely, this final room was, by far, the largest and grandest bedchamber at Winterset. And like the mistresses' bedchamber, in far finer repair than the rest of the manor.

"This is the master's bedchamber." I frowned at Mrs. Owensby.

"It is, sir." She was not even trying to hide her disrespect.

"Then why, Mrs. Owensby, was I made to sleep in the smallest bedchamber last night?"

"Because it is the *farthest* bedchamber from the master's bedchamber, sir."

I frowned, puzzled. "Do explain."

"I-I thought you would not wish to sleep in the same room that Mr. Lockwood died in," she said.

Out of respect for Mr. Lockwood? Or because she was being mindful of any reservations *I* might have? I wasn't squeamish about death, but she might be. "The period of mourning has long since passed," I said. "And seeing as I am Winterset's master, I would like my things moved to the master's bedchamber. Directly."

She nodded, appearing resigned.

With the main house tour complete, she led me back through the long gallery toward the stairs. I still wanted to see the attic, but not with her as my guide. It would keep until later, when I could explore in solitude.

As we walked, I glanced at the art dotting the walls. There were so many portraits and all of the same man. "Who is this man?" I asked Mrs. Owensby.

"That is your previous tenant, Mr. Lockwood, sir."

"And why are there so many portraits of him?"

"His daughter, Miss Lockwood, was an artist. She enjoyed capturing his likeness."

That suddenly made the portraits much more interesting. I stopped to inspect one of the paintings. It was not as perfect as the professionally painted ones that hung in the entrance hall, but Miss Lockwood *had* been skilled.

Hands clasped behind my back, I continued down the gallery, glancing at each portrait.

She'd painted her father from every angle: straightforward, in profile—both sides—and even one from above, which showcased a bald spot. An odd detail to commit to canvas, and it made me slightly uncomfortable. There was something too real, too raw.

A pity her talent would never be fully developed.

How would she have painted my portrait? What would she have seen in me?

Mrs. Owensby cleared her throat, and I stepped away from the portraits to follow her out of the gallery. We didn't speak as we retraced our steps through the corridor nor as we descended the grand staircase.

But when we reached the entrance hall, Mrs. Owensby turned to me with an earnest look. "Winterset has been a most beloved home and haven to many generations," she said, her tone somber. "And now it is entrusted to your care. I hope you will do whatever is necessary to see her properly cared for, sir."

Although Mrs. Owensby had not expressly said it, her concern was apparent: she viewed me as an unwise and unworthy master.

How could she not?

I had been foolish. Not in the way she was accusing me of, but I had been a fool.

Mrs. Owensby watched me as if waiting for a response. But as my servant, she was not owed an explanation, and I wouldn't provide her one. The burden of my mistakes was mine alone to bear.

"Thank you for the tour, Mrs. Owensby."

"You're welcome. I'm sure it has given you much to consider."

Truer words had never been spoken.

Mrs. Owensby returned to her tasks in the kitchen, and I glanced around the entrance hall. With the curtains now fully opened, the space did not seem so dismal as it had yesterday in the low light. The hall was still smaller than I preferred, but the stained-glass windows lining the landing, the intricately carved banisters, and the glittering chandeliers made the space feel somewhat refined.

Even the portraits were not so fearsome as yesterday. I walked to the spot to view Miss Lockwood's portrait, wanting to see the beautiful face that had haunted my dreams last night, but the wall where her picture had hung was vacant. Where had it gone?

"Mrs. Owensby," I called. Once she'd returned to the entrance hall, I indicated the vacant space on the wall and asked, "Where is Miss Lockwood's portrait?"

"It was removed, sir. As you requested."

In a way, I was pleased that my servants had carried out my instructions, but why did they have to start with the one portrait I actually wanted to see again? "Why do the others still hang here?"

"It will take Bexley some time to accomplish the task. He must remove, carry, and store each painting in the attic one by one."

Sadly, that did make sense.

"Shall I make you finger sandwiches for luncheon?" Mrs. Owensby asked.

"Yes. Thank you."

With a nod, she turned toward the kitchen.

"One last thing, Mrs. Owensby," I said, and she turned back. "Please send Charlie to my study. I would like to instruct him to move my things. I will sleep in the master's quarters tonight."

"You needn't trouble yourself, sir. I can instruct him for you."

I'm sure she could, but she would likely instruct Charlie to move my belongings to the stable. "No, thank you. I am quite particular and prefer to give him the instructions myself."

Mrs. Owensby nodded with resignation, then continued toward the kitchen.

Alone again, I went to the study and closed the door. It was a modest-sized room with oak bookshelves lining the far wall and a large desk occupying the space directly in front. To the right, a fireplace, and to the left, a bow window. The walls were papered in a dark-green damask print and decorated with paintings of local landscapes. Had Miss Lockwood painted these too? I searched for the artist's signature but could not find it anywhere on the canvas.

I stood behind the desk next to the leather chair but didn't sit.

Such a small thing, sitting. But I'd dreamed of this moment—of being master—more than any other. For as long as I could remember, Father could always be found sitting in his study, poring over his ledgers, reading a book, smoking his pipe, and I'd come to associate this type of room with authority, manhood, ownership.

I didn't feel worthy to sit behind this desk. Not yet. Not unless I decided to take up the duty.

With an exhale, I braced my hands on the desk and hung my head.

And that was how Charlie found me.

"Long morning?" he asked.

"The *longest* morning." I pushed off the desk to stand at my full height. "Winterset is in even worse repair than I'd imagined. The entirety of the east wing should be condemned."

"Surely not," he challenged with a smile and sat in the chair before my desk.

I slipped off my coat, laying it over the back of my chair before loosening my cravat and cuffs. "The manor is in utter disrepair. There is water damage in the drawing room, a ghost in the attic, and I cannot be sure, but I think I hear rats in the walls." Not to mention the candles. I could not stand their stench.

"A ghost?" Charlie grinned. "It can't be *that* bad."

"It is. And I don't know how I'm going to change anything in the future. My money is nearly gone, and with it, any hope I had of marrying this century."

"I'm sure *someone* would have you. A dairymaid, perhaps?"

I glared at him, unamused. "Thank you for that."

"Anytime, Granger." Charlie sank further into his seat, lacing his hands behind his head and giving me a self-amused smile.

"I detest it when you call me that."

"That is precisely *why* I call you that."

I did not truly hate the moniker; it was a great deal better than *sir*, which propriety demanded he address me in public, but in private, I preferred for him to call me by my given name, as would a true friend.

"Well, what will you do?" Charlie asked, sobering.

"Had I the funds, I would return straightaway to my bachelor lodgings in London."

"You may not like what you've found here, but I know you, Granger. You won't give up so easily."

I didn't want to give up, partly because of my pride—no man liked to fail—but also because I had nowhere else to go. And what about the rest of the estate? I didn't even know yet what state the tenant cottages were in. If they were in as poor condition as the manor, it would ruin me.

I blew out a breath and dragged a hand through my hair. "I need to track down Mr. Moore and get my money back," I said.

Charlie nodded. "How should we go about it?"

How indeed.

Fool that I was, I hardly even remembered what the man looked like. How could I hope to find him? I pursed my lips, thinking. "My letters to Mr. Moore were addressed and delivered to the postmaster in town. Perhaps he has identifying information on the man who picked them up."

"We shall question him, then." Charlie glanced at the mantel clock. "It's not too late today; let us ride out, survey the tenant cottages, and then visit the postmaster."

"Yes." I nodded. "Let's go directly after luncheon." I felt a bit better for having a plan in place.

CHAPTER SEVEN

Kate

My STOMACH GROWLED. *LOUDLY*.

I didn't know the precise time because my attic "bedchamber" did not have a window, but given the severity of my hunger, it had to be well after breakfast, maybe even luncheon. I cursed Mr. Jennings for robbing me of both my dinner last night and my breakfast this morning.

I also blamed him for my boredom.

I didn't even have any light to draw by; I'd not anticipated having to hide for so long this morning, so I'd burned my candle to the bottom while drawing.

Last night, Mrs. Owensby had made me promise to stay in this priest hide until she came to fetch me. She did not want me to have any near run-ins with Mr. Jennings again. Since there was no knowing where he would be lurking, I laid in my little attic bedchamber, staring at the sliver of light that snuck in beneath the door.

Would it be so great a crime if I opened the door a crack? I wouldn't *leave* the priest hide, so my promise would still be intact, and then, at least, I would have enough light to sketch by.

I rolled out of bed and felt my way in the dark for the hidden knob on the wall. Once found, I opened the small panel door, which took me to *another* small chamber: the decoy priest hide. Crossing to the wall opposite, I came to another hidden knob that led me to the main attic.

It was an ingenious design: the real priest hide being hidden behind the false one. Care had even been taken to make the first priest hide, the decoy, appear as a real room, with a small window and bed. In the past, when priest hunters had searched the house and found the first priest hide bedchamber, they had not thought to look for another one directly behind it. Or at least, that was the idea.

I opened the door, but the tiny window in the decoy room did not let in enough light to see much of anything, so I cracked open the second door, which opened to the rest of the attic. That let in a little more light, but not enough. If only I had not promised to keep it closed. Drat! The minimal light would have to suffice.

Sitting on my bed, I grabbed Papa's book and my bit of charcoal and opened to my unfinished drawing of the daisy weed. The flower was still pressed between the pages, but it didn't look at all like it had when I'd begun the sketch; it was dry and thin and flat. The petals were translucent, and the stem was a stiff spine. I'd have to complete the picture from memory.

I sketched the remaining petals and leaf and was adding cross-hatch shading to add depth and dimension when I heard the lower door open and footsteps ascending the attic stairs.

I froze.

I was expecting Mrs. Owensby, but it *could* be Mr. Jennings. It was too late to make any movement.

I eyed the open door between my bedchamber and the decoy priest hide, wishing I'd kept it closed.

"Kate?" Mrs. Owensby called quietly, and I exhaled in relief that it was her. A moment later, she peeked inside my room, sparing only a second to frown at the open door. "Are you all right, dear?"

"Yes," I said, my voice scratchy from lack of water. "What time is it?" I asked.

"Past luncheon. You must be starving. Hurry, and you can have a change of scenery and eat lunch in the kitchen. Mr. Jennings and his manservant are out of residence, surveying the property and tenant cottages on horseback. They won't return for hours."

Famished, I quickly put on my slippers and followed Mrs. Owensby down two flights of stairs to the kitchen. A plate of finger sandwiches and fruit was already waiting for me on the table. I bit into a cucumber sandwich and closed my eyes. Food had never tasted so good.

As I ate, Mrs. Owensby and Bexley huddled over me like protective parents, their faces concerned.

"What is it?" I asked. "Is something wrong?"

"Oh, Kate," Mrs. Owensby said. "I don't think we can keep up this charade."

My pulse picked up. "Has something happened? Is he suspicious?"

"No, but you must agree that things have not gone according to plan."

I set aside my food, considering this for a moment. "Actually, save having to sit still in such small places for long periods of time, I think things are going quite well. Mr. Jennings has not found me, nor does he seem suspicious."

"Did you not hear how he questioned me yesterday when he saw your portrait? He *is* curious about you, Kate."

"I heard him ask a few questions, but you commanded the conversation brilliantly. Thanks to your quick thinking, Mr. Jennings believes I am dead."

"For now," she said. "But you already nearly exposed yourself when you giggled."

"That was one mistake. I will not make another."

"Oh, you will not? You were sitting at the table in plain view when Charlie came down the stairs yesterday. And today, I found you sitting in the priest hide with the door open." She gave me a displeased look.

I trained my gaze on my plate, guilty.

"Kate, we have done our best, but he seems in no hurry to leave. I think—*we* think . . ." Mrs. Owensby glanced at Bexley no doubt to bolster her confidence. "There is a better option than hiding. We think you should reveal yourself to Mr. Jennings."

"You cannot be serious."

"I am quite serious. Mr. Jennings seems like a decent fellow. I believe he will prove to be a friend, not a foe."

"You *believe*," I said, "but you cannot be certain. None of us can. We have only just met Mr. Jennings. And as you well know, any man can put on a pleasant facade for a few days." Longer if it suited his interests.

She gave me a sympathetic look of understanding but continued. "You did not see the way Mr. Jennings stared at your portrait yesterday. He was quite taken with you, Kate."

"That hardly recommends him." I daresay it did the opposite.

Mrs. Owensby's gaze softened. "Not all men are abhorrent, Kate. I have a good feeling about Mr. Jennings."

"A good feeling? How so? This is the same man who shirked his obligations to Winterset these past two years. Mrs. Owensby, you have a gift for seeing the best in people, but in this situation, I must beg you to see reason."

"And I must beg *you* to do the same. Hiding from Mr. Jennings forever is an impossible endeavor. If you reveal yourself to him now, you can appeal to his sympathetic sensibilities and request his assistance in relocating to someplace safer."

My mind spun in disbelief, and I looked at Bexley. "Do you truly agree?"

"Mr. Jennings has behaved as a gentleman thus far," Bexley said. "It is possible he may prove you an ally."

"Think of it, Kate," Mrs. Owensby hastened to add, her voice hopeful. "You could begin a new life elsewhere. Far away from Mr. Cavendish and everyone who knows you."

"I do not want a new life, nor do I wish to live elsewhere." Winterset was my home. My servants were family. And even if I did want to leave, where would I go? At least here I had a roof over my head. Telling Mr. Jennings was too risky.

"You must wish for more," she said. "Freedom. A family."

What person did not wish for those blessings? But I could not have a family without a husband. And I most certainly did *not* want one of those. Nor would I ever. Of *that*, I was certain. "I am content with my life, Mrs. Owensby."

"Content but not happy," she countered.

"What need do I have for happiness when it is so quickly turned into misery?"

"That is the way of life, my dear. Everything must have its opposite, or all will be meaningless. Please, won't you consider my advice?"

I had no desire to, but I owed my guardians at least that much, so I nodded. "When will Mr. Jennings return?" I asked.

"He and his manservant have only just ridden out," Bexley said. "So they will likely be gone for a few hours."

"Good," I said. "That gives me some time, then."

"Time for what?" Mrs. Owensby eyed me.

"To *consider*." I popped the last bite of sandwich into my mouth and quickly rose. I needed as much time as possible to poke around Mr.

Jennings's things. After all, he had been poking around mine all day, and what better way to learn about a man than to go through his personal effects?

Since arriving, he'd spent most of his time in his bedchamber and the study. I would quickly search those rooms and discover what I could about him in the time permitted.

I started in Papa's study.

Well, Mr. Jennings's study now, but I couldn't bring myself to think of it that way. I'd spent too many hours sitting in this room, snuggled in the leather armchair in the corner, sketching Papa as he balanced his ledgers. I'd wait hours for him to take a break so we could walk together in the walled garden.

I wished I could remember the last time I'd sat here with him. It could not have been long before his death, but I could not remember it. Had I known it would be the last time, I would have committed every detail to memory: what he was wearing, every word he spoke. I would have asked him questions and recorded his answers. But of course, I had not known, and now that last day was lost forever.

The study smelled different now, too, less like Papa's pipe and more like Mr. Jennings's cologne.

I walked to the desk and ran my fingertips along the desktop, which was something I would not have been able to do when it had been Papa's. Stacks of ledgers and letters had forever cluttered his desktop. Now the study was too tidy. The only things on the desk were an open notebook, a bottle of ink, and a quill pen.

I reached for the notebook but then hesitated. I'd come here with this precise intention, but it was wrong to read a person's private thoughts—even if the notebook *had* been left in plain sight. Mr. Jennings's lack of care was not an invitation, and I knew better than to think it was.

But Mrs. Owensby wished for me to put my trust, my very life, in this man's hands. How could I even consider doing that without first ascertaining his character? I had already made that mistake once with a man, and I would not make the same mistake again. Decided, I sat in Papa's chair and pulled the notebook toward me.

Mr. Jennings had precise, elegant penmanship. I couldn't help but admire the sophisticated slant of his scrawl and the perfect spacing between his letters.

His only entry appeared to be a list of needed repairs and refurbishments for Winterset. It was such a long list. My gaze drifted down the page.

Purchase wax candles

As soon as I read the first entries, I couldn't help smiling, pleased that my plans had made Mr. Jennings uncomfortable. But then I read the next item on his list and frowned.

Vanquish ghost

I scoffed. Unlikely.

Replace carpets
Repair uneven floorboards
Return Lockwood portraits
Repair water damage on western wall
Remove wall papers in the drawing room

Water damage? *What* water damage? The man must be senile. And he most certainly would *not* replace the wall papers; I'd spent months hand-painting the plain papers, and I was proud of the outcome. He should consider himself lucky to sit in such a beautiful room.

Repair window casement
Replace mattresses
Repair curtain rods
Remove wall papers in eastern wing bedchambers
Repurpose the gallery into a billiard hall
Turn the white room into a hat room

I sucked in a breath. The white room was *my* bedchamber. I understood why Mr. Jennings might think it would make a good dressing room; it was large and bright and conveniently connected to the master's bedchamber. But why would he wish to cannibalize the best room in the house for a few hats?

It was difficult to ascertain much of anything about Mr. Jennings's character from reading his checklist, so I searched his desk drawers. The top drawer was full of folded papers. Letters, I realized. Dozens and dozens of them, filed neatly in a row.

I pulled one out, intending to read it, but it was still sealed, so I put the letter back in the drawer and retrieved another. But that one was also sealed. As was *every* letter in that drawer.

How peculiar.

Why would Mr. Jennings keep these letters if he did not read them? And in his top desk drawer, no less. They must be important to him to keep them so close, but why had he not read them? I glanced at the back of one of the letters, hoping to identify the senders, but I did not recognize any of the seals. There appeared to be three different seals, but they seemed to all be written on the same creamy white paper.

Curiosity consumed me, and before I could think better of it, I cracked one of the seals and unfolded the letter.

It was wrong. I *knew* it was wrong. But also necessary. I needed to know more about this man to protect myself and, more importantly, my servants.

The letter was dated two years earlier, and it started simply:

Oliver,

What a pleasant name for such an *un*pleasant man. I continued reading.

It has been three weeks since I stood on the steps of Summerhaven and watched you leave on your Grand Tour. How I longed to run after you that day, brother, to convince you to stay, but you were decided, and I could do nothing to stop you.

Father died a few days after your departure.

Did you know? Do you care?

You missed his funeral.

On that day, Mother, Hannah, and I sat in our family's pew, waiting for you. Both women anxiously watched the door, hoping you would appear, but I knew you wouldn't. I understand why; Father was cruel and cold to you your entire life. But funerals aren't for the dead, Ollie; they are for the living. And we wanted you there. We needed you. I know you have not heard that enough; I am sorry for that. But I am also angry at you.

You might not think that fair, but I am. I am angry and sad and guilty and grief-stricken because of what has become of

us, because you aren't here to help me fix the family that Father has broken.
Come home, Ollie. We miss you terribly.
Your brother, first and forever.

xDamon

I would have given *anything* to attend my papa's funeral. But Mr. Jennings had abandoned his family days before his father's death. He had to have known it was coming. How could he not? But he could not even be bothered to open his brother's letters.

How cold. How cruel.

I could not, *would not*, trust Mr. Jennings.

Consideration done, I refolded the letter and placed it back inside the drawer with the other unopened letters.

My mind was made.

No matter what Mrs. Owensby or Bexley thought, I would *never* come out of hiding to Mr. Oliver Jennings. I would do whatever was necessary to drive him from the premises. Simple pranks like tallow candles and overboiled beef weren't enough though. I needed to give him a better reason to leave.

But what more could I do?

As Mrs. Owensby had said, he seemed in no hurry to leave; in fact, his list of repairs made it clear he planned to stay.

I had to change that.

I scanned the list again, trying to conjure up a plan to drive him away, and my gaze snagged on one line:

Vanquish ghost

Perhaps Mr. Jennings was more frightened of the *fantastical* than he seemed.

What if I played into his fears? I could pretend to be a ghost and haunt him. Mrs. Owensby had planted the seed in his mind. I only needed to water the idea to bring it to life. It was mad, but it just might make him leave.

I picked up the quill pen and drew a line through each renovation I disagreed with, making the thickest, darkest line across *Vanquish ghost.*

CHAPTER EIGHT

Oliver

The postmaster was no help at all.

I sighed as I exited his office and stalked to where Charlie stood in the lane with our horses.

"Did you learn anything to help you locate Mr. Moore?" Charlie asked.

"Not a thing." I swung up into my saddle, and we started for Winterset. "Apparently, each of my letters was retrieved from the postmaster by a different man, and the postmaster had not recognized any of them. Whoever this Mr. Moore is—perhaps he is not even one man but many men—is clever and careful.

"As soon as I informed Mr. Moore that I was returning to England to take up residence, he disappeared. My last letter with instructions to ready the manor was not even collected. The postmaster had to have it delivered to Winterset."

"I'm sorry, Granger."

"As am I."

"At least the tenant cottages are in good condition," Charlie said, attempting to cheer me.

"Truly," I said. It was a small miracle that the structures were sound, the lanes that led to the cottages were clean, and most importantly, the inhabitants were healthy. "I am more than grateful, but what about the manor? What about Mr. Moore and my money?"

"You must forget Mr. Moore," Charlie said. "You have followed the only lead, and he is gone. Dwelling on the past will not profit your future."

"As much as I hate to admit it, you might be right," I said.

"Of course I am right."

I gave him a long look. Charlie was not usually so vehement. "For as certain as you are of your own opinions, Charlie, you should have been born a duke."

"I was. Didn't I tell you?" Charlie quipped.

"No." I laughed lightly. "I daresay you did not."

He shrugged. "My mistake."

"All right, then, *Your Grace*. In your lofty opinion, what should I do about Winterset?"

Charlie sobered, his teasing manner falling away. "Like I said, I think you should set aside what has happened in your past and focus on the future."

"You make it sound so simple."

"It *is* simple. You have enough money to begin repairs, and the income that *you* will now be collecting from your tenants will carry you from month to month. You will have to economize, to be sure, but if you are prudent, you can do this."

"Prudence is not a virtue my father instilled in me." If anything, it was the opposite. As the second son of an earl, I'd lived a life of luxury and opulence.

"You cannot tell me you aren't excited about renovating Winterset," Charlie said, the clip-clop of our horses' hooves punctuating his sentence.

"*Excited* is far too optimistic a word." I stared at the road before us.

"Eager, then?" Charlie pressed on.

"Quite the opposite."

"Tell me you are, at the very least, curious."

I couldn't deny that my mind was muddling through possibilities for the estate. "I suppose."

"Curiosity." Charlie grinned. "That will do well enough."

"Will it?"

He nodded. "Curiosity has inspired many men to accomplish many great things."

Even if I accomplished the daunting task of bringing Winterset into this century, it would not be considered a great accomplishment but merely fixing my previous mistakes. "I'm still not convinced that it can be done. With the state of my finances, how would I even hire a steward?"

"You could manage things yourself," Charlie said.

I eyed him skeptically. "You mean, act as my *own* steward?"

He shrugged as though the idea weren't completely absurd. "You are better at numbers than three stewards combined."

"Three stewards combined? That makes no sense."

"See! You are already catching errors."

I huffed a laugh. "Shall I act as my own butler as well? I could cook and clean too?"

"Oh, no." Charlie made a show of shaking his head. "Mrs. Owensby would *never* allow that."

"At least we agree on something." I sighed. "To pull this off, I would have to live like a pauper."

"You might," Charlie said. "But I daresay that is more agreeable to you than the alternative."

I considered the alternative: returning to Summerhaven and begging my brother for assistance, money that, thanks to our father, Damon did not have to spare. And even if he did, why would he give it to me? He thought me vain and selfish. I had been when last he'd seen me. But I'd experienced much over the last two years on my Grand Tour, and I believed myself better for it. But my current situation would do nothing to improve Damon's opinion.

My family was better off without me.

I thought about the long list of repairs I'd written in my notebook. "Who will do the work?" I wondered aloud.

"*You* will," Charlie said.

I scoffed. "A gentleman cannot work on his own estate."

"That is your father speaking, not you. I daresay you prefer a little hard work to dwelling in squalor."

"Your faith in me is misplaced, Charlie."

"No," he said simply, and there was something about his belief in me that made me wish to live up to it, however impossible.

When Charlie and I left earlier that afternoon, I'd instructed Bexley to remove the ivy from the gate and clear a small path. As we entered through Winterset's front gate, I was pleased to find he had done as I'd requested.

Walking my horse through the gate unimpeded felt like a small victory. One that brought me a surprising amount of pleasure and pride.

The gravel drive and surrounding grounds were still a disaster though. I'd not yet had time to explore past the courtyard, but I assumed the walled garden and grounds behind the manor were in just as poor condition.

When we reached the putrid fountain, we climbed down from our horses, and Charlie took our mounts to the stables. We had no stablehands to tend to the horses, but thankfully, the stables were in decent condition. Nothing compared to the fancy one Damon had begun building—had undoubtedly *finished* building by now—at Summerhaven but serviceable.

As I walked to the front door, I let my gaze roam over the house and surveyed the facade. First, the base, which blessedly appeared level, then the ground and first floor, and finally, the attic. The stone structure appeared sound. Luckily, it was made of sturdy stone, not wattle and daub, but whoever had designed this house seemed to care more for function than form. The wings were not symmetrical, and the mismatched windows were unevenly placed. I counted at least three separate styles. Had the architect not considered the outside design when deciding where to put the windows? There was no rhyme or reason to their placement.

I shook my head and continued up the front steps.

At the door, Bexley greeted me with a bow and collected my things. Another improvement from our first encounter yesterday. "Mrs. Owensby is nearly finished with your dinner, sir. When would you like it served?"

"As soon as possible, please. I will take a tray in my study tonight." Normally, I would dress for dinner and eat in the dining hall, but with Charlie preoccupied in the stables, I had no one to assist me in dressing. And I hated to admit it, but I was anxious to open my ledgers and begin calculating the cost of repairs.

"Of course, sir," Bexley said and moved toward the kitchen.

I crossed the entrance hall to the study and stepped inside. It was a fine room with a nice view of the grounds. Or rather, it would have a nice view once the grounds were cleared, the windows were washed, and the season spring.

Standing behind my desk, I looked down at my notebook and froze. What the devil?

Several of my notes had been crossed off. I could still read the words, but that was not the point. Someone had entered this room without my permission, read my notes, and defaced my notebook.

I reached for my top desk drawer and pulled it open. Relief flooded me when I saw that my letters were still neatly stored in the drawer.

I quickly closed it and began pacing behind the desk. I scanned the room. Nothing else appeared out of order, but I felt ill-at-ease, like someone was watching me. I looked at the open door, half expecting to see Mrs. Owensby or Bexley standing at the threshold, but they weren't there.

I rubbed my forehead, then reached for my notebook to study which items had been crossed off.

~~Vanquish ghost~~
Replace carpets
Repair uneven floorboards
~~Return Lockwood portraits~~
Repair water damage on western wall
~~Remove wall papers in the drawing room~~
Repair window casement
Replace mattresses
Repair curtain rods
Remove wall papers in eastern wing bedchambers
~~Repurpose the gallery into a billiard hall~~
~~Turn the white room into a hat room~~

There didn't seem to be a commonality between all the items redacted. I looked over the list again. A few were directly related to the Lockwoods, such as removing their portraits, but not all. *Vanquish ghost*, yes; *remove wall papers*, no.

Had *I* made these redactions? I'd been overwhelmed by all the needed repairs, but no, I would remember doing something like this. Someone had been in this room, someone who had a preference for how things should be run at Winterset. And I had a good idea who it was.

Not two minutes later, Mrs. Owensby appeared at the study door with my dinner tray. She placed it on my desk in front of me, then stepped back, looking up to meet my gaze.

"Mrs. Owensby. Has anyone been in this room?" I asked, my voice stern.

Her brow furrowed. "No, sir."

"You are sure?" I held her gaze and pointed at my notebook. "My notes have been defaced."

Her eyes widened. "You don't think *I* did that, do you?"

"Bexley was working to clear the gate of ivy all afternoon. Charlie was with me. And you were—"

"At the market."

My confidence wavered.

"I needed to purchase provisions," she continued, "f-for your meals. Meat, vegetables. Everything is in the kitchen. I can show you, if you desire."

Lud, I'd scared her again.

"Not necessary," I said. "I am not angry, Mrs. Owensby. I only wish for an explanation for how this happened." I indicated the notebook.

"May I?"

I pushed it across the desk and gave her a few moments to examine it. "Well?" I said, keeping my tone even so as not to frighten her again. "Do you have any explanation?"

"I don't think she likes your plans for Winterset," Mrs. Owensby mumbled.

"She *who*?"

"Kate. That is, Miss Katherine Lockwood. Your previous tenant's daughter."

Miss Katherine Lockwood.

The beautiful young lady in the portrait. *She* was the ghost? I suddenly did not mind so much Winterset being haunted. I might even welcome it.

Kate.

Her name matched my vision of her: Headstrong. Confident. But also lovely.

I cleared my throat, pushing away the thought. "To be clear, Mrs. Owensby, you believe it was a ghost, Miss Katherine Lockwood, who defaced my notes?"

"I wouldn't put it in quite that way, but yes, sir. I believe it was she who did this. Though she should not be blamed."

I pinched the bridge of my nose and took a deep breath. Surely Mrs. Owensby didn't expect me to believe an apparition was capable of committing this crime. I had no desire to embark on yet another circular conversation with my housekeeper, but alas, here we were.

"A ghost cannot pick up a quill pen, much less write with one," I said. "And I cannot imagine why a ghost would mind whether or not I removed damaged papers from the walls in the drawing room."

"Seeing as *she* painted the papers, I can."

I took back my notebook from Mrs. Owensby. "I suppose that explains why she took exception to my turning the art gallery into a billiard hall and the white room—*her* room—into a hat room."

"I would say so." Mrs. Owensby's chin quivered as she nodded.

Suddenly, it dawned on me. It was Mrs. Owensby's show of emotion that led to the realization that it *was* Mrs. Owensby who had redacted my notes. She'd not done it maliciously but, rather, out of grief. "Miss Lockwood must have been very dear to you," I said, softening.

"As dear to me as if she were my own daughter."

My irritation turned to compassion. "How long did you care for her, Mrs. Owensby?"

"From the time she was a newborn babe."

Mrs. Owensby probably thought she was *still* caring for her charge by protecting Miss Lockwood's paintings, bedchamber, and family portraits. "Seeing my plans to undo some of Miss Lockwood's work must be difficult for you, but in some cases, it cannot be helped." I explained about the water damage. "But I give you my word that I will preserve as much of Miss Lockwood's memory as possible. In a show of goodwill, please have Bexley rehang the young lady's portrait."

"That is most kind of you."

It wasn't, actually. It was a selfish wish. The young lady's eyes captivated me, and I preferred to have the luxury of looking at her portrait until it could be returned to the young lady's kin.

"Yes, well. The painting will still need to be given to her next of kin when they are located, but until such time, please rehang her portrait in the entrance hall."

"Thank you, sir. I will. I do hope that will please her."

I hoped it would please *Mrs. Owensby*—at least enough to stop her antics. "And I hope we can now peacefully coexist."

"As do I," she said, sounding earnest.

"Very good." Although I disapproved of Mrs. Owensby's actions, I felt better knowing why she'd done what she had. And I was confident that in confronting her, I'd no longer have to deal with Miss Lockwood's "ghost." "I believe we understand each other."

She nodded. "Do you require anything else?"

"Nothing, thank you."

She quit the room with a curtsy.

Alone again, I quickly ate dinner—boiled beef and root vegetables—then picked up my quill pen and notebook and moved to the window, where the day's dwindling light was the brightest. The list was extensive: broken beams, faulty casements, and water intrusion in the drawing room. The major repairs needed to be completed before winter, or more damage would be inflicted. And I still needed to examine the attic to determine the extent of the damage there.

It took over an hour to estimate each repair's cost and calculate the total price.

It would take a considerable amount of money, but it could be done if I made most of the repairs myself and acted as my own steward. I would have to prioritize the needed repairs over the lofty renovations I'd dreamed of, but if I sacrificed, I could secure Winterset's future and my own, if I chose to.

It was the right choice, perhaps the only choice, so why did I feel such apprehension?

The truth?

I was afraid.

Not of the manual labor, though I did not relish the idea, but of failing again.

I'd made one decision on Winterset's behalf: entrusting the estate's care to Mr. Moore, and that had proven disastrous. How could I trust myself not to make any more mistakes?

Part of me wanted to run away from this burden. But to where? To whom? Winterset was all I had. My one foothold in Society. My only hope for the future.

There *was* no escape.

Winterset needed me, and *I* needed Winterset.

Charlie was right. No matter how inadequate I might feel, I could not turn my back. I did not want to, I realized. Not really. I wanted to protect this home, to make something more of it, as my maternal ancestors had. And although I would never admit it to Charlie, the prospect of repairing Winterset, as daunting as it was, was beginning to excite me.

So, I would stay.

I would stay where I was needed, and I would work to make this manor my home.

A place where I belonged.

CHAPTER NINE

Kate

I turned onto my side in bed, trying to get comfortable in the dark of night, but I couldn't stop thinking about how Mr. Jennings had blamed Mrs. Owensby for redacting his notes. I'd been hiding in the priest hide built into the bookcase, hoping to hear Mr. Jennings's reaction when he returned. Knowing that both Mrs. Owensby and Bexley had been otherwise engaged all afternoon, I hadn't expected Mr. Jennings to blame either of them. But, of course, he had. Logically, there was no one else to blame. If he'd wanted to, he could have released them from his employment.

And it would have been *my* fault.

From now on, I would ensure that the things Mr. Jennings saw and heard could not be traced to the servants. I'd been lucky that he'd shown Mrs. Owensby empathy instead of anger.

As much as I hated to admit it, Mr. Jennings possessed *some* admirable qualities. But that did not mean we could *peacefully coexist*.

I rolled onto my back.

Hmph. It didn't seem fair that Mr. Jennings should be sleeping so soundly in his bed when he was the cause of my unrest.

It was time for *my ghost* to cause another disturbance.

How though?

I thought back to the countless stories my maid Molly had told me about the pranks she and her siblings used to pull on one another. I'd never laughed so hard as when she'd told me the story of how her eldest brother had thrown water on their youngest brother in the dead of night.

Perhaps *I* could wake Mr. Jennings. I couldn't get too close to him, so throwing water on him was out of the question, but there had to be some way of waking him without being discovered.

Earlier today, Mr. Jennings had had his belongings moved to the master's bedchamber in the west wing of the house, directly over the drawing room. The drawing room housed the pianoforte. What if I sneaked downstairs and played the pianoforte? All the servants were safely accounted for in their beds, and Mr. Jennings's own manservant would be able to vouch for this, so Mr. Jennings could not blame them.

Excited, I rolled out of bed and crept down the attic stairs to the landing. It was dark, but I didn't need a candle. I knew every twist and turn of these halls, every piece of furniture and squeaky stair too.

It didn't take me long to pass through the corridor and descend to the ground floor. Returning to the attic would be more difficult, as I would have to sneak back through the narrow, secret passageways in the walls, but it would be worth the effort to see his face.

I slipped into the drawing room, padded soundlessly to the pianoforte, and propped open the lid. Thankfully, the moon was full and gave me enough light to see the keys.

Seating myself on the bench, I felt a bit guilty, knowing my actions would also wake the servants. However, it was, in a way, for their protection. Mr. Jennings needed to know that it was *me* who was disturbing his peace, not them.

What to play?

I swirled my finger along the top of the piano, thinking. Something dark and brooding. Something *haunting*.

Mozart? No, Mozart's melodies would lull Mr. Jennings peacefully from sleep, and I wished to rip him from his rest.

For that, only Bach would do.

Toccata and Fugue in D Minor. The pounding minor melody could wake the dead.

I gingerly placed my fingers on the keys, then struck the first chords, shattering the silence. I played the piece as loudly and violently as possible, rending the night.

I should be able to complete at least a dozen measures before anyone appeared at the drawing room door. Mr. Jennings would likely get here first since his bedchamber was closest, but the servants would not be far behind.

I was not inordinately skilled at the pianoforte, but I was proficient. In the darkness, though, I missed several notes. But my mistakes only added to the eeriness.

Above me, there came a loud *thump*, like a man falling out of bed.

I snorted a laugh and continued playing or, rather, pounding the keys. It felt so good. After being silent for so many days, making myself heard felt liberating.

Mr. Jennings was moving around his bedchamber now. It wouldn't be much longer before he came downstairs.

I quickly completed a rapidly descending cascade of notes that was sure to set his heart racing, then held a final chord and rose from the bench.

I'd played a minute, at most, but I'd made myself heard.

Footfalls sounded on the grand staircase.

I hurried to the hidden jib door and pressed it open to reveal the secret passageway—a derelict servants' corridor that snaked through the walls of the entire house. I stepped into the shadows and pushed the jib door back into place. A few paces down the darkened corridor, there was a small gap where the panels met, which provided a view of the drawing room.

Only a few moments later, Mr. Jennings skidded into the hall. He held a candlestick, which highlighted the fact that he wore only his nightshirt. It gaped at the neck, revealing the portion of his chest that a cravat would typically cover.

I swallowed hard.

He raked his free hand through his curls, the golden locks gleaming in the flickering candlelight. He squinted into the darkness at the pianoforte. "What the devil?"

Not long after, his manservant, Charlie, ran into the room, looking just as bedraggled as Mr. Jennings. "Granger?"

"I'm here," Mr. Jennings said.

Charlie glanced around the drawing room. "Were you . . . playing yourself a lullaby?"

Mr. Jennings scowled. "Don't be daft. The music woke me, same as you."

And a moment later, a disheveled Bexley and Mrs. Owensby entered the room.

"Sir?" Bexley said. "Are you quite all right?" Bexley's voice was gravelly with sleep. And behind him, Mrs. Owensby clutched the neckline of her night dress.

"The pianoforte," Mr. Jennings said, pointing an accusing finger at it. "It played."

"You mean, *you* played?" Mrs. Owensby said.

"No, *it* played. I only just came down to see who was playing at this ungodly hour and found the room empty."

"We were belowstairs," Charlie said. "Perhaps it was . . ." His sentence drew out, then died, having no plausible explanation.

I smiled.

No one was hurt. No one was blamed. I'd succeeded!

Mr. Jennings checked the windows, the pianoforte, behind the furniture. But there was nothing to find. Well, nothing except for me, of course, but I was hidden within the wall.

They continued discussing what might have caused the disturbance, and I passed through the secret corridor undetected upstairs. It was cramped and dark and dusty, but I hardly noticed as I felt my way upstairs, so great was my glee.

And I wasn't even finished yet.

With everyone accounted for, I went to Mr. Jennings's bedchamber. I opened the window, and cool air whooshed into the room, billowing the curtains. His bedchamber would be freezing when he returned.

I turned to leave but paused when I saw something on Mr. Jennings's dressing table: his fob watch, key, and seal. It was his seal that interested me most. I picked it up and moved to the hearth to inspect it in the firelight.

The inscription read: *Veritas, Honestas, Libertas*. Truth, Honor, Freedom. The motto was laid over a rose.

Perhaps I would hold on to this until Mr. Jennings learned to live by the virtues it symbolized.

I closed my fingers around the seal and slipped into the corridor. I walked to the end and opened the small window.

When Mr. Jennings opened his bedchamber door, it would create a wind tunnel and slam the door shut. He might be able to explain why the door slammed but not *who* had opened the window.

Pleased with my work, I climbed the stairs to the attic and got into bed. And for the first time in a month, with Mr. Jennings's seal safe in my hand, I slept soundly.

CHAPTER TEN

Oliver

The next morning, I took a breakfast tray in the drawing room. As I ate a too-hard, tasteless biscuit, I stared at the pianoforte. I did not believe for one second that Miss Lockwood's ghost was haunting me.

It was implausible.

Foolish.

And yet I could not explain last night's events: A pianoforte could not play on its own, nor could windows open themselves. Even now, in the light of day, fully awake and rested, I could not make sense of what had transpired.

Mrs. Owensby had surely redacted the list in my notebook, but there was no possible way she could have played the pianoforte or opened my window while she was sleeping belowstairs. Perhaps I had dreamed that the sound was coming from the pianoforte? But no, the servants had heard it too. It was baffling.

The only possible explanations were that I was going mad, or a ghost was indeed haunting my house. That I even considered the latter a possibility probably indicated the former. Had King George known he was going mad as it had happened?

There must be a simple explanation that did not include phantoms. This house and the people who lived within it held secrets, and I intended to discover every one.

I set my biscuit on the tray and rose from the sofa. The pianoforte lid was still open, so I peeked inside, but nothing was amiss. I circled the instrument but found nothing out of the ordinary.

I sat on the bench and stared down at the keys. I hadn't played in years.

As a young boy, Mother had insisted both Damon and I take lessons, wishing for our home to be filled with music. Damon had practiced regularly and quickly become proficient, but I hadn't progressed. I'd sat at the pianoforte for hours, but I'd pouted more than I'd practiced.

I placed my fingers on the keys.

I was only six when Father had had enough of my pouting. He'd just come inside from riding. He'd struck my knuckles so hard with his crop that they'd bled.

My knuckles still bore scars.

When I'd screamed in pain, Damon had come running. As the first son, he'd always borne the brunt of Father's teaching tactics, but as the spare, I had often been beneath Father's notice.

From that day on, whenever I'd practiced, Damon had sat beside me. He'd shown me the mathematics behind the music, and I'd learned to love playing. Not because I'd suddenly found the instrument diverting but because my brother had sat beside me.

And then he'd gone away to school, and when he'd returned, everything had been different. *He* had been different—more like Father, cold and cruel. And when he'd sat at that bench, he'd played not for pleasure but for praise.

I withdrew my fingers from the keys.

It would do me no good to think about the past. I'd once thought Damon and I would repair our relationship, but too much had passed between us now for our relationship to be mended.

I closed the lid and was about to rise from the bench when I saw something on the top of the piano. A swirl in the thin layer of dust, swirling around a smaller central circle. It almost looked like a flower.

Could Miss Lockwood's ghost have drawn this? Mrs. Owensby had said she had been an artist, but . . . Ghosts could not draw. They did not even exist.

Perhaps I *was* going mad.

I stood and stalked to my study. It was time to get to work.

Thankfully, nothing appeared out of sorts this morning. I walked to my desk and pulled out a paper from the top drawer to draft a letter to the local magistrate, informing him of my unfortunate experience with Mr. Moore.

I did not think Mr. Moore would be apprehended, and I did not wish for the magistrate to view me as a fool, but I could not hold back the information knowing it might save another man from the same fate as me.

Once the letter was finished, I folded the paper and reached for my seal. But I felt only my watch and key.

Thinking the seal might be stuck under the fob ribbon, I stood, smoothing the fabric. But the clasp where my seal usually hung was empty.

Had I removed it yesterday before I'd discovered my notebook? No. I hadn't gotten that far. My pulse began to race.

I could not lose my seal. It was an irreplaceable family heirloom and had been entrusted to my care.

I moved the heavy oak desk, lifted the threadbare carpet, and shook the velvet curtains but found nothing. Dropping to my hands and knees, I scoured every inch of the floor, wondering if it had fallen and rolled out of sight. But my search was fruitless.

Standing, I took a deep breath to calm my emotions. It had to be here. Where had I last seen it?

Could it have come off my fob ribbon when I'd removed it last night? I'd been in such a hurry to get to the drawing room that it was possible I'd knocked my things off my bedside table, and it had become detached.

I took the stairs two at a time, then ran to my bedchamber. I all but skidded into the room.

There was nothing on the night table nor on the ground below it. I glanced under the bed, but the floor there, too, was bare.

Frantic now, I overturned my mattress and searched under every piece of furniture. But I did not find my seal. It wasn't here. It wasn't anywhere.

It had most likely fallen off my fob ribbon while I'd been riding yesterday.

Another failure.

Blast! I slapped my hand against the wall and then leaned into it and closed my eyes.

A gentleman always keeps track of his belongings. Father's voice crept into my mind unbidden, and I drove it away with a shake of my head.

There was too much to do today to waste time wallowing: the attic still needed to be inspected, the Lockwood portraits stored, and the drive cleared.

Exhaling, I pushed myself from the wall and walked down the corridor to the attic door. I opened it and found a slender, spiral staircase. There was no rail, but a thick rope hung in the center of the spiral. I gripped it for stability and started up the stairs.

A scurrying sound came from above.

"Mrs. Owensby?" I called, but there came no response. It was likely only a rat.

At the top of the stairs, I let go of the rope and stepped into the attic.

The space had only a few small windows, so it was darker than the rest of the house. It was also quite cluttered. Broken pieces of furniture were strewn about the space, old rolled carpets littered the walkway, and bulky picture frames were tilted against the wall. There did not seem to be any sense in how things were stored.

I tilted a few of the portraits away from the wall and glanced at the nameplates mounted on the bases.

Ah. Mother's family portraits.

Thankfully, they appeared unharmed. I continued down the long line, viewing the portraits, and after seeing no less than twenty, I realized I was searching for Miss Lockwood's portrait.

It had not yet been rehung, as I'd instructed yesterday, but I'd thought of her likeness, her bright eyes and coy smile, more than once. Ironic, considering I'd had her portrait removed to *avoid* thinking of her.

I turned my attention to inspecting the ceiling.

With hardly any room overhead, I ducked under beams as I moved through the cramped space. For once, luck was on my side. There were no signs of water damage or rotted wood. The windows, too, appeared in good condition, with no evidence of mold or rot around the casement.

I exhaled in relief, my breath fogging the autumn-chilled window, and something caught my eye. I exhaled again, slowly this time. In the middle of one of the diamond-shaped panes was another swirl similar to the flower design I'd found drawn in the dust on the lid of the pianoforte.

I stared at it for a few seconds, then wiped it away. Mrs. Owensby had likely made both designs while moving about the house.

The window boasted a view of the garden, or rather, the tall hedge maze that I assumed led to the garden. I was sure it was as overgrown and ill-tended as the rest of the grounds, so I was glad it was hidden from view.

I turned my attention to the attic floor to assess the severity of the rodent infestation. I walked the entire length of the attic, my eyes sweeping side to side, but I strangely saw no signs of rodents. There were no droppings, nests, or chew marks, which was unexpected, considering how often I'd heard them in the walls the past three days.

I turned to make my way back down to the attic door, but I must have turned too swiftly because the toe of my Hessian boot caught the corner of a traveling trunk, leaving behind a large scuff on my boot.

"Deuces!" I sat on the trunk and tried to buff the mark with my sleeve, but the scar was too deep. Groaning, I gripped the edge of the trunk to stand and felt something rough beneath my fingers.

I ran my thumb over the rough spot, wiping away the dust, and there, on the lid, were carved the initials *KL*.

Katherine Lockwood.

My back grew warm, like someone was watching me. I glanced over my shoulder, but no one was there.

Who had I expected to find? Miss Lockwood?

What a fool I was. Sometimes, she felt so real, though, so alive. Perhaps it was only because Mrs. Owensby was determined to keep the young lady's memory alive, but there were times when it almost felt as though Miss Lockwood were standing in the room with me.

I lowered myself onto one knee before the trunk and opened the lid.

It was filled with women's clothing. Miss Lockwood's, presumably. A blue dress folded neatly on top, the fabric surprisingly fresh and clean. I held it up to the light to admire—*er,* examine. It was lovely. And so petite.

"Mr. Jennings?" Mrs. Owensby's voice called up the stairs.

My heart raced as it had when I was a boy and Father had caught Damon and me creeping around Summerhaven's forbidden east wing. I guiltily dropped the dress and closed the trunk lid.

"Mr. Jennings?" she called again. "The attic door was open. Are you up there?"

"I'm here," I called back, quickly standing and searching for something to do to make my being here less suspicious.

But *why*? This was *my* house, *my* attic. Even this trunk was mine until Mr. Lockwood's next of kin could be found. Still, I felt silly standing here doing nothing, so I sat atop the lid and pulled out my notebook and pencil.

Mrs. Owensby appeared at the top of the stairs and walked over to where I sat. "What are you doing up here?" she asked, breathless.

"Can a man not sit in his own attic?" I smiled.

"He can, but why would he wish to?" She glanced around the attic as if looking for explanation.

That was the question, wasn't it? "To . . . rest."

She gave me a skeptical look, unconvinced.

"I was checking the soundness of the roof, and I grew tired."

"I see. And how have you found the roof?"

"Watertight."

"Good. Then you will have no need to come up here again."

I raised an eyebrow at her impertinence. I stood and, crossing my arms, looked down at her.

"That is to say," she quickly amended, "it is good that you will not have to add a new roof to your list of repairs and waste your time up here, where no one will ever see your progress. Shall we?" She motioned toward the stairs.

She was acting even odder than usual, like a vexed governess handling a naughty child.

"I'll be down shortly, Mrs. Owensby," I said, standing my ground.

But she stood *her* ground.

What was a man to do? I cleared my throat. "We have much to accomplish with very little time before winter arrives; the drive must be cleared of overgrowth to allow the cart entrance, the Lockwood portraits removed and replaced with these." I indicated my ancestor's portraits leaning against the wall. "Speaking of portraits, I did not see Miss Lockwood's portrait rehung in the entrance hall, nor did I see it stored up here in the attic. Do you know what has become of it?"

Mrs. Owensby cast her eyes about the attic, whether to look for it or avoid my gaze, I couldn't be sure. "I suppose it has been . . . *misplaced*," she said.

"Well, see that it is found and rehung immediately. I should like to keep the portrait safe until it can be delivered to the young lady's next of kin."

Mrs. Owensby nodded but said nothing more on the subject.

I continued listing the chores that needed to be completed today. "You and Charlie will work inside the house to remove the pictures. Both the gallery and the white room must be emptied," I instructed. "And Bexley and I will work outside to clear the drive."

I thought it best to separate Bexley and Mrs. Owensby and keep an eye on them until I could explain all that had transpired in this house or until these peculiar incidents stopped happening.

"Very well," she said. "We best get to it."

Still, she seemed too eager. She did not even object to my requests or to being paired with Charlie instead of Bexley. Why? What was she hiding?

"Please inform Bexley and Charlie. And as I said, I will be down shortly."

Unmoving, she worried her lower lip.

"You may go now, Mrs. Owensby."

With a nod, she reluctantly retreated down the stairs.

Mrs. Owensby was undoubtedly hiding something in this attic, perhaps protecting something that had belonged to Miss Lockwood. What? I wasn't sure yet. But now, more than ever, I was determined to find answers.

CHAPTER ELEVEN

KATE

WHEN I WAS FINALLY BRAVE enough to creep out of my attic bedchamber, the faintest hint of Mr. Jennings's cologne lingered in the air. Lemon, sandalwood, and cedar. A heady combination. Masculine.

He'd gotten too close. *Dangerously* close.

Had I taken my pranks too far or not far enough?

Nothing I had done to get him to leave had worked. What else could I do to make him uncomfortable here?

I was pondering what I might do to increase his discomfort when I heard voices outside.

I went to the window, and careful to stay in the shadows, I peeked out.

In the courtyard below, Mr. Jennings and Bexley stood on the drive, holding shovels.

He'd written in his notebook that the drive needed to be cleared, and I'd just heard him tell Mrs. Owensby that he planned to clear the drive, but I supposed he would have Bexley clear the drive while he supervised. Did he really mean to do it himself? While wearing his fine coat? He would split the seams! And where were his gardening gloves? His hands would be littered with blisters by the time he was finished.

I shook my head, laughing at his obvious inexperience.

He didn't know the first thing about gardening. This would be entertaining.

The men moved in opposite directions, Bexley toward the house and Mr. Jennings toward the gate.

Mr. Jennings didn't hesitate, thrusting his shovel into the ground and removing a clump of weeds. His shoulders strained against the seams of his coat.

I leaned against the wall next to the window and watched.

Mr. Jennings possessed unexpected strength for a man of gentle breeding. He moved confidently, attacking the weeds. He had muscular arms and a straight back, and he did not lack determination. He might not know anything about gardening, but he did not look bad doing it.

But after only a few minutes of laboring, it began to rain. And not a little.

Mr. Jennings looked down at the few feet of ground he'd managed to clear. Even from all the way up here, I could feel his frustration.

Poor man. Even Mother Nature was on my side.

Mr. Jennings looked at the sky and cursed, then called to Bexley. Though I could not make out Mr. Jennings's words over the sound of the rain, I assumed he was telling Bexley that they'd have to stop working for the day, unfortunately for me. Watching him struggle had been such an enjoyable diversion. But Mr. Jennings did not leave the courtyard. He only removed his coat and cravat and handed them to Bexley. Mr. Jennings's waistcoat came off next, leaving him in only his shirtsleeves and breeches.

Bexley walked back toward the house, out of my line of sight, and Mr. Jennings returned to his task. Rain soaked his white shirt, and the material clung to his shoulders, arms, and chest.

He stopped shoveling several times to wring water from his shirt, but the effort was futile, and he finally surrendered. Reaching over his shoulders, he removed his shirt over his head in one swift motion and tossed it aside.

I stared, captivated.

Raindrops pelted his broad shoulders and slid down his smooth, sculpted chest and abdomen, each droplet tracing the contours of his powerful physique. His breeches, weighted with water, hung low on his hips, accentuating his trim waist and tapering torso.

Mr. Jennings turned to continue his task, executing each thrust of the shovel with controlled precision. His biceps bulged.

"Kate!"

I jumped at the sound of Mrs. Owensby's voice directly behind me and turned to face her. How had I not even heard her approach?

"Saints above!" she snapped. "Come away from the window before Mr. Jennings sees you."

When I took one last glance at Mr. Jennings's fine form instead, Mrs. Owensby grabbed my elbow and *pulled* me away.

"What could possibly be so interesting?" Mrs. Owensby peeked over my shoulder out the window and sucked in a scandalized breath. "Katherine Lockwood!"

"You were right," I said. "He *is* nimble."

"I ought to box your *eyes*."

"Can eyes *be* boxed?" I asked.

She huffed at my impertinence. "After Mr. Jennings's perusal of the attic this morning, I should think you would have learned to be more careful."

"I *was* being careful. I was keeping close watch of Mr. Jennings."

She looked at me in disbelief. "And what about his manservant, Charlie? Did you not think to be wary of him?"

I had not.

"He is currently removing your family members' portraits from the walls downstairs and will shortly be carrying them up here to store."

Her words alarmed me. "I was momentarily distracted, but since Mr. Jennings was outside, I did not think I was in danger."

"You are in great danger, hiding here without Mr. Jennings's permission, and you must never forget it."

"I'm sorry. The day was just so long, and . . ." I hung my head. There was no excuse.

Mrs. Owensby's expression softened. "I hate the thought of you sitting up here in the attic all alone, but if you will not leave Winterset and you will not reveal yourself to Mr. Jennings, you *must* stay hidden."

I nodded contritely. "I will be more careful."

"Good. Now, I am supposed to be drawing Mr. Jennings a warm bath and fetching his French-milled lavender soap."

I rolled my eyes. "Did he also order you to collect fresh rainwater to fill his royal bath?"

"You mustn't say such things," she scolded, though I saw the start of a smile on her lips. "Mr. Jennings is working hard to clear the drive. Not many masters would do such a thing."

"True, but Mr. Jennings let the weeds grow in the first place." Had he cared one wit for his estate, he would have hired a steward to manage Winterset two years ago.

"Regardless, Mr. Jennings will still need a warm bath after he is finished outside."

"Well," I crossed my arms, "I'm not sure his fancy soap will be strong enough to remove all that soil. Perhaps you should replace it with the lye soap you use to launder his clothes?"

She shook her head. "It is a bit too harsh."

"Not harsh enough to hurt him. I just don't want him to get too comfortable here."

"Oh, Kate."

"Tell him you accidentally used his soap to clean his laundry and bring the bar to me for safekeeping." I was curious. What made it so superior? I had to see it.

Mrs. Owensby seemed uncertain but warily nodded, then turned to leave.

"One last thing," I said, stopping her. "After a day spent outside in the rain, Mr. Jennings will likely be chilled to the bone. You must season his soup with plenty of pepper to warm him from the inside."

"You are a force to be reckoned with, Kate." Mrs. Owensby sighed. "Now, go and hide before Charlie comes up," she instructed and left the attic.

I did as I was told and hid all afternoon, listening to Charlie climb up and down the attic stairs, storing the portraits.

Eventually, Mrs. Owensby returned with a dinner tray: steaming soup with a side of bread and butter. Also on the tray was Mr. Jennings's soap.

The bar was buttery soft and smelled divine, like all the best scents in the walled garden combined.

The rain continued into the night. I loved the soft sound, but then it became a storm. Lightning lit the sky, and thunder ripped through the silence. I'd never liked storms. Such powerful, unpredictable forces of nature had always frightened me. Sleeping in the attic so close to the stormy sky was terrifying.

When I was young, Papa used to take me into the library during storms. He'd pull me into his lap and read to me until the storm stopped or I fell asleep, whichever came first. How I wished he were here now.

Clutching my blanket, I tried to calm my fears by repeating Papa's promise: So long as I stayed within these walls, I was safe. But no matter how many times I repeated the mantra, I could not stop trembling.

Another bolt illuminated the sky, and unable to stand it any longer, I rose from my bed.

Mrs. Owensby's earlier warning rang in my ears. It was dangerous for me to go downstairs at this hour. Although I'd heard Mr. Jennings retire to his bedchamber not long ago, he was likely not yet asleep. But the storm seemed a great deal more dangerous than he did at present. I did not like to disobey Mrs. Owensby, but the storm was severe. It sounded like a bolt could come crashing through the roof at any moment. I could not stay here.

I crept down the attic stairs, pressed my ear to the door, and listened. The house was quiet, so I sneaked down the stairs to the library and quietly closed the door.

The storm was quieter inside this room with the noise dampened by all the books lining the walls. Lightning flashed, illuminating the study table in the center of the room, the overstuffed armchairs by the hearth, and the rolling ladder on the bookcase, but only for a moment. Thunder rolled in the distance, but it was not so loud in this room. I felt safer here, closer to Papa, if only in my memory.

I ran my hands over the books. I should take one or two more while I was here. The pages of my current "sketchbook" were almost full, and who knew when I would be able to come down here again. I always selected my books from the uppermost shelves. They seemed to be the least often read and, therefore, the least likely to be missed.

Without slippers, the ladder rungs were cold beneath my bare feet, and my white linen nightgown tickled the tops of my toes. I felt along the books for the slip of paper marking the last spot I'd retrieved a book and pulled out the next. The book was thin, so I grabbed another. Taking two books at a time left a considerable gap on the shelf.

Perhaps, I should—

But before I could finish the thought, there was a noise at the door. The turning of the knob.

My gaze darted to the door, which was slowly being pushed open, and then swept around the room, looking for a place to hide. The secret passageway was the only place, but I could not descend the ladder quickly enough to conceal myself.

The door creaked open to reveal Mr. Jennings, candlestick in hand. Everything happened in rapid succession: lightning flashed, our eyes locked, Mr. Jennings jumped back, and his candlestick fell to the floor, catching the carpet on fire.

CHAPTER TWELVE

OLIVER

I QUICKLY STAMPED OUT THE fire. It took only a moment, but by the time the flames were extinguished, the ghost was gone.

"Blast!"

She'd been wearing white and floated several feet from the ground. I'd never believed in such things, but now...

"Is someone there?" I called. But of course, there came no reply.

I squinted into the darkness, searching for some explanation, but there was nothing to explain the lady in white nor the wide eyes that had flashed in the darkness.

On the opposite side of the study table, near the bookshelf where I'd seen the ghost, was a bellpull to call the servants. I could hear them in the kitchen, talking as they went about their end-of-day duties, so I knew they were still awake. I walked over and took hold of the bellpull but then hesitated. This would be the second night in a row I'd alarmed the servants, claiming a ghost. They would think me mad.

Ghosts did not exist.

And yet I'd *seen* her.

I was most assuredly going mad. I needed a break from this house and everyone inside it.

I also needed a drink.

A *strong* drink.

The village tavern wasn't far, but even so, I could not safely set out in this weather. I returned to my bedchamber and dressed warmly. I waited there for the lightning to subside, which thankfully took only twenty minutes or so, then I went to the stables, saddled and mounted my horse, and guided him to the tavern.

The tavern was tiny but bustling with energy. Men, likely waiting out the storm, sat at tables, drunk with cheap ale. Serving girls scrambled to get them their drinks. There was not a single open seat, only a few stools at the bar. I moved in that direction, pressing through a sea of bodies.

I made it only a few paces when somebody shoved me, and I stumbled forward into a man with a missing front tooth, causing his drink to slosh slightly over the side of the cup.

The man scowled me. "You lost, gent?"

I didn't dignify his question with a response. In London, I'd encountered more than a few working men who hadn't liked sharing "their" space with a gentleman. I'd learned the best way to handle men like this was to ignore them. I turned toward the bar, but he grabbed my arm, whipping me back to face him.

He'd put his glass down on the nearest table, and his fists were now raised for a fight.

I'd never been opposed to brawling. Thanks to Gentleman Jackson's boxing saloon, I could defend myself well enough, but this was my first visit to town, and I had no wish to make enemies. "I have no quarrel with you," I said, stepping back.

His response was a quick jab to my shoulder.

I raised my fists to defend myself.

The toothless man moved to strike again, but another man, a gentleman by the look of his dress and manner, stepped between us.

"Come now, Mr. Fletcher," he said to my assailant. "Is that any way to treat a gentleman?"

The man cowered. "No, mi'lord."

"I thought not. Be on your way." He gestured with his head for the man to leave.

The toothless man shot me a scathing glare, then slunk back into the crowd.

I looked to my rescuer and took his measure. He appeared to be about my age. He possessed a confident bearing and sharp gaze. A peer of the realm, likely, although I did not recognize him.

"Follow me," the gentleman said to me before I could inquire, and he led the way to a private table tucked into a nook in the corner, ducking under a low-hanging beam.

"Lord Markham," he introduced himself upon sitting. "Baron of Blackhurst Abbey."

"Oliver Jennings," I said, taking the seat opposite him. "Second son of the late Earl of Winfield."

"Ah. The Winterset heir." He relaxed back into his chair. "We've all been wondering when you would take up residence."

"Not soon enough," I muttered to myself, then to him, "I took a tour of the Continent."

"Ah," he said. "And what brings you in here tonight? Not the nicest weather for a tour of the town."

Water dripped from the ends of my hair onto the table, validating his statement. "*That* is a long story," I said.

He shrugged. "I have time."

I gave him a mirthless chuckle. "I think I'll need some drink in me before sharing that story."

"Fair enough." Lord Markham laughed and beckoned a serving maid to our table. "What will you have, Mr. Jennings?"

"Something strong."

He grinned knowingly at me before turning his attention to the serving maid who'd arrived beside him. "Brandy for the Winterset heir. And port for me."

"Right away, my lord," she said and departed with a curtsy.

Markham stared after her retreating form until she was swallowed up in the crush. "So," he said, turning back to me. "Where did you go on your tour?"

"The usual places: France, Italy."

"I'm surprised we never crossed paths. I toured the same places the year before last. My favorite was Italy."

"Italy was remarkable," I agreed. "But France was my favorite."

"Ah. Yes. French women are quite . . ." Lord Markham's sentence stalled with a wolfish grin, "beautiful."

They had been beautiful, but this line of conversation made me uncomfortable. It reminded me too much of the man I used to be. "I'm sure the young ladies here in town are just as lovely," I said, steering the conversation.

He shrugged. "They are sufficient, I suppose."

"That does not sound promising."

He laughed lightly. "Well, they are not *French,* if you know what I mean, but they are fine enough to look at for an evening. But don't look too long at any young lady, or you might find yourself engaged." He winked.

If only that were my problem.

The serving maid returned with our drinks and set them on the table.

Lord Markham grabbed his glass and raised it. "To French beauties," he said, and we drank.

"This drink is certainly strong." I grimaced.

"The strongest," he agreed. "Burns all the way down, doesn't it?"

"That it does." I swirled the amber liquid and took another sip. "It will get the job done, though, and that's all I care about tonight."

"Here, here." He knocked on the table, and we both took another drink. "So what finally lured you back to England?" he asked.

"Duty."

He nodded his understanding. As a baron—a *young* baron—I was sure he did.

"And now that you're here, what are your plans?" he asked.

"I have many. But first, I must renovate Winterset. Then I hope to find a bride."

"A marriage-minded man?" He met my gaze over the rim of his glass. "Best not say that too loud, else the matchmaking mothers will have you married by sun up."

"It would not matter if they heard. My suit is not such a prize. My elder brother Damon holds the title, not I."

Lord Markham set down his glass. "That makes you second in line, does it not?"

"It does. But being second does not count for much."

"Maybe not in London, where there is a peer on every corner, but people up here are not so prejudiced."

I raised an eyebrow. "Oh?"

He took a sip of his port and set it down. "I daresay we are the only two unmarried gentlemen under the age of thirty-five in this county. Truly, you have a fine house and a titled family. Here, you are as good as an earl. As long as you attend Sunday services every week, you will have your choice of women."

The thought that my suit might be enticing to the young ladies here was hard to believe. I'd spent my life being Damon's shadow, watching every lady of our acquaintance prefer him over me simply because he was the heir—except for Hannah, at first, but I'd been too daft to see what I had in front of me.

"I will have to take your word." I took another sip.

He shrugged. "You are not so far from a title as you think. People die all the time."

I choked on my brandy.

"Don't look so scandalized," Lord Markham smirked. "Death is a fact of life that can only benefit us second sons."

Try as I might, I could not find a dignified response to the first part of his statement, so I focused instead on the latter. "You are also a second son?" I asked.

"I am. My father passed away last year from consumption, and my elder brother died six months later in an unfortunate hunting accident." Lord Markham stared down at his drink.

"My condolences," I said. Having lost my own father, and to the same disease, I knew all too well the pain that lingered. Perhaps Lord Markham's speaking so casually on the subject was his attempt to minimize his pain. I could forgive him for that.

"It was tragic, to be sure, but I count myself blessed. After all, I am a baron now." He paused, taking in my expression. "That face again. You cannot tell me that you haven't considered the possibility of inheriting."

It was impossible *not* to. Negligent, even. Should any harm befall Damon, I was next in line. It was my duty to be prepared. To my shame, there'd been a time when I thought I might make a better earl than my brother.

But I'd never wished for it.

No matter our issues, I did not, and would never, want that.

"Judge me for speaking plainly if you wish," Lord Markham said, "but we second sons must look out for ourselves. It is the only way we can survive in this blasted Society."

"I am not judging you," I said. I couldn't. Lord Markham and I were too similar in situation. I understood him, and perhaps I'd found someone who had the potential to understand me.

We finished our drinks, and the serving maid brought another round, which we happily drank while exchanging amusing tales from our time on the Continent. The pattern continued, and as the night wore on and the brandy kept coming, I felt more and more relaxed, happy to forget the burdens of Winterset and the ghost who inhabited it.

"Come now, Jennings," Markham said, slapping the table. "You must tell me this story that has brought you out tonight in the rain."

I glanced side to side to be sure I wouldn't be overheard, then leaned forward and lowered my voice to a whisper. "My house is haunted."

Markham snorted a laugh. "I think you've had too much to drink."

"Think me mad if you wish, but I *saw* her. This very night. Floating in my library."

He grinned. "What did she look like?"

"A *ghost*." I grabbed back my drink, sloshing it over the side, and took another swallow. "White night rail, long curly hair . . . and this, I remember clearly: beautiful, bright eyes."

His gaze narrowed. "Have you seen her before?"

"Yes. Well, no, not in person, but I've seen her portrait, and I've heard her. She stole my seal. Actually, I can't be sure she did, but Mrs. Owensby believes she did, and even though I did not believe Mrs. Owensby at first, I think I might now."

"You have *definitely* had too much to drink. We'd best get you home."

I groaned at the thought of having to return to Winterset. "I would rather sleep at this very table. My ghost enjoys interrupting my slumber," I muttered.

Markham shook his head and beckoned over the serving maid. He gave her instructions, something about a carriage, or my horse . . . ? I was too full of drink to really follow their conversation.

"Come on, old boy." Lord Markham stood and gestured for me to do the same.

I scooted out of the booth and stood, forgetting entirely about the low beam above our booth, and hit my head. Hard.

"Blast!" I cursed.

Markham chuckled, and then he looked at me, and his expression turned serious. "You are bleeding." He gestured to my forehead.

I touched two fingers to the spot and felt the slick blood.

Lord Markham handed me his handkerchief.

I pressed the square to my wound and hissed at the sting.

"That's going to hurt tomorrow," he said.

The alcohol in my system dulled the pain now, but he was right. In the morning, my head would hurt.

Markham wove through the crowd toward the door. I followed, still pressing the cloth to my head to stanch the blood. We had nearly reached the door when someone bumped into me. Ale poured down my front, soaking me.

Could this night get any worse?

Brushing myself off as best I could with one hand, I looked up to see the toothless man again. My blood boiled knowing he'd purposefully caused the collision.

But before I could do anything about it, Markham grabbed my elbow and led me away. "Come with me before you start a brawl," he said as we made it outside and to a waiting carriage. "Get in."

"But my horse—"

"Is already being tied to the rear of my carriage."

Gads! I hadn't even noticed. I stepped up into the conveyance and slumped into the seat.

"My driver will see you safely home," Markham said.

"What about you? You're as drunk as I am."

"I'm not actually. I am going back inside to settle our tab. Go home and sleep it off. I'll see you tomorrow morning at church. You may share my pew so all the matchmaking mamas can get a good look at you."

He closed the door, and the carriage jerked into motion, moving toward Winterset.

CHAPTER THIRTEEN

KATE

At least an hour had passed, maybe two, since Mr. Jennings had seen me in the library, and I still shook as I paced the attic. Had he not dropped his candle, he would have—well, I did not know what he would have done. Dragged me to the constable? Thrown me out in the rain?

I continued pacing.

Mr. Jennings would likely return any moment.

What was I to do?

I could not stay. He knew I was living in his house now. But neither could I leave; as dangerous as Mr. Jennings might be, Mr. Cavendish was infinitely worse. Mrs. Owensby's plea that I reveal myself to Mr. Jennings and beg his protection echoed in my mind. But it was too late for that now. I'd stolen food, shelter, and his precious seal. Men had hung for less.

Noises came from outside. Gravel crunching as a carriage came down the drive and then a man's voice. Mr. Jennings's. Was he . . . *singing*?

I rushed to the window and peeked outside, but with the thick cloud cover still left from the storm, it was too dark to see anything.

The singing grew louder as he neared the house. Was that French? No, Italian? It was impossible to tell because his words were slurred.

He was drunk.

I'd been certain he'd gone to town to fetch the constable, but it seemed he hadn't visited the jail, only the tavern.

Perplexed, I crept down the attic stairs to the landing and peered through the rails.

Below, Mr. Jennings staggered into the entrance hall.

"*Signora Owensby!*" Mr. Jennings singsonged. "*Venga in fretta!*"

I fought a smile at his deep, lilting voice.

A moment later, a bedraggled Charlie entered the hall, no doubt startled awake by the singing. "Granger?" He held up his candle and, seeing his master in such a sorry state, burst out laughing.

"Does my singing *amuse* you, Charlie?"

"Indeed it does, sir," he said, and using his candle, he lit a few lamps.

"Well, at least you are honest, which is more than I can say for you." He pointed at Mrs. Owensby, who had just entered the hall looking half asleep and in her nightclothes, and Bexley on her heels. "You are always talking in circles, you are." Mr. Jennings turned in a circle, arms caged as if dancing a waltz.

Oh my. He was more than drunk; he was utterly possessed.

"I am tired of being toyed with," Mr. Jennings said, stopping his drunken spinning; however, in an attempt to regain his balance, he all but ran into Mrs. Owensby.

"Sir," Mrs. Owensby said, hand outstretched to steady him. "You are blee—"

He batted away her hand. "Do not try to placate me, Mrs. Owensby. I am in a foul mood. I refuse to be the cat to your mouse any longer. Or no, that isn't right." He paused, looking to be in thought. "You are the cat, and I am the . . . the . . ."

"Mouse?" Charlie supplied.

"Where?" Mr. Jennings's gaze snapped to the floor. "Blasted things have been creeping through the walls at all hours, and now they have the gall to scamper across my floors in plain sight?"

"No." Charlie sighed. "*You* are a mouse."

"The devil I am!"

Charlie groaned. "You are insufferable when you are intoxicated, Granger."

"Does he drink to a stupor often?" Mrs. Owensby asked Charlie.

"No," Charlie said. "Almost never."

Mr. Jennings sighed dramatically. "*Si vous aviez mes problèmes, vous seriez ivre mort aussi.*"

He spoke both Italian and French then. Impressive.

"Sir," Mrs. Owensby said again but more sternly this time. "I must beg you to listen. You have injured your forehead and may require stitches."

Mr. Jennings touched his forehead and winced.

"Charlie," Mrs. Owensby said. "Come help me."

Charlie obediently started toward them, but the nearer he came, the slower he stepped.

"If you will just press the cloth to his cut," she instructed Charlie, and he seemed to sway.

"No, ma'am. I—" Charlie started, but his plea faded as he fell to the floor.

"Charlie!" Mrs. Owensby shrieked.

Bexley stooped to help Charlie. "I don't think he's too fond of blood."

"He detests it," Mr. Jennings said. "It made him a terrible second in the ring."

So, Mr. Jennings was a pugilist. That explained his athletic form.

"Take Charlie belowstairs to rest," Mrs. Owensby instructed Bexley.

"I hate to leave you alone," Bexley said. "Mr. Jennings is in such a state."

As if cued, Mr. Jennings launched into another aria, his deep vibrato filling the entrance hall. I hated to notice, but his voice was quite pleasant.

"I will be fine," Mrs. Owensby said. "Although I do not have the stamina to tend to two patients tonight. If you will, see Charlie back to his bed and watch over him, and I will see to Mr. Jennings's injury."

Bexley agreed, and when Charlie came to, still quite pale and shaken, Bexley assisted him belowstairs to recover for the night.

"Come, Mr. Jennings," Mrs. Owensby said. "Let's get you into the library. You can warm yourself by the fire, and I will better be able to see and help you."

Mr. Jennings shook his head. "The library is haunted."

"What?" Mrs. Owensby said to him, but her gaze lifted to the banister, where I was hiding.

Of course Mrs. Owensby knew I'd sneaked down to watch the spectacle.

"I saw Miss Lockwood's ghost, Mrs. Owensby. This very night, floating in the library."

I blinked in surprise. He didn't know I was alive? Miracle of miracles! Our scheme had worked! I was safe.

Mrs. Owensby glanced in my direction again, her face pinched with anger. "Then I will assist you to the drawing room, sir." She draped his arm over her shoulder to support his weight.

Still crouched behind the stair rail on the landing, I wasn't sure what to do. I did not wish Mrs. Owensby to be left alone with an injured, intoxicated man. But besides his sultry serenading, he did not *seem* dangerous.

One never could be too sure, though, so I tiptoed down the stairs to the drawing room door and slipped inside. I hid myself in the shadowy corner of the room near the door. Even though he thought me a ghost and was quite clearly drunk, I did not wish to try my luck.

Mrs. Owensby lowered him into an armchair by the dying fire. Needing more light, she added another log, stoked the flame back to life, and then lit the lamps, illuminating the room.

By the time she turned back, Mr. Jennings's breathing had evened out, and he was still with sleep.

Mrs. Owensby leaned close and inspected his wound.

From my position, I could see only the top of Mr. Jennings's head poking over the back of the armchair, but his injury was severe enough to elicit a wince from her.

She straightened and moved toward the drawing room door, where I hid.

"Is he all right?" I whispered as she passed.

"Kate!" Mrs. Owensby startled and looked over her shoulder at Mr. Jennings to ensure he hadn't heard her, then turned back to me. "No, I'm afraid not. His wound is deep and wide and requires stitches. I am going to tell Bexley to fetch Doctor Foster."

My insides clenched. A memory of Doctor Foster standing over Papa's lifeless body flashed through my mind. Although the doctor was not directly responsible for Papa's death—Mr. Cavendish was—he had done little to help the situation. "Doctor Foster is likely as drunk as Mr. Jennings," I said.

"We will have to hope that is not the case tonight," she said. "I can't sew Mr. Jennings's wound; my eyesight is too poor, and my hands are unsteady."

I held Mrs. Owensby's gaze. "I will do it."

"Don't be absurd, child. What if Mr. Jennings wakes and sees you?"

"He has *already* seen me," I reminded her.

Mrs. Owensby frowned her displeasure.

"Luckily," I added, "he believes I am a ghost. And even if he does see me again tonight, he is too drunk to remember it accurately in the morning."

"Perhaps," she conceded, "but you have never stitched a wound before."

"No," I said, "but I am proficient enough at embroidery."

"Stitching skin is vastly different from stitching silk, Kate."

I grimaced at her words but pushed the feeling aside. "I don't trust the doctor not to do more damage, Mrs. Owensby. And we shouldn't delay Mr. Jennings's care."

She bit her lower lip, seeming to consider.

"Please let me do this," I said. "Think of it as my penance for all my pranks."

"I don't like it," Mrs. Owensby said, "but you're right; his care should not be delayed. Use his cravat to wipe away the excess blood while I fetch supplies," she said and hurried toward the servants' quarters.

Alone now, I walked slowly and quietly through the drawing room, never taking my eyes off Mr. Jennings. His head was propped against the armchair wing, and his curls fell across his forehead, covering his wound. His arms were draped over the armrests, and his legs were splayed on the floor.

Heart pounding, I retrieved a chair from the corner and sat close to him.

My goodness. Had he *bathed* in drink? I should not be surprised if he slept until spring.

Feeling more confident that he wouldn't wake, I moved to loosen his cravat. It was intricately tied, and it took me a minute to work out the knot and then another to unwind the cloth. My fingers brushed the soft skin of his neck. Despite his wet clothing, his skin was warm.

Using one hand, I pushed back the golden curls that had fallen across his forehead to reveal the gash above his left eyebrow. It was not long but appeared deep. What had happened? Had he gotten into a fight? Fallen?

I folded his cravat in my free hand and lightly touched the linen to his temple. The blood wiped away easily, but it took more effort to clean his cheeks, where it had already begun to dry.

He really was handsome.

But just because he was handsome did not mean he was good. In my experience, good looks often seemed to indicate the opposite; the more handsome the man, the worse his behavior.

The sheer symmetry of his face demanded artistic admiration. Most people had one eye that was slightly lower than the other, a nose that was a little crooked, or ears that protruded unbecomingly. But Mr. Jennings possessed strong, sturdy features that were implausibly balanced: eyes equidistant from a straight nose, high cheekbones, and plump, red lips.

"I think that will do," Mrs. Owensby said, startling me.

Realizing Mr. Jennings's cheeks and forehead were clean and had likely *been* clean for some time, I withdrew my hand.

Mrs. Owensby handed me the needle and thread, then stood directly behind me to assist.

Thankfully, Mr. Jennings's skin was split straight and should be easy enough to sew closed. I would be as gentle as possible, but no matter how careful I was, it would likely leave a scar.

Only half a dozen stitches were all that would be needed, and then I could retreat back to the attic. My hands shook as I gripped the needle. Despite all my pretended confidence, I was afraid.

Mrs. Owensby whispered some basic instructions and made a display of how and where to sew the flesh. "Quickly now," Mrs. Owensby whispered, "before he wakes."

With a nod, I focused on the task.

I could do this.

I *had* to do this.

Bracing my elbow on the chair's left wing, I touched the needle to his forehead.

He shifted in his sleep but did not wake.

I concentrated on making tight, even stitches, and little by little, I closed the wound.

"Not a ghost," Mr. Jennings murmured.

I froze, my face mere inches from his. His eyes were open, though only just, and he studied my face. My heart hammered in my chest. He would haul me to the authorities now and—

"An *angel*." He lifted his hand and brushed the back of it to my cheek. He touched me softly, but his skin was rough, likely from work and lye soap. I felt a pang of remorse. He dropped his hand back onto his lap like it was too heavy to hold up. A straight scar stretched across his knuckles. It was thin and faded. He'd likely received it when he was a boy. What had happened to him? I wondered. "Do you see her, Mrs. Owensby?" His eyes locked on mine, and I dared not move an inch.

"S-see *who*, Mr. Jennings?" Mrs. Owensby said.

"Miss Lockwood's ghost," he said.

"I see no ghost," she said, and his brow furrowed. "Do not move! You must relax your forehead, or you will pull out your stitches."

"You truly cannot see her?" He reached out to touch my cheek again, but Mrs. Owensby swatted away his hand.

"Eyes closed!" she ordered.

"*Le plus bel ange*," he murmured, then closed his eyes, complying.

I quickly made the last stitch and tied the knot, then looked up at Mrs. Owensby. She motioned for me to hide behind the curtains.

Once I was safely out of view, she said, "There. Good as new."

Mr. Jennings's eyes fluttered open, and he blinked several times at the spot where I'd stood. "Where has she gone?"

"Where has *who* gone, sir?"

"Miss Lockwood. I could have sworn she was—" Mr. Jennings's sentence stretched thin as if he were attempting to make sense of what he'd seen—*me*—and what he'd heard—*Mrs. Owensby*. When he couldn't, he shook his head. "I fear I am going mad, Mrs. Owensby."

I felt bad for my behavior. I'd not meant to cause Mr. Jennings any real pain, physical or mental.

"Nonsense," Mrs. Owensby said and helped him stand. "You are only drunk as a fish. You will feel better after a good night's rest."

He huffed a laugh, though it held no amusement. "Miss Lockwood would never allow it," he said. "I've not had a decent sleep since stepping foot in this wretched manor."

Wretched manor?

Winterset was many things, but it was not *wretched*. It was my home. My haven. How dare he speak of it so disdainfully.

I'd thought he was beginning to see Winterset for how wonderful it was. He'd made an exhaustive list of repairs and had even worked the land with his own two hands. But no. Mr. Jennings was just as selfish as the day he'd walked into Winterset, and it was past time he left. If he wasn't happy here, then he shouldn't be here.

Any kindness I'd felt toward him instantly evaporated, and my resolve to drive him from this *wretched manor* strengthened.

I would make him rue the day he stepped foot in this house.

And I knew exactly how to do it.

CHAPTER FOURTEEN

Oliver

"What did you DO?" Charlie said the next morning.

"I don't remember." Other than a few foggy facts, such as going to the tavern and meeting Lord Markham, I remembered very little of what had happened last night. I felt awful, though, like I'd been dragged behind a carriage.

I scowled at my reflection in the mirror, staring at the stitches on my forehead. For the most part, they were straight and smooth, but near the knot, my skin was slightly puckered.

"You might want to delay attending church services a week . . . or two?" Charlie suggested.

"Lord Markham made it quite clear that my reputation depends upon my attendance." *That* I remembered clearly.

"Right, then," Charlie said. "Perhaps I can style your hair across your forehead so that your curls will conceal the cut."

"It is worth a try," I said. "Would you also pick up some salve from the apothecary? I'd like to try to minimize the appearance of the scar."

"You sure, Granger? I've heard women find scars attractive."

I laughed out loud. "I sincerely doubt that, *Your Grace*."

"It's true," Charlie said.

"Just fetch the salve."

Charlie held up his hands in surrender, then got to work taming my curls. He combed several locks forward and pomaded them in place. It was not my favorite hairstyle. I preferred a more submissive style and, well, *less* curly, but at least it concealed my blemish.

"I should like to wear my new topper today." It was my most fashionable hat; perfect for meeting new people.

"I'll fetch it for you right now," Charlie said, already moving toward the white room, where my hats were now stored.

Fatigued, I sat on the end of my bed and tried to remember what had happened after I left the tavern last night. Who had tended to my wound? I remembered hearing Mrs. Owensby's voice, but when I closed my eyes, it was Miss Lockwood's face that I saw.

Nothing made sense.

My memories were muddled.

Several minutes passed, and Charlie still hadn't returned with my hat. What was keeping him? I did not wish to be late to the service.

"Charlie?" I called.

A moment later, he walked back into my bedchamber with my favorite topper in his hands. "I don't know what to make of it," he said.

"Make of *what*?" I asked, standing.

He tipped the hat so I could see inside. Was that . . . *dirt*?

"What the devil!" I strode across the room and took the hat. I attempted to brush away the dirt, but the motion only ground the soil further into the fibers.

"I have no explanation," Charlie said. "But I did not do this."

"I believe you." Enough oddities had happened in this house that I could not *not* believe him.

"Can it be cleaned?" I asked.

"Perhaps," he said. "But certainly not before church."

I cursed. Although I was disappointed, I had others, though this was my favorite and most expensive hat. "Fetch me another."

Charlie's gaze met mine, wary. "I'm sorry, Granger. But they are all like this."

A pit formed in my stomach. "No. *No, no, no.*" Not my hats.

I ran through the connecting sitting room to the white room, skidding to a stop. I peeked inside each hat and found that every one of my twenty-seven hats had been turned upside down and were filled with dirt and a twig.

My hats were being used as planting pots.

I gritted my teeth. I'd spent a small fortune on these hats. Charlie had been meticulous in his care of them. I tunneled a hand through my hair.

"Stop!" Charlie said. "Your forehead. Your *hair*."

I carefully withdrew my hand and checked my pocket watch. Services started in less than half an hour, and we needed to leave immediately. "I can't go without a hat."

"Perhaps there is one in the attic," Charlie suggested. "I can search, if you'd like?"

"Seeing as mine are unwearable at present, yes. Thank you." I didn't relish the idea of wearing another man's hat, but attending church without one would be inexcusable.

"Right. Of course. Give me a minute to look, and I will meet you in the entrance hall," he said and hurried down the corridor toward the attic stairs.

I inspected my appearance one last time before I went downstairs. My hair did not look terrible, and my stitches were hidden. I had a little time before Charlie would be down, so I went to assess the damage my candle had caused to the carpet last night.

Sunlight streamed through the library windows. The carpet had been smoothed back into place, but there was a hole where my candle had dropped and caught fire. Another thing to add to my endless list of repairs.

I eyed the bookshelf across the room where I'd seen the lady floating. Like the drawing room, this room did not seem so strange in the light of day—just some furniture, a bunch of books, and a rolling ladder. Although, what was that on the floor *beneath* the ladder? A book?

How had it fallen?

I glanced at the shelves directly above. On the top shelf, there was an empty space, and another book was partially pulled out of its place too.

I walked around the study table in the center of the room and stooped to pick up the book.

Disquisitions on the Decline and Fall of the Roman Republic by James Cowper. It was a dense book, and I couldn't picture Mrs. Owensby or Bexley reading it for pleasure. I opened the book, meaning to flip through pages but paused on the first page, confused by what I saw. Was that a drawing of a flower?

I turned the page and then another and found they were all filled with charcoal drawings of flowers. Roses and lavender and daisies covered every page. I stared down at the simple sketches. They were quite good. I could not help being impressed.

Who had done this?

The artist had not signed their work, but I knew of only one artist who had lived in this household: Miss Katherine Lockwood.

"Granger?" Charlie stood at the library door, holding a hat by the brim at his side.

I distractedly waved him inside. "Come look at this, Charlie."

He walked over, and after I handed him the book, he examined several pages. "Are all the books like this?"

The thought had not even occurred to me. I pulled a book off the nearest shelf. To my disappointment, there were no sketches inside it, nor in the several more books I skimmed from the lower shelf. But the book with the drawings had likely fallen from the *top* shelf.

I climbed the ladder and grabbed a book from the highest shelf. It, too, was filled with drawings, as were the ones next to it and the ones next to that.

"Are they all ruined?" Charlie asked.

"I would not say they are *ruined*." I smiled at a particularly good rendering of a rose. "Only *altered*. Here." I handed him the book. "See for yourself. The sketches are quite impressive."

Charlie flipped through the pages and frowned. I understood why too; books like these in my library were expensive. A treasure that only a privileged few could afford to own. And Charlie loved the written word.

"Impressive indeed, but books are not meant to be drawn in but read. And these, I'm sorry to say, are quite unreadable."

"I can still read the words despite the sketches atop them," I insisted, and he raised an eyebrow at me. "I'm not saying it wouldn't take effort, but it *is* possible." Even if it were not, though, I could not bring myself to be bothered by these sketches. They were a window into a lady's soul whom I would never know.

"First, your hats, and now, your books." Charlie shook his head. "You are taking this surprisingly well, Granger."

"I should tell you something, Charlie," I confessed. "I fear you will think me mad."

Charlie looked up at me, listening.

"Last night," I began slowly, "I saw a ghost. Miss Lockwood's ghost."

Charlie raised a disbelieving eyebrow. I couldn't blame him; I scarcely believed it myself.

"I know how it sounds. Ghosts don't exist, and yet I *saw* her, Charlie. She was floating right here in this very library." I pointed at the bookshelves near where the ladder was placed.

"Perhaps you only dreamed about her?" Charlie said.

"Perhaps," I said. "But I don't think so."

Charlie's brow furrowed. "In that case, I worry what else of yours will be ruined before this day is done."

"Well," I said, stepping down the ladder and checking my pocket watch, "my reputation if I miss church."

Charlie handed me the top hat he'd found with an apologetic expression.

Nothing was wrong with it, per se. It was in good condition and not *very* out of style, but it was brown, and my clothing was black.

"People will think I employ a blind man to serve as my valet." I laughed lightly.

"Well, it is either this or one of my caps," Charlie said with a shrug.

"This will have to do, then." I plopped the topper on my head, and we walked to the door.

We entered the churchyard only a few minutes before the service was to begin. Thankfully, Lord Markham was still standing in the courtyard. I stopped to greet him, and Charlie continued inside to join the other servants in attendance.

"I was beginning to think you weren't coming," Lord Markham said.

"Yes, well, I ran into some trouble this morning with my wardrobe. It's quite a long and altogether boring story."

"I doubt that entirely." He eyed my hat with a smirk.

As soon as we walked inside, I removed my hat, careful to make sure my hair fell at the right angle to conceal my wound, and held it low at my side as we entered the chapel.

It was a small but adequately sized chapel with twenty pews on either side of a broad aisle, each filled with parishioners.

All their eyes were on me.

As the second son of an earl, I was accustomed to being noticed, if not seen; usually, when people looked at me, though, they were really only looking *around me* for a glimpse of Father or Damon. Today, however, they were looking *at me*; matchmaking mothers and their doe-eyed daughters took my measure as if to determine my worth.

Perhaps I *would* have my choice of young ladies to court here.

I could only hope they'd not seen the sorry state I'd let Winterset fall into.

We continued down the aisle to Lord Markham's pew in the front row. Once we were seated, the vicar took his place at the podium.

He was an older man with a droning voice that induced sleep more than spirituality. But knowing people were watching me, I did my best to appear alert and attentive throughout the sermon. After an hour and a half, the verbose vicar finally took his seat.

A closing song was sung, a prayer said, and finally, the meeting ended.

Lord Markham leaned close. "Come, Jennings. There is a young lady I would like to introduce to you."

"By all means, lead the way."

CHAPTER FIFTEEN

Kate

SUNDAYS WERE NOW MY FAVORITE day of the week. With Mr. Jennings and his manservant at church, I could read in the library, draw in the garden, or even play the pianoforte in the drawing room if I wished. Currently, I did not wish to. But I could. Because for a few glorious hours, I could do *anything* I wanted.

And the first thing I wanted to do was take a bath.

It had been such an effort last night to fill Mr. Jennings's hats with soil. How vain did a man have to be to own so many hats? I'd had to wash my hands thrice, and they were *still* filthy from the effort.

After the last week, lurking around the house with the constant fear of discovery, I now walked the familiar corridors with a lightness in my step, a freedom I'd nearly forgotten.

I sank into the bath Mrs. Owensby helped me prepare and breathed deeply, enjoying the sweet scent of Mr. Jennings's lavender soap. It was wrong of me to use it, but I could not resist. I would find a way to repay him for the stolen indulgence. Maybe I would let him sleep soundly tonight.

After my bath, I quickly dressed and gathered my art supplies. It had been a full week since I'd spent time in the garden, and I didn't want to waste a second. The vicar was well versed, but even he could not talk all afternoon. I likely had only two or three hours at the very most to do everything I loved. When the sun reached its zenith overhead, I needed to return inside.

I exited through the servants' entrance and hurried to the hedgerow maze. It didn't take long to navigate to the gate, and once inside the garden, I found my favorite spot under the willow and sat. Sunlight caressed my cheeks, and a sense of peace washed over me. The rustling leaves and babbling birdsong whisked away my fears, if only for a moment.

The garden had changed since I'd last lingered here. Not a single flower remained in bloom, not even any daisy weeds.

I glanced around, searching for something interesting to sketch. The craggy stone wall? The weeping willow? The swaying swing? Nothing inspired me.

And then a leaf fluttered to the ground in front of me. The colors were so bright. It looked as though it had soaked up every shade of the sun: red and yellow and orange. Paint was my preferred medium, but I'd run out over a year ago. I missed having a brush in my hand more than I could say. I couldn't capture the leaf's intricate details or incredible color with a dull bit of charcoal. I worked for a few minutes before the leaf blew away in the breeze.

Drat!

I glanced at the sky to gauge the time. The sun was still low, not even close to overhead, so I turned the page to begin a new sketch, a portrait, perhaps. I tipped back my head and closed my eyes, trying to envision a face to draw, but I saw only Mr. Jennings. I blinked, trying to dislodge the image, but it did not drive away the desire, and I found my charcoal inching toward the paper.

I'd never been very gifted at drawing a person's likeness from memory, and sketching Mr. Jennings would be incredibly challenging. We'd only been face-to-face twice before, and not nearly long enough for me to remember the unique details of his features. But once I started drawing an oval for his head, then guidelines for his facial features, it did not take long to forget my failings and lose myself in creating.

I defined his jawline and ears, then created swirls for his hair, trying to capture the wild way it had fallen across his forehead in the rain. Finally, I drew his nose, mouth, and eyes, sketched stitches on his forehead last, and held it up to view.

Individually, his features looked accurate: the flop of his curls, the rise of his cheeks, the perfect bow of his lips; collectively, though, something was off. I could not tell what was wrong precisely, but I'd not quite captured him.

What a disappointment.

Had Michelangelo ever felt this way? Da Vinci?

It was hard to imagine the masters I admired ever despising creating as much as I, but they must have. One could not create something so vast as the Sistine Chapel or so enduring as *The Last Supper* without feeling some degree of frustration.

Setting my art supplies aside, I rolled my neck and shoulders, sore from hunching over for so long, then shook out my aching hand.

It had been a long time since I'd lost myself in the bliss of creating, and I felt untethered. Like I'd awoken in the middle of a dream.

Needing a little more time to ground myself before returning to the attic, I glanced at the sky. The sun was still not directly overhead, so I had some time left to linger. Not long, but a few minutes.

I laid back and closed my eyes, enjoying the birdsong, the breeze, and the scent of the grass and garden, soaking in every last second of this respite.

CHAPTER SIXTEEN

Oliver

"Lord Markham," a lady greeted as we passed, her lovely daughter at her side. "How do you do?"

He gave the lady a polite nod in passing but did not stop to make my introduction, as I would have liked. Once we were out of earshot, he leaned close and said, "Mrs. Parker and her daughter are amiable enough, but you have no interest in tying yourself to *Mr.* Parker. He lost everything at sea six months ago and would love to saddle his daughter's future husband with his debt."

"How unfortunate," I said.

"Indeed."

We passed another pretty pair, and again, Lord Markham did not slow, only tipped his head in a hasty salutation. "The chit is lovely, but her family is unsuitable. You undoubtedly heard all *eight* of her unruly younger brothers and sisters during the service."

I had not heard them, actually, but even if I had, I would not have minded. Having grown up in a small family and often feeling alone, I was a bit enamored by the thought of one day having a larger family. I hoped to make the family's acquaintance in the near future.

Finally, about halfway down the gravel walk to the gate, we stopped near a fashionably dressed family.

"Good day, Lord Markham," the gentleman greeted Markham.

"And to you, sir," he said, then turned to me. "Mr. Jennings, allow me to introduce to you Mr. Dalton, Mrs. Dalton, and their lovely daughter, *Miss* Dalton."

"A pleasure to make your acquaintance, Mr. Jennings," Mr. Dalton said, doffing his hat in greeting.

"The pleasure is all mine," I said to him.

"How long are you in town?" Mrs. Dalton asked, taking my measure. I hoped the expensive cut of my coat and the intricate knot of my cravat would impress her. My hat certainly would not.

"Indefinitely, madam," I said.

"I should have said sooner," Lord Markham cut in. "Mr. Jennings is the son of the late Earl of Winfield. He is the Winterset heir. Our new neighbor."

"Oh." Mrs. Dalton's demeanor brightened. "We heard you had arrived. It's nice to meet you."

Mr. Dalton chuckled. "I daresay this news will make many mothers here quite happy."

"I believe what my husband *meant* to say"—Mrs. Dalton eyed her husband with censure before turning back to me with a smile—"is that everyone will be glad for the opportunity to make the acquaintance of such a fine gentleman." She looked at her daughter. "Don't you agree, Hyacinth?"

"I do, Mother." She smiled up at me through her lashes. "*Quite* glad."

"Had I known how *lovely* it is here, I might have been persuaded to come sooner," I said, still looking at Hyacinth.

Miss Dalton's cheeks pinked prettily.

"And did you enjoy the service today, Mr. Jennings?" Mrs. Dalton asked, reclaiming my attention.

I chose my next words carefully, wanting to be honest but not unkind. "The vicar's sermon was . . . thorough."

"Indeed." She grinned, and I felt like I'd passed a test.

A sudden autumn gust caught Miss Dalton's bonnet and blew it across the courtyard.

"Oh!" she exclaimed, watching it tumble away.

"Allow me." I went after it, but the hat kept tumbling. A gravestone finally stopped it, and I braced one hand on the lichen-covered stone to steady myself before I bent to retrieve the bonnet. As I did, I glanced at the epitaph, half expecting to read Katherine Lockwood's name. It seemed plausible she would haunt me even here. But it wasn't hers, so I grabbed the bonnet and stood.

"That was quite a chase," Miss Dalton called, catching up to me. "Thank you."

"Happy to be of service." I gave her the bonnet.

She placed it back upon her head and, feigning innocence, looked up at me. "Would you mind?" She held out the ribbons.

"You wish for *me* to tie the bow?" I blinked. She must know how improper it would be for me to help her in such a way.

"I would do it myself, but it is so difficult without a looking glass. You don't mind, do you?"

"I . . . haven't much practice in bow tying," I excused.

"It is quite simple, I assure you." Miss Dalton stepped closer and extended the ribbons toward me. "Please?"

Saints, she was persistent. What should I do?

Damon had more practice with eager women such as she. Until this moment, I'd envied the attention he'd always garnered. Wherever we went, women all but threw themselves at him. But now, being wanted simply for *what* I was, not *who* I was, felt rather reductive—like I was nothing more than a hat to be plucked off a shelf and worn about town.

Seeing no polite way to refuse her, I hastily took the ribbons, tied a bow, and then put a proper distance between us again. "It is a little lopsided, I'm afraid."

"I'm sure it is perfect. Thank you, Mr. Jennings. You are too kind."

I forced a smile and surveyed the churchyard. "Do you know if the Lockwood family is buried in this cemetery?" I asked Miss Dalton.

"Oh," she said, sounding surprised.

My change of subject might have been a bit abrupt. "I only ask because they were my tenants, and I have not had a chance to pay them my respects," I explained.

"How gracious of you. I believe their plots are over there. I will show you, if you'd like."

"I would. Thank you."

I stepped forward, but she stood still. "Would you be so kind as to lend me your arm? The walking path is uneven, and I don't want to take a tumble."

I begrudgingly offered her my arm, and she sidled up to me.

Their plots were not far from where we stood, only a few paces away. "Here they are." She gestured to two gravestones.

Eustace Lockwood
Beloved Father and Husband

My throat tightened. "How did he die?" I looked up at Miss Dalton.

"According to the *church's* record, Mr. Lockwood died in a 'misadventure.'"

"And the truth?" I raised my eyebrow in question at her.

"A duel," she said somberly.

"A *duel*?" I couldn't contain my shock. Having died in the same year as his daughter, I had assumed they'd perished in a carriage accident or succumbed to the same sickness. A duel had not once crossed my mind. "Do you know the reason for the challenge or who issued it?" I asked, anxious for answers.

She shook her head. "I do not."

I nodded and moved to the next gravestone, expecting to read Miss Lockwood's name on it, but it wasn't hers.

Eleanor Lockwood
Beloved Wife and Mother

"I believe she died in childbirth," Miss Dalton said, her voice quiet.

"How very tragic," I said, feeling a pang of sadness that Kate had never known her mother.

Miss Dalton nodded.

"And what about Miss Lockwood? Where is she buried? Her grave must be nearby." I glanced at the inscriptions on the neighboring gravestones but did not see Miss Lockwood's name.

"Miss Lockwood is not buried here," Miss Dalton said.

"Oh? May I ask why not?"

"That is a rather delicate subject, one surrounded by much speculation."

I furrowed my brow. "Will you tell me?"

She was more than happy to oblige. "Well, Mama said that upon her father's death, Miss Lockwood was overcome with grief and cast herself off a cliff into the sea and drowned."

I sucked in a shocked breath.

"Her body was never recovered. Although even if it had been, she would not have been buried in the churchyard, considering the circumstance of her death."

I gripped the top of Mr. Lockwood's gravestone to steady myself. I'd known Miss Lockwood was deceased from nearly the first moment I'd stepped foot into Winterset, but hearing proof of her death, when only hours earlier I'd seen symbols of her life in my books, hit me harder than I thought possible.

"If her body was not recovered, how did anyone know what became of her?"

"Her pelisse was found on the seashore. It was bloody."

"But her body was *not* found," I said. "You're sure?"

"I am certain, sir."

"Miss Dalton," Lord Markham said, approaching with Mr. and Mrs. Dalton in tow. "You weren't telling Mr. Jennings ghost stories, were you?" He glanced down at Mrs. Lockwood's gravestone. "You must be very careful, Miss Dalton. Mr. Jennings already believes Winterset is haunted. You don't want to scare him away, do you?"

My gaze flashed up to meet his. Saints above, what had I said to him the other night in the tavern? "I don't actually believe Winterset is *haunted*," I assured the Daltons.

"You seemed *quite* insistent."

"Yes, well, I've developed a bit of an overactive imagination from reading so many ghost stories." Or, rather, living in one.

"I *love* ghost stories," Miss Dalton said.

"As do I," Lord Markham said. "I say, Jennings, Winterset would be the perfect location for a ghost-story reading."

"A reading?" I said. "At Winterset?"

Lord Markham nodded, his eyes moving meaningfully to Miss Dalton, then back to me. I remembered part of our early conversation from the tavern, about my wanting to marry. He was giving me an opportunity to make her an invitation. "With all those secret passageways and priest hides in the walls," Markham continued, "your manor is a uniquely qualified setting for a ghost-story reading, don't you think?"

Priest hides? Secret passageways? At Winterset? Not wanting to repeat the humiliation of not knowing the history of my own house, I tried not to let my confusion show and gave a slow nod.

And then I remembered something Mrs. Owensby had said when showing me the manor about priests having perished while in hiding at Winterset, and I felt like a fool. A priest could not hide if he had no *place* to hide. She'd gone on and on about the house's history, showing me room after room, but she'd left out arguably the most important parts: the priest hides and passageways.

Every curiosity that had occurred since I'd arrived flooded my mind: the scratching sounds in the walls, the pianoforte playing in the dead of night, the redacted notes, the books filled with sketches, the ghost I'd seen in the library.

Heavens.

What if my *ghost* was not a ghost but a living, breathing *lady* hiding within Winterset's walls? And what if that lady were Kate?

Her body had never been found. It was possible.

The longer I thought about it, the more sense it made; Kate had grown up at Winterset, so she would know about the priest hides and passageways. And after her father died, with no family or friends, she would not have had anywhere else to go.

It seemed so obvious now.

It hadn't occurred to me before because until this morning, I'd believed her dead. I'd had no reason to question her survival. But now that I knew her body had not been recovered and about Winterset's priest hides and passageways, it made sense that she was alive and hiding at Winterset. I'd *seen* her with my own eyes, "floating" in the library, for pity's sake.

I could not be sure. Perhaps I only *wanted* it to be true. I had to talk to Charlie.

"Jennings?" Lord Markham said, pulling me from my thoughts and making me realize Mr. and Mrs. Dalton were eyeing me strangely. "What do you say? Will you host a reading for us?"

"I'm . . . afraid Winterset isn't ready for visitors yet." I glanced around the churchyard for Charlie, eager to return to Winterset and search out all the priest hides. "Mr. and Mrs. Dalton, Miss Dalton, I apologize, but I must go."

"I'm not suggesting you host it tonight," Lord Markham said, holding out a hand to stop me. "We all know you need time to get your estate in order." He laughed lightly.

The Daltons also laughed.

I pretended to laugh.

I was sure Markham hadn't meant to, but I felt instantly humiliated. *Gads.* Winterset *was* a laughingstock.

Perhaps I should host this reading to prove my worth. "On second thought, I would be delighted to host a reading . . . in one month. Now, if you will excuse—"

"A month?" Lord Markham interrupted. "Wars are fought and won in less time."

It was true, but a month was already a stretch. I felt my frustration rising. And even if I were able to make Winterset hospitable for guests, I did not have a proper staff to host such a party. I had only two servants—well, three if I counted Charlie—but that was not enough. It would be impossible to repair my house, hire staff, and plan an event. But how could I not? "I am making many renovations," I said. "And Mrs. Owensby will need time to prepare a menu."

"Nonsense," Mrs. Dalton said. "Your Mrs. Owensby could plan and prepare a feast fit for a king in less than an hour."

Were we speaking of the same Mrs. Owensby? Mine was barely proficient in plating a sandwich. Finally, I spotted Charlie across the courtyard and stepped away. "Fine," I acquiesced, if only to break away from the group. "A fortnight."

"A fortnight." Markham grinned. "I am holding you to it, Jennings."

I was sure he would.

CHAPTER SEVENTEEN

Oliver

Bexley greeted me at the door with a bow and presented a salver. On it, another missive. "This was delivered while you were out, sir."

I took the missive and, recognizing Damon's handwriting, stuffed it in my pocket. "Bexley, have Mrs. Owensby meet me in my study straightaway."

"Is everything all right, sir?" he asked.

"I am not certain. Please summon Mrs. Owensby for me."

"Right away, sir."

Before going to my study, I went to the library and retrieved one of the books with the drawings inside. As I strode to my study, I flipped through the pages, stopping on a sketch of a willow tree. I perched myself on the edge of my desk and examined the drawing. The tree trunk was drawn in the center of two pages, and the weeping boughs spread to fill both pages. It was extraordinary.

"Good afternoon, sir. Would you like your lunch served in—" Mrs. Owensby's sentence cut off when she saw the book I held, or more precisely, *the drawing* in the book.

"No lunch for me today." I snapped the book closed and set it aside. "But I had an interesting conversation at church today and wanted to ask you about it. Did you know that Winterset has several priest hides? Secret passageways too?"

"O-of course, sir."

"Why did you not point them out when you showed me Winterset?"

She bit her bottom lip. "They are derelict, sir. I didn't think you would find them interesting."

"Ah. Another misunderstanding between us. Let us rectify this one immediately. Why don't you show them to me." I stood, gesturing to the door. "And be sure not to forget a single spot this time."

"Certainly, sir. I should be happy to show them to you, but first I must—"

"Whatever else you were doing can wait. I would like to see these secret spaces now."

She swallowed hard. "Certainly, sir. There is an entrance to the old servants' passageway right behind you."

"The bookcase? How clever." I walked around the desk to inspect the case but did not see any latches or hinges to pull it open.

"The small blue book," Mrs. Owensby said. "Tip it toward you to release the latch, and it will swing open toward you."

I did as she said, but the door did not open.

I tried again, pulling more firmly this time, but it barely budged.

"Allow me to show you?" Mrs. Owensby asked.

I nodded my approval and took a step back to allow her space to open the bookshelf.

She tipped back the little blue book just as I had twice before, but unlike me, she held on to the book and used her strength to pull the door open.

A musty smell filled my nose. Mrs. Owensby stepped inside the small space, turning in a small circle and moving her arms as if to clear the space of cobwebs, or perhaps evidence.

Cobwebs did indeed cover the walls of the cool, dark corridor, and two centuries' worth of dust coated the floorboards, save Mrs. Owensby's fresh footprints, of course. It was hard to imagine anyone hiding inside my walls. A shiver snaked down my spine. I shuddered and secured the door back into place.

"Show me the rest of the priest hides," I said.

She nodded. "Follow me."

I did, but first, I pushed the desk against the bookcase so that it could not easily be opened from the inside.

In the entrance hall, standing in front of the wall of portraits, Mrs. Owensby pointed out another priest hide. "Push the top of that timber."

Thinking it would stick like the last one, I used my strength, and it swung swiftly out and struck me in the shin.

Blast!

I jumped back. After walking off the pain, I lightly pressed the timber and looked inside the dark cavity.

This priest hide was much smaller than the entrance to the servants' corridor in my study. *Much* smaller. It was a wonder anyone could fit inside at all.

I crouched to look inside and saw something. A frame?

I reached inside to pull it out, letting the timber fall back into place as I stood, and held up the frame to view the image.

Miss Lockwood's missing portrait. The same one Mrs. Owensby claimed had been misplaced, but it had *not* been misplaced. It had been hidden.

I rehung the portrait in its proper place and stepped back to ensure it was level. My goodness, Miss Lockwood was beautiful. Miss Dalton did not hold a candle to her.

"This stays here." I gave Mrs. Owensby a reproving look. "Show me the dining hall next."

She led me there and pointed at the threadbare tapestry hanging on the wall. "There is an alcove behind it."

I pulled back the material and stepped inside. Curious about what it would feel like to hide here, I let the tapestry fall back into place. The space was immediately dark, save for a few pinpricks of light that poked through holes. I peeked through one. It had a perfect view to see the head of the table. My skin prickled at the thought of Miss Lockwood's watching me take my meals. But despite my strong suspicion, I hadn't found any evidence of another human hiding in my house.

I stepped back out. "Show me the drawing room now." I wanted to know how someone could play the pianoforte one second and disappear the next.

With a nod, Mrs. Owensby led me into the drawing room and pointed out a hidden jib door. I pushed on the panel, and it slid open to reveal the derelict servant's passageway. This passageway was as dark and dusty as the one in my study, though the cobwebs here were broken and brushed aside, and the dust on the floor had been disturbed by human footprints.

I blinked, not believing my eyes, but they did not disappear. I stepped inside the corridor, determined to discover where the footprints led.

"Mr. Jennings, please, wait."

But I did not wait.

I did not even slow as I walked the length of the corridor and climbed the steep stairs. At the top, a door opened to the first-floor landing, and directly before me was the attic door.

Mrs. Owensby had not followed me through the passageway but was using the grand staircase to climb.

I did not wait for her to catch up but opened the attic door and climbed the steep spiral stairs.

Once in the attic, I walked along the walls, searching for seams and pressing on panels, hoping to find another priest hide, but they were well disguised, purposely so.

I'd already made a full circle of the room's walls when Mrs. Owensby entered the attic, out of breath and looking anxious.

"Where is the entrance?" I said.

"Perhaps you should not—"

"The priest hide, Mrs. Owensby. Where is the door?" I knew there was one up here, considering how strangely she'd acted the last time we'd occupied this space together and how severely she was shaking now.

She didn't move right away, and my confidence wavered. I could be wrong. While Miss Lockwood's survival and hiding here made sense, I'd seen nothing other than a few footprints today to prove as much.

But then Mrs. Owensby stepped past me and pressed on a wall panel that looked as innocuous as all the others, and a door swung silently open.

My heart picked up its pace. Miss Lockwood could be sitting inside this room. I tugged my cuffs to straighten my shirt sleeves and walked inside the room, anticipating our introduction.

But the room was empty.

This was, by far, the largest priest hide. The room where a priest would have slept. It boasted a neatly made bed, a wardrobe, and even a tiny window. Dust covered the furniture, and cobwebs hung in the corners. Miss Lockwood had not slept here. The room was undisturbed.

Disappointed, my heart slowed to its normal rhythm. I was about to leave when I noticed something strange: footprints leading directly into the wall.

For a moment, my mind conjured up an image of a ghost passing through the wall. But then I just as quickly dismissed the idea because an incorporeal being did not have feet with which to make these footprints.

Could there be *another* room directly behind this one?

I knocked on the paneling, and sure enough, it sounded hollow. It took a moment to find a latch, but when I did, the door easily opened.

I blinked against the darkness. There was no window in this room.

"Hello?" I said softly, gently, but there came no answer. She wasn't hiding here.

It took a few seconds for my eyes to adjust to the darkness. This room was significantly smaller than the first, just large enough for a bed and bedside table, but it appeared lived in.

Linens covered the bed, a book spread open on a pillow. I picked up the book and thumbed through the pages. Like the other books in the library, drawings of flowers covered the pages. I closed the book and set it back on the bed.

On the table was a woman's hairbrush and a bar of soap.

My soap, I realized from the familiar scent.

I tucked the bar into my coat pocket, then sat on the bed and opened the bedside table drawer, wondering what else my stowaway had pilfered. Something rolled to the front. I felt for it, and once it was in my hand, I did not even have to hold it up to the light to know what it was.

My seal.

I trained my gaze on Mrs. Owensby, who was silently watching from the doorway.

"I know how this must seem, sir, but if you will let me explain."

"Oh, I *demand* that you do. But first, I want to know where she is."

"W-who, sir?"

"Come now, Mrs. Owensby. You've had enough entertainment at my expense, don't you think? No more lies."

"I have never lied to you, sir."

"Not overtly, but you have withheld the truth. Is that not lying?" I asked, and she looked away, guilty. "I was told today that Miss Lockwood's body was never recovered. So I will ask you again, and plainly this time so there is no room for confusion or miscommunication: Where is Miss Lockwood?"

As if Mrs. Owensby could no longer bear the weight of her guilt, she bowed her head and sniffed. "I don't know. Kate was supposed to be back up here well before you returned home from church, but sometimes she gets distracted drawing, and . . ." She shrugged.

I blinked.

I'd been convinced Miss Lockwood was alive, but now I had confirmation: She was alive, and not only alive but also *here*.

Relief rushed through me. "I want to see her."

"W-what do you mean to do with her?" Mrs. Owensby said quietly, sounding scared.

"I only want to have a conversation," I said.

"Would you allow me to speak with her first?"

"No." If Mrs. Owensby spoke with Miss Lockwood, I was certain Miss Lockwood would disappear. And more than anything else, I wanted to meet Miss Lockwood, to unravel her many mysteries. To understand why she had hidden here and to help her. But I could not do any of that with Mrs. Owensby working against me.

"Do you enjoy your employment here, Mrs. Owensby?" I asked.

"I do, sir. Winterset is my life's work," she said.

"I will offer you a choice then: If you swear not to say a word to Miss Lockwood about my knowing about her and all this"—I indicated the priest hide—"then you may continue working here."

"I don't understand."

"You will go about your duties as though nothing has changed."

Her eyes narrowed when she looked at me. "But why?"

"Miss Lockwood has played me for a fool long enough. It's time the tables were turned." I would find ways to draw her out without scaring her or making her feel endangered. I doubted it would take long for her to reveal herself once I turned some gentle pranks her way.

Mrs. Owensby studied me. "If I say nothing to Kate, then you will allow her to keep hiding here?"

"I have already discovered her, so she no longer needs to hide from me."

"It isn't *you* that she is hiding from, Mr. Jennings. Not really."

My brow tightened. "Who, then?"

"Mr. Cavendish. The evil man who killed her father," Mrs. Owensby answered, but I only had more questions.

"Miss Lockwood is in danger?" I asked.

"So long as she stays hidden here at Winterset, she is safe, sir. He does not know she is alive, but if he did know, I believe she would be in danger, yes. Which is why you must promise *me* two things."

"Go on."

"First, you will do nothing to harm Kate."

"I can easily promise you that. And second?"

"You will not say a word about Kate's existence to anyone."

It was possible Mrs. Owensby was toying with me again, playing on my sense of honor and duty to keep her ward close to her. But fear shone so brightly in her eyes, a genuine expression that could not be playacted. While I was not entirely convinced Miss Lockwood was in any *real* danger—Mrs. Owensby had not been the most reliable source of information—I was a gentleman, and it was my duty to protect *any* young lady who might require it. "You have my word as a gentleman," I said. "Now, will you tell me where she might be?"

Mrs. Owensby's gaze drifted to the window. "I suspect she is in the walled garden. It is her favorite place, and it has been a week since she has been outside."

A week. I winced. All this time, she'd been right here.

Mrs. Owensby turned to leave.

"One more thing," I said, stopping her. "Contrary to personal experience, I have it on good authority that you are an exceptional cook, Mrs. Owensby. Salmon sounds delicious for dinner."

"Yes, sir. It shall be ready by seven."

"See that it is." I stood. "Now, if you will excuse me, I must finish blocking the entrances and exits to the passageways and priest hides, and then, I think I will walk in the walled garden."

CHAPTER EIGHTEEN

Kate

A COOL BREEZE WOKE ME from my garden nap. White puffy clouds dotted the sky, and the sun was high overhead.

Oh no!

I sat up with a start. If the sun was that high in the sky, I'd stayed longer than I should have. *Much* longer. Mr. Jennings would be returning from church any moment, if he was not already home.

I grabbed my art supplies and rushed to the gate. I wished I could linger a little longer in the garden, but sadly, I didn't have a single second to spare. It would be another week before I could safely return. Sneaking inside the manor this late in the day was already risky.

I locked the gate behind me and started through the hedgerow maze.

Should I go through the main entrance or the servants' entrance? I wasn't sure whether Mr. Jennings had returned from church yet, but if he had, he might be sitting in his study or lounging in the library. But I could not enter through the servants' entrance either. His manservant could be sitting in the kitchen with Mrs. Owensby. Apparently, he was an aspiring poet and enjoyed sharing his work with her while she cooked.

What was I to do?

I was entering the last row of the maze when I heard a sound and stopped short.

There, entering the maze, was Mr. Jennings.

Thankfully, he was looking down at the ground, or else he would have seen me.

I turned on my heel to retreat, and a twig snapped beneath my feet.

"Is someone there?" Mr. Jennings said.

He'd heard me but hadn't yet seen me, so I dashed away down the row.

"Hello!" he called.

If I could navigate a few more rows, I would reach the edge of the maze that bordered the courtyard. If I made it there, I could wedge myself through the plants to freedom.

But Mr. Jennings's footfalls sounded such a short distance away. Only one row over, from the sound of crunching leaves and snapping sticks. If I slowed even a fraction, he would catch me.

Fear propelled my legs faster.

Only one row stood between me and safety.

I sprinted down the last row toward a dead end. The hedges were planted so closely together and their branches so tightly woven that the plants looked like a green wall. Glancing at the ground, I found a small space between bases and turned sideways to squeeze through. Sharp sticks scratched my uncovered skin as I slid through the hedge, but I hardly noticed the sting as I exited to safety.

Mr. Jennings would not be able to wedge himself through the hedgerow, nor could he climb over it as he had the front gate; the little limbs would not support his weight. He would have to retrace the path to the exit, and by that time, I would be safely inside the manor.

I'd not run more than half a dozen steps across the courtyard toward the house when I heard a thud and an ungentlemanly curse.

He must have run headlong into the hedge when he'd turned the corner at full speed.

I ran to the house's main entrance. A glance confirmed no one was in the entrance hall, so I went unnoticed up the grand staircase and through the attic door.

My heart pounded as I climbed the attic stairs to safety. I hurried into the first decoy priest hide and closed the door, sighing with relief, then sucked in a sharp breath.

The second door to the real priest hide was slightly ajar.

I did not remember leaving it open; I was always careful to close it behind me, but I had been excited for a day of freedom. Perhaps I'd forgotten to check that it was securely closed. Or possibly, Mrs. Owensby had come up to check on me and left it ajar by accident?

I slowly pushed it open and peeked inside.

At first glance, the room appeared exactly as I remembered leaving it: my bed was neatly made, and my book sat on my pillow. Although I did not remember closing it, it seemed I had. Other than that, though, all was as I remembered leaving it this morning.

Sitting on my bed, I took a deep breath.

And then another.

Was that . . . salmon?

I'd been in such a rush to run upstairs that I hadn't even noticed it.

Why was Mrs. Owensby making Mr. Jennings's favorite dish? Was she making it poorly? Pulling another prank on the poor fellow. The taste of putrid fish could turn him off the dish forever.

I sniffed the air again.

It did not smell putrid. It smelled good—*very* good, like lemon and garlic and butter.

My mouth watered.

I hadn't eaten fine food like that in years. Not since Papa passed.

Maybe Mrs. Owensby was trying to torture me. She had been quite angry when she'd learned that Mr. Jennings had seen me in the library. I'd explained it was good because he now thought me a ghost, but she'd still been vexed. What would she say when she learned about him chasing me through the hedgerow in broad daylight? I would have to hope my disappearing act today would strengthen his belief that I was a ghost.

My stomach growled.

Hmph.

Whether she meant it as such or not, this was a punishment.

Why hadn't I thought to eat something in the kitchen while Mr. Jennings was away? I sighed and reached under my bed for the small stack of crackers I'd stashed. I'd placed it there for situations like these, when I was stuck upstairs for an extended period. I took a bite, but the stale cracker did not satisfy me.

It was going to be a very long afternoon, waiting until it was safe to sneak downstairs for food. I could only hope that Mrs. Owensby would save me some of that salmon.

I passed the rest of the day lying in bed, replaying the day's events in my mind; reliving the luxury of the warm bath, the peace in the garden, and even the thrill of running away from Mr. Jennings.

At some point, I must have drifted off to sleep, though, because some time later, I awoke to the sound of Mr. Jennings's bedchamber door closing below me—a sure sign that he was dressing for dinner. I hurried into the servants' passageway.

I'd grown rather good at sneaking through the darkened passageway and quickly descended the stairs to the dining hall. I hadn't watched Mr. Jennings dine since the first night Bexley had cooked him overboiled beef and burned bread, but I had to know what Mrs. Owensby was up to tonight, and I needed food. I was famished.

At the dining hall, I pushed on the door to exit the passageway, but it didn't budge. So I pushed my shoulder into it, but it still didn't open.

No matter. I would exit the passageway in the drawing room.

But that one wouldn't open either, nor would the doors in the study or library.

Either Mr. Jennings had decided to redecorate, which seemed unlikely, or Mrs. Owensby was trying to send me a message; she had made it no secret that she didn't like me sneaking around the house, and presumably, she'd set out to prevent it.

Blast and bother!

I rushed back up the stairs and exited the passageway where I'd entered it near the attic door. I glanced down the corridor and was unsurprised to find Mr. Jennings's door still closed. The man took an age to dress for dinner.

Clinging to the shadows, I inched across the landing and descended the grand staircase. I had just reached the base when I heard Mr. Jennings's bedchamber door open.

I hurried through the entrance hall and slipped into the dining hall. I'd wanted to grab something to eat from the kitchen, then hurry back to my attic bedchamber before Mr. Jennings's valet came down, but I'd wasted too much time in the passageways, so I tucked myself inside the tapestry-covered alcove. It was as small as I remembered, but hiding here would be worth it even if I got only one bite of Mrs. Owensby's delicious dinner.

I leaned forward and looked through the hole in the tapestry.

Bexley strode through the entrance hall toward the dining hall to announce dinner, then returned with Mr. Jennings a moment later. I noted

Mr. Jennings's fine dress, styled hair, and easy manner. Bexley pulled out Mr. Jennings's chair and then took his usual place by the wall.

Mr. Jennings leaned back in his seat, appearing at his leisure. He looked much more at home since I'd first watched him dine.

After hearing my "ghost" in the garden earlier today, I thought he would be less at ease. But he did not look the least bit disquieted. He seemed comfortable. Comfortable in a way only a man at home could be.

I frowned.

Mrs. Owensby entered the dining hall, carrying a platter of scrumptious-looking salmon. A savory scent filled the air as she set it on the table in front of Mr. Jennings.

If Mrs. Owensby meant to torture me, she was certainly succeeding.

It took her three trips to the kitchen to retrieve all of Mr. Jennings's dinner, and although his face remained a neutral mask, I was sure he grew bored with waiting. He was a proper gentleman, after all, and likely not used to waiting. Despite Mrs. Owensby's protests that he not hire more staff, it could not be long before he demanded a footman, a cook, a few housemaids, a gardener, maybe more.

What would I do when he did? How would I hide?

Once the table was set, Mrs. Owensby took her place next to Bexley, and Mr. Jennings served himself some food. He took a bite and closed his eyes as he chewed. I wondered if his reaction meant Mrs. Owensby had overseasoned or overcooked the salmon. Even if she did mean to punish me, she couldn't have lost sight of our goal to make him leave.

"Mrs. Owensby," he finally said slowly, his tone inscrutable. "You've outdone yourself."

Not a prank, then. At least, not on him.

Mrs. Owensby smiled, pleased. "Thank you, sir. I am glad you like it."

"I more than like it. This may be the most delicious salmon I have ever tasted," he enthused. "In fact, I should like you to make it for the dinner party, which I am to host in a fortnight."

He was to host a dinner party? *Here?* He couldn't!

"Well, actually," Mr. Jennings continued, "I have agreed to host a *ghost-story reading*, not a dinner party, but I daresay that if I invite guests— there should only be five—to Winterset, then I should also feed them."

"Yes," Mrs. Owensby agreed. "I suppose you should."

"So," he said, "I would like you to make the salmon then. It really is delicious."

Though he could not see me, I scowled at him as he finished every. Single. Bite.

Mrs. Owensby moved to clear his plate. "Might I bring you dessert now? I've made trifle."

My mouth watered at the mention of my favorite dessert.

"If it is half as good as the salmon, I should be delighted." He smiled up at her.

She disappeared into the kitchen, returning only a moment later with the most delicious-looking dessert: layers of ladyfingers and creamy custard.

Mr. Jennings took a forkful and moaned. "This is . . . incredible."

Mrs. Owensby smiled. "That is kind of you to say, sir."

"I only speak the truth. You all must have some. You, Bexley, and Charlie."

Mr. Jennings wanted to share his meal with his servants? Such an unexpected and kind gesture.

"I couldn't—" She started to protest.

But he held up his hand, cutting her off. "You can. You will. Not a single bite of this delicious creation is to go to waste."

"As you say, sir," she said, carrying the bowl to the kitchen. Hopefully, she would save me some.

Finished with his food, Mr. Jennings sat back in his seat with a contented sigh and stared straight ahead at the tapestry in front of where I stood.

"Bexley, do you know anything about that tapestry?"

"I believe it is quite old, sir. Dates back to the Tudor era, if I'm not mistaken."

"It is quite lovely." Mr. Jennings stood and slowly walked the length of the dining table toward the tapestry.

I pressed my back against the alcove wall.

His footsteps clicked across the dining hall and stopped directly in front of where I stood. Only the thin fabric of the tapestry separated us.

"The silver threads in this tapestry do not shine in the candlelight as they ought," Mr. Jennings said, and his gloved fingers curled around the edge of the tapestry, coming within a few inches from my face. I held my breath as he rubbed the material between his fingers.

I was certain he was about to discover me, but then he dropped the fabric, letting it fall back into place. "It is quite dirty." He inspected the dust now covering his hand. "It should be removed immediately and cleaned."

"Immediately, sir?" Bexley asked.

"First thing tomorrow morning," Mr. Jennings clarified. "I want it made to shine when I host my dinner party and reading in a fortnight."

"It shall be done, sir."

"Very good," Mr. Jennings said, retreating a step backward.

It was then, as he quit the dining hall and walked toward the drawing room, that I noticed something dangling from his watch fob ribbon.

Was that . . . ? I squinted to see better.

No. It couldn't be. But somehow, it was: his seal.

Had Mrs. Owensby found it in my bedside table and given it to him? When? *Why?*

These questions plagued me for hours as I stood in the small alcove, waiting for Mr. Jennings to retire to bed. My feet grew sore, and my legs stiffened from standing so long. I felt faint, but finally, I heard him climb the stairs, and his door close.

I pushed back the tapestry, and although I wanted to go to the kitchen to partake of the delicious food Mrs. Owensby had prepared, without knowing where Charlie was, I couldn't risk it.

As I padded from the dining hall, I noticed somebody had pushed the buffet in front of the jib door. Then, as I tiptoed through the entrance hall, I saw something that stopped me in my tracks: my portrait, the one I'd hidden in the entrance hall priest hide, was hanging on the wall.

My mind raced to make meaning of all the oddities that had occurred today: Mr. Jennings appearing in the hedgerow maze, my attic room door being ajar, the passageways blocked, his seal, my portrait returned to its place.

He knew.

I did not know how he knew, but he did. He knew about the priest hides, about the secret passageways, about *me*.

And Mrs. Owensby knew that he knew. That was why she was acting so strange, why she was serving him salmon and smiling down at him.

My heart raced with the realization and the knowledge that if he knew I was hiding here, then I wasn't safe here. My servants seemed to be but not me. So instead of running upstairs to hide, I fled out the front door.

CHAPTER NINETEEN

Oliver

I slept better than I had in weeks. There had been no noises in the walls, no pianoforte playing, nothing. All was silent and still.

It was over.

There would be no more restless nights, no more tasteless meals, no more hats filled with soil. *I* was the master of this house now.

When I'd gone to bed last night, I'd thought about all the pranks I'd play on her, but now that it was morning, none of that seemed so appealing. I'd had my bit of fun with her by blocking the passageway entrances and viewing the tapestry behind which I was sure she stood last night. All I wanted now was to meet Miss Lockwood. A thrill ran through me at the prospect of us standing face-to-face *without* a tapestry between us.

I slipped out of bed and rang for Charlie. Knowing Miss Lockwood would likely be watching me from the shadows again today, I wanted to look my best. A fresh shave. My finest clothes. I *would* have worn my best hat, but she'd made that quite impossible.

A smile tugged at my mouth.

I'd never met a lady with such . . . tenacity. I could hardly wait.

But an hour later, when I went downstairs, there was no trace of her; the house was quiet, the furniture was in its proper place, and the curtains were neatly drawn.

Where was she?

I went to the kitchen to inquire of Mrs. Owensby, but *she* wasn't there either. I called for Bexley, but he had disappeared too. I walked the house looking for them, but they weren't in the drawing room, the dining hall, or the library. My study, too, was empty. As was the gallery, all four bedchambers, and the attic.

A pit formed in my stomach.

Were they *gone*?

Had they alighted in the night and left all behind?

Mrs. Owensby had said Miss Lockwood had nowhere else to go, no family or friends with whom she could seek refuge. Mrs. Owensby, Bexley, and Winterset were all Miss Lockwood had.

Despite my threat of punishment, Mrs. Owensby had likely told Miss Lockwood I'd discovered her at the first opportunity. Probably as soon as I'd retired to bed last night. Hence, the reason for my peaceful night's sleep.

My throat tightened.

What had I done?

Mrs. Owensby believed Miss Lockwood's life was in danger if she left Winterset, and I'd pulled pranks on the poor lady. My ultimate goal was to meet Miss Lockwood, but I'd gone about it all wrong. I should have attempted to *coax* her from the shadows, not *frighten* her from them.

Devil take me!

Miss Lockwood could be in danger.

Where would they have gone? *How* would they have gone?

Could they have taken my horses? The horses would provide them with a speedy getaway *and* prevent me from following after them. I ran to the stables and stopped short when I saw Bexley grooming my mount. If they'd fled, they had not taken my horse *or* Bexley.

Two women traveling without protection? I could not even bear to think about what harm might befall them. And I would be at fault.

"Where is Mrs. Owensby?" I asked curtly.

Bexley looked up from his task in surprise and gave a hasty bow in greeting. "Town, I'd say. She normally shops for provisions on Monday morning."

I narrowed my gaze on him. I thought Mrs. Owensby would have told him I'd discovered Miss Lockwood. But he seemed none the wiser. "Did you see her this morning?" I asked.

Bexley thought for a moment. "No, sir. But I believe she laid out your breakfast tray for Charlie to take to you this morning."

A biscuit with butter and jam and an apple. Something she easily could have laid out the night before.

"Is there something amiss, sir?" Bexley asked.

I opened my mouth to explain that they were missing but closed it. Could I trust Bexley? Did he know about Miss Lockwood? Or was it only Mrs. Owensby who was protecting and hiding her? I'd promised Mrs. Owensby just yesterday that I wouldn't tell anyone about Miss Lockwood's existence. If Bexley didn't know they were missing, there was likely a good reason.

"No," I said finally. "Nothing is amiss. I only wished for something else to eat. You may go about your work," I said and left the stables.

It didn't make sense. Miss Lockwood was smart; Mrs. Owensby too. They had to know their chances of survival were better here with me than outside Winterset alone.

They must still be here. If Bexley was to be believed, Mrs. Owensby would return from town later today. If not, I would know soon.

I needed only to be patient.

Attempting to distract myself, I went about my work, making plans for Winterset's repairs. Hours passed, and when I'd nearly given up hope of ever seeing Mrs. Owensby or meeting Miss Lockwood, Mrs. Owensby appeared at the servants' gate, her cart full of provisions.

I hurried outside. "Where is she?" I asked. "Where is Miss Lockwood?"

Mrs. Owensby eyes widened at the mention of her ward's name, and she hurried me inside the kitchen.

"Where is Miss Lockwood?" I asked again.

"I should think she is in the attic."

"She is not," I said.

Her brow furrowed in surprise, and then she moved more quickly than I thought her capable up the servants' staircase to Miss Lockwood's bedchamber in the attic. She took in the room, then turned to me.

"Kate would not leave Winterset," she insisted.

"All evidence supports the contrary." I wanted to ride out in search of Miss Lockwood and offer her my protection, as I should have done last night, but where would I search? She'd evaded my discovery in this one small house. I had no hope of finding her in a large country. I needed Mrs. Owensby's help. "I beg of you, Mrs. Owensby, if you know *anything*, you must tell me. She could be in danger. I only want to help."

"I know nothing, Mr. Jennings. I *said* nothing."

"Then how do you explain her sudden disappearance?" I asked.

"I would ask *you* the same question."

"You think *I* gave my knowledge of her away?"

"I don't know, sir. But I *do* know Kate, and she would not leave Winterset willingly."

I sank to the edge of the bed, bracing my elbows on my knees, and ran my hands through my hair. "Does Bexley know about Miss Lockwood's hiding here?" I looked up at her.

"Of course he does," she said.

"And you trust him?"

"I do, sir. With my life. Kate trusts him too."

"So where is she, then? I have searched everywhere within these walls."

"I don't know, but the more earnestly you search, the more ardently she'll hide. Kate is quite stubborn."

"I am beginning to see that," I mumbled to myself. "So I should let her continue hiding, then?" Ludicrous.

"No, sir. I am only saying that Kate has never liked being forced to do anything. I would think that includes coming out of hiding. You could *entice* her to reveal herself."

"How would I do that?" I laughed humorlessly. "Should I invite her to dinner?"

"It couldn't hurt."

I'd been jesting, but it wasn't the worst idea in the world. If I treated her as my guest instead of an intruder, perhaps she would reveal herself to me. It was worth a try.

"All right, Mrs. Owensby. We will do as you say." I instructed her to air out the bedchambers and put fresh linens on every bed. A guest could not sleep in the attic, after all. For dinner, I requested that she cook Miss Lockwood's favorite foods and lay an extra place setting on the table.

She did as I said, but Miss Lockwood did not join me that night.

After dinner, I asked about Miss Lockwood's favorite song and played the piece on the pianoforte. It was a soothing serenade that I hoped she would find inviting. But still, she made no appearance.

And as I lay in bed that night, surrounded by all that oppressive silence, I couldn't help feeling that Winterset had lost its soul.

CHAPTER TWENTY

Kate

I'd slept two nights in the potting shed and could not do another. I was cold and hungry and defeated. Mr. Jennings had won. I had no choice now but to beg his mercy, not for myself—I was already condemned—but for Mrs. Owensby and Bexley. They were blameless and should not be punished.

I waited for the sun to crest the horizon, then crept out of the cramped shed and started across the courtyard for the manor.

When I slipped inside, the house was quiet and still, so I ran up the grand staircase and to the attic to ready myself. Mr. Jennings likely would not care what I looked like, but I wished to look presentable and gather my most important belongings: Father's last letter to me and a miniature of Mama. I doubted Mr. Jennings would grant me time to do so before either kicking me out or calling the constable.

My hands trembled as I combed the tangles from my hair.

News of my reappearance would undoubtedly circulate quickly. How long would it take before Mr. Cavendish found out about my survival?

I knelt in front of my trunk and opened the lid. Memories from two years ago greeted me. The blue silk gown I'd worn the night of my engagement ball was neatly folded on top. I ran a gentle hand over the delicate lace neckline. It had been mended. I could hardly even see the tear.

I pushed the dress aside and sifted through the trunk. My hunter-green traveling dress was folded at the bottom. It was wrinkled but well-made and warm, ideal for wherever I might find myself tonight.

Father's letter, the one he'd written me to read the night my engagement was announced, was in the trunk lid pocket. I'd memorized it long ago, but I wished for a physical reminder of him. I held the treasured memento to my heart for a moment.

My throat constricted with grief. I would be leaving so much behind. There was no time to dwell though. Mr. Jennings would rise soon, and I wished to be waiting for him when he came downstairs. I replaced the contents and closed the lid.

I put on my traveling dress and tucked Father's letter inside it for safekeeping, then wove my curls into a simple plait and went downstairs to wait for Mr. Jennings in the study.

I stood near the back wall by the window, which would be out of his direct line of sight when he entered, but I didn't hide. There was no reason to anymore.

While I waited, I mentally rehearsed what I would say. I was duty bound to make sure my servants wouldn't be blamed for my mischief. Once I was certain of that, I would leave Winterset for good. I hoped Mr. Jennings would accept my defense of them. He did not seem like a cruel man, but I'd been deceived before, which was why I had to choose my words carefully.

At half past nine, Mr. Jennings strode into the study with a ledger tucked under his arm and went directly to his desk. He did not sit down though; he stood behind it, transfixed by whatever was on the page in front of him. A curl fell across his forehead, but he did not seem to notice. Neither did he notice me.

He was dressed in his usual restrained color palette of beige and brown and black, save for his shirt and cravat, which were white. It was like he was trying to tone down the natural beauty with which God had overly blessed him, but his dull wardrobe did nothing to deflect attention. It made his fine features—blue eyes, gold hair, red lips—more pronounced.

Mr. Jennings was handsome. *Aggressively* handsome. But a young lady who had stolen shelter and food and tormented him had no right to notice.

Another minute passed, and I grew anxious.

Not wanting to prolong purgatory, I shifted my weight, deliberately causing a floorboard to groan.

Finally, Mr. Jennings looked up, and his gaze met mine. He blinked several times, as if not believing what he was seeing. And then he *did not* blink, as if doing so would cause me to disappear.

Mr. Jennings straightened and slowly strode toward me, not stopping until he stood very near. My heart pounded as his eyes—so blue—searched my face. "For one who has wreaked so much havoc, you are positively petite, Miss Lockwood," he said, and then he did something entirely unexpected. He smiled.

I frowned.

"Please, have a seat." Mr. Jennings indicated the high-backed armchair facing his desk.

I glanced at the chair, which was positioned entirely too close to where he stood. I didn't want to be so close to him when I didn't know his intentions.

I took a backward step.

"Or . . . you are welcome to stand." His smile softened into a straight line. "I assume you've come out of hiding because you've surmised that I knew about you."

I nodded.

"Out of curiosity, what gave me away? Mrs. Owensby?"

Not trusting my voice, I shook my head and glanced at his watch fob ribbon.

He followed my gaze to his seal and grinned. "Of course. I daresay you are a great deal more observant than I. And better at hiding things too. Though, to be fair, you *did* have the advantage. You knew Winterset's layout, the passageways, the priest hides. Not to mention the help you had hiding."

Worried about my servants' safety, I stiffened.

He noticed. "Which, I suspect, is why you are standing before me now."

My hands trembled at my sides, and I clutched my dress to still them. He noticed that too.

"Please don't punish them, sir. Everything they did, they did for me." But no, that wasn't quite right. That made it sound like they were equal partners in this idea when, in fact, I had been the mastermind. "I *made* them do."

"We both know *that* isn't true." He laughed lightly. "I daresay Mrs. Owensby could not be made to do anything she didn't wish. But I respect you for trying to protect them." He sat on the edge of the desk, extending his legs and folding his arms. "Please. Go on."

I searched for the right words, but his casual manner disarmed me.

"Perhaps you can explain why you are hiding in my house," he supplied when I did not speak.

"This is the only home I've ever known," I said. "After Papa died, I had nowhere else to go. I am sorry for staying—"

"Are you?"

Was I?

Everything I'd told him was true. I had nowhere else to go, but was I sorry I'd stayed? No. I wasn't. I loved Winterset. It was my home. "I am sorry for the circumstance that demanded I take from you," I amended.

"And that circumstance is . . . ?"

Of course he wanted to know my reason for hiding here. He deserved to know, considering this was his house. But where to start? What to say? Even thinking about that night, about Papa, made me feel unsteady, and I began to sway, or perhaps that was only because I hadn't eaten anything besides a few apples and some water in three days.

"I fear you are about to fall over, Miss Lockwood. Won't you please sit down?" He stepped toward me, hand outstretched.

I shrank away.

Mr. Jennings dropped his hand and swiftly stepped back, bumping into the desk. He navigated behind it, keeping his eyes on me as he did so, and tugged the bellpull.

No. Not yet. He couldn't have the constable called. I hadn't had time to convince him to punish me and not my servants.

I opened my mouth to plead my case.

"Wait a moment, please," he said.

How could I beg his mercy if he would not allow me to speak? Perhaps that was his purpose. He was done hearing from me. How could I blame him? I'd stolen so much from him. And worse, I'd essentially just told him I wasn't even sorry for it. "Please, sir—"

"Not yet," Mr. Jennings said, not unkindly but sternly enough to stop me from speaking.

A moment later, Mrs. Owensby entered the study. "You rang, sir?"

"Yes. Good morning, Mrs. Owensby. As you can see, I require an introduction." Mr. Jennings gestured to me.

Mrs. Owensby looked at me, and I expected her expression to be scathing because I'd disappeared for two days, but she did not look upset. She looked relieved.

"I would be happy to, sir," she said. "Mr. Jennings, allow me to introduce Miss Katherine Lockwood, daughter of your late tenants, Mr. and Mrs. Lockwood. Miss Lockwood, this is Mr. Jennings, second son of the late Earl of Winfield and—"

"That will do, Mrs. Owensby," he interrupted her. "Thank you."

My brow furrowed. That was it? Why didn't he ask her to fetch the constable?

"You may go now," he said. "But please leave the study door open and remain close by in the entrance hall."

With a nod, Mrs. Owensby did what he said.

"Now," he said, turning to me. "Mrs. Owensby assures me you have a good reason for hiding here. I would very much like to know what it is."

"*Mrs. Owensby* told you I was hiding here?" I glanced over to where Mrs. Owensby was pacing the length of the hall, wringing her apron in her hands.

"Not exactly," Mr. Jennings said. "I discovered your hiding spot. She merely confirmed your existence. But that is beside the point. You were about to tell me why you were hiding in my house," he prompted.

"I was not, actually."

"You weren't?" he said, sounding surprised.

"No, sir. I am only here to ask you to spare the servants," I said. "To beg your mercy. They don't deserve punishment."

"You've already spoken on their behalf," he said. "Won't you say anything for yourself?"

"No, sir." I had no right to ask anything more of him. No matter my reasons, I was guilty.

His head tilted to one side.

What did he see? I wondered. An intruder? A thief?

"You are wearing a traveling dress," he finally said. "Why?"

"It seemed most appropriate, considering you must send me away."

"Must I? You and Mrs. Owensby said you have nowhere else to go. Where is it I am meant to be sending you?"

"I assumed you would either toss me out into the streets or to wherever it is that the constable takes thieves." Not that I planned to allow either of those things to happen. Once I ensured my servants' safety, I would depart. I could make my way to London and become a governess or a lady's maid.

Mr. Jennings's eyes widened. "You think I want you thrown into prison?"

I had no idea what Mr. Jennings wanted. I lifted my chin, trying to be brave.

"Miss Lockwood," Mr. Jennings said in a low tone that sounded almost disappointed. "I have no desire to toss you out on the streets or have you thrown into prison."

"How could you not? I trespassed your home. I stole from you."

"You also ruined all my hats," he grumbled.

"That, too, which is why you must fetch the constable. I understand. I only ask that you punish *me* and not my servants."

He appraised me. "You are adamant that I mete out a punishment?"

"Yes, sir. But *only* me."

He considered this for a moment, then slowly nodded. "Very well, if that is your wish."

Relief rushed through me like a raging river. I hung my head and blew out a breath. Whatever happened to me now, at least my servants would be safe.

"For your punishment," Mr. Jennings said slowly, as if still trying to decide how he should punish me even as he spoke. "I . . . should like you to join me for dinner."

"Dinner?" I glanced up at him.

"Seeing as you so obviously loathe me, I should think my company will be quite a punishment." His mouth twitched.

Was that . . . ? Did Mr. Jennings have a sense of humor?

"We will have a proper conversation about . . . everything," he said.

Everything.

What I'd done to him.

What he planned to do with me.

A conversation was more than I could hope for, yet the thought of sitting across the table from the man who held my fate in his hands frightened me. What was his motive? He'd said he didn't want to see me tossed out on the streets or thrown into prison, but he couldn't want me living in his home either. Was he toying with me? He did not *seem* sinister, but I knew better than to let down my guard.

Mr. Jennings dipped his chin to catch my gaze. "That was my poor attempt to invite you to dine with me. But I can see by your reaction that I severely butchered it, so please allow me to try again." He lightly cleared his throat. "Miss Lockwood, I would be honored if you would join me for dinner tonight. Will you?"

My stomach pleaded with me to accept, even as my head begged me to decline.

I didn't know what to make of his invitation.

Of him.

He had not reacted at all how I'd expected. Instead of kicking me out or calling the constable, he'd shown me kindness. Though I'd done nothing to deserve it, he'd invited me to dine with him tonight and talk to him. I did not know what could possibly come from such a conversation, our circumstance being what it was, but I was curious. And whether I wanted to talk or not, I *did* need to eat. "That is generous of you, Mr. Jennings. Thank you. I will join you."

CHAPTER TWENTY-ONE

OLIVER

STANDING BY THE HEARTH IN the drawing room before dinner, I tugged my cravat. I'd told Charlie to tie it tightly, but he'd been overzealous. I wanted to look my best tonight. Not because I wanted to impress Miss Lockwood but because I thought if I looked the part of a gentleman, she might feel more at ease.

She'd been so nervous earlier in my study. I wanted her to feel comfortable tonight. More than anything, I wanted to help her. But to do that, she needed to trust me enough to tell me about this man, Mr. Cavendish, whom she was hiding from. And more importantly, how I could be of service to her.

I checked the time on the mantelpiece clock and compared it to my pocket watch. Miss Lockwood was late but not excessively so. It felt like it only because I'd arrived thirty minutes early.

Perhaps I was a bit overeager.

Since we'd parted in the study this morning, I'd thought of little else but what would be our first meal together. For the second night in a row, I instructed Mrs. Owensby to prepare Miss Lockwood's favorite.

I rolled my shoulders, stiff from standing straight for so long. I probably looked like a statue waiting here, cold and unyielding. I leaned against the hearth, resting one arm on the mantel to appear more casual, comfortable, approachable. But now I was too casual. I sat on the settee. Too relaxed. So I resumed my position at the hearth and squared my shoulders again.

I glanced around the room, reviewing what needed to be done to make this drawing room presentable for the ghost-story reading I would be hosting in less than a fortnight. But I couldn't concentrate. My thoughts were solely on Miss Lockwood tonight. Where could she be?

Ten more minutes passed.

Twenty.

Still, she didn't show.

Had Miss Lockwood changed her mind about dining with me? I would not be surprised if she had.

Bexley appeared at the drawing room door. "Miss Lockwood sent me to inquire whether you plan to dine with her tonight, sir."

"Of course. Do you know when she is coming down?"

"She is already seated in the dining hall, sir. Has been for some time."

"The dining hall? How long has she been waiting?"

"Half an hour, sir."

I swore under my breath. "Why was I not informed?"

"We assumed you wished for a bit of peace before dinner."

"Why would I—" I pressed my lips together. "Never mind. I have kept Miss Lockwood waiting long enough as it is."

I brushed past Bexley for the dining hall.

Miss Lockwood looked up from where she sat at the far end of the table and stood. "I knew it took you a long time to dress for dinner, Mr. Jennings, but I believe this is a new record."

I did not know what had changed, but she already seemed more comfortable than she had earlier. I was glad. "I am flattered you've taken note of my daily routines, Miss Lockwood."

Her eyes widened. "That is not—I have not—"

"I am teasing you, Miss Lockwood. My apologies, both for that and for keeping you waiting. I assure you, it was unintentional. I was waiting for you in the drawing room."

"Oh," she said, laughing lightly. "Papa and I were never so formal. We always met for meals right here in the dining hall. My apologies for making you wait."

"Not at all." I took my seat, which was much too far from Miss Lockwood to be conducive to any meaningful conversation. What had Mrs. Owensby been thinking when she'd laid our place settings?

I was about to pick up my place setting and move it closer to Miss Lockwood, but something stopped me. What if the distance was purposeful? What if Miss Lockwood had requested it?

She'd all but run out of the room today when I'd tried to move the chair toward her in my study. Perhaps she did not want to sit any closer to me. Now that I thought about it, was it an accident that she'd come to the dining hall instead of the drawing room before dinner? Was she trying to avoid me?

She was clever, that I knew, so I would not put it past her. But . . . why? What had I done to make her dislike me?

The kitchen door swung open, and Mrs. Owensby stepped into the dining hall carrying a platter of food. The Duck à l'Orange smelled just as delicious as it had the previous night, but I didn't have an appetite.

Mrs. Owensby glanced at the wide space between us, trying to figure out where to place the platter. Seeing the predicament, she took it upon herself to solve it by serving us both individually, then setting the platter in the center of the table.

"Do you require anything else?" Mrs. Owensby asked.

"No, thank you," Miss Lockwood and I said in unison.

"Forgive me," Miss Lockwood said.

"There's no need," I said.

She trained her gaze on her plate and took a bite of food. She closed her eyes and chewed slowly.

"How do you find your food, Miss Lockwood?"

"It is . . ." Her sentence trailed off as she looked down at her plate. "It is the finest meal I've had in two years. Thank you, Mr. Jennings."

Had it truly been that long since she'd had a decent meal? Until this moment, I'd not considered what she'd been eating. I felt instant remorse once again for having turned the tables on her, on trying to tease her by parading my fine salmon meal in front of her two days ago. "I'm so glad you like it," I said. "I requested Mrs. Owensby prepare your favorite foods when I invited you to dine with me." Should I have said that? Would she think that odd?

Miss Lockwood gave me a weak smile and took another bite, seeming to enjoy this one as much as the first.

I followed suit, and we ate in silence for several minutes.

"Shall we get this over with?" she said, setting down her knife and fork.

"Get *what* over with?" I asked.

"This dinner. Our conversation."

"Is your punishment so severe that you want nothing more than to *get it over with?*" I gave her a small smile.

"Yes. I mean, no. I just want to know what you plan on doing with me."

"I was planning on eating with you."

"Mr. Jennings." She frowned. "I am speaking of our situation."

"As am I. We have a fine meal laid before us, Miss Lockwood, and I, for one, should like to enj—"

"Our current *living* situation," she clarified.

"Oh, that." I waved a hand in the air, brushing away the topic of conversation.

"Yes, that."

"Well, it's simple really—"

"Our situation is anything but simple, Mr. Jennings," she said.

"You're right, but my desire to help you *is* simple. Miss Lockwood, I won't pretend to know your reasons for hiding here, but one day soon, I hope you will trust me enough to tell me. Even if you never do, though, I want you to know that I will do whatever I can to help you."

"But . . . *why?*"

"Because I am a gentleman. It is my duty to come to your aid."

This time, she said nothing.

"As to our current living situation," I continued, "I'm not sure there is anything to alter it right now. Unless you have distant relatives I don't know about."

"My parents were both only children, and all my grandparents have long since passed," she said.

"And I'm guessing you would not be here if you were in possession of a fortune."

"You are correct." She laughed, though it held no humor. "My dowry died with me."

"Well, then. Until such time as we can arrange a satisfactory solution for you, you will live here as my guest."

"That is incredibly kind of you, but how would we even go about this?" She chewed her lip.

"I should like you to be my guest. I'm sure you will be comfortable here, seeing as this was your home long before it was mine."

"It has always been *your* home, Mr. Jennings. My family merely let it for a time."

While that was strictly true, Winterset did not feel like my home. I wanted it to, but I wondered if it ever would. What made a house a home? I didn't know. "Well, you are most welcome to borrow shelter here a little longer, Miss Lockwood. I hope you will feel comfortable going anywhere you would like in Winterset. I would prefer, however, that you use the corridors and not the secret passageways." I gave her a pointed look.

"I will," she smiled softly. "Thank you, Mr. Jennings."

CHAPTER TWENTY-TWO

Kate

I'd lain in my little bed in the attic for several hours but was wide awake, fearing for my future.

A *guest*, by definition, was temporary.

Mr. Jennings had said I could borrow his home a *little* longer. Duty prevailed upon him to aid me, but his generosity could not last forever. When it ran out—and it *would* run out—what would become of me?

I had nothing.

No one.

Regardless of my circumstances, though, I could not stay here indefinitely as his guest.

The weight of the realization pressed heavily upon me. I would have to leave Winterset, and soon, probably. My throat constricted with emotion. Winterset's walls had always been my haven, but now I felt them closing in around me.

Clutching my blanket, I curled into myself.

I felt so helpless, so *hopeless*. But I could not afford to give in to such emotions. I needed to create a plan.

I took a calming breath and forced myself to think. Slowly, an idea began to take shape.

I could not stay here at Winterset as Mr. Jennings's guest, but perhaps if I could prove my worth, I might remain here as his servant. He *did* need more help.

If I proposed the idea, I doubted he would agree to it. For weeks, I'd been nothing but an unruly ghost in his attic, and that was to say nothing of his sense of propriety. But if I showed him how useful I could be as a servant, if I fixed everything I'd done to Winterset these past weeks, and I helped him chip away at the repairs on his list, how could he deny me employment?

Unable to quell my anxieties enough to fall back to sleep, I rose well before the sun warmed the horizon and readied myself for a day of work. Mr. Jennings was not normally an early riser, and once he was up, it took him a considerable amount of time to get dressed, but there was so much to be done before he came downstairs to breakfast. I quickly donned a simple day dress and apron—it was actually an artist's smock, but it would protect my dress just as well from dust as from paint—then wove my hair into a plait.

My first task would be easy: replace the tallow candles with the wax candles we'd stored in the attic before his arrival. Hopefully, when he awoke to a pleasant smell, he'd know that I meant things to be different between us. That I no longer wanted to be his foe but his friend.

The task took only an hour, and I felt accomplished. Sitting alone in the attic day after day had been so stifling. How pleasant it was to be moving about freely and finally have a purpose.

The second chore I wished to complete was building a fire in each room Mr. Jennings would use today: the dining hall, library, and study. He was probably accustomed to having his rooms warmed before he awoke, but since he'd arrived at Winterset, the servants had had only enough time to light a fire in the first room he planned to occupy. My helping would lighten the loads of Mrs. Owensby and Bexley, who had been carrying more than their fair share in their effort to protect me.

But as I knelt before the hearth in his study, I realized one regrettable fact: although I'd seen plenty of fires being built, I'd never actually done it myself. Bexley had made it look so easy, but it took me several attempts to succeed. Hopefully, I would become more proficient with practice.

After lighting the fire in the study, I trimmed the quill pens and refilled the inkwell. His desk was already impeccably clean; otherwise, I would have tidied that too.

With little time left before Mr. Jennings would arise, I focused my efforts on tending to some of the easier items on the list of repairs he'd made in his notebook, starting with improving the entrance hall's appearance. I tied back each of the curtains to allow light to stream through the stained-glass windows and rolled the old, threadbare carpets. Bexley would have to help stow them in the attic and bring down the better carpets, but the space looked better already.

At half past six, I heard Mrs. Owensby beginning her chores in the kitchen, pots and pans clanking as she began breakfast. In the dining hall, I heard Bexley setting the table.

I hurried to help him.

"Ah, good morning, Kate. You're up early." Bexley smiled.

"I couldn't sleep. Rather than fight it, I thought it would be better to get up and work."

"Work?" Bexley's bushy brow furrowed.

"Yes. Speaking of, I need your assistance with something in the entrance hall."

"Certainly." He set down the silverware and followed me to the entrance hall. He glanced around the room, which was both brighter and better kept than it had been yesterday. "*You* did all this?"

I nodded, feeling pleased with myself.

"It looks wonderful, Kate. I daresay Mr. Jennings will be pleased to see the manor looking so wonderful, but I don't know that he'll be pleased to learn that *you* did it."

"I hope he will warm to the idea. It may be the only way I can stay at Winterset long-term," I said, and Bexley gave me a sad smile of understanding, confirming my fears. "Besides, it feels good to be useful again." If Mr. Jennings would allow me to stay, it would be a small price to pay to ensure my safety.

"What is it you need my help with?" Bexley asked.

"I need these carpets moved to the attic and the better carpets brought back down."

"I would be happy to," Bexley said.

"Thank you, Bexley. I will finish setting the table."

It did not take long to lay out Mr. Jennings's place setting at the head of the table, and it was a good thing, too, because he was due downstairs any moment. I needed to make myself scarce.

In the kitchen, Mrs. Owensby was up to her elbows in flour, and a sweet scent swirled in the air.

"Breakfast smells amazing." I took a deep breath. "How can I help?"

"No need. Almost done."

With a nod, I sat at the servants' table to wait.

Mrs. Owensby eyed my paint-stained smock. "Shouldn't you take your breakfast in the dining hall with Mr. Jennings?"

Although Bexley had brought out two place settings to put on the dining table, I'd laid out only one. "I'd rather take my meals here in the kitchen," I said.

She seemed unsure but said nothing and returned to her task.

It wasn't long before heavy footfalls pounded down the grand staircase and through the dining hall. The kitchen door swung open, and Mr. Jennings stood on the threshold. "Miss Lockwood is mi—" He cut off his sentence when he saw me sitting at the servants' table.

I stood to greet him as a servant would and said, "Good morning, sir. I trust you slept well?"

He frowned. "I did, thank you. But when I awoke this morning and walked down the corridor to come downstairs, I noticed your bedchamber door open, and I saw your bed had not been slept in. Where did you sleep, Miss Lockwood?"

"The attic," I said.

"Why would you—" He shook his head sharply, and a curl fell across his forehead. He promptly pushed it back. "May I have a word with you, please?"

"Certainly, sir." I straightened.

"In the drawing room," he clarified and propped open the kitchen door.

Heart racing, I quit the kitchen. Behind me, I heard him say something to Mrs. Owensby, but I could not hear precisely what. I hoped he was not vexed with her.

He did seem upset though, and I wasn't sure why he would be, seeing as the house looked and felt much better than it had when he'd gone to bed last night, but I could tell from his tone that he was.

In the drawing room, Mr. Jennings gestured for me to sit on the settee. He leaned against the pianoforte and crossed his arms, taking in my makeshift apron. "Miss Lockwood, I seem to have left some things unsaid last night. I apologize."

"There is no need."

"I believe there is. Last night, I invited you to be my *guest*, and today, I find you sitting in the kitchen at the servants' table and dressed in an apron, no less."

"It is a painting smock, but it doubles quite nicely as an apron, don't you think?"

Mr. Jennings blinked at me, looking utterly perplexed. "It does. But *why* are you wearing it?"

"Well, last night, when you invited me to stay here a *little* longer as your *guest*, I realized neither of those things is permanent. Eventually, I will need to find another situation. I thought that if I proved useful, I could convince you to hire me as a housemaid."

"I have offered to *help* you, Miss Lockwood, not *hire* you."

"Hiring me *would* be helping me," I argued.

"My assistance to you is not dependent upon your usefulness to me. You must know that."

"I do, sir. But I also know that I cannot live here as your guest forever."

"Did I not invite you to?" he said.

"You did not, sir. You invited me to stay here as your *guest*, which, by definition, is temporary. And I daresay, my occupancy here is still more of an invasion on my part than an invitation on yours."

"A fact you seem more preoccupied with than I am. And strictly speaking," he hastened to add, "you did not *invade* my house—you are not Napoleon, Miss Lockwood. You just never vacated it."

I didn't know what to say to that, so I remained silent.

"I fear we haven't gotten off on the best footing." Mr. Jennings sighed.

"Considering I pretended to be a ghost and haunted you to get you to leave . . ." I bobbled my head side to side. "No, I don't think we have."

His mouth quirked up at the corners, revealing a single dimple in the center of his chin. "May I speak candidly?"

"I would prefer it."

Mr. Jennings pushed off the pianoforte and sat in the armchair opposite me. He rested his elbows on his knees, bringing us eye level. "I cannot in good conscience employ you as a servant. You are a gentleman's daughter, Miss Lockwood. Your father was my tenant. I will not take advantage of your misfortune. I invite you to be my guest here at Winterset for as long as you need. Indefinitely, if that is your desire."

"That is generous of you, Mr. Jennings. Still, I struggle to accept your invitation because I know I don't deserve your help."

He studied me as if searching for the right words. "Miss Lockwood, you do not have to *deserve* my help, nor do you need to earn your keep. You simply need to accept my invitation to stay. Will you?"

"I don't want to displace you in your home."

He raised an eyebrow. "I believe that has been exactly your goal," he said teasingly.

"It was," I admitted, my cheeks warming with shame, "but not anymore."

"I am relieved to hear that, seeing as this is the only home I have."

"It is the only home I have too," I said quietly.

"Well then, since it seems we will be sharing this space for the foreseeable future, can we declare an official ceasefire?"

"On one condition," I said.

"Name your terms."

"I would like to make recompense for my actions. I took a few pranks too far, and I feel bad about them. Allow me to clean your hats."

A laugh burst from his mouth. "No. Absolutely not."

I frowned. I thought he would be glad to have me clean them. It would be a tedious task and likely occupy much of his valet's time. "I only want to fix what I have ruined."

"And while I appreciate that, Miss Lockwood, I am not letting you within ten paces of even my *least* favorite hat."

"And here I thought we were going to be friends." I shook my head.

"We are. So long as you don't lay one finger on my hats."

I opened my mouth to argue, but he held up his hand.

"Those are my terms, Miss Lockwood."

"Very well," I conceded.

"Good. Now then." He stood, signaling the end of our discussion. "Won't you please join me for breakfast? To be clear, I'm inviting you to *join* me for breakfast, not *serve* me breakfast."

I gave him a rueful grin and stood. I was quite hungry after working all morning. But then I remembered the state of my dress: my messy apron and lack of gloves. "I'm not dressed for—"

"You look lovely, Miss Lockwood." He gave me a sincere smile.

"That is kind of you to say, even if it is untrue." I smoothed my stained apron, but it did not make it any more presentable.

"You don't need to change your clothing on my account. But if you prefer to do so, I would happily wait."

"I fear my meal might suffer for it if I do."

He pointed at himself. "You aren't suggesting *I* would do something to your food, are you?"

"Considering all the overboiled beef and burned bread I made the servants feed you, I would not put it past you."

"As enjoyable as that might be, we've declared peace, Miss Lockwood. What kind of person would I be if I pulled a prank right after promising not to?"

"Hmm," I said, making a show of taking his measure. "I should not like to test our truce so soon."

"Shall we?" He gestured for me to lead the way and followed me out of the drawing room.

As we passed through the entrance hall side by side, Mr. Jennings kept a respectful distance. He remarked on the stained-glass windows, noting how much brighter the entrance hall appeared with the curtains pulled back. And when we entered the dining hall, I noticed a place setting had been added to the table directly beside Mr. Jennings's.

He followed my gaze. "I asked Mrs. Owensby to add another place setting. Is that all right?" he asked in a low voice.

Was it?

Despite everything, I didn't feel uncomfortable. Or I did, but not because I was afraid of him. The opposite. Mr. Jennings had said he wanted to help me, and I believed him. Any discomfort I now felt was owed solely to anticipation, the unsteady footing of a new friendship, the wonder of what he would say next, and how I should respond.

"It is all right," I said finally. "Thank you."

With a nod, he assisted me with my chair. "Now, let's discuss your sleeping in the attic."

CHAPTER TWENTY-THREE

OLIVER

THE FOLLOWING MORNING, I WAITED in the dining hall for Miss Lockwood, hoping she would join me for breakfast, but she didn't. I checked the drawing room to ensure she was not waiting there for me, but she wasn't. So I resumed my seat at the table.

Mrs. Owensby placed my breakfast before me: rolls with butter and preserves and tea.

"Would you like anything else, sir?" she asked.

"Nothing, thank you. But do you know if Miss Lockwood is joining me this morning?"

"Miss Lockwood took a tray in her bedchamber this morning."

"Oh. Did she say why?"

"No, sir."

"I see. Thank you, Mrs. Owensby."

Was she avoiding me? The thought gnawed at me as I forced myself to eat. Something in our conversation last night must have unsettled her.

I had no desire to dine alone, so I quickly ate and went to my study. There was so much that needed to be done, so many issues that required my time and attention, but I could not concentrate. My thoughts circled back to Miss Lockwood and the exchange we'd had the previous day. Our conversation had started strained when I'd discovered her acting as a servant, but it had ended pleasantly enough. At least, I thought it had. Perhaps I was mistaken.

I retraced our conversation. Over breakfast yesterday, we'd discussed the specifics of our arrangement. Miss Lockwood had insisted on staying in the attic as if she were still a ghost. I refused, and she suggested she sleep belowstairs, but that idea was equally unacceptable. She wasn't a servant, and I wouldn't treat her as one.

We discussed other possibilities, including us both sleeping in our respective rooms, but the antechamber that connected our rooms presented a problem: It wasn't proper. An unmarried man and an unmarried lady could not sleep in connecting rooms meant for a husband and wife, and I did not want to make her uncomfortable.

Our discussion went nowhere until Mrs. Owensby intervened, suggesting we sleep in separate wings. Her suggestion had some semblance of propriety, so we agreed. I insisted Miss Lockwood take the mistress's bedchamber in the eastern wing, where she would be more comfortable, and I would sleep in the western wing, where I'd slept my first night at Winterset. As this was not a permanent situation, my belongings would remain in the master's bedchamber to avoid causing the servants unnecessary work; moving my clothing only to move them back again in a few weeks or months, whatever it would take to secure a new living situation for Miss Lockwood, would be foolish. It wasn't a perfect solution, but we were both satisfied.

Or at least, I'd thought we were. She'd seemed so happy yesterday as the servants had moved her belongings back into her bedchamber. She'd taken a dinner tray in her room and retired to bed early last night, but I'd supposed that was only because she'd been tired. She'd awoken so early to play the part of a servant. But now it was morning again, and she remained in her bedchamber. Had I misjudged her emotions?

I dragged my attention back to my notebook, but the words blurred before my eyes.

Deuces! I needed a distraction. I tugged the bellpull, summoning Charlie to my study.

Not five minutes later, he appeared at the door. "You rang, sir?"

"None of this *sir* business today, please. I need you to play the part of my friend today, Charlie."

He stepped inside and closed the door.

"Is something wrong?" Charlie asked, sinking into an armchair.

"No. Nothing. I'm just thinking."

"About . . . ?"

Miss Lockwood, I thought, but I said, "Winterset."

"Right," Charlie said, his smile as wide as the Thames. "*Winterset* is what has you out of sorts this morning."

I blew out a breath, but it did nothing to lessen the pressure building inside me. "I can't stop thinking about her. Her situation, that is. I want to get to know her so she trusts me enough to help her. But how can I do that when she is avoiding me?"

"You could write her a note," Charlie suggested. "Invite her to do something with you that she enjoys."

"The last time I wrote to a lady, it did not go so well." Amelia Atherton had denied my marriage proposal outright. And now that I thought about it, most of my relationships with ladies, while enjoyable, never ended well. Or I should say, they *always* ended. "I don't want to make a mess of things with Miss Lockwood. Given our unusual situation, it would be foolish. Besides, words are your forte, not mine."

"I'm not suggesting you write Miss Lockwood a sonnet, Granger." He smirked. "Only an invitation. Your unusual situation presents certain challenges, to be sure, but one invitation won't mess things up. It might even make her feel more at ease. I will fetch your stationery."

I rolled my eyes. "Thank you, *Your Grace*."

"You are most welcome, *Granger*."

Ten minutes later, and just as many drafts, I'd written Miss Lockwood a short note inviting her to walk with me that afternoon and handed it to Charlie to deliver.

An hour passed, and I anxiously paced the entrance hall. Charlie assured me he'd delivered the invitation, yet I'd received no response from Miss Lockwood. At a quarter past twelve, she finally appeared at the top of the stairs, dressed in a simple blue gown and pelisse with her hair pinned into a chignon. She looked lovely.

"I wasn't sure you were going to come," I said, my voice betraying my tension.

She descended the stairs, stopping on the last step. "I wasn't sure you truly wanted me to."

"I did. I *do*. Did I do something to make you think otherwise?"

"No," she said hastily. "You've been more than kind." Her cheeks pinked ever so slightly. "It's just . . . I feared you offered only politeness."

"Not at all," I said. "I invited you to walk with me today because I enjoy your company, Miss Lockwood. And I'm relieved you accepted."

She glanced away shyly. "Had you not, I might have run straight into another hedgerow," I said, trying to lighten the mood.

A small smile tugged at her lips. "Seeing as I led you into the first hedgerow, you may want to rethink your invitation."

"No," I said simply and offered her my arm.

She hesitated, and I realized my mistake.

"Forgive me," I said, returning my arm to my side. "I didn't mean to make you uncomfortable."

"You didn't," she said quickly. "You only surprised me. I'm out of practice at, well, everything."

"You don't seem to be. But even if you were, I'm glad you came. If you would still like to walk with me, Mrs. Owensby has kindly agreed to be our chaperone." I tipped my head toward Mrs. Owensby, who stood discreetly by the dining hall door.

"I would like to walk with you. And if you are still willing, I should be glad to take your arm too." She lifted her hand.

I eagerly held out my elbow. The feeling of her featherlight fingers on my arm made my heart race. Bexley opened the front door, and Miss Lockwood's grasp tightened on my arm.

"Bexley, will you please ensure the courtyard is clear?"

He quickly did so and returned promptly with a nod, signaling that it was safe. As we stepped outside, I wished just for a moment that the ivy I'd loathed upon my arrival still cloaked the front gate to offer her a sense of security.

"Where shall we walk, Miss Lockwood? You know these grounds far better than I."

"Would you like me to show you the walled garden?" She glanced up at me, her eyes hopeful.

"I'd like that. It's one of the few places in Winterset that I haven't seen yet."

She led me to the hedgerow maze. The path to the garden entrance was well-worn, something I hadn't noticed when I'd chased her. We reached a weathered wood door, and she produced a key from her pelisse. Entering first, she led me down a cobblestone path to a pond. Mrs. Owensby trailed behind us, but not distractingly so.

"I'm afraid the garden is going dormant, so there aren't any blooms, but what do you think of it?" she said, her voice laced with uncertainty.

I took in the tranquil scene: the weeping willow, the winding path, the small pond. The garden was not overly large, but it was well-appointed, peaceful, and protected. I understood why Miss Lockwood liked coming here. "It's beautiful."

Her expression softened. "I know it doesn't look like much now, but in a few months, this garden will burst into life again. The hawthorn blossoms will turn the hedges white as snow, and clusters of primroses will dot the ground. Robin song will fill the air. And the scent of blooming lilacs will be intoxicating."

"I knew you were a talented artist, but am I to understand that you are also a master gardener?" I raised an eyebrow.

She scoffed. "Hardly."

"How do you know so much, then?"

"My father taught me the basics of how to plant and prune, but everything else I have learned from your library."

"Do you enjoy reading?" I asked her.

"Immensely."

"It is a wonder, then, that you drew in my books," I teased, unable to resist.

She grimaced. "I ran out of paper and used the books I thought no one would ever read again."

"Miss Lockwood, I was teasing. I don't mind. Your drawings likely improved their value. They are lovely."

She blushed. "Thank you."

"I noticed you like to draw flowers." The books were filled with them.

"Actually, I prefer to paint people. Portraits. Capturing a person's likeness and the feel of their soul on canvas is magical." She smiled softly. "I don't think I've ever felt so much passion for anything."

Her eyes sparked with mischief. "You are passionate about your hats."

"Why, Miss Lockwood. Did you just call me *vain*?"

She shrugged playfully. "Only if the hat fits."

"I daresay it does." I laughed.

We continued in companionable silence until we reached a stone angel. At the base, an inscription read For Eleanor Lockwood.

It was a touching monument, but I was a bit surprised to find something so permanent here, seeing as the Lockwood's had only been letting Winterset, but it didn't bother me.

Miss Lockwood looked up at me and must have seen my wonder because she said quietly, "My father had this statue made and placed here in the garden in my mother's memory. She died in childbirth."

"I'm sorry you never knew her."

"Me too," Miss Lockwood said. "Had his death not been so sudden, I'm sure he would have had it removed upon quitting Winterset. I would understand if you—"

"It's lovely," I said and meant it. "It must stay wherever you are."

"Thank you, Mr. Jennings." She gave me a grateful smile and turned back to view the statue. "I may not have known my mother, but my father kept her memory alive with this garden. While we planted and pruned together, he told me stories about her. I can still see the crinkle of his eyes and hear the smile in his voice when he used to talk about her. I would give *anything* to see my father one last time and to meet my mother."

Her words struck me with unexpected force. She spoke so genuinely and with so much love. I'd never felt that way for anyone before, and certainly not for my father. I could barely meet her gaze, ashamed of the emptiness I felt in comparison.

She looked up at me. "You look upset. Have I said something wrong?" she asked.

"No. It's only . . . I have been to many places, seen many things, and met many people, but I have never experienced the kind of passion and love that you just expressed. You speak of your parents, your art, even this garden as though they are the air you breathe, and I feel . . . envious."

"I assure you, my life is nothing to envy," she said softly.

My heart squeezed.

There was so much I didn't know about her. But I wanted to know more. I wanted to know *everything*. I had so many questions, but I couldn't ask her outright. Her walls were as high as this garden's, and I had to climb carefully if I didn't want her to retreat.

So, instead, I said, "That is a beautiful memory. Thank you for sharing it with me."

We continued walking through the garden. It felt nice to walk with her like this. It was easy between us. When she let down her guard, she was witty and clever and sweet. The gentle rustle of the willow leaves and the soft sounds of the pond mirrored the peace between us.

Yet as we rounded a bend in the path, the weight of my responsibilities crept back into my mind. Specifically, the ghost-story reading I'd agreed to host loomed over me like a shadow. How could I host such an event when I was so concerned about Miss Lockwood's well-being?

"What are you thinking about?" Miss Lockwood asked, breaking my reverie.

"Nothing important."

"Your brow says otherwise, Mr. Jennings."

She was observant, as always. "I was just thinking about the ghost-story reading I am supposed to host."

"I forgot about that," she said softly.

"Forgive me, what I should have said was that I was thinking about how I might *cancel* it."

"You shouldn't do that."

"Shouldn't I?"

She shook her head. "I don't want to interfere with your plans any more than I already have." She smiled bravely, but I saw the worry in her eyes. "When are you hosting it?" she asked.

"A little less than two weeks."

"That doesn't leave you much time."

"Not much at all," I agreed, thinking of all the work that needed to be done.

"Do you have a plan to make the estate presentable?"

"Only a vague one," I admitted. "I thought I would concentrate my efforts on the places my guests will see."

"So, outside, you will focus on the courtyard and drive. And inside, the entrance, dining hall, and the drawing room?"

I nodded. "The drawing room will be the most difficult. The water damage under the window is extensive."

"Water damage?" She looked equal parts concerned and confused.

"Yes. The window seal failed. The frame is rotted, and the papers are ruined."

"Is *that* why you are planning to remove them?" she asked. "I thought you didn't like them."

"I love them. The design is beautiful."

She smiled at that. "Thank you. It took me nearly two months to paint them."

"I didn't realize."

"How could you have?" she said. "That room alone will likely take more than two weeks to repair."

"I know." I sighed. "And even if, by some miracle, I complete the repairs, new wall papers cannot be delivered so quickly."

"You could purchase plain papers, and I could paint them for you if you would like."

"I would like that very much. Thank you."

"Perhaps you could order new furniture to distract from the imperfections," she said.

"I doubt there is enough time."

"You're probably right." Her brow furrowed. "We could rearrange the existing furniture to hide the imperfections," she said.

I laughed. "The entire room is an imperfection."

"Hmm. Well, what if, instead of hiding the needed repairs, we highlight them? You are hosting a ghost-story reading, after all."

"You think I should make Winterset look worse?"

"Only the drawing room. We could bring down the old furnishings from the attic: the threadbare carpets and moth-eaten tapestries. Your guests would think the decor was purposeful. We will make the rest of the manor as presentable as possible."

She was excited, her eyes distant, as though she were picturing the room.

"That might work for the inside," I said. "But what about the grounds?"

"If you have the funds, hire men from town. They could cut back the overgrown plants in the courtyard, regravel the drive, and fix the fountain."

"Do you think they can do that in less than two weeks?"

"If you pay them, they'll find a way."

I did not have much money to spare, but there should be enough to cover the cost.

As our walk came to an end and we made our way toward the garden gate, I felt a growing sense of anticipation. I had been overwhelmed by the work that Winterset required, but now, with Miss Lockwood's help, I had something to look forward to.

CHAPTER TWENTY-FOUR

KATE

SITTING IN FRONT OF MY mirror the next morning, I pinned up my hair, or attempted to anyway. I wasn't doing a very good job of it. Mary had always made it look easy. It took me much longer than it should have, but finally, it was up. I didn't think it looked half bad, although I wasn't sure it looked half good either. It was the best I could manage on my own though.

I glanced at my timepiece.

Drat! It was already quite late.

I hoped I had not missed breakfast with Mr. Jennings again this morning. He would likely think I was still avoiding him if I did. After our walk in the garden and candid conversation yesterday, I was sure he would be waiting. But when I went downstairs, he wasn't there.

I suddenly felt silly for spending so much time dressing and styling my hair. Not that I had taken care of my appearance for him, per se, but, well, yes, I had.

Mr. Jennings was always fashionably dressed and had perfectly styled hair. I wanted to look less like I had been living inside a wall for the past two years.

A lone place setting sat on the dining table, but I did not wish to eat alone. So I scooped up the plate and silverware and went to the kitchen.

Mrs. Owensby looked up from kneading dough. She eyed my hair and dress with a knowing smile. "You look nice this morning."

My face warmed, and I wished I would have left my hair alone and worn my drabbest dress.

"How did you sleep last night?" she asked.

"Better than I have in two years," I admitted. Not only was my bed even more comfortable than I remembered from a mere week before, but knowing Mr. Jennings slept down the hall in the other wing and that he'd pledged to protect me made me feel safe.

"I'm glad to hear it," Mrs. Owensby said and served me a pastry and a steaming cup of chocolate.

A sound caught my attention, and I looked up from my meal.

Mr. Jennings's valet stood in the kitchen, looking slightly startled at the sight of me. Although *I'd* seen Mr. Hanover before, *he'd* not seen me. We'd never met face-to-face.

He stepped toward the table. "Miss Lockwood, I presume?"

I nodded. "And you are Mr. Jennings's valet."

"Charles Hanover," he supplied.

"How do you do, Mr. Hanover?"

"Call me Charlie," he said. "Please."

"All right. Would you care to join me, Charlie?" I gestured to the table.

"I should be glad to." He took the seat across from me.

Mrs. Owensby set a plate of food in front of him, and he thanked her.

I wasn't sure what I expected from Charlie . . . casual conversation, perhaps, but he only pulled out a small notebook and pencil and began writing. As he worked, I noticed a reddish-pink stain on the side of his right hand, like he'd smeared his hand through paint. Was he an artist like me? I glanced at his notebook. No, he was writing, not drawing. And when he set down his pencil and picked up his fork, I realized it was not a stain but a port-wine birthmark.

Charlie alternated between writing and eating for several minutes but said nothing.

"What are you working on?" I asked, and when he looked up, I indicated his notebook.

"Oh, it's nothing. Just a poem."

"You are a poet?"

"Hardly. My poems are terrible. I write only for enjoyment."

"Like my art."

He gave me a pointed look. "*Not* like your art. I have seen your sketches, Miss Lockwood. And they are very good."

I could tell by the off-handed way he'd delivered the compliment that he hadn't said it to flatter me, but it unsettled me all the same. He'd seen something personal, something *I'd* not shown him, and it made me uncomfortable. I supposed that made me hypocritical, but I couldn't help it.

"Would you read me one of your poems?" I asked.

He hesitated.

"You have seen my art," I reminded him. "It feels only fair."

"All right." He pushed the notebook to me. "But remember I warned you."

I glanced down at his notebook and read:

A teapot's hat was much too small
And did a jig upon the wall,
Where saucers hummed a merry tune,
As if they were the size of moons.

I looked at Charlie again.

"Mr. Jennings is right; your eyes *are* expressive." He chuckled. "I told you my poems were terrible."

I should probably have felt embarrassed for not hiding my thoughts better, but Mr. Jennings had told his valet my eyes were expressive? The thought made me smile.

I swallowed down my glee with a sip of my chocolate. "No, no. It is a well-written poem. I like the cadence. I'm not sure I understand it." How did teapots jig upon the wall? And what made singing saucers the size of moons?

"*That* is because it does not make any sense." Charlie smiled. "I write whatever comes to mind and move on. It's a terrible poem but a fun exercise. Would you like to try it?"

"I'm not much of a writer."

"I meant with drawing." He handed me the pencil.

I glanced down at the notebook and ran my hand over the blank page. It had been so long since I'd had plain paper to draw on.

"You have ten seconds. Don't think, just draw. Ready?" He indicated his notebook with a nod. "Begin."

I lowered the pencil to the page and drew the first thing that came to mind. As luck would have it, a gentleman's top hat. A very poorly proportioned one.

I laughed and showed Charlie.

"Interesting."

"I know." I grimaced. "It's terrible."

"That is not why I find it interesting. This looks like one of Mr. Jennings's toppers."

It did look like one of his toppers. My cheeks warmed. "Where *is* Mr. Jennings this morning?" I said, trying for nonchalance but achieving the opposite.

"Town," Charlie said simply, either not catching on or commenting at my eager interest.

"For what purpose?" I asked.

"I couldn't say."

Couldn't or wouldn't? "He's probably gone to buy another ridiculous hat."

Charlie's mouth tugged up at the corner. "Knowing him, you're probably right." He opened his mouth like he intended to say something more, but his attention focused on something over my shoulder, and he stood.

I followed his gaze behind me and saw Mr. Jennings standing at the kitchen door. My heart jumped at the sight of him. He looked so handsome in his greatcoat that I nearly missed the plethora of parcels tucked under his arms.

"Perhaps he *did* go to town to buy new hats," Charlie whispered, and I laughed lightly.

"Something funny?" Mr. Jennings asked, glancing between Charlie and me.

I pressed my lips together, trying not to laugh, then looked at Charlie.

"I let Miss Lockwood read one of my poems," he said. "She wasn't impressed."

Mr. Jennings smiled. "Ah."

"What are those?" I glanced at the parcels.

"*Those* are the reasons I missed our breakfast this morning. Come, I'll show you."

Curious, I followed him to the drawing room. He closed the pianoforte lid and spread out the parcels upon it. Each was wrapped in brown paper and tied with string. He unwrapped the first parcel and looked at me excitedly as I opened its contents.

"Oh!" I gasped, tears filling my eyes at the sight of so many paints and brushes. I touched them reverently.

"Would you like to open the rest?" He pushed one toward me.

I quickly opened one to discover a new sketchbook and pencils. The next parcel contained canvases. The one after that held the plain wall papers I'd requested.

"I went to the store to buy only the paint and papers for the walls, like we talked about yesterday," he admitted. "But then I couldn't stop thinking about our conversation, about how much you love to paint and sketch, and I realized you probably needed some supplies, and . . ." He glanced down at all the materials, then sheepishly at me. "I may have gotten carried away. If any of these are wrong—"

"Not wrong," was the most I could manage around the lump in my throat. "Forgive me," I said, blinking back tears. "It's just been such a long time since I've had any art supplies. I feel like I've been reunited with a long-lost friend."

He handed me his handkerchief. "If I have forgotten anything, you need only ask."

"You have left nothing undone." I dabbed the corners of my eyes. "But even if you had, I am already so deeply in your debt. This is incredibly generous of you, Mr. Jennings. No one has ever done anything so thoughtful for me. Thank you."

"You are most welcome," he said. "Oh! I almost forgot." He produced one last parcel from his coat pocket and handed it to me.

I eagerly untied the twine and opened the package. A sweet, citrusy scent filled the air.

"Lemon drops? These are my favorite!"

"Mrs. Owensby might have mentioned that when I asked her what your favorite confection was this morning."

I touched his arm in gratitude. I couldn't help it!

Mr. Jennings looked down at my hand.

I quickly let it drop and stepped back, feeling self-conscious. "You have no idea what this means to me."

He gave me a warm smile. "I'm glad you like it."

"*Thank you*, Mr. Jennings. For the supplies, the sweets, for everything."

"It was nothing."

"Not to me." I held his gaze, hoping to convey just how much this meant to me. How much I appreciated these gifts, how much I appreciated *him*. But I held his gaze a moment too long, and it felt almost intimate.

My cheeks warmed with embarrassment, and I looked away. "When can we get started on the wall?"

"Whenever you would like," he said.

"Now. I wish to start now."

"Then we will. I must warn you, though, that it will take at least a day of preparation to remove the ruined papers and rotted wood and likely another day to replace it with good wood."

"Why, Mr. Jennings, that sounds like a challenge. If we all work together—you, me, Bexley, Charlie, and Mrs. Owensby—I believe we can have it done by dusk."

"Dusk?" He shook his head. "Perhaps by dawn, *if* we work all night."

"Then we better get started immediately," I said.

Mr. Jennings smiled fully, the dimple in his chin making a rare appearance. "Yes, we'd better. I will get the others so we can get started."

CHAPTER TWENTY-FIVE

Oliver

"You were right," I said to Miss Lockwood, amazed. "I did not think it possible, but you were right." It had taken the five of us all day, but we had done it: we'd stripped the old papers off the wall, removed and replaced the rotted wood around the window, and even rehung the plain wall papers, and all by dusk.

Miss Lockwood grinned up at me. "Honestly, I didn't think it was possible either, but I am thrilled that we did."

"As am I. It will take some time for the papers to dry, but you should be able to start painting them in a day or two."

"I can't wait!" She clapped her hands excitedly.

"In the meantime, are you ready for dinner?"

She glanced down at her dress and then at me. "Not in the least." She laughed, pulling scraps of wall paper off her dress and out of her hair. "And . . . neither are you."

I looked down at my shirt sleeves and waistcoat. I'd removed my coat earlier so I would not ruin it. Curled pieces of the wall paper looked an awful lot like feathers. "Why did you not tell me I looked like a half-plucked chicken?" I ruffled my fingers through my hair, and so many scraps fell to the ground that it looked like it was snowing.

"You don't," she giggled.

"Oh, don't I?"

"No, you look more like you are molting," she said, and I shook my head at her, smiling. "I *am* quite hungry though."

"So am I. What do you say we throw propriety out our newly fixed window and eat dinner as we are?" I suggested, wanting to preserve the easiness we'd built between us.

"Yes! *Please.*"

I offered her my arm, and she readily took it. Progress.

In the dining hall, a simple dinner was already set on the table: finger sandwiches and fruit. Mrs. Owensby had worked alongside us most of the day, so something quick and simple was just the thing.

Famished, we sat and served ourselves.

"Mm," Miss Lockwood moaned. "Finger sandwiches have never tasted so good."

"Delicious," I agreed, and then neither of us said anything more until we'd had our fill.

Usually, Miss Lockwood excused herself as soon as she finished eating, but tonight, she sat back in her chair with a satiated smile.

I did not want to hope, but perhaps she was not ready to bid me good night. It was not late. And although I was physically exhausted, I was not mentally tired. I tried to think of something we might do together so she would linger with me a little longer. "Would you care to join me for a game of . . . chess?" I proposed the first two-person game that came to mind.

To my relief, her eyes lit up. "I would love to."

In the drawing room, she led me to the corner where the chessboard was neatly stored. I set it on the small game table, trying to ignore the pang of self-doubt that tugged at me. It had been ages since I'd last played, and I was never particularly adept. The game had always been Damon's strong suit, not mine. I should have suggested a different pastime.

We arranged the pieces, the familiar clinking of wood against wood filling the quiet room. Miss Lockwood went first, confidently advancing a pawn. I mirrored her move, though with far less conviction. With each turn, I felt more and more like a schoolboy fumbling through a lesson than a gentleman engaging in a friendly game. She captured my rook with ease, and my queen was left unprotected far too soon. My strategy, if it could even be called that, was quickly unraveling.

Miss Lockwood, ever gracious, did not comment on my missteps, but I noticed the way her gaze lingered on the board, her lips pursed in quiet observation. As she reached to move her next piece, she paused, her fingers hovering above a pawn. "Do you enjoy playing chess, Mr. Jennings?" she asked, her tone gentle but inquisitive.

"I . . . don't," I said, feeling a tinge of embarrassment.

"So you suggested it because . . . ?"

"I thought you might enjoy it," I said sheepishly.

Miss Lockwood's lips curled into a mischievous smile. "May I tell you a secret?" She leaned forward, motioning for me to do the same. "I don't care to play chess either."

Her candidness made me chuckle. "Then why did you agree?"

"Because I thought *you* enjoyed the game."

Relief washed over me, and I relaxed into my chair. "What a pair we are, Miss Lockwood. What games do you enjoy? Cards?"

"Yes," she nodded. "Very much."

"Shall we switch games, then?" I suggested.

She bit her lip.

"Unless you are tired," I said.

"I'm not tired. Well, I am. But that's not it. It's just . . ." She sighed and stood. "It will be easier if I show you." She retrieved the playing cards from the cupboard and handed me the stack.

I glanced down at the cards. She'd painted them. Miniatures. "Who are they?" I asked.

"People I used to know. Their faces were starting to slip from my mind, and I didn't want to lose them completely, so I used the last of my paint to create their images. I made sure the numbers and suits are still visible," she said. "But I am sor—"

"Don't apologize," I stopped her. "I'm not upset. I'm impressed, by your talent and your ability to survive so long in isolation."

Even in the flickering candlelight, I could see her cheeks flush. I indicated her vacant seat, and to my relief, she resumed it.

I spread the cards out on the table to look at her paintings. I recognized a few faces: the vicar and the baker, but most were unfamiliar. They were lovely. "How long did these take you to make?"

"About a month. I painted one or two a day. Once they were completed, it made playing patience much more fun. I imagined whichever person was on the card as though they were sitting across from me, and I felt less lonely."

I could hardly bear to think of her sitting alone, painting the faces of the people in her town whom she planned never to see again. I stared down at the cards so Miss Lockwood could not see the emotions I was sure were written on my face.

"Do you have a favorite game?" she asked.

"Several," I said, "but perhaps we shouldn't play with these." They were too precious. I gently stacked the cards and set them aside.

"Nonsense," she reached for the deck. "They are just a few silly pictures. If you are worried about dirtying your hands, you needn't. I used watercolor, so the paint cannot rub off. The pigment has soaked into the paper fibers."

That wasn't why I was worried. I did not want to ruin them. But Miss Lockwood's eyes pleaded with me to agree to a game. To tell her through my actions that I wasn't vexed. So I said, "I'm not particular. Do you have a favorite game?"

Her shoulders relaxed. "What about whist? Papa and I used to play it after meals."

"I enjoy playing whist." I carefully shuffled the cards. "My brother, best friend, and I used to play all the time before—"

"Before . . . ?" Miss Lockwood prompted.

"Nothing. Just *before*." The memory of playing cards with Damon and Hannah had slipped so suddenly into my mind and then out my mouth that I hadn't had time to censor it.

"Are you and your brother close?" she asked.

I dealt the cards. "We used to be when we were young."

"Not now?"

"No."

"Why not? What happened?"

"That is a very long and uninteresting story," I said.

"I doubt that. Will you tell me about him?"

Uncomfortable, I rearranged my cards. I had no desire to talk about him, but maybe my vulnerability would inspire hers, and I relented. "What would you like to know?"

"To start, his name."

"Lord Winfield. However, he refuses to use his proper title and insists everyone continue to call him by his courtesy title Lord Jennings." It was so like him to think himself above Society's customs.

"Those are his *titles*," Miss Lockwood said. "But what is his name? What do *you* call him?"

"Nothing, if I can help it." I'd meant my words to sound teasing, but even to my ears, they sounded petulant.

Miss Lockwood's lips scrunched to one side in confusion, or perhaps reproof.

"His name is Damon, but I have not spoken to him in over two years."

"You have a living, breathing brother, and you have not spoken to him in *two years*?" She blew out a breath. "I don't understand."

"Perhaps I will explain it to you one day." I offered her a smile, hoping to end the conversation.

"Not now?"

"No reason to ruin a perfectly good game. It is your turn, by the way."

"Hmm." She set down a pair of cards. "Well, if you won't tell me about your brother, at least tell me about your best friend you mentioned."

"I should be happy to. Hannah is—"

"Hannah?" Miss Lockwood looked up from studying her cards. "Your best friend is a *woman*?"

"Well, she wasn't a woman back then; she was a girl. But yes, growing up, my best friend was female."

"Oh." Miss Lockwood trained her gaze on her cards. "How nice."

"It was nice. But now she's married to my elder brother, so I suppose they are best friends now." I pressed on before she could ask questions. "Hannah visited Summerhaven, my childhood home, every summer. Our mothers were best friends, you see."

Miss Lockwood nodded, listening. "Are you close in age?"

"Hannah's mother and me? Not particularly."

Miss Lockwood looked to the heavens. "You know what I meant."

I smiled at her. "Yes. Hannah and I are close in age. Only a year separates us."

"You two must have been very close."

"Indeed."

"So . . . how was it that Hannah came to marry your brother, then?"

"Well, I suppose because he is better at chess than I am."

Her brow furrowed, and then a thoughtful expression took over her face. "Is that why you aren't close with your brother? Because of Hannah?"

"No," I said too quickly, then added, "Well, she is part of the reason, but not in the way you are probably thinking." I hesitated but said, "My brother and I were not on good terms long before they fell in love, but the way in which he courted her did nothing to aid my affection for him."

"Do you approve of their union?" she asked.

"I do." Sometimes, I still couldn't believe they were married. They'd hated each other as children—or so I'd thought—and I disapproved of how their relationship started, but I did not begrudge their union. How could I? They were a perfect pair. My feelings for Damon were complicated, but I honestly only wanted for their happiness.

"But . . . ?" Miss Lockwood squinted as if doing so would help her see my past more clearly.

"But nothing," I said, having no intention of sharing any more details with her. It was far too humiliating. "You are working too hard to puzzle this out, Miss Lockwood. We should turn the topic of our conversation to you now."

"I'd rather we keep talking about you."

"You are quite persistent, aren't you?"

"To the point of impertinence." She shrugged one shoulder. "Forgive me if I am overeager for something new to discuss. I have not spoken to another soul besides Bexley and Mrs. Owensby in two years."

"I daresay you are using your circumstance to your advantage, Miss Lockwood."

"One must play the cards one has been dealt, sir." She smiled coyly.

"*Sir?*" I protested. "Come now, Miss Lockwood, we have been living together for weeks now. Please, call me Oliver."

She scoffed. "I will do no such thing."

"What will you call me, then?" I asked, amused. "I am growing so tired of *sir*."

"I should think *Mr. Jennings* would be quite acceptable," she said, smoothing her plait playfully over her shoulder.

I tilted my head side to side, pretending to weigh the merit. "Under normal circumstances, I would agree with you. But our situation is not normal now, is it? Therefore, you shall call me Oliver, and I shall call you Kate." I reached across the table and teasingly tugged the end of her plait.

She stiffened, then shot to her feet.

Surprised by her swift response, I stood too. I searched our surroundings, glancing over my shoulder out the window, worried that someone might have ventured past the window and seen her. But I saw nothing.

"I am going to go to bed now." Her voice was thin and distant.

"Are you unwell?"

"No, yes." She shook her head. "I just have to go. Excuse me." She sidestepped out from behind the table and pushed in her chair.

I immediately offered her my arm to assist her.

She looked at my arm like I was offering her a snake, her eyes wide with fear.

Because of me? Because I'd suggested we use our Christian names? Because I'd tugged her hair?

"I will take my breakfast in my bedchamber tomorrow," she said.

"Of course, if that is your wish. But what has happened? Have I done something wrong?"

"Nothing." She raised her chin and blinked rapidly as if to hold tears at bay.

Not knowing what else to do, I took a backward step to allow her space and bumped into my chair. It clattered to the floor. I stooped to pick it up, and when I rose, she was gone.

CHAPTER TWENTY-SIX

Kate

Two years.

Two *years* and one teasing tug had sent me right back into the nightmare.

I pressed my back against my bedchamber door and slid to the floor, the cold seeping through my gown as if trying to anchor me to the present. But the past had its grip on me, tightening with every thought.

I hated Mr. Cavendish. With every breath and bone in my body, I hated him.

If only I had seen who Mr. Cavendish truly was, if only I had bothered to ask more questions and demand answers, Papa might still be alive today.

Footsteps sounded in the corridor, and seconds later, someone knocked on my door.

"Kate?" Mrs. Owensby's voice filtered through the door. "May I come in?"

I let her into my bedchamber.

Her eyes roamed over me, checking for injury. "Are you all right, dear? Mr. Jennings said you might need me."

"I'm fine. It's only . . ." I sat on the edge of my bed and released a long breath. "Mr. Jennings touched my hair."

"My dear girl." Mrs. Owensby sat beside me and wrapped me in her arms.

"He probably thinks me mad." I rested my head on her shoulder. "I probably am. No sane person would fake their death. Nor hide in a house that does not belong to them for two years."

"Mr. Jennings doesn't think you are mad, but he is worried about you. Have you told him what happened to you?"

I shook my head.

"Why not?"

"Well, when he first asked me the day I revealed myself to him in his study, I was only concerned about protecting you and Bexley. It seemed irrelevant."

"And after?"

"I don't know. I want him to know why I'm hiding here, but I don't know how to say the words. How am I supposed to slip the most shameful moment of my life into conversation? Things with Mr. Jennings have been going so well. When I am with him, I feel almost happy. I don't want to lose the ease between us. If I tell him, I worry he'll look at me differently. That he'll treat me differently."

"I cannot tell you how he will react, but you needn't be afraid. He is a kind man with a good heart and will do all he can to help you and keep you safe."

I felt the truth of her words. Mr. Jennings had been nothing but kind to me since the day he'd stepped into this house. He'd shown me respect and put my needs and comfort above his own. Over the past few weeks, I'd come to trust him.

It would be difficult to tell him what had happened to me, but I wanted him to know my story. And it could not wait another moment, lest I lost my resolve. I abruptly stood. "Thank you, Mrs. Owensby. I don't know what I would do without you." I kissed the top of her head and hurried out the door.

I crept into the corridor to the grand staircase. Candlelight flickered from the study door into the entrance hall.

Mr. Jennings sat at his desk with his head in his hands. His hair was disheveled, an unruly mess of curls poking through his fingers. His waistcoat was unbuttoned, and he'd removed his cravat and discarded it on the floor. The sight of him so undone made my heart ache.

I stepped out of the shadows and into his study.

Mr. Jennings's gaze snapped to me. He stood quickly but didn't approach, watching me with a mixture of concern and restraint.

"Might I have a word?" I asked.

He nodded, gesturing to the pair of armchairs on either side of the fireplace, and we sat.

I took a deep breath, and without preamble, I said, "I met my former intended, Mr. Cavendish, when I was only seventeen."

Mr. Jennings's eyes widened in surprise. Whatever he'd thought I was about to say, I was sure it wasn't this.

"We were introduced at a dinner party. I thought him dashing in his formal attire. He liked my eyes." I laughed bitterly. "Probably because I was blind to his true nature."

Mr. Jennings remained silent, his attention fully on me.

"Over the next few weeks, he courted me, and we fell in love, or so I thought.

"Papa had reservations about our relationship: Mr. Cavendish was several years my senior and had acted inappropriately by dancing three sets with me at a ball. But Papa saw how besotted I was with the man, and after much discussion, he accepted our courtship."

Mr. Jennings's jaw clenched, but he said nothing.

"We became engaged and set our wedding date. It felt like a dream. But then, at our engagement ball, I found him kissing a maid in the garden. His betrayal devastated me, and I refused to marry him. I turned to walk away, but he—" I hesitated, the memory of that night hitting me with such force that I had to pause to steady my breath. "He dragged me back by my hair."

Mr. Jennings's eyes darkened, understanding dawning in them as he glanced at my hair.

"He was furious that I dared deny him and demanded that I marry him," I continued. "He said that I belonged to him, that I must marry him whether I wanted to or not, and that I would not play him for a fool. Looking back, I see now that he did not love me but rather my dowry.

"I screamed for help, and Papa came, along with others who had already been looking for me. But before they reached us, Mr. Cavendish tore my dress, disheveled my hair, and kissed me forcefully to make everything appear as though *we* had been taking the moonlight together. He even loosened his cravat to make it look more convincing."

Mr. Jennings pressed his eyes shut. He worked his jaw but said nothing. He seemed to know that if he interrupted me, I might not have the courage to finish my story.

"When Papa and the others finally reached us, Mr. Cavendish told everyone *we* had succumbed to our passion. I tried to tell the truth, but he silenced me with whispered threats and stepped in front of me as though he were protecting my virtue. I felt utterly powerless in that moment, but Papa believed me and challenged Mr. Cavendish to a duel to defend my honor." My voice trembled when I added, "Papa died defending me."

A tear slipped down my cheeks, and Mr. Jennings silently handed me his handkerchief.

"Papa's last words to me were a promise: that if I stayed within these walls, I would be safe. But not an hour after he passed, Mr. Cavendish came to Winterset and demanded that I fulfill our marriage contract. He told me he would not allow me to tarnish his family's name and threatened that if I refused him, I would meet the same fate as my father."

Mr. Jennings's hands tightened into fists in his lap.

"I don't know how Mr. Cavendish deluded himself into believing I could marry him after all he had done. Perhaps he thought that in ruining my reputation and killing my father, I would have no choice *but* to marry him. I don't know. But I could not marry that man, so I staged my death and disappeared. The villagers found my pelisse—stained with Papa's blood—at the bottom of the cliffs on the seashore and assumed I was dead.

"I'm told that Mr. Cavendish played the part of distraught bridegroom, spinning a spectacular story to make it sound like it was my father who had become unhinged after finding me kissing Mr. Cavendish in the garden. He made everyone believe my father was mad, not himself. He convinced people that he was passionately in love with me and had been trying to *save* me from my father. Like he was some sort of knight come to rescue me from a monster. But nothing could have been further from the truth; *he* is the monster. Sometimes, when I close my eyes, I still see Mr. Cavendish's cold eyes and the malicious curl of his lips."

Mr. Jennings swore beneath his breath, his expression pained. "Miss Lockwood—"

"Kate," I said.

"Kate," he repeated, his voice soft and sincere. "I am so sorry for what you've endured. But I swear to you, you have nothing to fear from me. I will never let any harm come to you. No one should bear such a burden alone."

He stood and moved closer, pausing a step away from me. The hesitation in his eyes spoke volumes. He was giving me the space to trust him. When I didn't recoil, he slowly knelt before me. "I cannot imagine the strength it took for you to survive this, to carry on when your world was crumbling. But you are not alone anymore. I will protect you."

His words washed over me, a balm to the wounds I'd kept hidden for so long. There was no pity in his eyes, only compassion and kindness.

Tears welled in my eyes again, but this time, they weren't born of pain or fear; they were the tears of a woman who had finally found a safe harbor after years adrift.

"Thank you," I whispered and reached for his hands, needing the reassurance of human touch.

Oliver's hands were warm, his grip secure. "We'll face this together," he promised. "You have my word."

"Why are you being so kind to me?" I asked. We'd only known one another a short time, and for half of it, I had made his life miserable.

"Because I know what it is to feel alone. To feel unseen," Oliver said quietly.

And for the first time since Papa died, I felt something other than guilt or fear.

A fragile hope.

Oliver knew everything now, and yet he didn't turn away. Instead, he drew closer, offering protection, understanding, and empathy. As he held my hands, I allowed myself to believe that a future beyond the nightmare I had been living might be possible.

CHAPTER TWENTY-SEVEN

Oliver

After Miss Lockwood—Kate—retired to her bedchamber, I sat in my study. The only thought on my mind was how I might protect her from this monster Mr. Cavendish. I'd known men like him before. Men who charmed and took and ruined. They were as cunning as they were cruel.

I had once been cruel, courting women only for what they could bring to the marriage. I'd never ruined reputations, but I'd likely broken hearts. First, Hannah's, and then Miss Digby's, perhaps even Amelia's. My past actions filled me with shame. I wished I could go back in time and do things differently. I wished I would have behaved as a gentleman and been a better man. While I could do nothing to change my past, I hoped that in helping Kate, I might find a measure of redemption and begin to shape a future filled with purpose and integrity.

When Mrs. Owensby told me that Kate's life was in danger if she left these walls, I'd believed she *thought* Kate was in danger, but I saw no real threat.

I saw it now.

While no immediate danger existed, if ever Mr. Cavendish were to discover Kate's survival, I did not doubt he would make good on his threat. A man who'd gotten away with murder once would assume he could get away with it again. And seeing as no one outside this house knew Kate was alive, it would be all too easy.

The longer I sat in my study, the more my thoughts festered.

Was Mr. Cavendish still living close by? Did he suspect that Kate might have survived? Her body had never been found, so he might. All night long, thoughts plagued me. And when morning dawned, I had the beginnings of a plan to protect her: I would go to town today under the guise of borrowing a book for my ghost-story reading, and while there, I would learn everything I could about this Mr. Cavendish. I would be cautious and keep my questions subtle, so I would not raise suspicions.

I tugged the bellpull to call Charlie. Not long after, he appeared at my study.

"Granger?"

"Good morning, Charlie." I motioned him inside. "Come in and close the door."

He entered and sat. "Did you sleep?" he asked.

I rubbed my forehead, heavy with fatigue. "I couldn't after my discussion with Miss Lockwood last night. Which is why I've called you here. I need your help." I quickly relayed the pertinent facts about the danger Mr. Cavendish posed to Kate and my desire to learn everything I could about him so that I could protect her. "While I'm out of residence, would you look after her? I'd rather she were not alone today."

"Certainly," Charlie said.

After our conversation, Charlie saddled my horse, and I quickly readied myself and hurried out the door.

The sky was gray and ominous as I rode into town.

A premonition? A warning?

The wind was fierce, the weather unforgiving. I tugged up the collar of my greatcoat to guard against the cold, but it did little good.

Outside the lending library, I tied my horse to a post. A bell rang overhead as I entered, and the bookkeeper, a gray-haired gentleman with small, round spectacles looked up from his book.

"Ah, Mr. Jennings." He stood to greet me. "Welcome."

"I see my reputation precedes me," I said.

"No, sir, only your good name. How can I help you?"

"I need a book for a reading I am hosting. A ghost story."

"We have plenty. They are quite popular these days. Follow me." He led me to a bookcase and showed me which shelf to search.

As I glanced over the titles, I feigned interest in ghost stories, asking if he knew about any local ones to cover my true intentions. But my inquiries led nowhere, and I left the shop with nothing but a borrowed book.

As I exited, I heard a familiar voice say, "Mr. Jennings."

I turned and saw Lord Markham. "How do you do, Lord Markham?"

"Very well, thank you. Is that a book for our ghost-story reading?" He indicated the book tucked under my arm.

"It is," I said, brandishing the book.

"I'm looking forward to the reading. How are preparations coming along?"

"*I* am ready, but Winterset is not."

"Well, ready or not," Lord Markham chuckled, "this reading will happen. I promised to hold you to it, remember? And even if *I* did not, Miss Dalton and her mother would." He lowered his voice. "Word has it they are already assembling Miss Dalton's wedding trousseau."

Miss Dalton.

Gads!

I had not thought about the young lady since the day we'd been introduced at church.

Would that I could get out of this whole affair—both the reading and her interest in me—but if I canceled, she and her mother might call on me unannounced, and that would be much worse. Whether I liked it or not, I was stuck.

Bexley met me at the door and took my hat and coat. "Welcome home, sir. How was your visit to town?"

"Unproductive." I sighed, the weight of the morning's disappointment still heavy on my shoulders. "Where is she?"

"The drawing room, sir. With Charlie."

"Thank you." I walked in that direction.

As I approached, the sound of laughter—Kate's laughter—floated in the air, slowing my step. I paused at the threshold, the scene inside the drawing room catching me off guard. Kate sat comfortably on the settee, her face lit with amusement, and Charlie stood in front of her, reading a poem in an animated voice.

". . . And so the moon, with her silver spoon, stirred the stars into a fine, twinkling broth!"

Kate laughed, the sound bright and uninhibited. Her eyes sparkled with genuine delight, and her cheeks were rosy.

How had Charlie managed to make her laugh so freely?

A sharp pang of something unfamiliar twisted in my chest. Irritation, perhaps? But why? It would be irrational. *I'd* asked Charlie to look after Kate while I was out of residence, after all.

I was probably overtired.

"Ah, but beware the midnight spoon, for it stirs the heart as well as the stars!" Charlie concluded with a bow.

"Bravo!" Kate leaped to her feet, clapping as if she couldn't contain her joy. She seemed so much lighter today. It was as though Charlie had unlocked a sense of happiness in her that I had struggled to reach.

I cleared my throat, drawing their attention.

"Mr. Jennings!" Kate gasped softly in surprise and smiled up at me. "How long have you been standing there?"

"Only a moment." I pushed off from the doorframe and walked fully into the room. "Good poem?"

"It was a *terrible* poem." Kate looked at Charlie, and they shared a laugh. "But also amusing. Will you join us?"

"Perhaps a little later," I said to her, then to Charlie, "I need to speak with you in my study for a moment."

"Certainly," he said and closed his notebook. "Don't let the silver spoon stir up too much trouble while I'm gone," he said to Kate, then followed me out of the room.

She laughed.

My chest tightened. A casual familiarity had grown between them in my absence. It was as though they shared some private world where I did not belong.

This was more than irritation, I realized. This was something visceral, something that was twisting painfully inside me.

I glanced at Kate before leaving the drawing room.

She watched me, her expression unreadable, and I wondered if she sensed my turmoil.

I gave her a small smile, hoping to reassure her, then led Charlie to my study.

I closed the study door more abruptly than I'd intended.

Charlie raised his eyebrows. "You all right, Granger?"

"What did you mean by your last remark to Miss Lockwood?" I asked. "About the silver spoon?"

"Nothing." Charlie laughed. "Just a line from one of my ridiculous poems that she found funny."

"I see." It would be problematic if they weren't getting along, so part of me was glad they were, but another part of me disliked how Charlie already seemed to know Kate in a way I didn't.

"What was it you needed to talk to me about?" Charlie asked.

"I wanted to tell you that I didn't learn anything more about Mr. Cavendish in town today."

"That's all?" Charlie asked.

"I thought you would want to know, seeing as I enlisted your help in *protecting* Kate."

He studied me intently but said nothing.

"You may go now, Charlie. I'm sure we both have plenty to do before dinner."

I lingered in the study after Charlie left, staring at the closed door. Our conversation had done nothing to soothe my agitation; it had only inflamed it.

Hoping to clear my head, I returned to the drawing room, intending to find Kate and suggest a walk. But she wasn't there. I quickly searched the common areas in the house, but I couldn't find her.

I returned to my study and forced myself to focus on work, drowning out my unsettled emotions with calculations and correspondence. The hours slipped by, and finally, evening shadows signaled it was time to dress for dinner.

When I entered my bedchamber, Charlie looked up from brushing my dinner coat.

I shrugged off the coat I had on, but it stuck on my arm. I struggled for a moment, but my shoulders were too tense to make much progress.

Charlie moved to help me, but I held up a hand, stopping him. I finally slipped my arms from the sleeves, then balled up the blasted garment and threw it on the bed.

Charlie glanced at the coat and then at me.

"You look like you want to say something," I said.

"You would not like what I have to say."

Because he had feelings for Kate?

"Do *you* want to say something?" he asked.

To him? "No." I moved to the mirror.

Charlie sighed. "We were reading poetry to pass the time, Granger. And only because you asked me to watch after her while you were gone."

"If you're insinuating that I'm jealous, I'm not."

"Aren't you?" Charlie challenged.

"No," I said with all the energy of a sulking schoolboy. "But you're right. I don't want you to court her."

"That much is obvious. Your reasoning, however, is not."

"She's been through a lot," I explained. "If you pursue her and it ends badly, she has nowhere else to go."

"That isn't why," Charlie said. "And just so we are clear, I would never do that to you."

"That's not what I'm saying."

"What *are* you saying?" Charlie asked.

I couldn't answer that. Not because I didn't want to but because I had no idea what I was saying. My mind was a mess.

"Do you want to know what I think?" he asked.

"Not particularly."

"I think you *are* jealous," Charlie said anyway. "You like Miss Lockwood more than you're willing to admit; you enjoy feeling needed by her, and I think you like how it feels to belong here with her. And that scares you because you know this situation can't last. *That's* what I think."

"Well, you're wrong, *Your Grace*," I ground out.

"Am I?"

"Yes. No." Deuces! I didn't know anymore. "I'm not going to throw her out, Charlie. She doesn't want to leave."

"*She* doesn't want to leave, or *you* don't want her to leave?"

I said nothing.

"Have you asked Miss Lockwood what she wants?" he pressed.

"I don't need to. I know how she feels about Winterset. It's her home. She has no one she can turn to for help."

He gave me a disapproving look. "This is *your* home. *You* can help her."

I held his stare as his words sank in. Blast! He was right. About all of it. I *didn't* want Kate to leave. I'd told myself I was helping her hide here because that was what she wanted. But was it? She could likely live a safer and more fulfilled life elsewhere. And I could have—no, I *should* have—offered to help her leave.

But I hadn't.

Because the thought of Kate leaving bothered me more than her staying.

Charlie was right, I *did* like Kate. More than I should, probably. She was living under my protection, for heaven's sake.

I clawed at my cravat, which was suddenly too constricting, and ripped it from my neck.

Charlie scowled at the crumpled cloth. "Do you know how long it took me to starch and iron that?"

I slumped onto the edge of my bed, resting my elbows on my knees and my head in my hands.

When had this happened? And more importantly, what was I to do about it?

CHAPTER TWENTY-EIGHT

Kate

My pulse pounded.

    I'd overheard every word of Oliver and Charlie's conversation. I hadn't meant to, but I was drawing in the antechamber that connected the master's and mistress's bedchambers when they had entered to dress for dinner.

    Earlier, when I'd seen Oliver leaning against the drawing room doorframe, I'd had a sudden desire to draw his portrait. He'd looked so handsome with his hair all windswept and cheeks ruddy from his ride. So when he and Charlie had gone to the study to talk, I had sneaked upstairs to the antechamber, where no one would see me draw Oliver's likeness. When I'd heard their voices, I'd stood to leave, but then they'd said my name, and I'd stayed.

    Oliver cared for me, that much was clear, but he was also conflicted, torn between what he wanted and what he thought was right. I'd known since the day I'd found out he was coming to Winterset that I could not continue living here with him forever in his company and care, but more and more every day, I wanted to.

    A knock came at my bedchamber door, cutting off my thoughts, and my heart leaped.

    I hurried to my feet, quietly closing the antechamber door behind me, and then hid my notebook under the edge of my mattress.

    "Kate?" Mrs. Owensby said, knocking again.

    I opened the door.

    "You're not ready for dinner." She eyed me, her gaze sharpening when she saw my hands.

My *charcoal*-covered hands, I realized too late. "I *may* have gotten distracted drawing and lost track of time," I confessed.

She shook her head in disapproval. "Now, Kate—"

"I didn't *mean* to," I said, and it was true. We'd been apart all day, and I'd looked forward to dining with Oliver tonight. But I was also relieved that I would not have to face him. How could I sit so near him knowing what I did and not turn a deep shade of vermilion?

"What shall I tell Mr. Jennings?" Mrs. Owensby asked.

"Tell him . . . that I . . ." I bit my lip and shrugged.

She sighed. "I'll tell him you are tired tonight and are taking a tray in your room. But he will expect you to come down for breakfast tomorrow, so don't stay up too late drawing."

Unfortunately, I did stay up too late drawing, but I wanted to see Oliver badly enough that I had no trouble getting out of bed and being on time for breakfast. Still, he was already waiting for me in the dining hall.

We said good morning, and he helped me with my chair and served me food. Then he sat and opened his newspaper. There was a tightness in him that hadn't been there before yesterday. His shoulders were stiff and his jaw set, and he was concentrating far harder than normal on his newspaper.

What was he thinking about? What Charlie had said, no doubt.

Should I tell him I'd overheard their conversation so that we could discuss our options? It was obvious my presence was making him uncomfortable, but I worried that he was strategizing how to change our situation. I also worried that he wasn't. I didn't know what I wanted: to stay or to go, and that worried me too.

"What are you reading?" I asked, trying to make conversation.

"Forgive me for being rude." He lowered the paper and moved to set it aside.

"Don't stop reading on my account. I know you enjoy reading the newspaper over breakfast."

"I must confess, it is a little disconcerting that you know that fact about me. I wonder . . ." Oliver glanced at me sideways, as if looking at me fully would be too difficult. "What else do you know about me?"

My face warmed. There was no way he could know I'd overheard his conversation, could he?

He raised a brow at me. "I can see from your reaction that I have much to be embarrassed of."

"No," I said too quickly. "You have always behaved like a perfect gentleman."

"Now I *know* you are lying." He chuckled.

"Well, save the time you were clearing the drive and you cursed heaven for the rain."

"You were watching me work that day?" he said, looking at his plate.

"There was little else to do in the attic." I shrugged.

"Interesting." He finally met my gaze fully. "I worked shirtless that day."

"I looked away before you took it off," I lied, and I was sure he knew it because my face felt like it was on fire.

"I'm sure you did." He gave me a wicked grin, then picked up his newspaper again. "What section would you prefer to read?" He thumbed through the pages. "The political column? Current events?"

Was he teasing me?

When I didn't answer, he looked at me in question, and I was surprised to see that he seemed in earnest, if not nervous. Maybe he didn't know what columns interested young ladies. "The fashion or Society column would be preferable."

He sucked in a breath through his teeth. "I'm afraid you can't have either of *those* columns. Clearly, they are *my* favorites." He made a show of straightening his already straight cravat.

I couldn't help but laugh. "Ah, yes. Perhaps you could pick out a few new toppers. I'm sure you don't have enough already."

"It's true," he agreed. "Someone confused them with flowerpots, if you can believe it." He grinned and handed me my preferred columns.

We passed the rest of breakfast reading in companionable silence. I'd grown fond of Oliver's teasing manner and the relaxed banter we shared, but I liked the easy silence we shared just as much.

When he decided it was time for me to leave, I would miss mornings like this. I would miss *him*.

After we finished our food, I hoped he would ask me to walk in the garden again, but he excused himself and went upstairs to work on the repairs in one of the eastern bedchambers. I would have asked if he wanted my help, but I got the impression that he was avoiding me.

So I passed the morning hours by myself in the drawing room, sketching with the supplies and paper Oliver had gifted me. As much as I loved creating, I would have rather worked with Oliver on the repairs. It had been so enjoyable to work with him on the drawing room. Which made me wonder, Were the wall papers dry enough to paint?

To my delight, they were!

Eager, I spread out all the supplies Oliver had purchased for the project and covered the floor with a Holland cover. It had taken me months to paint this room the last time, but I did not have months, so I had to be smart about where I started in case I could not finish in time for his party.

I decided to start with the swath of wall right under the newly repaired window.

It felt heavenly to hold a paintbrush in my hand.

I dabbed some paint onto a tray and mixed the colors to create the correct shade, then started painting the pattern.

Later that afternoon, when Oliver finally came downstairs, I was still sitting on the floor. I pretended not to hear him. It was childish, but I felt confused by both my feelings and his, and I disliked how he'd avoided me all day.

"You've made good progress," he said.

I took a moment to finish the pattern I was working on, then turned to look at him.

He stood in the doorway, leaning against the frame again. He wasn't wearing his greatcoat today, but he looked just as handsome in his waistcoat and rolled shirt sleeves. And the book tucked under his arm only added to my attraction.

He grinned.

Oh dear, I was staring at him.

I turned back to my task. What had he said? "Not as much progress as I'd like. But I'm working on the parts your guests will see first, so you don't need to worry."

He walked closer and crouched next to me, observing the pattern. "It looks wonderful, Kate. I am impressed."

"Thank you."

Oliver stood and held out his hands to help me stand too.

"How are the repairs on the bedchambers coming along?" I asked as we walked to the settee.

"Good. It took all morning, but I rehung the peeling wall papers and fixed the curtain rods. I still need to level the uneven floorboards, but it's looking better."

"I'm glad."

We sat, and Oliver balanced the book on his knees.

"New book?" I asked.

"Oh, no. I borrowed it for the ghost-story reading. I was hoping you might help me select a passage."

Of course I knew about the reading; it was the reason I was painting the walls, but seeing the book that would be used that night somehow made it feel realer.

He sensed my unease and said, "You don't have to."

"I want to," I said.

"But . . . ?"

"But nothing. It's just been a long time since Winterset has had any visitors."

He nodded, sobering. "I made the invitation before I knew about you. I would cancel it if I could, but—"

"Don't be silly," I said, trying to sound nonchalant.

"I've only invited a few people. And I promise I won't let anyone come near wherever you will be hiding."

"I'm not worried," I said, although I was, but it was more than that. I wanted to attend his reading, not hide in the attic while he hosted it.

"This dinner party . . ." I began.

"Ghost-story reading," he corrected with a wink, and then he winced like he wished he could take back the gesture. I didn't know why. I loved it when he winked at me. It made my stomach flutter.

"Did *I* inspire the event?" I batted my lashes.

"You know you did."

I tried not to notice the sober way he said it or the tender look in his eyes.

But I did.

The flutter in my stomach became a flurry.

Whatever this was that we were teetering on was getting harder to balance.

"Well then, I suppose I must help you select a passage."

Oliver opened the book, his fingers brushing gently over the pages as he thumbed through them.

We took turns selecting and reading aloud passages ranging from eerie to absurd. Laughter came easily between us, and for a while, I forgot about our complicated emotions.

And then we came upon one particular passage, and my laughter faded. The description of a hidden treasure, lost for centuries and guarded by the spirits of those who had sought to protect it, reminded me of something—something I hadn't seen or thought about in many years.

"This one," I said excitedly. "You have to use this one. It's perfect! I know how you should decorate the drawing room to set the right atmosphere."

"Tell me how, and I will," Oliver said, his playful expression softening.

"I'll show you," I said, pulling him up to stand. "Follow me to the attic."

CHAPTER TWENTY-NINE

OLIVER

THE STEEP SPIRAL STAIRS CREAKED beneath our feet as we ascended to the attic.

"So, what exactly is in the attic?" I asked.

"You mean, besides ghosts?" Kate smiled over her shoulder at me, and I felt it everywhere.

"Certainly not, seeing as I have vanquished all the ghosts from this house," I teased.

"My dear Oliver," she tsked. "It is precisely the ghosts I want to show you."

"Now I am intrigued."

When we reached the top of the stairs, it was cold, but with a few windows, it was somewhat light. Still, I could not imagine how Kate must have felt having to hide up here. I glanced at the hidden door that led to the tiny, dark priest hide she'd used for a bedchamber. It pained me to think of her sitting all alone in the dark, so I shifted my gaze and saw her traveling trunk—contents of her past life all packed away. Life had been so unfair to her. Cruel.

"This way." Kate looked over her shoulder at me, smiling as she moved toward the northwest corner of the attic.

I attempted a smile in return, but seeing this attic now made me feel so sad. She deserved so much more.

We passed the portraits tilted against the wall, then ducked under a low beam. She slowed when we reached the attic corner. The *barren* corner.

I glanced around the space skeptically.

"Look closely," she said and pointed at the wall.

Squinting, I could see the faintest outline of a piece of furniture and a smoke stain on the wall above it. But I couldn't guess what might be remarkable about this corner. I looked at her in question.

"I believe Mrs. Owensby told you about Winterset's tragic history?" she said.

"She did . . . Am I about to *become* part of this tragic history?" I eyed her teasingly.

"What?" Kate laughed. "Of course not!"

I glanced at the wall again, thinking I might find evidence of another priest hide, but saw nothing. "So, you brought me up to this hidden part of the attic to . . . ?"

"Show you some of the things the priests left behind."

That got my attention. "They left things behind?"

"They did." She took a tentative step forward, tapping the floor with her toe. She did so a few times until she heard a hollow sound. She knelt and lifted the floorboard to reveal a small space. There was something inside, but it was covered with cloth.

Kate carefully peeled back the cloth, then looked at me as if to gauge my reaction.

It took me a moment to understand what I was seeing. Candlesticks, a platter, a cross; the vessels once used for mass. "I can't believe it," I said, kneeling beside her. "How long have these relics been here?"

"Likely since the time of Queen Elizabeth." Kate grinned at me.

"Over three hundred years." I shook my head in disbelief. "Incredible. May I?" I looked at her in question.

"Of course. This house and everything inside it are yours."

Not everything.

When I made no move to retrieve the relics, Kate lifted one of the candlesticks toward me. I knelt beside her and took it. I turned the sacred item over in my hands. It was heavy. Silver. "There is a small fortune here," I said. "It is a wonder these items have not been sold."

"I believe they would have been had anyone before me discovered them."

"What did your father think of these?"

"He didn't know," I admitted.

"You never showed him?"

"He forbade me from coming up to the attic. With the exposed nails and uneven floorboards, he thought it was too dangerous. And if I'd told him about these, he would have known I'd been disobedient."

"You have *always* been sneaky?" I grinned at her.

"I have always been *curious*." She corrected.

"Curious Kate," I said, trying the moniker on for size. "I like it."

"I don't. I already feel bad about disobeying him. You have no need to tease me, *Odious Oliver*."

"*Now* who's teasing?" I bumped my shoulder lightly into hers.

Even in the dark, I saw how her cheeks pinked. I liked it. I liked that I'd been the one to put it there.

I turned back to the relics, put the candlestick back in its hiding place, then ran my hands reverently over the other items: the lavabo dish used for washing hands, a chalice that once held wine as well as the matching communion cups, and the patten that had held the bread.

"I truly cannot believe these are here," I said.

"There's more." Kate slid back and lifted another floorboard. "This is where the most precious items are hidden."

I sucked in a breath when my gaze landed on the monstrance. It had an ornately engraved base that rose like a candlestick to a sunburst top. In the center of the sun, there was a cylindrical eye where the lunette once held the consecrated bread. It was quite literally breathtaking.

I reached out to touch the relic at the same time Kate did, and our hands brushed. The unexpected touch sent a wave of warmth through me. But I stilled, remembering how she'd fled when I'd touched her hair in the drawing room after our card game. It was then I noticed how close we were sitting. So close our knees nearly touched. Did she notice? Did she mind?

She didn't shy away from me, and her eyes did not seem fearful, only searching, as her gaze rose to my forehead. To my scar. Did she find it repulsive?

I pushed my hair forward to hide the imperfection.

"Don't," she said, and her hand rose between us. "May I?"

I hesitated, not because I didn't want her to touch me but because I did. Charlie's words replayed in my mind. Kate was living under *my* protection. I should not be sitting here alone in an attic with her like this. And yet . . . I nodded.

She leaned forward and brushed back the curls from my forehead with one hand. I could smell rose water on her wrist. Soft and sweet. She brushed her thumb lightly over my scar, studying it.

My heart raced.

Charlie had removed the stitches, but in their place was a one-inch scar. A straight line of fresh, white skin.

"It's healing nicely," she said, sitting back and setting her hand in her lap.

"I believe I might have you to thank for that?"

"You don't remember?" Her beautiful brow furrowed.

"The details of that night are fuzzy." I'd tried to recall the events of that night many times but had not been able to. "Could you remind me?"

"I would be happy to," she said. "Tell me, have you any formal musical training? You have quite the vibrato."

"I *sang* that night?"

"You did." She grinned. "In both Italian *and* French, no less."

"You jest."

"I promise I do not." She laughed to herself.

Lud! What she must have thought of me, returning to Winterset in such a state. *Singing!* And with a head wound, which she'd had to stitch. "I only remember one thing about that night," I admitted. "Your eyes."

She looked away, feigning interest in the relics. "Yes, well, they have always been too big for my face."

Was she in earnest? "If you are fishing for a compliment, you needn't. Your eyes are beautiful, Kate. Truly, I thought of nothing else for days."

She met my gaze.

I'd said too much. I knew it, and so did she. "Forgive me. I should not have said that. I can only imagine what you thought of me that night."

"I thought that I had never wanted to paint a portrait more," she said.

"Because you wished to erase this unsightly scar?"

She shook her head. "*Because* of it."

Was she lying? Trying to make me feel better about the imperfection? I'd applied salve to it every day since my accident to help minimize the scarring, but I suspected it was here to stay.

"It tells a story, Oliver. One *you* may not wish to remember but one *I* will never forget." And there was something about the way she said that, about the way she searched my face that undid me.

"I overheard what you said to Charlie last night," she said. "While you were dressing for dinner," she clarified as if it were not already painfully clear what conversation she was referring to. I tried to recall exactly what was said and then, remembering, decided I'd rather *not* remember. I trained my gaze on the priest treasure.

"Why did you tell Charlie not to pursue me?" she asked softly.

Was she asking because she wanted him to pursue her? Or was she asking because she wanted to know my motive for asking him not to? *I* was confused about my motive for doing so, so it stood to reason that she would be too. But I had a history of not reading women well. I tried to gauge her thoughts, but her expression was inscrutable. "Does it bother you that I asked him not to?"

As soon as I'd asked the question, I wanted to snatch it back because I was not sure I would like her answer.

But then, ever so slowly, she shook her head. "No," she said finally, and I felt like I could breathe again. "But I would like to know why."

"You *know* why." My gaze sank to her lips.

We sat only a breath away from each other; it would be so easy to kiss her. I wanted to—the devil, I wanted to—but what did *she* want?

I didn't know for certain.

And until I did, I had no right kissing her. There was too much unsaid between us. She'd heard our conversation so she must know something about how I felt for her. But I didn't know what was in her heart. I didn't want to do the wrong thing again and scare her away. Worse, what if she felt she *had* to kiss me in order to stay here? The thought made me feel sick.

I sat back at the same time she closed her eyes and leaned toward me.

I wanted to lean in too. I wanted to kiss her. But it wasn't right yet. It took every ounce of my resolve, but I managed to say, "We should return downstairs."

"Oh." Kate's breath caught, and her eyes snapped open. She promptly sat back, her cheeks bright red. "Forgive me, Mr. Jennings," she said, looking at the ground.

"There is no need. Kate, I—"

"I forgot myself for a moment," she pressed on. "I promise it won't happen again."

Oh, how I hoped that were not the case.

She stood and retreated toward the door.

"Please, wait a moment," I said softly, but she sharply shook her head and continued toward the door.

"Kate," I called after her, but she did not stop.

I wanted to run after her, to pull her into my arms and kiss her so soundly that we both forgot these past few moments.

But I couldn't.

Well, I could, but I wouldn't. I cared for her too much to treat her so selfishly. So I stood there and watched her go.

CHAPTER THIRTY

Kate

Sitting on the window seat in my bedchamber, I glanced out the window. The sun had set, and soon Oliver's guests would arrive. I'd avoided Oliver for several days. It wasn't hard to do, seeing as how busy he was working on Winterset, and tonight, I would be hiding in the attic, so I would not see him.

I didn't regret admitting that I'd overheard his conversation, but I did feel foolish for leaning in to kiss him. For wanting the very same thing he'd warned Charlie not to want with me: a relationship.

How could I not? He was kind and charming and handsome. He was honorable and hardworking. He was everything a man should be. Everything I wanted.

When we had sat in the attic together, I'd thought he wanted me too. He'd knelt so near me that our arms had been touching. He'd gazed so deeply into my eyes and at my lips. Perhaps he did want me but had more sense to stop himself than I. How could we be together when I could not even show my face in Society? I had not been thinking about that when I'd leaned in to kiss him.

Logically, I knew nothing could happen between us. Oliver was my host and my protector. And I was what? His guest? His ghost? How had I forgotten our situation so completely? How humiliating! How could I ever hope to look at his handsome face again?

I didn't know then, and two days of rumination had only made my mind more tangled.

With a sigh, I stood and started gathering the things I needed for the attic: my warmest shawl, my candlestick, and a book. I was halfway to the door when I heard footfalls coming down the corridor. Strong, sturdy footfalls that stopped right in front of my door.

Oliver?

I waited a moment for someone to knock, but nothing came. Another moment passed and then a soft swish as paper slipped beneath my bedchamber door.

A note.

I rushed to retrieve it, and when I saw my name written in Oliver's handwriting, I could not open it fast enough.

> *Dearest Kate,*
>
> *I write you this letter with trepidation. For I know once these words are said, they cannot be unsaid. But I fear you believe something that is untrue, and I cannot bear it. You asked why I told Charlie not to pursue you. The answer is quite simple: I could not endure watching another man court you. I care for you, Kate, more than I should as your protector.*
>
> *There it is. The truth.*
>
> *Since the first day I stepped foot in Winterset, you have haunted me. Day and night, my thoughts turn to you unceasingly—your strength of character, your courage, your ability to see beauty in a world that has shown you so much ugliness—and I am utterly enamored.*
>
> *And it is because I care for you that I could not kiss you. I wanted to. Oh, how I wanted to. But when you looked up at me, so trusting, and leaned toward me, so willing, Charlie's words rang in my ears: that you might only be here because I want you here. And I could not be so selfish. When we finally met face-to-face in my study, I should have offered to help you find a safer situation. At the time, I thought I was helping you by allowing you to stay at Winterset. I told myself that you wanted to stay here, but I didn't know—I don't know—because I did not ask you. I should have. I am sorry.*
>
> *So I will ask you now: What do you want, Kate?*
>
> *Whatever you wish—to stay, to go, to stay and have me go—I will give it to you, asking nothing in return.*

I have attempted to write this letter no less than a dozen times, and still, I am unsatisfied. I do not know your reasons for what almost took place in the attic, but I do hope. Forgive me for being so bold.

Yours, however unworthy,

xOliver Jennings

As soon as I finished reading his beautiful letter, I started reading it again, from the beginning to take it all in. Then I pressed the letter to my chest. He cared for me. He *hoped* for me. My heart felt like it might burst with joy.

I all but ran down the stairs, wanting to talk to him before his guests arrived, and I found him in the library.

When I entered, he looked up, and realizing it was me, he stood swiftly, clearly surprised to see me so soon.

Dressed in his finery and hair perfectly styled, he was dashing. No, that was doing it too lightly. He was devastating.

"I read your letter," I said, pulling the door *almost* closed behind me.

He nodded slowly, looking more nervous than I had ever seen him.

"Did you mean what you said?" I asked.

"Every word," he said in a low voice. "If you want to leave Winterset, I will help you."

How could he still not understand my meaning? Nevertheless, I needed to hear him say the words. "Do you *want* me to go?"

He looked surprised by my question. "No. I only want you to know that you have options, Kate. Whatever you want, you need only ask me."

My heart raced so swiftly that it felt like it might beat right out of my chest. "Did you mean what you said about your feelings for me?" I asked.

"I did," he said, swallowing hard. "I *do*."

"I care for you too."

He searched my eyes for meaning. "Tell me what you want, Kate."

"I want to stay here, Oliver. With *you*."

Oliver's eyes flickered with emotion. A mixture of hope and hesitation. "Are you certain?" he asked.

"I am."

He took a slow step forward. "Under normal circumstances, I would court you. But given our situation, I don't know how to go about this."

"Nor I. But together we will figure it out."

"Perhaps we can meet in the dining hall for breakfast," he suggested.

"And in the drawing room before dinner," I said.

He nodded. "We can walk in the garden every afternoon."

"And play cards by candlelight every evening."

He smiled. "I would like that very much."

"Me too."

"And if you change your mind—"

"I won't."

He stepped even closer to me. Close enough that I could feel the heat of his body and see the desire in his eyes. I had not imagined it. He wanted me too.

Oliver ducked his head slightly toward me. To say something more? To kiss me? I would never know because we were interrupted by a knock at the library door. Jarred back to reality, Oliver cleared his throat and put proper distance between us. "Come in," he called.

Bexley peeked inside the library, his gaze moving between us. "Your guests should be arriving soon, sir."

"Thank you, Bexley," Oliver said, and then he turned to me. "May I walk you upstairs?"

I took his offered arm.

We silently ascended the stairs, and when we reached the top, he led me down the corridor to the attic door. The space was not wide, nor was it well lit.

When we reached the door, he touched my elbow, gently turning me to face him. "I dislike that you must hide in the attic," he said.

I did, too, but saying so would not change the fact that it was necessary. "I've hidden in the attic for two years. What is one more night?"

He looked pained. "Promise me you'll stay hidden. If anyone sees you—"

"I promise," I said. "You've worked hard to make this night a success. Don't waste it worrying about me."

"I will *always* worry about you," he whispered.

"You needn't. I will be fine. Your guests will arrive soon. You should go," I said, though I did not want him to.

"I should," he agreed, though he did not move.

"Oliver." I forced a smile I didn't feel. "Go."

He took a slow backward step.

"Wait," I said, stopping him. "Your . . . cravat is crooked." It was a pathetic excuse to prolong his parting—Oliver was nothing if not precise with his appearance—but he immediately came closer and lifted his chin.

My hands rose to his cravat. The fabric was stiffly starched and free of wrinkles. If I touched it, it would crease. I couldn't do that to him tonight. Candlelight flickered in his eyes. "Forgive me, I was mistaken. Your cravat is perf—"

Oliver tugged his cravat.

"Oliver!" I gaped at his crooked cravat. "Your guests."

"Help me retie it?" he murmured.

I lifted my hands to his cravat again, but they were trembling too much to do any good.

I could feel the heat of his body through his shirt. We were standing so close. So close that if I were to look up, our mouths would meet in a kiss. I wanted to kiss him, and the rapid way his chest rose and fell with each of his breaths hinted that he wanted the same. But I had misjudged one moment between us, and I did not want to make the same mistake again.

I glanced away, giving Oliver the opportunity to retreat, but he cupped my chin and gently drew my gaze back to his. He brushed his thumb across my cheek, and the sensation made me shiver with pleasure.

I leaned into his touch, inhaling the spicy, sweet scent of the cologne on his wrist. He smelled so good. He always smelled good, but tonight, he was intoxicating.

He looked at me like I was something precious, something he treasured.

But he didn't kiss me. He seemed afraid that one wrong move would send me fleeing into the shadows. After the trauma I'd experienced with Mr. Cavendish, I had not thought I would ever feel so safe with a man again. But the time I'd spent with Oliver had changed me. I wasn't frightened anymore. I wouldn't run. Not from him.

I lifted my still trembling hands to his shoulders.

The simple contact seemed to reassure him. He lightly rested his hand on my waist, pulling me closer with a careful restraint that only made me want him to kiss me more. He dipped his head but hovered a breath away, giving me a final opportunity to retreat.

I tilted my chin just enough to show him that I welcomed his kiss, that I wanted it.

Finally, he lowered his mouth to mine.

Oliver's kiss was soft and sweet and achingly slow, and I savored every second, the tenderness of his touch, the warmth of his lips, the gentle pressure of his fingertips on my face and waist. It was a kiss that asked for nothing but offered everything.

When Oliver finally drew back, he rested his forehead against mine. We lingered like that as long as we could. Until we heard a carriage coming down the lane outside.

Oliver reluctantly stepped back, trailing his hand down my arm before finally letting go. He smoothed his crumpled cravat and tied a quick knot. He then turned and retreated down the corridor. At the end, he looked over his shoulder at me and smiled. It was small but more certain than before our kiss.

My heart swelled with happiness.

Everything felt foreign and fragile, like we were walking a path we didn't quite know how to navigate, but we were both eager to see where it would lead.

CHAPTER THIRTY-ONE

OLIVER

STANDING ON THE DRIVE, I watched the Daltons' carriage come toward me. I'd hoped Markham would arrive first so that he could act as a buffer between Miss Dalton and me, but unfortunately for me, he did not.

As soon as the Daltons' carriage came to a stop, one of the men I'd hired to help as footman tonight stepped forward to let down the step and open the door. I had also hired a few stablehands to assist with the horses and carriages in the stables but no one additional.

When I'd made my invitation, before I'd known about Kate, I'd planned to hire more staff. But after she'd come out of hiding, I hadn't felt comfortable bringing additional people inside the manor. I hated how hard my servants would have to work to put on this dinner and reading tonight, but Kate's safety came first.

Mr. and Mrs. Dalton alighted first, followed by Miss Dalton's younger sister, Miss Arabella Dalton. It had been lucky indeed that Miss Dalton had a younger sister. Otherwise, our numbers would not have been equal, and I would have had to invite more guests. Finally, Miss Dalton poked her head out the door.

Knowing the part I must play, I stepped forward and tapped the footman on the shoulder and asked him to move aside so that I might assist the young lady myself. I did not relish having to play the part of a doting suitor tonight, but I was a gentleman.

Miss Dalton gracefully placed her gloved hand in mine and stepped down. I tucked her hand into the crook of my elbow, and we started up the stairs.

"You look lovely tonight, Miss Dalton," I supplied the expected pleasantry, and while it *was* true, she was not as lovely as Kate.

"I am glad you think so, Mr. Jennings. I had this dress made especially for this occasion."

I hoped she hadn't spent too much, for the effort was wasted on me. Her excitement, however, was a good reminder to tread carefully tonight. I didn't wish to give the girl false hope, at least no more than I already had.

We'd just reached the portico to wait with the rest of her family when Markham's carriage entered the gate.

I made idle conversation with the Daltons as the conveyance traveled down the short drive and around the fountain, then finally came to a stop.

The footman opened the door, and Markham stepped down. His eyes skimmed over the chimneys, the cornice, the canted windows. My manor likely did not hold a candle to his own—he was a baron and likely lived in a far grander house than Winterset—but I was proud of all the improvements I'd made since my arrival; the drive was freshly graveled, the fountain clean and working, and the ivy neatly trimmed.

When Markham finally dropped his gaze and started up the stairs, I said, "Welcome to Winterset, Lord Markham."

"I have been waiting a long while to hear those words," he said.

"Two weeks is not so long." I gave him a good-natured laugh.

"No, indeed. I'm just impatient for some entertainment."

"Well then, let us not delay any longer. Mrs. Owensby is preparing us a fine meal, and then we shall have our reading."

"Capital," Markham said and offered the younger Miss Arabella his arm.

Bexley stood at the door to take my guests' coats, but when the moment arrived to do so, he stood stock-still, eyes wide and mouth ajar, gaping at my guests.

Gads! My guests were not even inside yet, and already, my servants were acting strangely.

"Bexley." I cleared my throat. "The coats, if you please."

Bexley shook his head as if coming to his senses and took the proffered items before quickly disappearing inside to stow them.

"My staff is a little out of practice," I jested, trying to lessen the discomfort and earning a few laughs from my guests.

"So it seems," Mrs. Dalton said. "We should be glad to host you next, Mr. Jennings."

"You are too kind," I said, but I would not be accepting any future invitations from them.

I led my guests inside, and their gazes roamed the entrance hall. Not much had been done to improve this space, save for replacing the carpets and candles, but contrary to my first impression, not much had actually been needed in this hall. Winterset's entrance was not as grand as some larger houses, but it was impressive.

Moonlight poured through the centuries-old stained-glass windows, illuminating the images and casting shadows along the arched corridor that ran the length of the landing. And on the ground floor, candelabras highlighted the hand-carved banister of the double staircase and the gallery of gilded frames.

"You have a fine home, Mr. Jennings," Mr. Dalton said.

"Very fine, indeed," Mrs. Dalton said, glancing around. "Lacking a few feminine touches, but I suppose you are wise to let the future Mrs. Jennings"—she glanced meaningfully at her daughter—"see to such things."

Miss Dalton smiled up at me as though already envisioning herself in the role.

My stomach twisted at the thought. "This way." I directed my guests to the drawing room to wait for dinner to be announced.

"Oh my!" Miss Dalton gasped. "Mr. Jennings, this room is . . ." Her sentence stalled as she eyed the threadbare carpets, moth-eaten tapestries, and gruesome paintings. We'd hung the most graphic ones on either side of the stage.

"Terrifying?" I supplied.

"Well, *yes*."

"I'm glad you think so."

She stared at me like I'd gone mad.

"Is it not the perfect setting for our reading?" I asked.

Mr. Dalton laughed. "You mean to say you did all this"—he swept his hand over the room—"on purpose?"

"What is a ghost story without a haunted room to read it in? Please, have a look around."

The Daltons readily took my invitation, walking to where the historical relics were displayed on the pianoforte.

Only Markham remained at my side. He lowered his voice. "Hope you are ready for a quick courtship, old boy."

My gaze cut to him.

"Don't look so alarmed." He chuckled. "I *did* tell you not to pay too much attention to any one young lady."

"Yes, but this is only our *second* meeting," I said only loud enough for him to hear.

"Mothers have seen their daughters married with less. Don't you like her, Jennings?"

"I hardly know her."

"She has a pleasing face and a decent dowry. What more do you need to know?"

My conscience condemned me for having once believed something similar. How shortsighted and selfish I had been.

Markham clapped me on the back, and we joined the Daltons at the pianoforte to view Kate's relics.

"This is quite a collection you've got," Mr. Dalton said.

"It is," Markham agreed. "A small fortune."

"Yes, well, the monetary value of these items is nothing compared to their historical significance," I said and began reciting what history I could recall from Mrs. Owensby's tour during my first week at Winterset. To my surprise, I remembered quite a lot: I told them of King Henry VIII and the Roundheads, of the Elizabethan priest hunters, and of my ancestors who came to own the home. I told them of the many improvements they'd made and how I hoped to be part of this incredible history.

The Daltons seemed impressed, but I hadn't said it to impress them. I honestly felt what I said. My maternal ancestors had an honorable history, and day by day, as I'd worked to improve the house and protect Kate, I was proud to become a part of that legacy.

Not long later, Bexley appeared at the door.

I all but held my breath, waiting for him to speak, hoping he would not make another blunder. He was a bit stiff and did not linger, but to my relief, he seamlessly announced dinner and quit the room.

My guests and I filed out of the drawing room in pairs: Miss Dalton and I, Lord Markham and Miss Arabella, and Mr. and Mrs. Dalton.

I didn't like how strongly Miss Dalton smelled of bergamot or the way her fingers dug into my arm. Or perhaps I just didn't like having anyone other than Kate on my arm.

In the dining hall, I pulled out Miss Dalton's chair—*Kate's* chair—and Miss Dalton sat.

I'd made sure Mrs. Owensby had prepared Kate a tray before the guests arrived, but I hated that she had to eat it in hiding.

As soon as we were all seated, the dinner service began.

It had been a long while since I'd attended a dinner party, and I'd never hosted one, but I found it rather enjoyable. Conversation flowed as freely as the wine, and dinner was delicious.

Only one thing was missing.

Kate.

She should be seated beside me tonight. She'd planned nearly everything about this night: the decorations, the dinner menu, even the passage we would later read. This was her night, and it was not fair that she did not get to enjoy it. Would we ever find a way to make it safe for her to come out of hiding? I hoped so. She deserved so much more.

"What do you think, Mr. Jennings?" Mr. Dalton looked at me expectantly.

"Forgive me, my mind wandered. What was it you asked?"

"Your thoughts on keeping hedgehogs as pets," he repeated, his tone serious.

I glanced at Markham, who was fighting a grin, and cleared my throat. "I . . . suppose if one is fond of prickly companions, it might be worth the effort."

Mr. Dalton nodded, and the rest of the company continued the conversation.

To my relief, the hired footmen did their job admirably, and before I knew it, dinner had progressed to dessert. When we'd had our fill, we retired back to the drawing room for the reading.

Mrs. Owensby had positioned the settee and armchairs in an arc, facing the wall that would serve as the back to our "stage," as Kate had planned. The stage was nothing more than a threadbare carpet and the backdrop only a tattered tapestry, but it worked well enough.

The Misses Dalton and their mother whispered as they sat on the settee in the center, and Markham and Mr. Dalton made themselves comfortable in the armchairs.

I stood at the front of the room. "I'm pleased you were all brave enough to attend this ghost-story reading tonight. Winterset has a long and tragic history, and I have it on the best authority that ghosts haunt these halls. We shall have to hope they behave tonight."

Charlie, who'd entered the room unnoticed behind my guests, began to play an eerie song on the pianoforte. The ladies were startled, but when they saw that it was a servant, not a spirit playing the instrument, they giggled at being so easily scared.

"Tonight," I continued in a low and ominous tone, "I offer you a reading from *The Wraiths of Dunmore Abbey* by Mr. Laurence Fairfax, a gripping ghost story that may stretch the limits of your sensibilities. Prepare yourselves to hear a terrifying tale."

I retrieved the book from the top of the trunk and turned to the bookmarked page.

"Once upon a time," I began in a low voice. "In a home very much like this one, there lived a man, though some believed him more a monster than a man . . ."

As I read, the women clasped hands, hanging on my every word. I varied the tone and volume of my voice to build tension. When I reached a particularly suspenseful passage, I paused.

The silence stretched into the stillness, and then there came a scraping sound from inside the wall behind me. My guests' eyes widened, not knowing it was only Bexley inside the derelict passageway.

Page after page, I read, and my guests hung on my every word. When I reached the climax of the story, Charlie played the pianoforte at a feverish pace, then stopped suddenly, and Mrs. Owensby screamed, splitting the night.

I snapped the book closed, signaling the end of the reading and gestured for Bexley, Mrs. Owensby, and Charlie to join me onstage to take a bow.

Everyone applauded enthusiastically.

"Bravo!" the women cheered.

"Most entertaining!" Mr. Dalton said.

And Markham nodded his approval.

I breathed a sigh of relief.

We'd done it.

The night had gone off without a hitch. I could not wait to tell Kate about it tomorrow morning. To hold her in my arms again, to kiss her.

I walked my guests to the drive and was handing Miss Dalton into the carriage when Markham discovered he'd forgotten his gloves.

"Blast! I'll return shortly," he said and ran back inside.

The Daltons lingered longer than I liked, reissuing their invitation to dine with them next. I evaded acceptance, and when they finally left, Markham's carriage inched forward on the drive.

But he hadn't returned.

I went inside to find him, but the drawing room was empty. I checked the dining hall next, but he wasn't there either. I passed through the entrance hall to recheck the drawing room when I heard a sound in my study.

Markham? I walked to the door and found him standing by my desk. His back was to me, so he didn't see me right away. His shoulders were rounded, and his head was down as though he were looking at something in his hands.

"Are you lost, Lord Markham?" I asked.

He turned to face me. In his hands was a piece of paper, but it was too dark to see what was written on it. "What can I say? It is a big house."

"It's not, actually."

"Well, saying so is far less embarrassing than admitting I have no sense of direction."

"What are you doing in my private study, Lord Markham?"

"*That* is an excellent question. I'm so glad you asked. I believe you are hiding something that belongs to me, Jennings, and I had to investigate for myself."

"Something that belongs to you? Your gloves? I assure you I didn't take them, if that's—"

"Not my gloves." He huffed a humorless laugh. "You know, I never thought it odd that Miss Lockwood's body wasn't found until you appeared in the tavern raving like a lunatic about seeing a ghost." He shook his head and laughed lightly. "She really played me for a fool, didn't she?" He sneered down at the paper in his hands—the heavily *crumpled* paper—and I realized it was one of the many drafts of my letter to Kate that I'd discarded. Proof of her survival.

I grew cold but tried to cover it.

"Don't get me wrong," Markham continued, stalking closer, like a cat toying with its prey, "I understand why you'd want to keep Miss Lockwood for yourself. She is *uncommonly* beautiful. Unfortunately for you, though, she already signed a marriage contract with me."

"Cavendish," I said, finally seeing his true identity.

"Yes." His mouth curled into a sinister smile. "I believe we finally understand one another. Where is she, Jennings?"

"I don't know what you're talking about," I said through gritted teeth.

"Yes, you do." He shoved the letter into my chest. "And if you know what's good for you, you will return what rightfully belongs to me."

"I can't. I sent her away," I said, thinking quickly. "That is why I wrote her a letter instead of telling her."

He grinned like he found my attempt to protect her amusing. "I find that difficult to believe, but fine. I'll play along. I will give you one week to retrieve my property and return it."

"And if I don't?"

"Well, I would say you'd live to regret it, but you probably won't."

I wouldn't regret it, or I wouldn't *live*?

His gaze raked down my form with chilling coldness, and I knew the answer. "Within the week, Jennings," he said, then shouldered past me into the entrance hall.

I followed immediately after him, watching to ensure he climbed into his carriage. As soon as his conveyance was outside the gate, I shouted for the servants.

They joined me seconds later. "Sir?" Bexley said.

"Cavendish is Lord Markham?"

"He is, sir," Bexley said gravely.

"How is that possible?"

"Well, he *was* Mr. Cavendish, but after the deaths of his father and elder brother, he inherited the family title and is now called Lord Markham."

"I know how titles work. What I am wondering is why I am only now finding this out? Why did you not tell me sooner?" I looked to Mrs. Owensby, who was wringing her apron.

"You didn't disclose your guest list. You never made any mention of him to us before tonight either."

I hadn't. Why would I have? There had been no reason to talk to my servants about my new friend. But then my mind went back to Bexley's reaction upon Markham's arrival. How had I been so blind? "When he showed up tonight, you recognized him. Why did you not say anything?"

"I wanted to, sir, but when I went to stow your guest's coats and I told Mrs. Owensby and Charlie about his being here, we decided it was best not to alert you. If we had, you might have acted differently and made him suspicious. We did not want to risk Kate's safety."

I raked my hands through my hair. Considering how I felt right now, they'd been right not to tell me. Had I known Markham's true identity earlier tonight, I would not have been able to keep my composure.

"How did you learn who he was?" Charlie asked.

"Markham found a letter I wrote to Kate in the bin, thus proving she is alive. He has demanded that I deliver her to him within the week."

"You can't," Mrs. Owensby all but cried.

"I *won't*." But now that he knew Kate was alive, how could I possibly keep her safe?

CHAPTER THIRTY-TWO

KATE

L<small>IGHT CREPT UNDER THE PRIEST-HIDE</small> door, signaling morning.

At last!

I'd been awake for hours, eager to hear every detail of Oliver's ghost-story reading, but I'd forced myself to lay in bed until the sun had risen to allow Oliver to rest after his late night spent entertaining. I also did not want to appear *over*eager.

What I would have given to attend last night—to have heard him read the passage we'd selected, to have been seated beside him as we'd eaten the delicious meal we'd planned, and to kiss his sweet lips after all our guests had left. I would have worked for a month, a *year*! I would have even allowed Mrs. Owensby to style my hair.

But Oliver's recounting of the night would have to suffice.

I pushed back the covers, shivering against the cold, and quickly donned my slippers and dressing gown. I felt along the wall until I found the handle and pushed open, or rather, *tried* to push open the door. But it didn't budge. I tried again, this time pressing my shoulder into the door. It opened only an inch, then snapped shut with the heaviness of something blocking it.

My heart picked up its pace, panicked at being trapped in such a small, dark place.

I took a steadying breath and made myself think logically. Could something have fallen in front of the door? Maybe I needed to use some force to move it out of the way.

I planted my feet on the floor, and using all my strength, I gave the door a hefty push. This time, it easily swung open, and I fell through the threshold into Oliver.

His arms came around me as I fell forward, and we ended up in something of a dipped embrace.

I blinked up at him. Sun streamed through the window behind him, highlighting his golden curls. His *messy* golden curls. As he set me back on my feet, I took his measure: mussed hair, puffy eyes, rumpled clothes. The same clothes he'd worn last night, minus his coat and cravat, which had been removed and discarded in a pile by the door. He was usually so composed, so perfectly styled and put together; this morning, though, he was anything but.

I liked seeing him undone.

"Did you *sleep* here last night?" I asked.

"Against the door," he confirmed. "I would not suggest it. Very uncomfortable, and I had quite a rude awakening."

"You can hardly blame *me* for that. I did not know you were there, and a door's main purpose is to be opened, is it not?"

"Indeed, you are right. I only have myself to blame for this stiff shoulder." He rolled his shoulders as if trying to drive away the pain.

I tried not to notice how the muscles in his arms bunched and flexed, but it could not be helped. I knew I should look away, but his arms were just . . . so . . . admirable in those thin shirt sleeves. I made myself meet his knowing gaze and forced the focus of our conversation back on him. "So . . . *why* were you sleeping outside my door?"

"I wanted to make sure you were safe."

I smiled, pleased that he'd thought of me last night. "I am safe," I assured him.

Oliver nodded, glancing over his shoulder. What was he looking for?

"Are *you* all right?" I asked. "You seem out of countenance this morning."

"Yes, well . . . It's just . . ." He rubbed the back of his neck. "You should sit." He led me to the main part of the attic and gestured to the lid of my trunk. He remained standing.

"You are worrying me." And when he did not immediately start to assuage my fears, I knew something was wrong. Did something happen last night to make him regret our kiss?

"I have made a grave mistake, Kate. I invited Mr. Cavendish to the ghost-story reading."

"You *what*?"

"I didn't know his true identity," Oliver hastily explained. "You'd only ever called him Mr. Cavendish, and I knew him only as Lord Markham."

I tried to make sense of Oliver's confession. "You are saying *my* former intended Mr. Cavendish is *your* new friend?"

"I am."

"You must be mistaken. Mr. Cavendish was not in line to inherit his father's title. Could you have hosted his father or elder brother?"

Oliver shook his head. "Both his father and brother have passed away. Mr. Cavendish, Lord Markham, inherited the title sometime in the last two years."

"How is this plausible? How, within the space of two short years, have three men—my father, his father, and his elder brother—close to Mr. Cavendish died?"

"I have my suspicions," Oliver said.

So did I, and it did not bode well for my own survival. "All right." I took several deep breaths to stave off my mounting panic. "Everything is going to be all right. Mr. Cavendish was here, but he doesn't know I'm alive. Nothing needs to change."

Oliver looked like he might be sick. "He does know."

"He couldn't possibly."

"The night I went to the tavern, the night I saw you in the library, I told Markham that I believed Winterset was haunted. That I'd seen a ghost."

"That does not necessarily signify anything. I saw you that night, Oliver. You said so many things in your drunken state that did not make sense."

"It doesn't matter. What I said made him suspicious. And last night, he sneaked away from the party, into my study, and found a discarded draft of the letter I wrote to you. He knows you are alive, Kate. And he wants you back."

Dread washed over me in waves. I clutched the edge of the trunk to steady myself.

Oliver crouched in front of me and spoke softly. "I am so sorry. I promised to protect you and then led him directly to you."

"It is not your fault."

"It *is* my fault," he said.

I shook my head. "If I hadn't been in the library that night, you would not have had anything to tell. It was my fault more than yours."

"No. I was so eager to be befriended by Lord Markham that I was blinded to his true identity. But I should have opened my eyes. I should have seen who he truly was. I am such a fool."

"Don't punish yourself too severely. I fell for his act too. Mr. Cavendish, or I suppose it is Lord Markham now, is clever and cunning."

Oliver stood and began pacing the floor in front of me. "We must do something to ensure your safety," he said. "We must lock the gates and cover the windows and—"

"That might have worked well to protect me *before* he knew," I interrupted, "but not now. If he wants me back, closing the gate won't stop him from coming to claim me."

"You are right, of course." Oliver rubbed the scar on his forehead. "So we must . . . we must . . ." He let out a frustrated breath when an immediate plan did not reveal itself. He then raked his hands through his hair. And when *that* didn't prove successful in coming up with a strategy, he started pacing again.

He began suggesting ideas that ranged from the impossible—bringing the law to bear against Markham—to the absurd—changing my name and appearance and returning as a woman from foreign lands.

I simply listened, knowing what Oliver did not: there was no solution that would allow us to be together safely. No matter what we did, Markham would not give up.

"Oliver," I finally said, trying to stop him.

"I'll find a way to fix this."

"Oliver," I said again.

"I only need a little time to think of some way to keep you safe here."

I stood in front of him, stopping him. "You *can't* keep me safe here anymore," I said. "And if I stayed, *you* would not be safe. Three men have already died. I will not endanger another."

"Then . . . I will come with you," he said, his voice desperate.

"I wish you could come with me, but you cannot. Winterset is your home, Oliver. It is your livelihood and your future. No matter how much we might wish otherwise, I have to go, and you have to stay."

Oliver opened his mouth to protest, but I held up my hand, silencing him. I cared for him too much to allow him to sacrifice his well-being for me. "You said if I ever changed my mind about wanting to stay with you here at Winterset, I need only tell you."

He stilled, comprehension filling his eyes.

"I want to leave, Oliver. Please, help me."

CHAPTER THIRTY-THREE

Oliver

THERE WAS ONLY ONE PLACE that I knew Kate would be safe: Summerhaven.

It was not a permanent solution—she'd likely be safe there for only a few weeks, until Markham surmised that I'd sent her there—but the distance from danger would buy us a bit more time to find her a long-term solution.

Kate would leave first thing tomorrow morning, as we had decided. Charlie would accompany her to ensure her protection, but the rest of us—Mrs. Owensby, Bexley, and me—would remain here to maintain an appearance of normalcy.

Rain pelted my study window as I sat at my desk, and I pulled out a piece of paper to write a letter to my family.

I'd been estranged from them for more than two years now, but I knew that if I asked for their help, they wouldn't hesitate. Not because of their feelings for me but because it was Damon's nature to help those in need. Hannah's and Mother's too. If I asked, Damon and Hannah would hide Kate and keep her safe indefinitely. And Mother would help her find a permanent situation. She seemed to know everyone in England.

I need only find the right words to ask.

A daunting task, considering I hadn't read any of their letters or written to them in over two years. It wasn't that I didn't want to read their letters. I did. More than anything, I wanted to feel like they loved me. Like they needed me. Like I belonged.

But I didn't.

My whole life, I'd been the spare son. The child my parents had borne to protect the family's legacy in case their first son met some untimely fate. I was the secondary plan, the reserve, the afterthought.

In my last months at home, none of my family members had even thought to tell me of Father's failing health or that Summerhaven had been on the brink of ruin. I'd only learned the truth when I'd read a letter that Damon had written to Hannah in an effort to prove his unworthiness and win her heart—something I still felt ashamed of.

I was a burden to my family.

That was why I'd separated myself.

It hurt like the devil every day, knowing I did not belong, but I knew they were better off without having to worry about me.

That didn't matter right now though. Only Kate mattered. And I would do anything to protect her, including humbling myself to ask for my family's help.

I dipped my pen into the inkwell and began:

Dear Damon,

I write you this letter in desperation . . .

From there, I poured out my soul about my feelings for Kate, then described her perilous situation with Markham. I begged Damon to help her. Then I gave Charlie the letter as well as money to hire a private messenger to deliver it immediately. It would likely arrive only a day before Kate did, but at least they would have a little time to prepare for her comfort.

And in case Markham was monitoring my movements, I wrote a second letter, a decoy letter, to a fictitious family in France, demanding that they send Kate back to Winterset within the week, which I instructed Charlie to deliver to the postmaster.

The rest of the day passed in a blur of panic and packing. I stayed at Kate's side all day, afraid to let her out of my sight even for a moment. Markham had said he would give me a week to deliver Kate to him, but I didn't trust him to keep his word. Which is why I had Bexley stand guard at the front door, Mrs. Owensby watch the servants' entrance, and Charlie patrol the grounds with a gun.

When night finally came, Kate retired to the priest hide in the attic to sleep—the hidden spot seemed safer than her bedchamber—and I retired to my study.

Outside, it stormed. Lightning struck, illuminating the room, and several seconds later, thunder rumbled in the distance. The worst of the storm would likely pass tonight, but it would make Kate's journey much more difficult in the morning. It would probably deter other long-distance travelers though, and that thought brought me comfort.

If we could just make it safely through tonight.

I walked to the window and pushed back the curtain. With the cloud cover and heavy rain, I couldn't see much outside. But every time another bolt of lightning flashed, it illuminated the grounds: the barren trees, the empty fountain, the stone sentinels that sat atop the gate posts.

Then a different sound caught my notice. A noise inside. A patter of footsteps.

I went directly to the study door and peered into the entrance hall, locking eyes with Charlie, whom I'd asked to take the first shift guarding the front door. Charlie nodded toward the library, and I followed his gaze just in time to see Kate slip inside.

Worried, I followed after her, lightly knocking on the library door and then peeking inside. "Kate?"

She was curled on the small sofa, a blanket around her shoulders, shaking. "Oliver?"

"I heard you run to the library and wanted to check on you. Are you all right?"

She nodded that she was, but her eyes were wide with fear.

"May I sit with you?" I asked.

"I would be grateful," she said, scooting to one side of the sofa to make room for me. "I find storms so frightening," she said even as another bolt of lightning flashed.

I crossed the room to the window and closed the curtains, then walked back and sat beside her.

"Thank you," she said softly. "During storms like this, Papa used to sit with me here in the library. The books dampen the sound, and the storm feels less fierce. I know it's silly to be scared of a little weather, but—"

"Not silly," I said. "Weather like this is frightening. Any sailor would agree."

She gave me a small smile, but she still seemed so scared.

"What can I do?" I asked.

"Papa used to read to me to distract me."

"I should be glad to read to you. I'm sure you've read every book in this library, but what about the ghost story I borrowed from the lending library? Would you like me to read that to you?"

"A ghost story would only frighten me more. Would you tell me about your Grand Tour?"

My chest stiffened. I had no desire to relive that part of my life, for many reasons, but for her, I would. "What would you like to know?"

"Where did you go?" she asked.

"France. Italy. A year in each."

"You were gone a long time. Why?"

Thunder rumbled outside, and she stiffened. I instinctively put my arm around her shoulders, and she relaxed into my side. "Because I needed to get away. From home. From the man I was becoming," I answered honestly.

"What sort of man were you becoming?" she asked.

"The type of man who traveled with twenty-seven hats," I said, and she smiled. But her smile wouldn't last long, not once she realized her original perception of me was more accurate than her present one. "I was the type of man who cared more for himself than for others," I admitted. "The type of man who valued leisure and luxury more than love."

Kate stared up at me, listening.

"Every day, I awoke only to amuse myself: Hyde Park, Tattersalls, Vauxhall Gardens . . . All of it was mine for the taking. My plan for the future was to marry a woman with a large enough dowry to support my lifestyle." I admitted my greatest shame, and she sucked in a breath.

"Then," I pressed on, "at the invitation of my mother, Hannah came to visit. And over the course of that summer, she helped me see who I'd become. I didn't like what I saw, but neither did I know how to change. I thought I might be able to with her help, but it was too late. She'd fallen in love with my brother.

"Damon married Hannah, my father's health was failing, and then I was notified that Winterset had become vacant—or so we were told—a house that I wasn't sure I even wanted, much less was worthy of. It was a dark and depressing time in my life. I felt lost and alone, and instead of staying and facing my problems, I fled to France."

Another bolt of lightning flashed. Kate flinched and turned toward me. I wrapped my other arm protectively around her. When the initial fright had worn away, I thought she would sit back in her seat again, but she didn't. She rested her head on my shoulder and looked up at me, her eyes silently asking for me to continue.

Although I disliked sharing this part of my life, I sensed that the sound of my voice was soothing her, so I resumed my story.

"Paris and its many pleasures offered me a momentary escape from pain, but my days had no meaning, my life no purpose. Paris was a beautiful city, but besides Charlie, I was alone. I missed my family and my home, but I felt unwanted and unneeded by both. I wasn't ready to return to England and take up my responsibilities. I believed Winterset was better off in Mr. Moore's hands, so I stayed away."

"Who is Mr. Moore?" Kate said.

I didn't want to tell her. It was deeply humiliating. But she hadn't pulled away from me when I'd told her about the other things. Perhaps it would be all right. Longing for her understanding and absolution, I took a deep breath and hesitantly said, "When Winterset became vacant, I knew it was my duty to come and care for it, but I wasn't ready to take up the responsibility; I wanted to be, but I wasn't. And then Mr. Moore appeared in London, claiming to be Winterset's butler, and proposed that I hire him to act as my steward. His knowledge and love for the estate impressed me, and so I did."

"That is why your letter was addressed to Mr. Moore?" she said.

I nodded. "I paid Mr. Moore handsomely every month for two years to see to Winterset's upkeep, so you can imagine my surprise when I arrived here and saw the condition of the manor and grounds. I thought Mr. Moore was . . . Well, it does not matter what I thought because I was wrong."

"I do not know of any Mr. Moore."

"I don't think he actually exists. Someone saw an opportunity and took advantage. Perhaps it was someone who knew me in London."

"Or someone who knew my father," Kate suggested.

"It's possible. But I doubt we will ever know."

"Perhaps I could help identify him," Kate said. "What did Mr. Moore look like?"

"He was a man of average height and weight. Dressed cleanly. Well enough spoken to be convincing in his playacting."

"Did he have any distinguishing features?"

"I don't remember any," I said. "But to be honest with you, I was deep in my cups at the time. Beyond the barest description—one that could describe almost any man—I don't remember much."

"Have you looked for him?" she asked.

I nodded. "Right after arriving at Winterset, I went to the postmaster. Mr. Moore had been retrieving my letters and the money from the postmaster for two years, so I thought the postmaster might be helpful, but I learned nothing useful from him. Apparently, a different man came to pick up each of the letters. And after I wrote to Mr. Moore that I was returning to England, he disappeared completely. He didn't even pick up my last letter."

"I know. A post-boy delivered it to Winterset. We opened it to determine the sender."

"And you read it, I assume."

She winced. "Yes."

"Curious Kate." I shook my head, tsking.

She gave me a wry smile. "Could you hire a thief-taker?" she asked, changing the subject.

I sighed. "I considered doing so, but without a physical description of him or any leads, chasing Mr. Moore would be a fool's errand. Mr. Moore and my money are long gone."

She sighed, then was quiet for a long moment. "I thought you'd left Winterset to rot," she admitted. "I thought you didn't care."

"I can see why you would think that. But I promise you that I only stayed away for so long because I was trying to do right by Winterset."

"Why did you not say something sooner?" she asked softly.

"Because I was swindled, Kate. In my first hour of ownership, I placed my inheritance in the hands of a thief. And it was—it *is*—humiliating." I glanced at her, and her eyes showed a gentleness that made me feel even more unmanned.

"When did you go to Italy?" she asked.

"After a year in France, Charlie suggested we tour Italy. I wanted a change, too, so I agreed. I let a modest home in a small farming village. At first, I thought I might go mad from boredom. Life there was simple and slow, but as the weeks turned to months, I learned to love the solitude. "I saw how much the people loved their land, and I began to long for my own. I wanted to come to Winterset and make something of it and of myself. But it took me another year to trust myself again. To become a man I believed was worthy of Winterset.

"I was wrong to stay away for so long, Kate. I know that now. I should have come here as soon as I inherited Winterset and cared for my estate. I should have been a better man."

"Even the best men make mistakes," she said softly.

Perhaps, but I'd made so many.

"When I first read your letter to Mr. Moore, the one stating that you would soon be arriving, I thought you were proud and conceited."

"I *am* proud and conceited." I grinned at her.

"Perhaps," she said. "But you are also kind, gallant, and the most generous man I've ever known."

I shook my head. "I am every bit the lout you believed me to be when I first arrived."

"No, Oliver. You're not."

"I *am*, Kate. You would not even be in a position to have to leave tomorrow if it weren't for me." I trained my gaze on the ground, ashamed.

"Look at me, Oliver." Kate gently touched my cheek, guiding my gaze back to hers. "Since that day you climbed over the fence wearing that ridiculous topper, you have done nothing but care for this house and everyone inside it. You are the *best* of men, Oliver Jennings."

"You're wrong," I said. "My own family does not even think so."

She looked at me for a long moment, seeming to debate whether or not to say something, and then finally said, "I don't think that's true. Have you read their letters?"

"How did you know about their letters?"

"Before we met, when I was trying to ascertain your character, I went into your study, and I saw them in your desk. It was the same day I redacted your notes. I read one of the letters."

"Ah," I said.

"Are you very upset?" she asked.

Was I? I took measure of my feelings. I wasn't mad that she'd read a letter. I was embarrassed that she knew I hadn't read their correspondence. I wondered what damning information it might contain about me, but I wasn't upset. "No," I said. "I'm just surprised."

"I only read the one, but it was obvious how much your brother loves and misses you."

My throat tightened. "I'm sure you are wrong."

"If I am, then why would they continue to write?"

"Duty. Obligation."

She shook her head. "The words written in his letter said nothing of that."

"What *did* it say?" I asked.

"You should read his letters and find out for yourself." She raised an eyebrow at me in challenge.

"No good can come from digging up the past. It's better for me to look to the future."

"Sometimes, it is," she agreed. "And sometimes, you have to look back to know which way to move forward."

Kate clutched my lapels, and I looked down at her in my arms. Her eyes were filled with love and longing, a mirror of my own.

My heart felt like it would burst with the feelings it held for her. I wanted to hold her like this forever.

But no matter how much I wanted that, tomorrow morning, our lives would start down different paths, and I did not want to make our parting any harder. I would be the man she believed I was. I would be honorable and bid her good night.

"The storm has stopped," I said.

She listened for a moment, then nodded. "I didn't even notice."

"It's late," I said. "You must be tired."

Another nod.

I shifted her in my arms to help her stand, then stood myself. I walked her up the stairs to her bedchamber, and at the door, I bid her good night.

CHAPTER THIRTY-FOUR

Kate

"The carriage has arrived," Mrs. Owensby said early the next morning. "Are you ready to go?"

I glanced around my bedchamber. For two years, I'd dreamed of what life might be like outside Winterset's walls. I'd dreamed of more. But now that the morning for me to leave had arrived, it felt like a nightmare. I didn't want to leave my home. I didn't want to leave my servants. I didn't want to leave my Oliver.

"Will you tell the driver to wait a moment? I want to look around one last time."

"Of course," Mrs. Owensby said. "We will be waiting for you on the drive."

Alone, I spared one last look at my bedchamber, taking in the white walls, the canopied bed, and the antechamber door that led to the master's room—Oliver's room. My stomach clenched. I would never get to use that door, but someone would. One day, he would marry. I wished that woman could be me, but no amount of wishing would make it my reality. The realization filled me with sorrow.

Last night in the library, as he'd held me in his arms, I'd wanted to tell him how I felt about him. But it had not felt like the right circumstance. And now, this morning, I was leaving. We'd run out of time.

I stepped into the corridor and closed the door behind me. I'd walked these halls my whole life; how could this be the last time? How could I leave my home? How could I leave *him*? Winterset held every happy memory of my past, and Oliver was everything I'd ever wanted for my future.

Standing at the top of the stairs, I paused, trying to commit every sight, sound, and smell to memory: the color of the stained-glass windows, the sound of the creaking staircase, the familiar scent of home.

When I reached the entrance hall, Oliver was sitting in his study at his desk.

The very place we'd first talked face-to-face.

I stepped inside, and he looked up.

He took in my traveling dress. It was the same dress I'd worn the day we'd met. He smiled, and I thought he might be remembering our first moments together too.

He stood slowly.

But I didn't hesitate.

I walked to the side of his desk and wrapped my arms around his waist.

His arms came around me in a gentle embrace, and we silently held one another.

It had been a very long time since I'd felt so safe, so happy, so loved. I tilted my chin to look up at him. His eyes, so blue, held so much sadness.

A tear slipped down my cheek, and he wiped it away. I leaned into his touch and closed my eyes, trying to soak in everything about this moment: the feel of his calloused fingers, the subtle scent of his cologne, the warmth of his hand.

When I opened my eyes, I saw that his eyes were filled with tears too.

How could I do this?

How could I leave him in so much sadness?

No matter how much I might wish it otherwise, my future was anywhere *but* here.

Oliver kissed my forehead in goodbye, and it broke my heart.

I loved the feel of his lips, but it wasn't enough. If these were our last moments together, I wanted to make the most of them. "Oliver," I whispered, and when he pulled back slightly to look down at me, I slid my hands up his lapels to rest on his shoulders.

He gently cupped my face, brushing his thumbs lightly over my cheeks. The sensation made me shiver with pleasure.

Unable to bear the distance between us another second, I rose onto my tiptoes and kissed him.

The kiss was tender at first, only featherlight touches of our lips.

And then something shifted. Our mouths moved more urgently, rushing to convey everything we didn't have time to say.

He kissed me deeply, desperately.

And I relished every second.

It did not last long though; it couldn't. The carriage was waiting, and I had to leave before it was fully light to be safe.

When our kiss was over, Oliver rested his forehead against mine and trailed his hands down my arms, interlocking our hands, and I said, "I wish . . ."

"Me too," he whispered.

We didn't say anything more. What was there to say other than goodbye? And I never wanted to say that.

He led me to the front door and down the stairs to the drive, where Mrs. Owensby, Bexley, and Charlie were waiting. Mrs. Owensby opened her arms, and fighting back tears, I fell into them. Bexley stood behind us, embracing us both from behind. They were so much more than servants to me. They were family. They hugged me tightly as we said our bittersweet goodbyes, and then they let me go.

Charlie opened the carriage door and climbed inside first.

He would not ride in the carriage with me the whole time, only until we were outside of town. Then he would serve as an outrider to ensure my safety.

Oliver held out his hand to help me inside.

"Please, don't forget me," he whispered. "I don't think I could bear it."

"I won't," I whispered. "I promise."

He pressed a long kiss to my hand and then reluctantly closed the carriage door.

I held my hand to the window, and he did the same on the other side. Then he stepped back and alerted the driver to go.

Oliver stood there in front of Winterset as we pulled away. I wanted to watch him as I left but knew it was too dangerous. Someone might see me. I took one last look at Winterset, my servants, and finally, Oliver.

And then I closed the curtain and cried.

CHAPTER THIRTY-FIVE

Oliver

The wind whipped across the portico, chilling me as I watched the carriage disappear down the lane. Everything I cared about was inside that carriage, and I hated having to remain behind. I'd grown to love Winterset in the weeks I'd been here, but I resented having to remain here to care for it without Kate.

"Come inside, Mr. Jennings, else you will catch your death," Mrs. Owensby said, and when I didn't move, she clutched my arm and *pulled* me inside.

Bexley shut the door behind me. "They'll be all right, sir. Charlie will protect her during the journey."

I was certain he would, given the gun I'd tucked into his breast coat pocket. And Damon would look after her while she was at Summerhaven. But who would look after her in her new life?

I stalked to my study and slammed the door.

Only five minutes ago, we'd stood in this room together. And now she was gone.

Frustrated by my inadequacy, I swiped my arm across my desk, clearing it.

At the cacophonous sound, Bexley stepped inside. "Are you all right, sir?"

"Two years, Bexley! Kate hid successfully here for *two* years. And then I arrived, and—" I cursed under my breath. "I told her I would protect her, but I only put her in danger."

"You *are* protecting her now, sir, by sending her to Summerhaven."

"No. I am only hiding her in a new location."

"You are giving her a chance to live a fuller and freer life," Bexley said. But he was wrong. Kate wasn't free. She was farther from danger but also farther from those who knew and loved her. I braced my elbows on my desk and cradled my head in my hands. She deserved so much more.

"You've done right by her," Bexley said.

"Have I?" I said, my voice tight. "I feel like I have made a grave mistake."

"In my experience, heartache always feels like a grave mistake."

"I miss her already," I said.

"As do I," he said.

"And I," Mrs. Owensby said, entering my study with a tea tray. "But we trust her decision to leave, and you must trust it too."

"I am trying," I said, "but—" My voice caught, and I couldn't finish my sentence.

Mrs. Owensby poured me a cup of tea and set it on the desk in front of me. "Kate will be all right. You will be too. You'll see. Just give it some time."

Time.

If only Kate and I had had more of it, things might be different.

CHAPTER THIRTY-SIX

Kate

The journey took four days, thankfully all without incident, and finally, we had almost arrived at Summerhaven. With rolling green hills and an expansive blue sky, the southern part of the country was big and bright and beautiful. I'd never seen a place more picturesque.

Charlie rode by the carriage on his horse. I was grateful for his sacrifice to ensure my safety, and I hoped he'd not experienced too much discomfort.

The carriage passed over the stone bridge, through the iron gate, and finally started down the tree-lined drive to Oliver's childhood home.

Summerhaven was, without a doubt, the most magnificent manor I'd ever laid eyes on, so large that I could not see the whole of it out my side glass. The stone exterior sparkled in the afternoon sun, and the windows reflected the lush parkland it was built within.

Oliver's family was waiting on the steps to greet me. A handsome man with dark hair and a discerning gaze—Lord Jennings, I guessed from Oliver's description—and a lovely woman at his side. Hannah. Standing in front of them was a more mature woman. Oliver's mother, Dowager Lady Winfield. They looked so similar.

The carriage came to a careful stop. A liveried footman opened the door and let down the step, then reached up to hand me down.

I smoothed my dress, though it made no difference. It was horribly wrinkled and two years out of fashion. What would the earl and his wife think of me? Did I even remember how to properly greet an earl, much less one who refused to be called by his title? My first and only Season had been cut short, and during that time, I'd not been introduced to someone so high-ranking in Society. And this particular earl was predisposed to dislike me, seeing as he and Oliver were estranged.

I'd been so focused on leaving Winterset that I had not thought about arriving at Summerhaven. Oliver had sent them a single letter, pleading for them to take me in and help me find a new situation someplace safe, but that had likely arrived only yesterday. I was fortunate they were outside to greet me at all. I was a stranger to these people.

I pressed my back against the cushion and closed my eyes.

"Miss?" A footman peeked inside the carriage. "Is something the matter?"

"No. Nothing," I said, my voice shaking. They probably thought me mad.

"May I help you alight?" He extended his hand another inch. I reached forward, but instead of taking his hand, I grabbed the door and pulled it closed, causing the footman to quickly retract his hand.

I couldn't do this.

I wanted to go home to Winterset. To Oliver. But I could never go back.

My eyes burned with tears, but I blinked them away. A minute passed, or maybe it was mere seconds before a soft knock startled me.

The older woman stood at the carriage door, offering a small smile. She pointed at the door as if asking permission to enter, and I nodded.

"Miss Lockwood?" she asked, her voice gentle.

"Yes, my lady," I said, my voice thin and trembling.

"I'm Lady Winfield, Oliver's mother. May I join you for a moment?"

I slid to the side to make room for her.

She climbed into the carriage and sat directly across from me. Lady Winfield had kind eyes and a soft smile, like Oliver, which made me feel more at ease. "I remember the first time I made the journey from Winterset. I grew up there, you know."

"You did?"

She nodded.

"I already miss it," I sniffed.

She set a hand on my knee, offering quiet comfort. "When I first saw Summerhaven, my new home by marriage, I felt incredibly overwhelmed. I imagine you might too."

"I do," I admitted.

She nodded in understanding. "I know it isn't the same, but I want you to know that you are most welcome here."

I gave her a grateful look. "Thank you."

She squeezed my knee, giving me a little of her courage. And for a few seconds, I felt a bit braver. But as soon as I glanced out the side glass and saw the earl and his wife, it faded.

Lady Winfield followed my gaze. "Perhaps you might feel more comfortable if I told you about my family before you meet them?"

I nodded.

"That is my eldest son, Lord Winfield, Earl of Summerhaven—although he has not properly claimed his title." She sighed as if it had been the topic of many tiresome conversations. "He prefers to be called by his Christian name, which is Damon, but I suggest you call him by his courtesy title, Lord Jennings."

"Oliv—I mean, Mr. Jennings," I corrected myself, "mentioned that."

"Oliver is fine. I am quite partial to the name, seeing as I gave it to him." She winked and then returned her attention outside. "That lovely young lady is my daughter-in-law, Lady Winfield. Although she will likely respond only if you call her Hannah." She gave a slight shake of her head.

"My darling twin granddaughters are napping in the nursery, but you will meet them later."

"Twins?" I said.

Lady Winfield nodded. "Yes, they are my reward for rearing such strong-willed sons."

I smiled but felt sad. Oh, how I wished Oliver were here to introduce me to his family. I doubted he even knew about his new nieces. The thought hurt my heart.

"Would you like to meet my son and his wife now?" she asked.

Although I was still afraid, I felt braver. "I would."

Lady Winfield alighted first, and I stepped down after her. We climbed the stairs together to where the earl and his wife stood. I sank into a deep curtsy.

"Miss Lockwood, I presume?" the earl said.

"Yes, my lord." I rose and found him fighting amusement.

Had I done it wrong?

"Stop it." Lady Winfield—Hannah?—nudged her husband. "You are making our guest nervous."

His dark brows pulled together, and then he sobered, standing straighter. "My apologies, Miss Lockwood. I meant no offense. Truly, I was only remembering the last time I welcomed a young lady to my home after a long journey." He grinned at his wife. "She quite ruined my boots. You aren't feeling ill, are you?"

"No, my lord."

Hannah huffed at her husband, but her adoration of him was apparent. "You must forgive my husband, Miss Lockwood. He seems to have lost his manners again."

They were so nice, so *normal*.

"Welcome to Summerhaven," the younger Lady Winfield said.

"Thank you, Lady Winfield," I said.

"Please, call me Hannah." It was as Oliver's mother had predicted. "It will be quite confusing if you call us both Lady Winfield." She smiled at her mother-in-law, who stood beside me, and I could see why Oliver had been friends with Hannah. She was warm and friendly and made me feel comfortable. "Now, let us get you inside."

Lord Jennings offered Hannah his arm and assisted her up the stairs to the door, and the elder Lady Winfield and I followed behind.

As soon as I stepped over the threshold, I sucked in a breath. With black-and-white marble floors, a sweeping grand staircase, and a vaulted ceiling so high I had to strain my neck to see the whole of it, the entryway was incredible.

And Oliver had grown up here.

It was no wonder that he'd initially been unimpressed by Winterset. The entire expanse of it could fit inside one wing of this house.

"Your home is lovely," I said.

"Thank you," Lord Jennings replied. "If you'll briefly excuse me, I'll go instruct Caldwell, our butler, to take your trunks to the . . ." He looked at his wife in question.

"The lilac room," Hannah supplied with a smile.

"The lilac room," Lord Jennings repeated, and he kissed Hannah's hand before parting.

Hannah watched him go with a look of love in her eyes, then turned back to me and Lady Winfield. "It'll be a few minutes before your trunks are brought up. Would you like us to give you a quick tour while we wait?"

"I would love that."

But before we even took one step, a woman appeared and curtsied in front of Hannah. "Pardon me for intruding, my lady, but you asked to be told when the girls awoke."

"They're awake already?" Hannah said, sounding surprised.

The woman nodded.

"Thank you, Betsy. I will be there as soon as I can."

Betsy curtsied and left.

"Allow me?" Lady Winfield asked.

"That would be wonderful," Hannah said. "Thank you."

Lady Winfield walked away, leaving Hannah and me to our tour.

On the ground level, Hannah pointed out the study, which was thrice the size of Winterset's; the dining hall, which boasted an impossibly long table; and a large ballroom, with a glittering chandelier in the center.

The most awe-inspiring room of all, though, was the gallery. From the vaulted glass ceiling that bathed the room in sunlight to the black-and-white marble checkered floor, I felt as though I'd stepped into one of the finest museums in all of England. The life-sized paintings of Lord Jennings's ancestors—*Oliver's* ancestors—were so vivid and lifelike that they seemed to jump off the canvas. I'd never seen paintings so stunning. How had the artist managed it?

"Your collection is impressive," I said.

"I think so too," Hannah said. "But my husband dislikes this room. He thinks the paintings are too grim and gruesome." Her gaze rose to a painting of a particularly bloody battle scene.

"Oh my." I held a hand to my mouth. "The artist really managed to capture the brutality of battle, didn't he?"

"Indeed he did." She giggled. "I assure you that not all the paintings are so graphic, especially not the contemporary ones. Let me show you our family portraits."

She led me to the opposite side of the gallery, and I marveled at the multitude of paintings.

"Here is Damon's and my wedding portrait," Hannah said proudly. "It was painted the same year we were married. Don't tell anyone, but I was carrying my daughters at the time, and I very much looked it." She smiled up at the portraits, clearly reliving a fond memory. "The girls' portraits will be painted when they are a few years older. And behind you is Ollie's portrait."

I'd not considered that his likeness might be hanging here, but of course it would be. He was the second son of the late Lord Winfield and brother to the current. This was his family seat.

I sucked in a breath when I saw the full-length rendering of him.

"Do you think it looks like him?" Hannah asked.

"I do." It was a near-perfect likeness. All that was missing was the small scar on his forehead.

"I think so too." Lord Jennings walked up behind us. "The artist captured Ollie's condescending gaze quite perfectly, don't you think? See the way he looks down his nose at me? It's as if he is standing right here in this room."

"Damon." Hannah frowned her disapproval.

To my surprise, he took his wife's censure in stride. "Forgive me, Miss Lockwood. I should not have said that." Then he added in a low voice, "Even if it *is* true."

Oliver? Condescending? I studied his portrait but could not see it. "Well, condescending gaze or no," I said, "*I* could not have painted his likeness half so well."

Hannah's eyes lit. "You are an artist?"

"*Aspiring* artist," I clarified. I'd carefully packed all the art supplies Oliver had given me in my traveling trunk and itched to use them again, if only to feel closer to him.

"I can't even draw a simple outline of a figure, much less paint a portrait." Hannah laughed at herself. "Consider me thoroughly impressed."

"Me too," Lord Jennings said.

"You would not be if you saw my most recent work," I said, thinking of my sketches in Oliver's books.

"I am sure you are a great deal better than you are giving yourself credit for. We women tend to be our own harshest critics, I think. You shouldn't sell yourself short, Miss Lockwood."

"Kate," I said. "If I am to call *you*, a countess, by your Christian name, it seems only right that you call me by mine."

"I would be honored."

"Your trunk should be in your room," Lord Jennings said. "Would you like to go upstairs now?"

"I would. Thank you," I said.

Lord Jennings and Hannah led the way.

At the gallery door, I glanced over my shoulder to steal one last look at Oliver's portrait.

We climbed the grand staircase to the first level.

"Summerhaven has two modern wings connected by a central original building," Lord Jennings explained. "However, only the west wing, which we now stand in, is in use."

Hannah pointed out several rooms: the morning room, the music room, and a parlor, and I peeked inside each as we passed. They were all empty, devoid of decoration and furnishings.

"You said this wing is in use?" I asked Hannah, thinking I might have misunderstood.

"Yes. You are wondering why they are all vacant?" she asked, and I nodded. "Suffice it to say, my husband sold every furnishing he could to marry me."

"A decision I do not regret in the slightest," Lord Jennings said over his shoulder.

"Selling your family furnishings or marrying me?" Hannah grinned at Lord Jennings.

"Selling the furnishings, my dear, obviously. They were all so *dreadfully* uncomfortable." He winked at his wife, and his teasing nature reminded me so much of Oliver that my heart squeezed for missing him.

"And this is your bedchamber." Hannah pushed open the door to reveal the aptly named lilac bedchamber. The walls were papered in a pale shade of purple. A four-post bed occupied the center of the room, and a mahogany vanity was positioned near the window. On the vanity was a vase of snowdrops. And through the window was the garden.

"Thank you," I said to my hosts. "Both for welcoming me into your home and for allowing me to stay in this beautiful room."

"What we have, we have to share," Lord Jennings said sincerely. "We hope you will feel welcome here, Miss Lockwood. Please stay as long as you need."

"Thank you, my lord."

He bowed and took his leave.

Hannah turned to me. "Dinner will be served at six," she said. "I would be happy to send my maid Nora to help you dress and style your hair if you'd like."

I hesitated. For two reasons: first, because it had been such a long time since someone had helped me with my hair, and I wasn't sure I could endure it. And second, because I wasn't sure it would be safe. The more people who knew about my being here, the more likely word was to spread. Servants had a tendency to talk, and I did not want word somehow getting back to Markham. It seemed impossible so far from him, but I didn't want to take any chances.

"I don't mean to overwhelm you," Hannah said, sensing my hesitancy.

"It's not that," I said. "It's only . . ." My sentence stretched as I tried to find the right words to voice my concern. "What if the servants talk?"

"We have told the servants that you are my cousin visiting from York." Hannah reached for my hand and led me to the edge of the bed to sit beside her. "I understand your fears. You have been through so much. But I promise you, you have nothing to fear here. When Damon received Oliver's letter asking for his help . . ." Her voice quivered. "You cannot know what it meant to him. He sprang into action immediately and has worked night and day to ensure your protection."

"I do not mean to be a burden."

"Oh no." Hannah shook her head. "You are not. On the contrary, you are an answer to our prayers. We have not seen nor heard from Oliver in over two years." A pained expression shadowed her face. "I regret the circumstance that has brought you to us, but you are not a burden, Kate. You are a blessing. You have started communication between the brothers again."

"I have done nothing," I said.

"But you have, Kate. More than you know." She squeezed my hand and stood.

"Thank you," I said, feeling more calm and confident after our conversation.

"I know we've just met," Hannah said, "but if it would make you feel more comfortable, I would be happy to help you dress for dinner and style your hair tonight. I won't claim to be as talented at it as my maid, but I *do* know something about taming curls."

Her kindness touched me. "I would like that very much. Thank you."

We moved to the vanity table. I sat, and Hannah stood behind me.

I could barely feel her fingers as they worked to remove the ribbon from the end of my hair, but my breaths came more quickly.

As if she could sense my anxiety, she offered me a kind smile in the mirror, then unwove my plait.

Once it was down, I handed her the hairbrush.

"You have beautiful hair," she said.

"Thank you."

She brushed my hair so softly it tickled. I'd forgotten how good it felt.

"There is something I would like to talk to you about," she said. "I do not want to overwhelm you any more than I already have, but I think if I were you, I would wish to know."

"All right."

"In a few days, Lord Jennings and I are hosting a ball. When we learned you were coming, we wanted to cancel it, but the invitations could not be recalled in time." She bit her lip as she began pinning up my hair. "We have many options, including hiding you here in your room out of sight. But it *is* a masked ball, so your identity would be hidden should you wish to attend."

"I want to," I said, surprising myself. I didn't want Markham to steal any more of my life than he already had. Even if that life would not be the one I wanted and wished for with Oliver, I would not let our sacrifice be for naught.

"I am so glad," Hannah said. "We will do everything to make sure you are safe and comfortable."

Perhaps it was foolish of me, but being so far from Winterset, I felt like I was living in something of a sanctuary at Summerhaven. I knew I should speak to Hannah about helping me find a placement so I could start my new life, but I was surprised by how unaccustomed I was to being near people. This ball might be the perfect opportunity to mingle with people and reacquaint myself with social niceties. And armed with a fake identity, a mask, and an army of protectors, I did not think my attendance was such a risk.

"I don't have anything to wear though," I admitted. The gowns from my come-out were more than two years out of fashion, not that that mattered much to me, but I didn't dare wear anything that anyone might recognize.

"I would suggest we have a ball gown made, but I do not think a week is enough time for our local modiste to make and fit such an elaborate dress . . ." Hannah continued pinning up my hair, deep in thought. "What would you think about borrowing one of my dresses? I believe you are near enough to the same size I was before carrying the twins. A few inches shorter than I, but we can easily have the dress hemmed."

"If it's not too much trouble . . ."

"No trouble at all! In fact, I think it will be great fun."

CHAPTER THIRTY-SEVEN

OLIVER

Four days after Kate left, I sat in my study, staring at a stack of paperwork. I'd hired a new solicitor to see to my estate, Mr. Wheldon, and he was insistent that I read and sign the papers.

Page after page, I fought for focus, but there was nothing for it. My thoughts constantly turned to Kate.

She should have arrived at Summerhaven by now. I wondered what she thought of it. It was so different from Winterset. Would she be overwhelmed by its opulence? What would she think of my family? I knew they would be kind to her, but what would they tell her about me?

There was a knock at the door, and Mrs. Owensby peeked inside. "I'm going to town now, sir. Do you want me to purchase anything specific for your meals this week? Perhaps some salmon?"

I hated the thought of sitting down to another meal alone. "Whatever you prefer, Mrs. Owensby." I did not care. I had no appetite.

With a nod, she closed the study door, leaving me alone again.

There had been many times in my life when I'd felt alone—growing up at Summerhaven, within my own family, studying at Eton, traveling on my Grand Tour—but I'd never been this *lonely*.

Sighing, I pushed aside the paperwork and tried to outpace my problems. Back and forth, I walked the length of the room, but it was a fool's errand; my problems were too big, and my study was too small.

I walked to the entry hall, but the change of space did nothing to lift my mood. Without Kate, the manor felt more like a mausoleum, the halls hollow, the house lifeless.

Perhaps I needed some fresh air. Outside, though, the day was dark and dreary, so I returned to my study.

I'd failed to keep Kate safe here, but at least I could care for her home. That was how I thought of Winterset: *her* home. So long as I lived here, her ghost would haunt me, reminding me of how I was the reason she'd had to leave.

Mrs. Owensby had said to give it time and I would feel better, but no amount of time could fill Kate's void.

I slumped back into my seat. If only Markham had not seen the letter I'd written to Kate, then . . . What? She would still be hiding here?

As much as I missed her, I would sacrifice my desire to be with her a thousand times over if it meant she would be free to live a more fulfilled life.

Missing her, I went to the library, retrieved one of my books that she'd used as a sketchbook, and brought it back to my study. Sitting at my desk again, I opened the first page. The book was filled with sketches of flowers—every one lovely.

As I flipped through the pages, a flattened daisy fell out.

Picking it up, I rolled the stem between my fingers, twirling the flower. There was a bend in the stem. Why had she saved it? Perhaps she'd drawn the daisy.

She had.

It was a simple sketch but beautiful.

Kate was so talented. When she was safely settled in her new life, wherever that might be, I hoped she would continue to create.

I lowered the daisy to the page, then stopped. It was too lovely to be locked between the pages of a book, so I placed it in the empty inkwell. Every time I looked at it, I would think of her.

I glanced at the timepiece on the mantel.

Only a few minutes had passed since the last time I'd looked. Time passed so slowly without her, every second excruciating. How had Kate passed the time here alone for two years? It had been only four days since she'd left, and I was already mad for missing her.

I thought back to our last conversation.

She'd said so many wonderful things about me. I hoped she would remember me that way, but I worried Damon might say something to shadow her feelings for me.

Kate had said that based on what she'd read in Damon's letter, she thought he loved and missed me. What had given her that impression?

I could not think of a single reason he might write something remotely positive about me.

Our relationship had not been good since he'd gone away to Eton, and I'd been but a boy then. As we'd grown, his derision had been so painful. He'd not even sat at the pianoforte with me anymore. I wasn't sure what I'd done to deserve his hatred, but he *had* hated me.

And then after university, he'd become so much like Father. So superior. He'd looked down his nose at everything and everyone, including me.

There was a short time, the summer he'd courted Hannah, that he'd tried to mend our relationship. But even then, it had been obvious he had not liked me.

What had he written?

I opened my top desk drawer and stared down at the stack of unopened letters. I didn't know why I'd kept them all this time, carrying them from France to Italy and then all the way back here.

I ran my hands over the papers. Which one had Kate read?

I pulled out the one nearest the front of the desk. The seal had been broken. This one, then. Before I could think better of it, I unfolded the missive, smoothed it on my desk, and skimmed the message.

> *Oliver,*
>
> *It has been three weeks since I stood on the steps of Summerhaven and watched you leave on your Grand Tour. How I longed to run after you that day, to convince you to stay.*

I skipped down.

> *Father died a few days after your departure. . . . You missed his funeral. . . . We wanted you there. We needed you. . . . Come home, Ollie. We miss you terribly.*
> *Your brother, first and forever.*
>
> *xDamon*

A lump formed in my throat, and I set the letter aside. Father was dead. I had assumed he was. Even before I'd left I'd known he didn't have much time remaining. But reading confirmation brought fresh pain. My whole life, he'd been callous to me. But he was still my father, and I had always wished that one day we'd be reconciled, that he would finally see and love me. Now it was too late.

Honestly, though, what did it matter?

I glanced at Damon's salutation again and wondered whether his emotions were born more from my leaving or from Father's funeral. I couldn't tell.

Curious, I plucked the next letter out of the drawer.

> *Ollie,*
>
> *Charlie wrote that you have arrived in Paris. He says you are safe but doing no better than you were during your lowest days in London. . . . Come home.*

Charlie. The traitor. I scowled at the letter and set it aside.

> *Ollie,*
>
> *Did you leave because you are upset that I married Hannah? After reading my letter to her, I thought you understood. You seemed so supportive of our union. But I can't help but wonder if that is why you have been away so long. I beg you not to be angry. Hannah is my whole heart. I am sorry for hurting you, for forgetting you. I swear I will never let it happen again. Come home.*

> *Ollie,*
>
> *It has been two months. I know you do not like me, and I understand why. I designed it that way, after all. But I have to believe that if you understood why I distanced myself from you, you would have more compassion and desire to make amends. Come home.*

> *Ollie,*
>
> *Hannah is with child. She would be mortified that I wrote that in a missive, but you are my brother, and I want you to know. It is my greatest fear that I will become like Father. I need you here to tell me when I am being woolheaded. No one else will set me straight like you would. Come home.*

Ollie,

If he were alive, Father would whip my back until it bled for saying this, but I enjoy working in the stables. The stablehands don't know what to make of me. An earl who mucks stalls? Unspeakable! I told them if King George could farm, I could clean a stable. You would likely side with the stablehands. But I love it, Ollie. I love working with my hands. I wish you could see what I've done to our family seat. Come home.

I had the sudden desire to tell him all about working on Winterset with Kate. About the papers we'd hung and the drive I'd cleared. I was so proud of what we'd accomplished. I wished he could see it.

Ollie,

It has been six months. Charlie wrote to tell me that you don't read my letters. I don't care. I will keep writing to you until the day I die. I will not forget you again, brother. Come home.

Ollie,

Hannah is due any day. I'm so scared, Ollie. I don't think I could survive if something were to happen to her. Soon, I'll have a son or a daughter—perhaps both. And you won't even know. The thought breaks my heart. Come home.

Ollie,

Summerhaven Stables is a success. A slow success but a success nonetheless. I wish you were here to share it with me. Be done with this self-imposed exile, brother. Come home.

Ollie,

I'm a father. And you are an uncle. I wanted you to know. I won't write anything more than that, though, because I want you to come home and see for yourself. Come home.

Ollie,

It's been one year since you left. I convinced myself that you would return to Summerhaven today. I don't know why. I sat up all night in my study, waiting for you to walk in the door. Obviously, you didn't. I tried to hide my disappointment from Hannah, but she knew. She always knows. I cannot hide anything from my wife. It is a wonderful feeling to be known so well by someone. But it made me realize that one day, you will marry, and I won't even know. Perhaps you already have. The thought guts me. Come home.

Ollie,

Charlie writes that you've moved to Italy. That you are doing better there. I'm glad. But, Ollie, you should be here. If you were here, we could ride the hills together every day, just as we did when we were boys. I miss those times, Ollie. I miss sitting with you at the pianoforte. I miss skipping stones across the river. Do you? Come home.

Ollie,

I want to tell you why I distanced myself from you when we were boys. I want to explain why I maintained that distance for so long. I want you to understand why I gave you the cut direct when we were at Eton and why I stopped sitting with you at the pianoforte. But I don't want to write it in a letter. I want to talk to you face-to-face. I want to look you in the eye. I want to beg for your forgiveness. And I want to wrap my arms around you and tell you how much I love you. How much you are needed and wanted in this family. I want you to know more than anything that you belong. Please, I am begging you. Come home.

Ollie,

It's been two years. I still have not formally accepted my title. I don't know that I ever will. How could I accept a title that has caused us both so much pain? Come home.

In every letter, he'd written *Come home*. Did he mean it? He'd told me he hadn't forgotten me, and after reading all his letters, I wondered if it could be true. I wanted it to be. There were so many things I wanted to speak with him about. I wanted to hear more about the stables and Father's funeral and my niece or nephew. I wanted to tell him things too. About my Grand Tour and Winterset and especially Kate.

I'd see him soon, I hoped. And maybe we could talk. I wondered if time and distance had caused too much of a rift for us to overcome. There was no way of knowing, not until I returned to Summerhaven. And I couldn't go yet, for Kate's sake. I wouldn't risk leading Markham to her.

There was one more thing I realized, though, reading Damon's letters. Although he'd repeatedly beseeched me to *come home*, Summerhaven was not my home.

It had felt like home when I was a boy: sitting at the pianoforte with Damon, running through the garden hedgerows with Hannah, and learning how to read with Mother. Even though Summerhaven might be my family seat, it had not felt like home for a long time.

I'd lived in many places, but none of them had been home to me. Even Winterset, which was the closest to it, hadn't felt the same since Kate had left.

What was home anyway?

I'd always known that one day I would live at Winterset. As I'd worked with Kate to repair it, it had begun to feel like a home. I'd mistakenly thought the repairs and improvements were what had made my feelings change. Then Kate had left, and now it felt like nothing more than a foundation and empty walls.

The place where I'd had a purpose, a place where I'd felt needed, loved, and like I belonged, had reverted back to being a building void of sentiment.

My whole life, I had been looking for home, not realizing it wasn't merely the place one lived. As I sat in my study, I realized . . . Winterset wasn't my home. Without Kate, it would never be more than an empty house.

I suddenly understood. I finally knew what Damon had known all along: home was not a place but the people you loved.

Kate was my home.

That was why it hurt so much being separated from her.

But what if we didn't have to live at Winterset?

My heart raced with the realization.

When my brother had been willing to give up Summerhaven for Hannah, I'd thought him mad. I'd thought he'd been bartering our family's future for a feeling.

I understood now why he'd been willing to risk Summerhaven. It was because it was just a house.

I didn't need a house or wealth or a title to be happy. In fact, it was my *lack* of a title and entailment on my estate that was my greatest asset. Unlike Damon, who was legally bound to keep Summerhaven, as second son, I wasn't limited by such strict rules.

Winterset was not entailed. I could sell the estate, and then Kate and I could start a new life wherever we wanted. We could move to the other side of the world if we desired, and Markham would never find us.

It seemed so obvious now.

I stood, eager to begin preparations to sell this house and begin my new life. My new solicitor would think me mad. I'd just hired him to help me get my estate in order, and now I wanted to sell it. But I didn't care what he thought of me.

I stepped into the entrance hall, and the front door swung open.

It was Mrs. Owensby.

A glance at her face told me something was terribly wrong.

"Mr. Jennings." She gasped for breath. She must have run all the way from the village. "It's Lord Markham," she began. "He's gone."

My pulse picked up. "Gone where?"

"His servant said he had business that he *needed to put an end to* in the south country."

Kate.

"When did he leave?" I demanded.

"Four days ago."

The day Kate had left for Summerhaven. He knew.

Our plan to protect her, the guise with which we'd whisked her away to safety, had not fooled him.

I had to get to Summerhaven.

I had to get to Kate.

CHAPTER THIRTY-EIGHT

Kate

THE MORNING OF THE MASKED ball, the modiste delivered Hannah's newly hemmed ball gown for me to wear. After changing into the lovely light-blue gown, I stood before the mirror and admired my reflection. I couldn't help it. Made of the softest silk and daintily decorated with glass beads, the dress was the most beautiful gown I'd ever worn. My only regret was that Oliver was not here to see me wear it.

"I knew it would fit you!" Hannah beamed at my reflection. "What do you think?"

"I think I've never worn anything so beautiful as this dress." Hannah was right. It fit me perfectly. Almost like it had been made for me.

"You look stunning," she said. "You will have your choice of dance partners tonight."

Her words were meant to excite me but had the opposite effect. I did not wish to dance with anyone but Oliver.

"Or . . . perhaps you do not like to dance?" she said.

"I enjoy dancing very much. It's only . . ."

"If you are nervous about remembering the steps," Hannah said when my sentence stalled, "I have dance cards. We could practice before tonight."

"You're kind to offer, but I had quite an exacting dance tutor. I doubt I could forget the forms even if I wanted to."

"You are lucky. I once went to a ball and could not remember the steps to a quadrille. Damon was the only reason I got through the dance without thoroughly embarrassing myself." She smiled to herself as if reliving a pleasant memory.

I fidgeted with the fingers of my gloves, unused to wearing them.

"Do you feel unsafe?" Hannah asked.

"I feel safe," I said, and I did. Charlie and my hosts had been most diligent in protecting me. "Especially since I will be wearing a mask tonight. It's only . . ." How much should I say? I knew only the smallest sliver of her history with Oliver. "I do not know if I will wish to dance with anyone."

"Oh," she said, suddenly serious. "I must apologize. After what you've been through, of course you wouldn't want to—"

"I don't want to dance with anyone who will be in attendance," I clarified.

"Oh. *Oh!*" Her eyes lit with understanding. "You do not wish to dance with anyone tonight because you wish only to dance with Oliver."

My face warmed. "It's silly, I know. We knew each other for only a short time."

Hannah shook her head. "Oliver is easy to love. I should know, seeing as I spent half my life in love with him."

Love. Oliver hadn't told me they'd been in love. Hannah was a lovely person, though, as pretty to look upon as she was kind. I could understand why he'd felt that way toward her, even if I didn't want to think about it. "He mentioned you were friends growing up," I hedged, hoping she might say more.

"We were," she said. "Close friends. So close that I thought we would marry someday."

I'd seen firsthand how happily married she was to Lord Jennings. Her words had not been said to inspire jealousy, but there was a whole history between the three of them that I did not know, and I could not help feeling envious. "Oh," I said, surprised.

"But our feelings never aligned. When Ollie proposed—"

"Oliver asked you to *marry* him?" The jealousy sprang up inside me like a sudden storm. He'd proposed *marriage*? He'd never said. He'd never even hinted.

"He did ask," Hannah said slowly, taking in my shock. "But he did not love me, at least not as anything more than a friend. I think he knew it even then but felt that marrying me was his duty."

I furrowed my brow. "How was it you came to marry Lord Jennings?"

"That story is long enough to fill a book." She smiled. "Damon is the match of my heart; he always was. It simply took me a while to see him.

My only regret is that my decision to marry Damon deepened the division that already existed between the brothers." She worried her lower lip. "I've upset you," she said. "I am sorry. I thought you knew."

"You have no need to apologize. You did nothing wrong. There is just so much I don't know about Oliver. So much I will never know." I would likely never even see him again. The sooner I accepted that, the happier I might be.

"I wish there were something more I could do to change your circumstances."

"You already are doing so much. You've taken me into your home and are helping me find a new place to live. I am so grateful to you and Lord Jennings. I just miss Oliver terribly."

Hannah set her hand on my shoulder. "Sometimes, things have a way of working out."

"And sometimes, at least in my case, they don't."

A knock came at the door. It was Lady Winfield, and she was holding both babies, one on each hip. "Oh, Kate. You look so beautiful."

"Thank you, my lady."

"Hannah," she said. "Would you like to look over the ballroom with me one last time to ensure everything is prepared before the guests arrive?"

"I would," Hannah said. "Will you excuse me, Kate? I'll be right back, and then we can style your hair."

"Of course," I said, and they excused themselves.

Alone, I sat at my vanity table and took a deep breath. So much had changed in such a short time. Most of it, for the better. But, oh, how I missed Oliver!

CHAPTER THIRTY-NINE

Oliver

After two torturous days, Summerhaven finally came into view. One more hill was all that stood between me and Kate.

I kicked my horse's flanks, and he sprang forward. "Faster, boy! Faster!"

The horse ran at a feverish pace, but it was not fast enough. I needed to see Kate *now*, to know that she was here and unharmed.

I'd prayed for her safety my whole journey, but what if—No. I would not allow myself to even think it.

I cursed the hill, the long drive, the steps, the locked door, all keeping me from Kate.

I pounded on the door. I pounded so hard my hands hurt.

Only seconds passed, but it felt an eternity before the butler appeared. Caldwell. I'd known him my whole life.

"Master Oliver." He blinked at me in surprise but quickly recovered. "Welcome home," he greeted.

"Thank you, Caldwell," I said as I hurried inside.

"Is she here?" I said, looking for some sign of her.

"Lady Winfie—"

"Kate. Where is Miss Lockwood?"

Caldwell opened his mouth as if to answer, but it was not his voice I heard but Damon's. "Ollie?"

I swung around to see Damon. He stood on the threshold of Father's study—Damon's study now, I supposed—wearing a shocked expression. "Ollie?"

"Where is she?" I said. "Where is Kate?"

Damon rushed to where I stood. "Upstairs. Getting ready for the masquerade ball tonight."

"She's safe?" I said. "You're sure?"

Damon nodded. "She's safe, Ollie. I swear it. We've watched over her night and day. She's here, and she's safe."

Feeling like my legs might entirely give out with relief, I bent over, resting my hands on my knees. My breaths came in quick succession, and when I stood again, I swayed.

Damon wrapped his arms around me, holding me steady in a hug. "I thought I would never see you again," he said, stepping back slightly but keeping his hands on my shoulders. "I cannot believe you are here, brother. I am so glad." His eyes studied me, then his gaze grew concerned. "Has something happened?"

"He knows," I said. "Markham's servant told my housekeeper that he's come to the southern part of the country to *put an end to something*. I thought that meant . . . I thought—" I choked on my words.

"You thought he meant to harm Kate," Damon said.

I nodded. "I need to see her."

"Of course," Damon said, then eyed me from hatless head to mud-encrusted boots. "But first, may I suggest you bathe? Put on a clean pair of clothes. Style your hair."

Glaring at him, I shrugged his hand off my shoulder. "I've ridden for two days straight, stopping only to switch out my horse for fear that I would get here too late. So help me, if you stand in my way the last few feet—"

"I have no intention of standing in your way." Damon sighed. "But you stink, little brother."

It was at that moment that the ballroom door opened. Mother and Hannah stepped into the entrance hall, speaking about something I could not hear and smiling. They each held a baby on their hips. Two little girls, one had dark, straight hair; the other had golden curls.

Mother looked my way first. "Ollie?"

Hannah's gaze snapped up to mine, and her smile grew. "Ollie!"

They sped to where Damon and I stood. The curly-haired baby that Mother held reached for Damon. He took his daughter in his arms even as Mother embraced me. She held me for a long time, her shoulders shaking with silent tears. "I'm so glad you've finally come home," she said. "You cannot know how much I've missed you."

"We all have," Hannah said.

The baby Damon held started to wiggle, clearly wanting to be put down. He gently bounced her, and Hannah did the same with the little girl she was holding.

Seeing them like this, as parents, as a family, was sobering. I'd missed so much, moments I could never get back.

"Ollie," Damon said in an animated tone. "Allow me to introduce you to your nieces. Hannah is holding Anne. We named her after Hannah's mother. And this precious girl"—Damon smiled down at his daughter and then looked at me—"is Olivia. After you."

My chest tightened. It felt like my heart had grown twice its size in seconds and suddenly did not fit inside me. I stepped closer to Damon and looked down at my namesake.

"She's beautiful," I said. "They both are."

Hannah's eyes welled with tears. "I've turned into such a watering pot since they were born." She fanned her face, and her nose slowly scrunched in disgust. "What is that smell?" She sniffed both babies' bottoms to see if either had soiled themselves.

"*That*, my dear, is Ollie," Damon said. "I tried to tell him that he must bathe before seeing Kate, but—" He cut off his sentence with a shrug.

"*But* I'm going to see Kate first," I said. "Where is she?"

Hannah gave me a knowing smile. "She's upstairs getting ready for the masquerade ball."

"As I said." Damon huffed.

"But Damon *is* right. Before you see Kate, you need to bathe. She will be happy to see you," Hannah said, then her brow furrowed. "Well, not *entirely* happy. You should have warned me in your letter that you didn't tell her our history. She was bothered when I told her you proposed marriage to me."

"How did *that* come up?" I said.

"Yes, dear. How *did* that come up?" Damon raised an eyebrow at Hannah, and Mother chuckled softly.

"Never mind that." Hannah brushed off the question. "We must get you ready so that when Kate sees you tonight, she will think you so handsome that she will forget all about it."

"You mean when she sees me *now*," I corrected.

"No, I mean tonight, after you've taken a bath. Besides, she isn't ready to see you yet either. I still need to fix her hair."

I stilled. "Kate lets you touch her hair?"

Hannah gave me a sad smile, as if she understood the significance. "She does, Ollie."

More than anything else they'd said to placate me, this brought peace. Kate felt safe enough here to have someone else style her hair.

A weight lifted from my shoulders. I had no idea where Markham was, but Kate was safe, and I planned to keep it that way.

"So . . ." Hannah said. "You will have a bath and get ready for the ball, which I'm vexed that you never responded to the invitation, but I will forgive you because we are short of men, and I need you to partner young ladies. I don't suppose you've brought proper attire? A mask?"

I raised my arms to show her everything I'd brought.

"I thought not," she said. "Well, I suppose you will have to wear something of Damon's, then."

"My shoulders are broader than his," I said.

Damon rolled his eyes. "And I am an inch taller."

Mother sighed. "Really, the pair of you."

Hannah groaned. "Well, you can't wear what you have on, and seeing how you have nothing else, you will have to make it work, won't you? Now, go and get ready. I must finish Kate's hair. The ball starts soon, and I want you to be waiting right here when she descends these stairs."

CHAPTER FORTY

KATE

"Oh, Kate." Hannah beamed at me in the mirror. "You look so beautiful."

I turned my head to look at my hair in the mirror. Hannah had styled my curls into a coiffure, and I loved the pearls she'd pinned in. "Is it vain to say I *feel* beautiful?"

"No, not at all. In fact, I am glad you do because I have a surprise for you."

"I am already so deeply in your debt; I could not possibly accept anything more."

"Yes, you can." Hannah smiled. "Trust me, you want to." She held out her hand to me. "Come on, he is waiting."

I did not think Lord Jennings had seemed especially impatient, but Hannah pulled me from my seat with such determination that I thought he might not like to be kept waiting.

We moved down the corridor, closer and closer to the grand staircase, and my stomach fluttered with fear, and my hands shook. It had been two years since I'd attended any social event, and although I wanted to be here tonight, my anticipation bordered on anxiety.

Voices drifted up the stairs from the entrance hall below. Sometimes, Lord Jennings sounded so much like Oliver—his tone, cadence, and pronunciation—that it hurt to hear his voice.

Hannah stopped at the end of the corridor and took my hand. "You are shaking like a leaf caught in the wind."

"I am a bit nervous to be attending a ball," I admitted.

"Would it surprise you to know I am nervous to host one?"

"Truly? You seem so calm."

"I paced my room all morning," she confessed. "I checked the girls for fever about fifty times, thinking I might find some excuse to bow out."

"You didn't."

"I did," she said, and we shared a laugh. "Kate, I believe tonight will be an enjoyable experience for us both, but if it isn't, we will use the twins as an excuse to leave early and retire upstairs. Is that agreeable to you?"

I nodded.

"All right, then." Hannah squeezed my hand. "It is time. I will go first, and then you follow."

"Could we not descend the stairs together?" I asked.

"Not tonight," Hannah smiled. "I want to see your face when you lay eyes on your surprise. So, count to thirty, and then come down."

I opened my mouth to tell her I was terrified that I might tumble down the stairs without her to hold on to, but she dashed away before I could. I counted to thirty to give Hannah time to descend the stairs and then again, trying to calm myself. But there was nothing for it; I was a bundle of nerves and would be until the night was over.

Ever so slowly, I made my way to the grand staircase. At the top, I smoothed my dress, straightened my gloves, and gripped the railing. I kept my gaze down as I descended, fearing that if I looked up, I might lose my footing and fall.

Halfway down, when I felt sure of my footing, I finally looked up.

My breath caught.

Oliver.

Standing in the middle of the room, set apart from the others, seemingly conjured here from one of my dreams. *Was* I dreaming?

I blinked, and he didn't disappear.

I drank in the sight of him. Oliver was devilishly dashing, dressed in buff breeches, a dark coat, and a crisply tied cravat.

His head tilted slightly to one side, mouth set in a slanted smile, as if my shock at seeing him were somehow amusing. He strode across the floor and took the stairs two at a time until he stood before me. His eyes, so blue, bluer than I remembered, searched my face.

"Are you really here?" I finally managed.

"I'm really here," he murmured.

I wanted to throw my arms around his shoulders and bury my face in his neck. And then I realized that if he was here with me, it meant he was not at Winterset, where he should be. "How are you—? *Why* are you—?"

"I had to see that you made it safely here and were all right. Are you?"

I wanted to answer. I *tried* to answer. But seeing him here when I'd thought I would never see him again, was too much to make sense of. I could only nod.

"Would it be too soon to ask you for your first set?" he said.

"Not too soon. It's yours. And my supper set, too, if you want it."

"I want *all* your dances, Kate, but tonight, I shall try to be satisfied with just the two."

My stomach swooped at his words, and I clutched the railing to steady myself.

Oliver offered me his arm, and I relished his nearness as he helped me descend the remaining stairs and walk to where Hannah and Lord Jennings waited in the entrance hall.

"I *told* you that you would want your surprise," Hannah whispered in my ear, and then to the group, "Here are your masks." Mine was made of heavily starched black lace and was decorated with glass beads. Oliver's mask was also black but was made of satin and had no embellishments. "Hurry and put them on. The guests will be here any moment," Hannah said.

Oliver held up his mask to me. "Help me?"

I nodded, and he turned to allow me to tie it. I took my time, enjoying the feel of my hands in his soft hair. When I was finished, he turned to face me, and I held up my mask. "Will you tie mine?"

"Do you want me to?" He glanced at my hair. "I understand if you would rather have Hannah—"

"You," I said and turned so that he might tie it.

I felt his warmth first as he stepped close and then a tickle of touch as he took the strings. His fingers were careful, too careful to be tying a proper bow. I understood why, considering how I'd reacted when he'd playfully pulled my plait that evening over cards. But so much had changed since then. I longed to feel his fingers in my hair.

I reached behind me and guided his hands into my hair.

Oliver inhaled sharply, his hands stilled for a second, then they resumed tying. When he was finished, he lightly trailed his fingers down the side of my face, touching a tendril near my temple. The sensation sent a wave of warmth down my neck that spread throughout my body.

"You look so lovely tonight, Kate," Oliver whispered in my ear. And then he straightened and stepped back.

Beside us, Hannah smiled up at her husband. I would not have noticed her nervousness had she not said anything, but I saw it now.

Lord Jennings wrapped his arm around her waist in reassurance.

A knock came at the door, and my heart jumped.

"That should be Lady Margaret or the Athertons. Our dearest friends," Hannah said. "I asked them to arrive early, thinking you might be more comfortable surrounded by a group of friendly faces."

I smiled, grateful. "I'm sure I will be."

"I've briefly told them your story so that they, too, might make you feel more comfortable," Hannah said.

"I am grateful. Thank you."

Lord Jennings nodded to the butler to open the door.

The Athertons were the first to arrive. As soon as they walked in the door and saw Oliver, they went straight to him, eager to welcome him home. After, Lord Jennings introduced me to Miss Atherton, who insisted I call her Amelia, and her brother, Lord Atherton, or Frederick, as he demanded everyone call him. With their fiery red hair and personalities to match, I liked them both immediately.

Lady Margaret arrived shortly after. She looked every bit the daughter of a duke and had the manners to match her station, but she was kind and warm and gracious, and I could not have liked her more.

Lord Jennings and Hannah led our small company into the impressive ballroom, and I held tight to Oliver's arm. Candlelight flickered in the full-length mirrors that covered the windows and bathed the room in light. We claimed a quiet corner.

As hosts, Lord Jennings and Hannah stood at the ballroom door to greet their guests as they arrived.

The room quickly filled with people, noise, and heat.

Someone appeared at Oliver's side, a gentleman, to pull him away. Oliver hesitated, glancing at me, and I motioned that he should go. He moved only a few paces away but stood within sight. I stayed with Amelia, Lady Margaret, and Frederick. They chatted as only old friends could, but somehow, they still made me feel seen, heard, and important.

I watched Oliver talk to the gentleman and a few other people. Friends, I realized, from their shared smiles. Oliver moved effortlessly, fluidly, from one person to the next, all eager to hear of his Grand Tour. He talked and teased, then turned to the next person waiting for his attention and did it all again.

It was mesmerizing.

He seemed so confident, so carefree.

I could not look away.

Lady Margaret, who stood beside me, followed my gaze. "Mr. Jennings is handsome, is he not?"

My cheeks warmed, and I was glad I wore a mask to hide it. "He does look quite dashing," I agreed, then added, "I daresay he knows it."

"I daresay he does." Lady Margaret grinned. "But perhaps his confidence is part of his charm."

Perhaps it was. The self-possessed way in which he carried himself was undeniably attractive. I just did not like that I was not the only one to appreciate his fine qualities.

Finally, the first set was announced, and Oliver came to claim his dance.

I could hardly believe we were standing in this crowded ballroom together, taking our places across from one another. The first dance was a reel, and we had but a moment alone to talk, with all the turning. We managed a few well-timed touches, but that was all.

The second dance was a country dance. We stood in two lines, women on one side and men on the other. When the music began, Oliver bowed, and I curtsied. We danced only a few forms together, but he was an excellent dancer. He executed everything perfectly and even seemed to enjoy it. I suspected that might be because he'd had many opportunities to dance and with whatever woman he desired.

Women were always watching him. Did he feel their stolen stares? Did he enjoy their attention?

Then it was time to move down the line and dance with the next man. Frederick. He was also a graceful dancer, though he did not seem to enjoy it. Poor fellow.

And down the line I went, moving farther and farther from Oliver.

Finally, I reached the end of the line. I curtsied to my last partner, and the stranger stiffly bowed. I felt his eyes upon me, hot as a brand. He did not say or do anything untoward, but I was so unaccustomed to the attention of men that I felt uncomfortable.

After we executed our last forms together, I was glad to resume my original position across from Oliver. Standing with him, I felt safe and serene again.

When the dance was over, Oliver offered me his arm and led me back to our group.

Amelia's brother, Frederick, asked for my next set. He was a proficient partner and an excellent conversationalist, but my gaze kept drifting to Oliver, who was dancing with Amelia. They seemed to converse continuously. They had an easy rapport, so I thought they must know each other quite well.

After their set, Oliver returned her to our circle and stood beside me. Too soon, though, the next set was announced. I didn't wish to dance with any other men, but Oliver continued dancing with other women. He was doing his duty as a gentleman, and as a favor to Hannah, but I still did not like watching it. Now, for a waltz, he partnered with a blonde-haired woman who had a petite figure and low-cut dress.

Amelia and Lady Margaret shared an annoyed look across our small circle.

"I do hate seeing Miss Digby claw at Oliver," Amelia said.

Frederick sighed theatrically. "Well, had you accepted his proposal, you would not have to."

I stiffened. Oliver had proposed to Amelia too?

Amelia took notice of my discomfort; everyone in our group did.

"You know that it was more of a *business* proposal," Amelia said to her brother, but it was obvious her words were meant for me.

I blew out a breath. First, he'd proposed to Hannah, then later to Amelia. "Is there anyone Oliver has *not* proposed to?"

Amelia winced. "Well . . . he has not proposed to Miss Digby."

"Not *yet*," Frederick said. "But the night is still young."

I liked Frederick's teasing tone nearly as much as his foppish fashion, but it was not enough to distract me from watching Oliver *waltz* with this Digby woman.

"You don't think he would marry her, do you?" Lady Margaret said.

"She would like nothing better," Amelia said. "But no matter how large her dowry, I don't think he would make the mistake of courting her again."

"He courted her too?" Was Oliver something of a rake?

I felt faint. No. I felt like I was seeing Oliver's future play out in front of me. One day, he would marry. He would take a woman to wife, a woman who was not me.

I looked around the room for Hannah. By some miracle, I caught her eye, and she must have seen my distress, because she excused herself from her current conversation and came to me.

"Is there somewhere quiet I can sit? I need a moment."

Hannah glanced to where Oliver was dancing with Miss Digby and frowned. "That woman." She took hold of my hand and led me from the ballroom. But the entrance hall was nearly as crowded as the ballroom, so we continued toward the library.

As soon as we stepped inside, Hannah shut the door, and I removed my mask and placed it on a settee. Without the cloth on my face, I felt like I could breathe again. The air was much cooler, and silence surrounded us.

"You mustn't let Miss Digby disturb you," Hannah soothed. "I know how irksome she is, believe me I do, but I've known Oliver my whole life, and he has *never* looked at anyone the way he looks at you."

"If only that were enough."

Hannah gave me a sad smile.

The library doors burst open, and Oliver walked swiftly inside. He looked frantic.

"Are you all right?" He rushed to where I stood, removing his mask and stuffing it in his coat pocket.

Hannah quietly excused herself and closed the door behind her.

"I am fine, thank you."

His brow furrowed. "What have I done? Tell me so I can correct it at once."

"You have done nothing wrong," I said.

"That cannot be true, else you would not be hiding here in this room and scowling at me."

"I am not scowling."

"You are." He raised his hand to my forehead and smoothed the skin between my brows.

I turned away from his touch.

"Kate." He stepped to the side and ducked to meet my eyes. "Talk to me."

I snapped my gaze back to his, and he reared back in surprise. "Do you really want to know what is wrong?"

"I do, very much."

"You have proposed to two women, Oliver. *Two*."

"And yet I remain unmarried." He gave me a small smile.

"For now. But I suspect someday, someday *soon* if Miss Digby has any say, you will ask a third and—"

Oliver's mouth lifted into a small smile. "You are jealous."

"No," I said in a clipped tone. Then realizing I had no reason not to tell him the truth—I still had to find another situation, and he still had to return to Winterset—I said, "Well, *yes*, if you must know." I was so incredibly jealous, my stomach hurt.

"You have no reason to be," Oliver said, stepping closer.

"Trust me, I do. You don't see the way young ladies stare at you."

"Kate," Oliver said. "It doesn't matter if young ladies look at me. *I* am only looking at you." He set his hand on my waist and drew me near. "Since the day I first stepped foot into Winterset and saw your portrait, I have seen no other woman but you. Even when I didn't know you were alive, I couldn't get you out of my head. No other woman that I have met, or that I will ever meet, will consume my thoughts the way you do. So no, you have no reason to be jealous."

Perhaps not tonight or even next week. But someday he would find another woman to consume his thoughts. A woman who wasn't hunted by a man with murderous intent. Oliver would propose to her and take her home to Winterset. My heart broke anew at the thought of it. "No matter how you may feel for me, circumstance prevents us from being together."

"I thought so too. But I was wrong." He took my hands in his. "I am in love with you, Kate."

"You love me?"

"To the point of madness," he murmured.

"I love you too," I whispered. "More than you could ever possibly know. That's why this is so difficult." I saw the love in his eyes, and it made what I had to say next nearly impossible. But I had to, for his sake. "No matter our feelings, we can never be together. I can't lose you the way I lost Father." I waited for him to release my hands and step away, but he only drew me closer.

"You won't lose me, Kate. So long as we are together, we can survive anything."

"What about Winterset?" I said, voicing another obstacle. "I can't live there, and you can't give it up."

"I can, actually. Winterset is not entailed. It is mine to do with it what I will. And *I* will to sell it. I do not need a house or wealth to be happy. I need only you."

I felt the truth of his words, how much he loved me, how willing he was to give up everything so that we could be together. But . . . "I cannot ask you to sacrifice so much to be with me."

"You *aren't* asking me. I am *telling* you; I will not live in that house another day without you. I choose you, Kate. Above all else. Since the day I watched the carriage carry you away, I have been in agony," he said. "Sending you away was the hardest thing I have ever done, and I do not wish to be separated from you again. Run away with me tonight, and let's start a new life together."

"You don't know what it's like to live in hiding, to always have to be looking over your shoulder."

"I don't know what that feels like," he said. "But I do know what it feels like to be separated from you. I know how it feels to wonder where you are and to worry about whether you are safe, and I cannot endure it another day. Please don't ask me to."

"Where would we live?" I asked. I could not imagine how a life together was possible.

"Wherever you like. Paris perhaps? The whole city is a work of art. You would love it there. Imagine it: walking on the cobbled stone streets along the River Seine, exploring art museums and gilded palaces and flowering gardens."

Over the last two years, I had tried so hard *not* to imagine life outside the safety of Winterset, but as we stood there in the library, I could see it so vividly: sitting in an expansive garden and painting Oliver's portrait. I could feel the soft breeze in my hair, the sun on my cheeks. "It is a lovely dream," I said.

"It does not have to be a dream. It can be our plan. If we left right now, we could board a boat, and the captain could marry us before we docked. We could be walking in Paris together as man and wife by tomorrow night." Oliver lowered onto one knee. "Marry me, Kate."

I looked into his eyes and saw his determination. He wasn't offering his love in passing. This was his life, his heart, laid bare before me. How could I deny him, deny myself, the chance to finally be happy? I couldn't. I must cast my fear of Markham aside and have faith in my future with Oliver.

"Yes," I said. "Yes, I will marry you!"

Oliver rose, taking me into his embrace. He looked at me for a long moment, the sheer relief of knowing our future would be together clear in his eyes, and then he kissed me.

It was not as hurried nor as timid as our first kisses. His lips pressed against mine with passion—a promise of what was to come, of the life we would share.

His arms tightened around me, and I clung to him just as fiercely. I felt so safe and loved when he held me like this. Warmth built between us, and he deepened the kiss.

My stomach fluttered with a rush of feelings. Love and longing, hope and happiness.

And when we finally parted, breathless and smiling, I knew I'd made the right decision in agreeing to marry him. Our life might not be what either of us had expected, but at least we would enjoy it together.

"Have your maid pack your belongings," Oliver said, his voice soft. "I will speak with my brother and ask him to help us make the arrangements to sell Winterset. I will have the carriage brought to the drive. And then we will away."

"Are we really doing this?" I whispered.

"Yes, love. We really are."

CHAPTER FORTY-ONE

Oliver

The last time I'd stood in this study, it had belonged to Father. Not much had changed. The only difference I noticed was that a painting of Hannah now hung on the wall instead of Mother's.

"It's strange for me too." Damon closed the door and sat, not in the chair behind the desk but in the one beside me.

His choice made me feel slightly off-center. I'd imagined that he would take the place of Father. But he hadn't. He'd chosen, as he'd said in his letters, to be my brother. First and forever? The possibility felt real.

"You have no idea how long I have hoped to sit here with you and have a conversation," he said.

"I do, actually. You laid out your feelings in painstaking detail in your letters. You quite lack brevity, brother."

I'd hoped to tease away the tension, but Damon's gaze remained steady, intent. "You read my letters?" he said, his voice quiet.

"Not until this week, after Kate left," I admitted.

He smiled slightly, but it was sad.

I looked down at my hands, ashamed. "I wish I would have read them a long time ago," I said. "But it was probably better that I didn't. You would not have liked what I would have written before now."

Damon rubbed his forehead. "Anything would have been better than your deafening silence."

I shook my head. "I've been immature and full of self-pity and spite for a long time, Damon. I hated you for two years."

"You hated me much longer than that." Damon frowned.

"It's true," I said. "I did hate you, but only because you hated me."

"I have *never* hated you, Ollie." Damon held my gaze.

"Then why did you act like it?"

"I distanced myself from you because I wanted to protect you."

"Protect me from what?"

"Father." Damon worked his jaw as if chewing over words he did not want to say. "Do you remember that day at the pianoforte?" he asked.

I looked down at my hands, remembering the bite of Father's riding crop coming down on my knuckles.

"I see that you do," Damon said. "Do you know why he did it?"

"To punish me for not practicing."

"No. He did that to you to punish *me*, Ollie."

I squinted at him, trying to make sense of his words.

"At first, Father's favorite method of making me do what he wanted was whipping me." He avoided eye contact. "But I got too good at bearing it. He quickly discovered that a more effective method of making me submissive was to hurt you instead. Father saw how much I loved you, and he used it against me. The only way I knew how to protect you was to distance myself from you."

As I viewed my childhood from this new angle, I was horrified.

"It was around that time that I went away to school," Damon said. "There I learned what the rest of my life would be like, how I was more Father's heir than my own person." Damon breathed. "And I was angry, Ollie. I was so angry all the time. About everything. When you came up to me in the schoolyard crying, I was worried word would get back to Father, and then he would somehow make you pay. That is why I gave you the cut direct."

"I really believed you hated me," I said.

Damon shook his head. "I hated Father. I hated being his heir. I hated myself. But not you, Ollie. *Never* you. And I am so sorry that I made you believe that. I'm sorry for how Father treated you because of me, for abandoning you when you needed a brother most."

"I'm sorry too," I said. "For everything you suffered. I didn't know. I never saw how hard Father was on you or the weight you carried being the heir. I . . . might have judged you too harshly."

"Might have?" Damon raised a teasing brow at me.

Knowing the truth of his actions, I could now see that I *had* been a harsh judge. But even so, it was difficult to reconcile what I had lived with this revelation. Damon had not hated me, no matter how much it had felt like it at the time. "I have wanted and yearned for brotherly affection most of my life. Still, it will take me some time to fully be able to see you in this new light. Not as my adversary but as my protector. More than anything, though, I do wish for us to be reconciled."

"Do you mean it?" Damon asked.

"I do."

He closed his eyes as if savoring my words. "So do I, Ollie." Standing, he pulled me up into a hug. He held me tightly, dispelling the distance that had existed between us for far too long.

But another matter still weighed heavily on my mind.

"I need your help," I said, stepping back.

"Anything," Damon said.

"I need your help selling Winterset so I might marry Kate."

Damon stared at me for a long moment, then threw back his head and laughed.

I scowled at him.

"I'm sorry." He struggled to regain his composure. "But do you not find it funny? You have hated me for two years for even *trying* to remove the entail from Summerhaven so that I might sell the smallest portion in order to marry Hannah, and now you are asking me to help you sell the whole of your inheritance to marry the woman you love."

"Hilarious," I said with dry wit.

He shook his head, his smile fading. "Do you have the deed to the property?"

I produced the document from my pocket and handed it to him.

He glanced over it. "Do you have a preferred solicitor, or will my man be sufficient?"

"You aren't going to try to talk me out of it?" I asked. "Tell me I'm being foolish, as I once told you?"

"I know what it is to love someone as desperately as you do, Ollie. The law stood in my way, but I will not stand in yours."

His words left me momentarily speechless. It had been so long since we'd had this bond, and I was grateful. "Thank you, Damon."

"You don't need to thank me, Ollie. We're brothers. It is a blessing to finally be able to help you."

"In *that* case, I would like to help you. Let's talk about your refusal to be called Lord Winfield."

Damon groaned. "Not you too."

"Explain to me why you refuse to use the title."

"Father tarnished it. Refusing to use the title he cherished more than you or me seems an excellent way for us to spite the man."

I rolled my eyes. "If you believe that, then you are an imbecile."

He blinked in surprise. "You don't agree?"

I shook my head. "You mustn't allow him to hold power over you, Damon. *You* are the Earl of Winfield now. Claim the title, and do something good with it."

"You sound like Mother and Hannah." Damon glowered.

"Yes, well. They are wise women."

"Yes, they are." Damon smiled. "And so is Kate."

"She is, Damon. I don't deserve her, but I will do anything to make her happy."

"She's a lucky woman to have you, Ollie."

We spent several more minutes together, discussing the sale of Winterset and my plans for the future. I also wanted to be sure Mrs. Owensby and Bexley would be informed of our plans so they would not worry and that their futures were taken care of. Damon agreed to hire them as servants here at Summerhaven until such time that it was safe for them to join Kate and me in our new life elsewhere.

"Well," I said. "I must go meet Kate." It was time to begin the rest of our lives together.

"I am not ready for you to go," Damon said, pulling me into a hug. "But I am glad for you, brother. Will you write?"

"I will," I promised. "As soon as I can safely do so. My letters will be devoid of identifying information, so you won't be able to write me back though."

He nodded solemnly, and we parted with one last hug.

Damon remained in his study, looking over the deed, and I shut the door behind me and started down the corridor.

As I walked, I smiled.

Damon and I were reconciled. Kate would soon be my wife. *My wife.*

As soon as I climbed into the carriage, I could take her into my arms, and I would not ever have to let go.

"Excuse me, sir?"

I glanced over my shoulder and saw a masked man walking behind me. "Yes?"

"Do you know where Duchess Montrose might be?" The masked man's voice sounded vaguely familiar, though I could not place it.

"I don't. I apologize. She is likely still in the ballroom," I said as I turned to take my leave.

"That does present a problem," the man said, stopping me. "You see, there is somewhere I have to be, but the duchess must have her smelling salts, should she swoon. Would you be so kind as to help me?" He held up a woman's full silk bag. Heavens, it looked heavy. What did women carry in those things?

"My apologies, but I, too, am on my way out. I'm sure a footman would be happy to help you." I pointed toward the entrance hall, where he might find someone. I did not wish to be rude, but neither did I wish to keep Kate waiting. She probably had her things by now and was in the carriage, or she would be soon.

"Please, sir," he said, begging my assistance.

I supposed it would not take me too long to help him. "I will take the reticule and deliver it to the duchess on my way out." I wasn't sure why he could not do that himself, but apparently, he could not. I held out my hand.

The man stepped close, extending the silk reticule to me, but when I reached for it, he drew it back. "First, you must congratulate me," he said.

"For what, sir?"

"For my upcoming nuptials. Soon, I shall be married to Miss Lockwood," he said.

Too late, I recognized his voice. Markham.

He swung the reticule at my head, and everything went dark.

CHAPTER FORTY-TWO

Kate

It took me less than thirty minutes to change out of my ball gown and pull the pearls from my hair. Nora packed my belongings and set the small satchel on the edge of the bed. I stared at it and marveled that my necessary belongings could fit inside one tiny bundle.

"You're sure you want to do this, miss?" Nora chewed her lower lip.

"I am. Do you have a piece of paper?" I wanted to write Hannah to thank her and tell her what Oliver and I had decided. Oliver was downstairs even now telling his brother our plans, but after everything Hannah had done for me, I thought she deserved to hear the details from me. It was the least I could do for the kindness she'd shown me.

Nora handed me a paper and pencil, and I moved to the vanity table. It took me only a moment to write the note. I didn't worry about my words; I just wrote. When I was finished, I folded the paper in half and wrote Hannah's name on the front.

"See that she receives this tonight." I handed Nora the note.

"Of course, miss."

"Thank you for your help, Nora."

She nodded again, and I could tell from the way she rubbed her lips that she wanted to say something.

"What is it?" I said.

"There are other ways to marry Mr. Jennings. If you wait until morning, I'm sure Lord Jennings could procure a special license. Waiting would protect your reputation and Mr. Jennings's too."

I didn't explain that I had no reputation to protect—dead ladies don't—but I did worry about Oliver's. I knew how much this marriage would cost him.

"Does your father disapprove of the marriage?" Nora asked.

"It's not that," I said but did not elaborate. Had Father been alive, he would have given us his blessing. "Running away, marrying in secret is the only way Oliver and I can be together."

I could tell Nora didn't understand, and she *definitely* disapproved, but she nodded.

"Thank you," I told her again as I lifted the small satchel and left the room. It took only moments for me to descend the stairs and walk out the front door.

A single carriage waited on the drive.

My stomach fluttered with excitement. Oliver was waiting for me inside that carriage.

I lifted the hem of my skirt and ran down the stone steps. I couldn't make my feet move fast enough.

The carriage door opened from the inside as I neared. There was no footman to help me inside, but the step was down, and Oliver reached out his gloved hand.

I slipped my hand into his, and he effortlessly pulled me up. He was sitting in the rear-facing seat, so I sat in the forward-facing one across from him. The carriage was dark inside, and Oliver wore a black hooded cloak, hiding his face, making this moment feel every bit the clandestine arrangement that it was. Perhaps I, too, should have taken more care to conceal my appearance.

Before I could worry too much, Oliver knocked his knuckles to the carriage ceiling, and it jolted into motion down the long drive.

Oliver relaxed back into his seat, and although I couldn't see his eyes, I could feel the intensity of his stare. I'd imagined that when I climbed into the carriage, he'd pull me into his arms and whisper words of love.

But he said nothing.

Not as we drove down the long drive or when the carriage swayed onto the main lane nor even after we'd traveled that road for a few minutes. And as I stared at him in the darkness, my delight was overshadowed by uncertainty.

Did Oliver doubt our decision?

And if he did, did I have the strength to tell him to turn back?

"Will you not say anything to me?" I asked him.

Oliver tilted his head stiffly to the side. And there was something in that small motion that didn't feel right. That didn't feel like Oliver.

But no.

I was sure I must be imagining it—worrying about what we were doing and creating doubts where none existed—but I wouldn't be able to calm down until I saw his face and looked into his eyes. Then I would know for certain that he still wanted to marry me.

"Remove your hood," I said.

He reached both hands up and gripped the sides of the hood and slowly pulled it back. But he was sitting too far back in his seat, and his face was still obscured by shadow.

"Lean forward," I said.

He hesitated for a fraction of a second, then slowly did what I said.

My gasp filled the carriage.

Not Oliver.

It was the stranger I'd danced with earlier.

Then with a swift motion, almost gloating, he removed his mask, and I wasn't surprised to see that he was no stranger at all.

It was Lord Markham.

I threw myself at the door and fumbled for the handle. I found it and opened the door. Despite the fast speed of the carriage, I would have leaped, but Markham stepped on my hem, preventing my escape.

He grabbed my hair and dragged me back inside the carriage, then tossed me into my seat. Towering over me, he used his weight to pin me in place and held my wrists in one hand.

I tried to free myself from his grasp, but I was no match for his strength.

He worked to untie his cravat and then ripped it from his neck. I worried he was going to put it around *my* neck, but he tied it tightly around my wrists. Then he tugged the cloth, and seeming satisfied that it was secure, he sat in the seat opposite me again and *smiled*.

"Hello, Miss Lockwood. It's been too long."

CHAPTER FORTY-THREE

Oliver

I'm standing at the edge of a cliff.
Sea mist swirls around me, and I breathe in the salty-sweet air. Below, waves crash on the rocks.
Kate is there, walking along the seashore, her ball gown billowing in the breeze.
I cup my hands around my mouth and call to her.
She looks up. Sees me. Smiles. She motions for me to join her.
But my body is heavy, my limbs filled with thousands of grains of sand.
I'm stuck standing on the cliff.
Kate looks up at me with a pinched expression, as if wondering why I haven't joined her yet.
Wondering if I ever will.
Wondering if I even want to.
She turns away. Steps into the sea.
Water surrounds her ankles, her knees, her waist.
She takes off a pelisse that she wasn't wearing a moment ago and lays it on the water. She hesitates for a single second, then disappears into the depths.
I scream for her to swim, to fight. But I already know that if I don't get to her . . .

A sharp gasp of breath and my eyes snapped open.
But I saw nothing. The world was black.
I blinked.
Where was I? What had happened? I tried to make sense of my surroundings.

I was lying on my side, my face pressed against something cold. The marble floor?

My head spun as I sat up, and I rubbed my throbbing forehead. There was a large lump.

I stood and felt along the wall until I found a handle. As soon as the door opened, I realized where I was: in the corridor not far from Damon's study. Spinning around, I saw that I had been inside the butler's pantry. On the floor lay a woman's reticule.

Everything came crashing back to me: proposing to Kate, our plan to run away, my discussion with Damon, the masked man in the corridor. Markham.

Kate!

My pulse raced with panic. How much time had passed? *Please let her be safe in her rooms, packing her things*, I prayed.

I staggered up the stairs toward the west wing, where Kate's bedchamber was located. I didn't know which one was hers though. "Kate!" I called frantically as I checked inside each bedchamber. "Kate!" She had to be here. I had to find her before Markham did.

A door opened farther down, and a maid peeked out.

I ran toward her. "Where is Kate?"

The maid looked at me in confusion.

"Miss Lockwood," I said. "Do you know where she is?"

"I thought she was with you, sir. I watched as she climbed into your carriage and drove away."

My stomach dropped. Markham had her. "How long ago?" I demanded.

"I don't know. At least an hour."

"An hour?" I cursed. They could be anywhere by now. "I need you to run to the stables and have two horses saddled immediately."

She nodded but stood there in shock.

"Go now. And hurry!"

She sprang into action, and I sprinted back down the stairs and burst into the ballroom, searching out Damon for assistance. I scanned the crush for him and Hannah and found them in the center of the ballroom, waltzing.

They were surrounded by a dozen other couples, but I couldn't wait until the dance was finished. I shouldered my way through the onlookers, decorum done away with.

The fuss caught Damon's attention, his eyes widening when he saw me at the center of the commotion. He led a confused Hannah to me and took us both to the side of the ballroom to speak.

"What has happened?" he demanded, gripping my arm in concern.

I quickly explained what I knew: Markham knocking me unconscious, waking in the butler's pantry, discovering Kate had been taken. "We have to go after her," I said.

"We will find her," Damon promised. "Do you have any idea where he might be taking her? Did he say anything to you?"

Damon's question triggered my memory of Markham's words right before he knocked me unconscious. "He told me to congratulate him," I said. "That he means to marry her." His intention hit me like another blow.

"They are likely on their way to Scotland, then," Damon said.

"Gretna Green." The small town just over the border where many couples went to make their clandestine vows. Damon was right; Markham was surely taking Kate there in an attempt to force the marriage. I ran toward the front door.

Damon's footfalls followed close behind mine as we rushed to the stables. There a stablehand had just finished saddling our horses. I said a quick prayer of thanks to the maid for following through on her word and seeing that our horses were ready.

We swung into our saddles and dashed down the drive in the darkness. At the gate, we went north, but we did not travel far before we came to a fork in the road.

"What is your plan?" Damon asked.

I glanced down each darkened road, hoping I might see a clue, but saw nothing. I could not be sure which route they'd taken.

"I'll go one way; you go the other," I said. "One of us will find her."

Damon did immediately as I said, starting down the left road as I began down the right.

The only thing I knew for certain was that time was of the essence.

CHAPTER FORTY-FOUR

Kate

The cloth binding my wrists bit into my skin. I wriggled my hands, trying to loosen the restraint, but it did not relieve the discomfort.

"Don't bother," Markham said. "Even if you got it off, I would put it right back on. I'd tie it tighter too."

"Why are you doing this?" I asked. "I left. I posed you no threat."

"Because the only thing I dislike more than being lied to, Miss Lockwood, is being made a fool. I won't allow that to happen again."

"What is it you plan to do with me?"

"That *is* the question, isn't it?" He released a heavy breath, fogging the window. "I could make you marry me. You are still quite pretty."

"You cannot make me marry you, Markham."

"I think I could. You would do anything to save your precious Mr. Jennings, would you not?

"Don't touch him," I said through gritted teeth.

"I thought so." Markham grinned. "Unfortunately, I am not offering you marriage. I thought about it and even made Mr. Jennings believe that was my intention. But you are mad, Miss Lockwood. I could never tarnish the title I have sacrificed so much to secure."

"A title that I suspect you did not rightly inherit but stole."

"I did not *steal* anything. I earned it. My father was an old man. He had no use for it. And my brother was an imbecile who did not deserve the honor. I had no choice. I *had* to protect the title. I made sure they felt no pain."

"Do you mean to murder me too?" I asked.

"Who said anything about murder?" Markham's laughter filled the carriage. "You have quite an imagination, Miss Lockwood. But no matter how tempting it might be, even I would not kill a woman. I do have *some* morals." He shook his head, still chuckling to himself. "You are right about one thing, however: I *do* mean to silence you. I cannot risk anyone discovering you are alive. Not only would that harm my reputation, but you might also tell someone of your suspicions about how I came to hold the title. You understand."

"So what will you do with me, then?"

"I am taking my *ward*"—he winked at me as if letting me in on a secret—"to an asylum for the insane."

"You cannot."

"I am a baron, Miss Lockwood, a wealthy one. I can do almost anything I want. Don't worry though; it is a quaint place set upon a cliff in Scotland. There you can say anything you like, and no one will believe a word you say."

"I am not insane."

"I disagree. No sane person would fake their own death and hide for two years. You *are* mad, Miss Lockwood. You must see this as the kindness it is."

"It is prison."

"That too." He smirked. "You must admit, though, my plan *is* brilliant, don't you think? I get to keep a clear conscience, and you get to keep your life."

"You won't get away with this."

"I have *already* gotten away with it. Don't forget, you have already been dead for two years."

"Oliver will find me."

"Oh, I am counting on it," Markham said, glancing out the side glass. "To be honest, I expected him already."

My gaze snapped to Markham's. "What do you mean?"

"You must consider me slow of mind if you think I did not expect him to come after you," he said. "Why do you think I waited to take you until *after* he arrived at Summerhaven? My dear, I all but told him where I was taking you. If your Mr. Jennings does not find you, he is a great deal denser than I've given him credit for. If that worthless, waste of a man ruins my chance to use my dueling pistols tonight, I will be most disappointed."

This was a game to him. He was enjoying this.

"What do you want?" I asked.

"Were you not listening to a word I said?" he hissed, the corners of his mouth curling in contempt. "I told you I want to use my dueling pistols, and I want you silenced in an asylum."

"I will be silent," I pleaded. "Only please, *please*, don't hurt Oliver."

Markham sighed and looked heavenward. "I don't know what women see in that man. In either of the Jennings men. An earl who refuses to use his title and a second son who is too weak to defend it." He looked disgusted. "I did try to school Mr. Jennings the first night we met in the tavern. And do you know what he did? He had the audacity to look down his nose at *me*, a peer of the realm. I would be doing the crown a favor to dispatch them both. Then the title could be given to someone deserving."

Until this moment, I'd been praying Oliver would come for me. That he would find me, subdue Markham, and bring me home. Now I prayed he would take the wrong road, that I would disappear into the night, and that he would remain safe.

But then I heard a noise outside, a horse, and the carriage swerved.

Markham looked out the window and grinned. "It appears your Mr. Jennings has finally found you. What do you think? Should I shoot him right away? Or should I make him suffer?"

I stared into Markham's soulless eyes. "You are a monster."

"Only to those who cross me, Miss Lockwood." Markham alerted the driver to stop. And as the carriage slowed, he leaned forward, feeling for his pistol box.

Seeing an opportunity, I slammed my knee into his nose.

"*Lud*!" Blood burst from his nostrils like water from a fountain. As he fumbled for his handkerchief, I slid toward the door, and when he tipped back his head to stop the bleeding, I opened the door and jumped.

As soon as I landed, I ran toward the back of the carriage, where Oliver was dismounting his horse. He ran toward me and caught me in his arms. He kissed my brow, my cheeks, my lips.

"Are you hurt?" He put a fraction of space between us and took in my tear-streaked face and the cloth tying my hands. Oliver cursed. "I'll kill him."

"No." I glanced over my shoulder at the open carriage door. "Markham h-has his dueling pistols and means to make you suffer. Please, let's go."

But Oliver's eyes suddenly tracked something over my shoulder.

I turned and saw Markham calmly alighting from the carriage, looking like he hadn't a care in the world. A pistol dangled in each of his hands.

"So good of you to finally join us, Mr. Jennings."

Oliver stood in front of me like a shield, working to untie my hands. "I want you to run, Kate," he whispered. "Run and hide in the woods."

"Not without you."

"I can't defend either of us if I am worried for your safety. If you love me, you will run and hide, Kate." He kissed my knuckles. "Please."

"I do love you."

"Then run. Go. *Now!*"

Terrified to be a distraction and endanger him even more, I ran as fast as my feet would carry me to the trees lining the side of the road and then a little farther to hide behind a fallen tree.

I watched from my vantage point as Markham approached Oliver.

"Shall we settle this like gentlemen, with a duel?" Oliver said to Markham.

Markham laughed. "I will tell you the same thing I told the late Mr. Lockwood: I am not going to fight you for what is rightfully already mine." Markham aimed the pistol at Oliver. "Any last words, Jennings?"

No. *No, no, no.*

"You are a coward, Markham. A second-born son of a baron without any courage. You do not deserve the title you bear. No *true* peer of the realm would kill a man in cold blood."

Markham seemed to consider this. "Perhaps you're right," he said. "Not about deserving my title, of course, but about killing you. Unfortunately, we don't have our seconds or a doctor."

"Does that frighten you?" Oliver challenged.

"Not at all, but it should scare you. I am an excellent shot. But if a duel is how you wish to die, I will not deny you. My driver will witness the duel so no foul play occurs." He motioned the driver down from his perch.

The man took his place off to the side, and Markham shoved one of the pistols into Oliver's chest. "Ten paces, turn, and fire."

Oliver checked the gun, and then they stood back-to-back and began counting their paces.

"One!" they called.

My pulse pounded with panic. This was a trap; I did not know how, but Markham was not a man of honor, and he would not let Oliver win. He would shoot him and delight in watching him suffer as he had done before with my father.

"Two!"

For so long, I'd been afraid of Markham. But as I hid in the woods, I realized that my love for Oliver outweighed my fear of Markham. And in that moment, I knew that in order to truly live, I could not be afraid to die. Markham may know much about malice and murder, but he knew nothing about love and sacrifice.

"Three!"

Digging deep within myself, I found the courage to face my fears and sprang from my hiding spot.

"Four!"

I sprinted toward the stretch of road where the men were taking their steps.

"Five!"

Then, five seconds too soon, Markham turned and aimed his pistol at Oliver's back.

CHAPTER FORTY-FIVE

Oliver

"Oliver! *Markham!*" Kate screamed.

I whipped around in time to see that Markham had turned before the end of the count, his pistol moving away from me and toward Kate, who was running toward me.

Markham meant to kill her, but before he could, I flung myself forward in a desperate attempt to shield her.

In that same second, a shot shattered the night.

Fire seared my shoulder as we fell to the ground.

Kate landed on her back, and I fell hard atop her.

She gasped for breath, from the impact and not from true injury, I hoped. I shifted my weight slightly to the side, and she sucked in an unobstructed breath.

She was alive.

I felt a moment of relief before remembering we were still in grave danger.

In the distance, Markham was already reloading his pistol. He looked at where we lay, and we made eye contact.

Holding his gaze, I raised up, aimed my pistol, and pulled the trigger.

Markham fell to the ground, unmoving.

The driver ran over to assist him, but Markham remained still.

I dropped the gun and collapsed over Kate once more.

She held on to me, hugging me and crying into my neck. "I love you," she said again and again and again.

"I. Love. You. Too," I ground out, the pain so intense now that it was difficult to speak.

"Oliver?" Kate said, sitting up to search me for injury. Which she seemed to find because her eyes widened with worry. "Oliver," her voice broke. "No."

I gently touched her cheek. "If I don't—Be. Happy," I whispered.

"Not without you." Her voice caught.

I gave her a pained smile.

"You're going to be all right," she murmured.

But I wasn't so sure. My whole body was shaking now. I was simultaneously sweating and shivering. "Promise. Me," I said.

She shook her head. "We just . . . We need to . . . stop the bleeding." She worked frantically to untie my cravat and wrap it tightly around my wound.

I gasped in pain.

"I'm sorry. I have to stop the bleeding," she said, knotting the cloth.

Stars dotted my vision, so intense was the pain.

"Driver!" Kate called and motioned him over. "Help me get him into the carriage. We must get him back to Summerhaven at once."

The driver did as she said, leaving Markham's body lying in the road.

As soon as we were safely stowed in the carriage, she cradled me in her arms, and we started swiftly back to Summerhaven.

"Stay with me," Kate pleaded.

I fought for consciousness, but what happened next came in fits and flashes, like a fever dream.

A sway.

A sudden stop.

Summerhaven.

A surgeon.

Something being poured into my mouth.

A sharp stinging in my arm.

And then sleep.

CHAPTER FORTY-SIX

Kate

ALL THROUGH THE NIGHT, I sat by Oliver's bedside.

He'd been shot in the shoulder, and although the wound had bled profusely, the surgeon had said his injury wasn't fatal. Oliver had lost consciousness in the carriage, not due to loss of blood but due to shock. Seventeen stitches later, the doctor predicted Oliver should make a full recovery.

Last night, I had not been so certain though.

I hadn't known right away that Oliver had been injured. I'd heard the gunfire, of course, but Oliver had sat up and fired his own pistol. I'd thought he was all right. I hadn't known he wasn't until I'd seen the blood.

So much blood.

Red had stained the right side of his shirt, but I hadn't been able to tell where it was coming from. His chest? His abdomen? His shoulder? The shocking sight had scared me, and suddenly, I'd been transported back two years to the morning of Papa's death, standing at his bedside, saying goodbye.

It was breaking morning now, and I was once again sitting at a man's bedside, but this time he would live.

Through the long, predawn hours Oliver's breaths were still quite shallow, and he was so still it scared me. But as the sun rose, his breathing grew stronger, until it was finally steady and sure.

Lord Jennings stepped into the room, startling me. "Did you sleep?" he whispered.

I shook my head.

"I can take a turn watching over him," he offered.

"Thank you, but I want to be here when he wakes." Surely the laudanum would wear off soon.

"Of course," Lord Jennings said. "May I sit with you a moment?"

I nodded, and he took the seat on the other side of Oliver's bed.

Last night, I'd learned that Lord Jennings had ridden out with Oliver to find me. At a fork in the road, they'd had to separate, but when Lord Jennings had heard shots fired, he'd started back for us. He'd found Markham lying on the road. The shot Oliver had fired in my defense had indeed been lethal.

I was finally and fully safe. Thanks to Oliver.

"He looks better this morning," Lord Jennings said quietly. "More color in his cheeks."

"Yes," I agreed. "But I'm still scared." Oliver had survived the shot, but now there was the threat of infection to worry about.

"He will be all right," Lord Jennings said. "Oliver is quite stubborn, you see, and I daresay he would not give up a life with you even if the devil demanded it."

I gave Lord Jennings a grateful smile.

"Also," he said, "the surgeon was skilled, and we are all here to help Ollie through his recovery."

"Thank you, my lord. I know that will mean so much to him."

Damon sat with me for several more minutes. "Well, I suppose I should excuse myself. Mother, Hannah, and Charlie are not so patiently awaiting an update. I will go tell them he looks much better this morning."

"Thank you," I said again, and he quietly quit the room.

I stared down at Oliver. I'd come so close to losing him last night. I did not know what I would have done if he had died. I loved him so much. I could not bear to think of life without him.

I raised his hand to my lips and kissed it.

Oliver's eyes fluttered open and found mine.

A shuddering sob escaped my mouth. "Oliver."

He gave me a weak smile. "You're here," he whispered.

"Always."

"Markham?" he asked.

"We don't have to worry about him anymore," I said.

Oliver closed his eyes, the relief of the nightmare's end visibly sinking in. When his eyes reopened, he tightened his grip on my hand and pulled me closer. "I know I don't deserve you, Kate, but I swear I will work every day for the rest of my life to give you everything you desire. I want to give you the world. I want you to have everything you have ever wanted: Paris or—"

I laid one finger over his mouth, silencing him. "I only want *you*, Oliver."

"You have me, love. Every beat of my selfish heart, every breath of my prideful lungs belongs to you. I am yours, Kate."

"And I am yours." I leaned over him and gently kissed his forehead, careful not to jostle him, then sat back. "I love you, Oliver. So much. And I am grateful for all the places you want to take me, but as lovely as Paris might be, I just want to go home. I want to return to Winterset with you."

"Nothing would make me happier, my love." He pressed a gentle kiss to the back of my hand. "How long must I wait to call you my wife?"

"How soon can we marry without causing a scandal?"

"Oh, darling. We have already caused the scandal of the century. I daresay there is not anything we could do to surpass it."

CHAPTER FORTY-SEVEN

Oliver

It had been two weeks since I'd been shot, and most mornings, my sore shoulder still woke me before the sunrise—a small price to pay for Kate's safety and survival. I was lucky that the bullet had passed clean through my shoulder and that the wound it had left behind had not become infected.

Not wanting to wake Charlie needlessly, I slipped on my dressing robe and walked to the window to watch the sunrise. How many mornings had I stood in this very same spot as a boy? I couldn't count.

It was strange being back at Summerhaven, sleeping in my boyhood bedchamber. So much had changed since last I'd lived here. *I* had changed. I'd seen so many places, met so many people. I was no longer the same selfish boy but a man ready for marriage.

Kate and I decided not to wait long to be wed, only until I was well enough to travel and the banns were read, but every passing day without Kate as my wife felt like an eternity.

Restless, I went downstairs to the drawing room and found myself standing at the pianoforte. I pulled out the bench and opened the lid. Sitting, I placed my fingers on the keys. Or at least, I tried. My right shoulder hurt too much to play, and I set my hands back in my lap.

"May I join you?" Damon said, startling me. He stood at the drawing room threshold, dressed for his morning ride.

"If you have time," I said.

"I always have time for you, Ollie." He walked to the pianoforte.

I slid over to make room for him on the bench. "It's been a long time since we have sat here together."

"Too long," he said. "Do you still play?"

"No."

"*Would* you play a piece with me?" Damon rephrased his question.

"Something easy? Anything you can remember."

"The only thing I even vaguely remember is Bach's *Minuet in G Major*. But I'm not sure I can play it with my shoulder as it is."

Damon nodded. "What if I play the right hand and you play the left?"

I wasn't sure I wanted to play. I'd never really enjoyed playing the pianoforte and that was *before* Father had imbued the instrument with negative memories and physical pain.

But . . .

As a boy, I *had* loved sitting here with Damon. I loved the silly songs we used to create, the laughs we'd shared. If only Father had not robbed us of those times, how different things might have been.

But I had no desire to revisit the dark memories of our past or make myself melancholy about what might have been. I wanted to begin making new memories. Pleasant ones that would start us down a new path.

So I set my left hand on the keys, and Damon placed his right hand on the upper ones.

Damon tapped his foot on the ground to count us into the song just as he used to when we were boys, and then we began playing.

It was not pretty. I played more wrong notes than right, and my pacing was all over the place. But none of that mattered. What mattered was that Damon and I were sitting here together making music.

We played only a few measures before memory failed me, and we removed our hands from the keys.

"Thank you," Damon said, his voice thick with emotion.

I knew just how he felt. The road back home had not been an easy one, but I was so glad that I was finally here—with him.

"I wanted to talk to you about something." He cleared his throat. "Your plans for the future."

I'd known this conversation was coming. He'd tried to bring it up several times already, and I'd successfully circumvented the conversation. I wasn't sure why.

"Hannah and I have talked, and we would love for you and Kate to remain here at Summerhaven with us. We were thinking that you and Kate could live in one wing, and Hannah and I in the other. And once

Winterset has sold, you could use the funds to build a new house right here on the property. I am still happy to oversee the sale of Winterset, if you wish."

Now my throat thickened. "That is a generous offer, brother. But I cannot accept it."

His face fell. "If you are worried about not owning the land that you build on, you needn't be. When the entailment is no longer in force, it's yours. I have already spoken to my solicitor and requested that he draft the documents."

"It's not that," I said. "I have loved being here with you, Hannah, the girls, and Mother. But with the threat of Markham gone, Kate and I want to return home to Winterset. I've grown to love it there, brother. I cannot wait to show it to you."

Damon didn't respond right away.

I could tell he was disappointed by the downturn of his mouth. I'd only just come to Summerhaven, we'd barely begun to mend our relationship, and now I would soon be leaving again. It hurt me, too, but I also knew Winterset was where I belonged. It was where Kate and I were meant to make our home and start our family.

"We will miss you, Ollie. Desperately. Kate too. But I am also so proud of the man you've become." Damon squeezed my good shoulder. "Promise me that we will remain in close contact and visit one another regularly."

"I promise," I said. "I would like nothing more." And I meant it. I was so glad to have my brother by my side again and to know that whatever came, we would face it as a family.

EPILOGUE

Kate

Six months later

"Hold still, husband." I squinted at the canvas. "I am almost finished."

"You said the exact same thing two hours ago, wife. I daresay Mrs. Owensby will be cross with us both for missing luncheon."

Two *hours*? Had we really been sitting in Winterset's walled garden so long? How time hastened when I had a paintbrush in my hand. "Well, had you not moved, I *would* have been finished. Now, stay still. I am trying to get the shape of your scar right."

He waggled his brow, moving his scar.

"Oliver." I laughed. "Please."

"You could leave it off."

I frowned. "You know how much I love it."

"I *do* know, although I still do not understand why."

"Please?" I smiled.

"You know I cannot deny you when you smile at me like that." Oliver made a show of sighing and settling back into position on the blanket. Despite his dramatics, though, I knew he loved every second we spent together. Since we'd married, he'd told me more times than I could count, but even if he had not said a single word, the way he looked at me left no room for doubt.

Now that he was finally still, I stared at his handsome face, then at the canvas. I'd painted his portrait many times over the past few months, but every time, I'd come to this part of his face, I'd overthought it.

It was only a small scar—an insignificant speck when compared to the thousands of other brushstrokes on the canvas—but it symbolized our story, and I wanted so badly to paint it perfectly so that he might be able to see himself the way I saw him.

I lowered my brush to the canvas. Ever so slowly, I painted his scar one small stroke at a time.

As soon as it was complete, I stepped back to view the portrait. It wasn't perfect, but I felt pleased.

"I think . . . it is finally finished," I said.

Oliver smiled. "May I see it?"

"I'm not sure you will like it," I admitted.

"I *already* like it, simply because you painted it, my love. May I?"

"Of course."

He stood and joined me to view the portrait. His eyes scanned the canvas, taking in every detail. Did he like it? Loathe it? His expression gave nothing away.

"This is how you see me?" he finally asked, meeting my gaze.

I nodded nervously.

"Well . . ." His brow flicked up. "It is no wonder why you love me, then. This man you've painted is *shockingly* handsome. I'm not sure he looks anything like me."

It may not have been a perfect rendering, but I was confident it looked like him. "Pray tell, what have I gotten wrong?"

Oliver stroked his chin as if he were an art aficionado. "The color of my nose is off, don't you think?"

I pretended to study his profile and then his portrait. "Now that you mention it, yes, I believe I do." I leaned forward, pretending like I was going to paint the canvas, but at the last moment, I turned and painted the tip of Oliver's actual nose instead. "Now it is *exactly* the same shade. Are you satisfied?"

Smiling, he caught my wrist and tugged us down to lay on the blanket. He rolled onto his side, then, hovering over me, lowered his freshly painted nose to nuzzle mine. "*Now* I am satisfied."

My laughter matched his, and I could not ever remember being happier.

He produced a handkerchief from his pocket and gently wiped the paint first from my nose and then his own. He stared down at me, his teasing gaze turning tender, and his eyes filled with admiration and affection. "It's beautiful, Kate. Truly, I am in awe of your talent."

A surge of joy washed over me, and I nestled closer to him, his strong arms enveloping me.

He wrapped one of my curls around his finger. "I have been thinking."

"What about?"

He traced the curve of my cheek with a gentle finger. "I'm not sure the name Winterset suits our home. What would you think about renaming it?"

"Rename Winterset?"

He nodded.

To be honest, I wasn't sure I liked the idea. Winterset was, well, Winterset to me. I could not think of another name that I would like half so much. "What name did you have in mind?" I asked warily.

"Winterhaven," he whispered, his voice sounding almost reverent.

Winterhaven. The name held a sense of safety and sanctuary, of hope and home. "I love it."

"And I love *you.*"

I smiled up at him. "Do you?"

"You know I do."

I did know. I felt it in the gentle way his fingers tunneled through my hair. I saw it in his doting gaze. I heard it in the tender timbre of his voice. Oliver lowered his lips to mine and kissed me deeply, his mouth fitting mine in a perfect match.

And as the sun began to set, casting a golden glow in our walled garden, we basked in the warmth of our love, knowing that every brush stroke, every color, every scar had led us to each other—had led us home.

ACKNOWLEDGMENTS

Some books come gently into the world, and others are fought for one word at a time. When I set out to write Ollie's story, I believed it would be a breeze. I knew his character so well—I thought. And Kate's story was so clear in my mind. Boy, was I wrong!

As eager as I was to tell this story, life threw a few curveballs at me. And while I tried to write, it wasn't always possible. If I hadn't had a plethora of people behind me, pushing me to complete this story, I don't think it would have happened. So it is with gratitude in my heart that I thank the following individuals for coaxing this book into existence.

First, thank you to my readers and reviewers. One of my favorite things about publishing books is the people I get to meet along the way. Thank you for reading my books, reviewing them, and reaching out to me! Whether this is the first book you've read from me or your fifth, I am so grateful you're here.

A huge thank-you to the experts who helped me learn more about the history of the houses they love. Particularly, Phil Downing, hall manager, and Derrick Hughes, dedicated docent, at Harvington Hall, for not only preserving history but also making it come alive. Thank you for answering my questions and finding space for me to attend an entirely sold-out event. Your generosity made all the difference in getting the details of this book right.

Also, thank you to my critique partners: Ellisa Barr, Teri Christopherson, Leah Garriott, Aubrey Hartman, Melanie Jacobson, Brittany Larsen, Lindsay Sanchez, Deb Stevens, Sabrina Watts, and Jen White. Without

ACKNOWLEDGMENTS

your enthusiasm and expertise, I would not have found the confidence to create this story.

Thank you to my beta readers: Jillian Christensen, Jentry Flint, and Samantha Hastings. You were each so gracious with your time and talents. Thank you for helping me make the most of this manuscript!

Next, I thank my publishing family at Shadow Mountain. Heidi Taylor Gordon, you are like my very own fairy godmother. Publishing a book in the Proper Romance line is truly a dream come true! Thank you for making it happen for me. Samantha Millburn, I am so blessed to have you as my editor. The number of em-dashes, as ifs, and comma splices you catch will never cease to amaze me. Thank you. Callie Hansen, thank you for directing the production of *Winterset*, and thank you, Heather Ward, for creating such a stunning cover. Thank you also to Bre Anderl for your incredible typesetting skills. Amy Parker, I owe so much of this series' success to you! I will never stop saying it. I'm so grateful to you! Also, thank you to Haley Haskins, Troy Butcher, Lehi Quiroz, Bri Cornell, and Tasha Bradford for helping me reach new readers.

Thank you to my parents Heidi Mackay and Ken Farrell. You have always been supportive of my dreams, and I am so grateful you are mine.

Kids, I love seeing the people you are growing to be. Each of you is creative in your own unique ways, and I love you so much. Thank you for sharing me with my characters.

And thank you to my husband Kevin. I could write another novel on all the ways you have helped me write this story, but instead, I will just say thank you for loving me so perfectly. You are my favorite person. This book and all others I've written have only been possible because of you.

And most important of all, I thank my Father in Heaven.

ABOUT THE AUTHOR

Photo by Sabrina Watts

TIFFANY ODEKIRK believes cooking should take less than thirty minutes, frosting is better than ice cream, and all books should end with "happily ever after." After earning her bachelor's degree, she worked in the nonprofit sector to help unhoused women and children. Tiffany is the author of five romance novels and has received a five-star *Readers' Favorite* medallion and a Benjamin Franklin Gold Medal Award (IBPA) for her Regency romance *Summerhaven*. These days, you can find her reading or writing a book in her Southern California home, where she lives with her handsome husband and four adorable children. You can also find her on Facebook, Instagram, and Bookbub @AuthorTiffanyOdekirk.

A HIDDEN PAST. A HOUSE WITH SECRETS. AND ONE CHANCE FOR TWO WOUNDED HEARTS TO FIND LOVE TOGETHER.

Northern England, Late Fall 1820

Katherine Lockwood is hiding for her life in the priest holes of abandoned Winterset Grange. When the estate's owner, Oliver Jennings, returns from abroad, Kate tries to scare him off by acting as a ghost and "haunting" the home. But Oliver, determined to restore his inheritance, refuses to flee.

Discovering the truth behind the haunting, Oliver is intrigued by Kate and offers her shelter. As danger closes in from the man who threatens her, Kate and Oliver must outwit this powerful enemy and navigate the risks of trust, love, and survival as they fight for a future together that they never expected.

"Readers who loved *Summerhaven* will absolutely devour *Winterset*!"
—Jentry Flint, best-selling author of *To Love the Brooding Baron*

"Kate and Oliver stole my heart with their wit and their flirty banter. *Winterset* is beautifully written and whimsically humorous. I couldn't put it down!"
—Samantha Hastings, author of *A Hopeful Proposal*

"*Summerhaven* is a lovely novel . . . that will grab your heart as you follow love down an unusual path."—*Readers' Favorite* five-star review

Proper Romance is a registered trademark.

Also Available in eBook and Audiobook

Cover art: © Lauren Rautenbach / Arcangel; duncan1890 / Getty Images
Book design: © Shadow Mountain
Art direction: Garth Bruner
Design: Heather G. Ward